man's yet its flexibility and rhythm give it potential for lyrical expression which is distinctly Rankin's own'
Scotland on Sunday

'Top notch ... the bleakness is unrelenting, but it quite suits Mr Rankin who does his best work in the dark' *New York Times*

'The internal police politics and corruption in high places are both portrayed with bone-freezing accuracy. This novel should come with a wind-chill factor warning' *Daily Telegraph*

'Detective Inspector Rebus makes the old-style detectives with their gentle or bookish backgrounds, Alleyn, Morse, Dalgliesh, look like wimps ... Rankin is brilliant at conveying the genuine stench of seedy places on the dark side of Scotland' *Sunday Telegraph*

'It's the banter and energy, the immense carnival of scenes and characters, voices and moods that set Rankin apart. His stories are like a transmission forever in the red zone, at the edge of burnout. This is crime fiction at its best' *Washington Post*

Born in the Kingdom of Fife in 1960, Ian Rankin graduated from the University of Edinburgh and has since been employed as grape-picker, swineherd, taxman, alcohol researcher, hi-fi journalist and punk musician. His first Rebus novel, *Knots & Crosses*, was published in 1987 and the Rebus books have now been translated into over a dozen languages and are increasingly popular in the USA. Ian Rankin has been elected a Hawthornden Fellow, and is a past winner of the prestigious Chandler-Fulbright Award, as well as two CWA short-story 'Daggers' and the 1997 CWA Macallan Gold Dagger for Fiction for *Black & Blue*, which was also shortlisted for the Mystery Writers of America 'Edgar' award for best novel. Both *Black & Blue* and *The Hanging Garden* have been televised on ITV, starring John Hannah as Inspector Rebus. *Dead Souls*, the eleventh novel in the series, was shortlisted for the CWA Gold Dagger Award in 1999. An Alumnus of the Year at Edinburgh University, he has also been awarded two honorary doctorates, one from the University of Abertay Dundee in 1999 and another, more recently, from the University of St Andrews. He lives in Edinburgh with his wife and two sons.

BY THE SAME AUTHOR

The Inspector Rebus Series

Knots & Crosses
Hide & Seek
Tooth & Nail
(previously published as Wolfman)
A Good Hanging and Other Stories
Strip Jack
The Black Book
Mortal Causes
Let It Bleed
Black & Blue
The Hanging Garden
Death Is Not the End (novella)
Dead Souls
Rebus: The Early Years

Other Novels

The Flood
Watchman
Westwind

Writing as Jack Harvey

Witch Hunt
Bleeding Hearts
Blood Hunt

Ian Rankin

Set in Darkness

An Inspector Rebus Novel

ORION

An Orion Paperback
First published in Great Britain by Orion in 2000
This paperback edition published in 2000 by
Orion Books Ltd,
Orion House, 5 Upper St Martin's Lane, London WC2H 9EA

A CIP catalogue record for this book is available
from the British Library

ISBN 0 75283 708 7

Typeset by Deltatype Ltd, Birkenhead, Merseyside
Printed and bound in Great Britain by
Clays Ltd, St Ives plc

For my son Kit, with all my hopes, dreams and love

Though my soul may set in darkness
It will rise in perfect light,
I have loved the stars too fondly
To be fearful of the night.

Sarah Williams, 'The Old Astronomer to his Pupil'

Part One

The Sense of an Ending

And this long narrow land
Is full of possibility . . .

Deacon Blue, 'Wages Day'

1

Darkness was falling as Rebus accepted the yellow hard hat from his guide.

'This will be the admin block, we think,' the man said. His name was David Gilfillan. He worked for Historic Scotland and was coordinating the archaeological survey of Queensberry House. 'The original building is late seventeenth century. Lord Hatton was its original owner. It was extended at the end of the century, after coming into the ownership of the first Duke of Queensberry. It would have been one of the grandest houses on Canongate, and only a stone's throw from Holyrood.'

All around them, demolition work was taking place. Queensberry House itself would be saved, but the more recent additions either side of it were going. Workmen crouched on roofs, removing slates, tying them into bundles which were lowered by rope to waiting skips. There were enough broken slates underfoot to show that the process was imperfect. Rebus adjusted his hard hat and tried to look interested in what Gilfillan was saying.

Everyone told him that this was a sign, that he was here because the chiefs at the Big House had plans for him. But Rebus knew better. He knew his boss, Detective Chief Superintendent 'Farmer' Watson, had put his name forward because he was hoping to keep Rebus out of trouble and out of his hair. It was as simple as that. And if – *if* – Rebus accepted without complaining and saw the assignment through, then maybe – *maybe* – the Farmer would receive a chastened Rebus back into the fold.

Four o'clock on a December afternoon in Edinburgh;

John Rebus with his hands in his raincoat pockets, water seeping up through the leather soles of his shoes. Gilfillan was wearing green wellies. Rebus noticed that DI Derek Linford was wearing an almost identical pair. He'd probably phoned beforehand, checked with the archaeologist what the season's fashion was. Linford was Fettes fast-stream, headed for big things at Lothian and Borders Police HQ. Late twenties, practically deskbound, and glowing from a love of the job. Already there were CID officers – mostly older than him – who were saying it didn't do to get on the wrong side of Derek Linford. Maybe he'd have a long memory; maybe one day he'd be looking down on them all from Room 279 in the Big House.

The Big House: Police HQ on Fettes Avenue; 279: the Chief Constable's office.

Linford had his notebook out, pen clenched between his teeth. He was listening to the lecture. He was *listening*.

'Forty noblemen, seven judges, generals, doctors, bankers . . .' Gilfillan was letting his tour group know how important Canongate had been at one time in the city's history. In doing so, he was pointing towards the near future. The brewery next door to Queensberry House was due for demolition the following spring. The parliament building itself would be built on the cleared site, directly across the road from Holyrood House, the Queen's Edinburgh residence. On the other side of Holyrood Road, facing Queensberry House, work was progressing on Dynamic Earth, a natural history theme park. Next to it, a new HQ for the city's daily newspaper was at present a giant monkey-puzzle of steel girders. And across the road from that, another site was being cleared in preparation for the construction of a hotel and 'prestige apartment block'. Rebus was standing in the midst of one of the biggest building sites in Edinburgh's history.

'You'll probably all know Queensberry House as a hospital,' Gilfillan was saying. Derek Linford was nodding, but then he nodded agreement with almost everything the

4

archaeologist said. 'Where we're standing now was used for car parking.' Rebus looked around at the mud-coloured lorries, each one bearing the simple word DEMOLITION. 'But before it was a hospital it was used as a barracks. This area was the parade ground. We dug down and found evidence of a formal sunken garden. It was probably filled in to make the parade ground.'

In what light was left, Rebus looked at Queensberry House. Its grey harled walls looked unloved. There was grass growing from its gutters. It was huge, yet he couldn't remember having seen it before, though he'd driven past it probably several hundred times in his life.

'My wife used to work here,' another of the group said, 'when it was a hospital.' The informant was Detective Sergeant Joseph Dickie, who was based at Gayfield Square. He'd successfully contrived to miss two out of the first four meetings of the PPLC – the Policing of Parliament Liaison Committee. By some arcane law of bureaucratic seman- tics, the PPLC was actually a *sub*committee, one of many which had been set up to advise on security matters pertaining to the Scottish Parliament. There were eight members of the PPLC, including one Scottish Office official and a shadowy figure who claimed to be from Scotland Yard, though when Rebus had phoned the Met in London, he'd been unable to trace him. Rebus's bet was that the man – Alec Carmoodie – was MI5. Carmoodie wasn't here today, and neither was Peter Brent, the sharp-faced and sharper-suited Scottish Office representative. Brent, for his sins, sat on several of the subcommittees, and had begged off today's tour with the compelling excuse that he'd been through it twice before when accompanying visiting dignitaries.

Making up the party today were the three final members of the PPLC. DS Ellen Wylie was from C Division HQ in Torphichen Place. It didn't seem to bother her that she was the only woman on the team. She treated it like any other task, raising good points at the meetings and

5

asking questions to which no one seemed to have any answers. DC Grant Hood was from Rebus's own station, St Leonard's. Two of them, because St Leonard's was the closest station to the Holyrood site, and the parliament would be part of their beat. Though Rebus worked in the same office as Hood, he didn't know him well. They'd not often shared the same shift. But Rebus did know the last member of the PPLC, DI Bobby Hogan from D Division in Leith. At the first meeting, Hogan had pulled Rebus to one side.

'What the hell are we doing here?'

'I'm serving time,' Rebus had answered. 'What about you?'

Hogan was scoping out the room. 'Christ, man, look at them. We're Old Testament by comparison.'

Smiling now at the memory, Rebus caught Hogan's eye and winked. Hogan shook his head almost imperceptibly. Rebus knew what he was thinking: waste of time. Almost everything was a waste of time for Bobby Hogan.

'If you'll follow me,' Gilfillan was saying, 'we can take a look indoors.'

Which, to Rebus's mind, really was a waste of time. The committee having been set up, things had to be found for them to do. So here they were wandering through the dank interior of Queensberry House, their way lit irregularly by unsafe-looking strip lights and the torch carried by Gilfillan. As they climbed the stairwell – nobody wanted to use the lift – Rebus found himself paired with Joe Dickie, who asked a question he'd asked before.

'Put in your exes yet?' By which he meant the claim for expenses.

'No,' Rebus admitted.

'Sooner you do, sooner they'll cough up.'

Dickie seemed to spend half his time at their meetings totting up figures on his pad of paper. Rebus had never seen the man write down anything as mundane as a phrase or sentence. Dickie was late thirties, big-framed with a head like an artillery shell stood on end. His black hair was cropped close to the skull and his eyes were as small and rounded as a china doll's. Rebus had tried the comparison out on Bobby Hogan, who'd commented that any doll resembling Joe Dickie would 'give a bairn nightmares'.

'I'm a grown-up,' Hogan had continued, 'and he still scares me.'

Climbing the stairs, Rebus smiled again. Yes, he was glad to have Bobby Hogan around.

'When people think of archaeology,' Gilfillan was saying, 'they almost always see it in terms of digging *down*, but one of our most exciting finds here was in the attic. A new roof was built over the original one, and there are traces of what looks like a tower. We'd have to climb a ladder to get to it, but if anyone's interested . . . ?'

'Thank you,' a voice said. Derek Linford: Rebus knew its nasal quality only too well by now.

'Creep,' another voice close to Rebus whispered. It was Bobby Hogan, bringing up the rear. A head turned: Ellen Wylie. She'd heard, and now gave what looked like the hint of a smile. Rebus looked to Hogan, who shrugged, letting him know he thought Wylie was all right.

'How will Queensberry House be linked to the parliament building? Will there be covered walkways?' The questions came from Linford again. He was out in front with Gilfillan. The pair of them had rounded a corner of the stairs, so that Rebus had to strain to hear Gilfillan's hesitant reply.

'I don't know.'

His tone said it all: he was an archaeologist, not an architect. He was here to investigate the site's past rather than its future. He wasn't sure himself why he was giving this tour, except that it had been asked of him. Hogan screwed up his face, letting everyone in the vicinity know his own feelings.

'When will the building be ready?' Grant Hood asked. An easy one: they'd all been briefed. Rebus saw what Hood was doing – trying to console Gilfillan by putting a question he could answer.

'Construction begins in the summer,' Gilfillan obliged. 'Everything should be up and running here by the autumn of 2001.' They were coming out on to a landing. Around them stood open doorways, through which could be glimpsed the old hospital wards. Walls had been gouged at, flooring removed: checks on the fabric of the building. Rebus stared out of a window. Most of the workers looked to be packing up: dangerously dark now to be scrabbling over roofs. There was a summer house down there. It was due to be demolished, too. And a tree, drooping forlornly, surrounded by rubble. It had been planted by the Queen. No way it could be moved or felled until she'd given her permission. According to Gilfillan, permission had now been granted; the tree would go. Maybe formal gardens would be recreated down there, or maybe it would be a staff car park. Nobody knew. 2001 seemed a ways off. Until this site was ready, the parliament would sit in the Church of Scotland Assembly Hall near the top of The Mound. The committee had already been on two tours of the Assembly Hall and its immediate vicinity. Office buildings were being turned over to the parliament, so that the MSPs could have somewhere to work. Bobby Hogan had asked at one meeting why they couldn't just wait for the Holyrood site to be ready before, in his words, 'setting up shop'. Peter Brent, the civil servant, had stared at him aghast.

'Because Scotland needs a parliament *now.*'

'Funny, we've done without for three hundred years . . .'

Brent had been about to object, but Rebus had butted in. 'Bobby, at least they're not trying to rush the job.'

Hogan had smiled, knowing he was talking about the newly opened Museum of Scotland. The Queen had come north for the official opening of the unfinished building. They'd had to hide the scaffolding and paint tins till she'd gone.

Gilfillan was standing beside a retractable ladder, pointing upwards towards a hatch in the ceiling.

'The original roof is just up there,' he said. Derek Linford already had both feet on the ladder's bottom rung. 'You don't need to go all the way,' Gilfillan continued as Linford climbed. 'If I shine the torch up . . .'

But Linford had disappeared into the roof space.

'Lock the hatch and let's make a run for it,' Bobby Hogan said, smiling so they'd assume he was joking.

Ellen Wylie hunched her shoulders. 'There's a real . . . atmosphere in here, isn't there?'

'My wife saw a ghost,' Joe Dickie said. 'Lots of people who worked here did. A woman, she was crying. Used to sit on the end of one of the beds.'

'Maybe she was a patient who died here,' Grant Hood offered.

Gilfillan turned towards them. 'I've heard that story, too. She was the mother of one of the servants. Her son was working here the night the Act of Union was signed. Poor chap got himself murdered.'

Linford called down that he thought he could see where the steps to the tower had been, but nobody was listening.

'Murdered?' Ellen Wylie said.

Gilfillan nodded. His torch threw weird shadows across the walls, illuminating the slow movements of cobwebs. Linford was trying to read some graffiti on the wall.

'There's a year written here . . . 1870, I think.'

'You know Queensberry was the architect of the Act of Union?' Gilfillan was saying. He could see that he had an audience now, for the first time since the tour had begun in the brewery car park next door. 'Back in 1707. This', he scratched a shoe over the bare floorboards, 'is where Great Britain was invented. And the night of the signing, one of the young servants was working in the kitchen.

9

The Duke of Queensberry was Secretary of State. It was his job to lead the negotiations. But he had a son, James Douglas, Earl of Drumlanrig. The story goes, James was off his head . . .'

'What happened?'

Gilfillan looked up through the open hatch. 'All right up there?' he called.

'Fine. Anyone else want to take a look?'

They ignored him. Ellen Wylie repeated her question.

'He ran the servant through with a sword,' Gilfillan said, 'then roasted him in one of the kitchen fireplaces. James was sitting munching away when he was found.'

'Dear God,' Ellen Wylie said.

'You believe this?' Bobby Hogan slid his hands into his pockets.

Gilfillan shrugged. 'It's a matter of record.'

A blast of cold air seemed to rush at them from the roof space. Then a rubber-soled wellington appeared on the ladder, and Derek Linford began his slow, dusty descent. At the bottom, he removed the pen from between his teeth.

'Interesting up there,' he said. 'You really should try it. Could be your first and last chance.'

'Why's that then?' Bobby Hogan asked.

'I very much doubt we'll be letting tourists in here, Bobby,' Linford said. 'Imagine what *that* would do for security.'

Hogan stepped forward so swiftly that Linford flinched. But all Hogan did was lift a cobweb from the young man's shoulder.

'Can't have you heading back to the Big House in less than showroom condition, can we, son?' Hogan said. Linford ignored him, probably feeling that he could well afford to ignore relics like Bobby Hogan, just as Hogan knew he had nothing to fear from Linford: he'd be heading for retirement long before the younger man gained any position of real power and prominence.

'I can't see it as the powerhouse of government,' Ellen Wylie said, examining the water stains on the walls, the flaking plaster. 'Wouldn't they have been better off knocking it down and starting again?'

'It's a listed building,' Gilfillan censured her. Wylie just shrugged. Rebus knew that nevertheless she had accomplished her objective, by deflecting attention away from Linford and Hogan. Gilfillan was off again, delving into the history of the area: the series of wells which had been found beneath the brewery; the slaughterhouse which used to stand near by. As they headed back down the stairs, Hogan held back, tapping his watch, then cupping a hand to his mouth. Rebus nodded: good idea. A drink afterwards. Jenny Ha's was a short stroll away, or there was the Holyrood Tavern on the way back to St Leonard's. As if mind-reading, Gilfillan began talking about the Younger's Brewery.

'Covered twenty-seven acres at one time, produced a quarter of all the beer in Scotland. Mind you, there's been an abbey at Holyrood since early in the twelfth century. Chances are they weren't just drinking well-water.'

Through a landing window, Rebus could see that outside night had fallen prematurely. Scotland in winter: it was dark when you came to work, and dark when you went home again. Well, they'd had their little outing, gleaned nothing from it, and would now be released back to their various stations until the next meeting. It felt like a penance because Rebus's boss had planned it as such. Farmer Watson was on a committee himself: Strategies for Policing in the New Scotland. Everyone called it SPINS. Committee upon committee . . . it felt to Rebus as if they were building a paper tower, enough 'Policy Agendas', 'Reports' and 'Occasional Papers' to completely fill Queensberry House. And the more they talked, the more that got written, the further away from reality they seemed to move. Queensberry House was unreal to him, the idea of a parliament itself the dream of some mad god:

'But Edinburgh is a mad god's dream/Fitful and dark . . .'
He'd found the words at the opening to a book about the
city. They were from a poem by Hugh MacDiarmid. The
book itself had been part of his recent education, trying to
understand this home of his.

He took off his hard hat, rubbed his fingers through his
hair, wondering just how much protection the yellow
plastic would give against a projectile falling several
storeys. Gilfillan asked him to put the hat back on until
they were back at the site office.

'You might not get into trouble,' the archaeologist said,
'but I would.'

Rebus put the helmet back on, while Hogan tutted and
wagged a finger. They were back at ground level, in what
Rebus guessed must have been the hospital's reception
area. There wasn't much to it. Spools of electric cable sat
near the door: the offices would need rewiring. They were
going to close the Holyrood/St Mary's junction to facilitate
underground cabling. Rebus, who used the route often,
wasn't looking forward to the diversions. Too often these
days the city seemed nothing but roadworks.

'Well,' Gilfillan was saying, opening his arms, 'that's
about it. If there are any questions, I'll do what I can.'

Bobby Hogan coughed into the silence. Rebus saw it as
a warning to Linford. When someone had come up from
London to address the group on security issues in the
Houses of Parliament, Linford had asked so many questions the poor sod had missed his train south. Hogan
knew this because he'd been the one who'd driven the
Londoner at breakneck speed back to Waverley Station,
then had had to entertain him for the rest of the evening
before depositing him on the overnight sleeper.

Linford consulted his notebook, six pairs of eyes drilling
into him, fingers touching wristwatches.

'Well, in that case—' Gilfillan began.

'Hey! Mr Gilfillan! Are you up there?' The voice was

coming from below. Gilfillan walked over to a doorway, called down a flight of steps.

'What is it, Marlene?'

'Come take a look.'

Gilfillan turned to look at his reluctant group. 'Shall we?' He was already heading down. They couldn't very well leave without him. It was stay here, with a bare lightbulb for company, or head down into the basement. Derek Linford led the way.

They came out into a narrow hallway, rooms off to both sides, and other rooms seeming to lead from those. Rebus thought he caught a glimpse of an electrical generator somewhere in the gloom. Voices up ahead and the shadowplay of torches. They walked out of the hallway and into a room lit by a single arc lamp. It was pointing towards a long wall, the bottom half of which had been lined with wooden tongue-and-groove painted the selfsame institutional cream as the plaster walls. Floorboards had been ripped up so that for the most part they were walking on the exposed joists, beneath which sat bare earth. The whole room smelt of damp and mould. Gilfillan and the other archaeologist, the one he'd called Marlene, were crouched in front of this wall, examining the stonework beneath the wood panelling. Two long curves of hewn stone, forming what seemed to Rebus like railway arches in miniature. Gilfillan turned round, looking excited for the first time that day.

'Fireplaces,' he said. 'Two of them. This must have been the kitchen.' He stood up, taking a couple of paces back. 'The floor level's been raised at some point. We're only seeing the top half of them.' He half-turned towards the group, reluctant to take his eyes off the discovery. 'Wonder which one the servant was roasted in . . .'

One of the fireplaces was open, the other closed off by a couple of sections of brown corroding metal.

'What an extraordinary find,' Gilfillan said, beaming at his young co-worker. She grinned back at him. It was nice

13

to see people so happy in their work. Digging up the past, uncovering secrets . . . it struck Rebus that they weren't so unlike detectives.

'Any chance of rustling us up a meal then?' Bobby Hogan said, producing a snort of laughter from Ellen Wylie. But Gilfillan wasn't paying any heed. He was standing by the closed fireplace, prying with his fingertips at the space between stonework and metal. The sheet came away easily, Marlene helping him to lift it off and place it carefully on the floor.

'Wonder when they blocked it off?' Grant Hood asked.

Hogan tapped the metal sheet. 'Doesn't look exactly prehistoric.' Gilfillan and Marlene had lifted away the second sheet. Now everyone was staring at the revealed fireplace. Gilfillan thrust his torch towards it, though the arc lamp gave light enough.

There could be no mistaking the desiccated corpse for anything other than what it was.

2

Siobhan Clarke tugged at the hem of her black dress. Two men, patrolling the perimeter of the dance floor, stopped to watch. She tried them with a glare, but they'd returned to some conversation they were having, half-cupping their free hands to their mouths in an attempt to be heard. Then nods, sips from their pint glasses, and they were moving away, eyes on the other booths. Clarke turned to her companion, who shook her head, indicating that she hadn't known the men. Their booth was a large semi-circle, fourteen of them squeezed in around the table. Eight women, six men. Some of the men wore suits, others wore denim jackets but dress shirts. 'No denims. No trainers' was what it said on the sign outside, but the dress code wasn't exactly being enforced. There were too many people in the club. Clarke wondered if it constituted a fire hazard. She turned to her companion.

'Is it always this busy?'

Sandra Carnegie shrugged. 'Seems about normal,' she yelled. She was seated right next to Clarke, but even so was almost rendered unintelligible by the pounding music. Not for the first time, Clarke wondered how you were supposed to meet anyone in a place like this. The men at the table would make eye contact, nod towards the dance floor. If the woman agreed, everyone would have to move so the couple could get out. Then when they danced they seemed to move in their own worlds, barely making eye contact with their partner. It was much the same when a stranger approached the group: eye contact; dance floor nod; then the ritual of the dance

15

itself. Sometimes women danced with other women, shoulders drooped, eyes scanning the other faces. Sometimes a man could be seen dancing alone. Clarke had pointed out faces to Sandra Carnegie, who'd always studied them closely before shaking her head.

It was Singles Night at the Marina Club. Good name for a nightclub sited just the two and a half miles from the coastline. Not that 'Singles Night' meant much. In theory it meant that the music might hark back to the 1980s or '70s, catering for a slightly more mature clientele than some of the other clubs. For Clarke the word singles meant people in their thirties, some of them divorced. But there were lads in tonight who'd probably had to finish their homework before coming out.

Or was she just getting old?

It was her first time at a singles night. She'd tried rehearsing chat lines. If any sleazeball asked her how she liked her eggs in the morning, she was ready to tell him 'Unfertilised', but she'd no idea what she'd say if anyone asked what she did.

I'm a detective constable with Lothian and Borders Police wasn't the ideal opening gambit. She knew that from experience. Maybe that was why lately she'd all but given up trying. All of them around the table knew who she was, why she was here. None of the men had tried chatting her up. There had been words of consolation for Sandra Carnegie, words and hugs, and dark looks at the men in the company, who'd shrivelled visibly. They were *men*, and men were in it together, a conspiracy of bastards. It was a man who had raped Sandra Carnegie, who had turned her from a fun-loving single mum into a victim.

Clarke had persuaded Sandra to turn hunter – that was the way she'd phrased it.

'We've got to turn the tables on him, Sandra. That's my feeling anyway . . . before he does it again.'

Him . . . he . . . But there were two of them. One to carry

16

out the assault, the other to help hold the victim. When the rape had been reported in the newspapers, two more women had come forward with their stories. They'd been assaulted – sexually, physically – but not raped, not insofar as the law defined the crime. The women's stories had been almost identical: all three were members of singles clubs; all three had been at functions organised by their club; all three had been heading home alone.

One man on foot, following them, grabbing them, and another driving the van which pulled up. The assaults took place in the back of the van, its floor covered with material of some kind, maybe a tarpaulin. Kicked out of the van afterwards, usually on the outskirts of the city, with a final warning not to say anything, not to go to the police.

'You go to a singles club, you're asking for what you get.'

The rapist's final words, words which had set Siobhan Clarke thinking, seated in her cramped cupboard of an office; seconded to Sex Crimes. One thing she knew: the crimes were becoming more violent as the attacker grew in confidence. He'd progressed from assault to rape; who knew where he'd want to take it from there? One thing was obvious: he had something about singles clubs. Was he targeting them? Where did he get his information?

She wasn't working Sex Crimes any more, was back at St Leonard's and everyday CID, but she'd been given the chance to work on Sandra Carnegie, to persuade her back into the Marina. Siobhan's reasoning: how would he know his victims belonged to singles clubs unless he'd been in the nightclub? Members of the clubs themselves – there were three in the city – had been questioned, along with those who'd left or been kicked out.

Sandra was grey-faced and drinking Bacardi and Coke. She'd spent most of the evening so far staring at the table-top. Before coming to the Marina, the club had met in a pub. This was how it worked: sometimes they met in the pub and moved on elsewhere; sometimes they stayed put; occasionally some function was arranged – a dance or theatre trip. It was just possible the rapist followed them from the pub, but more likely he started in the dance hall, circling the floor, face hidden behind his drink. Indistinguishable from the dozens of men doing the selfsame thing.

Clarke wondered if it was possible to identify a singles group by sight alone. It would be a fair-sized crowd, mixed sex. But that could make it an office party. There'd be no wedding rings, though . . . and while the age range would be broad, there'd be no one who could be mistaken for the office junior. Clarke had asked Sandra about her group.

'It just gives me some company. I work in an old people's home, don't get the chance to meet anyone my own age. Then there's David. If I want to go out, my mum has to babysit.' David being her eleven-year-old son. 'It's just for company . . . that's all.'

Another woman in the group had said much the same thing, adding that a lot of the men you met at singles groups were 'let's say less than perfect'. But the women were fine: it was that company thing again.

Sitting at the edge of the booth, Clarke had been approached twice so far, turning down both suitors. One of the women had leaned across the table.

'You're fresh blood!' she'd shouted. 'They can always smell that!' Then she'd leaned back and laughed, showing stained teeth and a tongue turned green from the cocktail she was drinking.

'Moira's just jealous,' Sandra had said. 'The only ones who ever ask her up have usually spent all day queuing to renew their bus pass.'

Moira couldn't have heard the remark, but she stared anyway, as if sensing some slight against her.

'I need to go to the toilet,' Sandra said now.

'I'll come with you.'

Sandra nodded her agreement. Clarke had promised:

you won't be out of my sight for a second. They lifted their bags from the floor and started pushing their way through the throng.

The loo wasn't much emptier, but at least it was cool, and the door helped muffle the sound system. Clarke felt a dullness in her ears, and her throat was raw from cigarette smoke and shouting. While Sandra queued for a cubicle, Clarke made for the washbasins. She examined herself in the mirror. She didn't normally wear make-up, and was surprised to see her face so changed. The eyeliner and mascara made her eyes look hard rather than alluring. She tugged at one of her shoulder straps. Now that she was standing up, the hem of her dress was at her knees. But when she sat, it threatened to ride up to her stomach. She'd worn it only twice before: a wedding and a dinner party. Couldn't recall the same problem. Was she getting fat in the bum, was that it? She half-turned, tried to see, then turned her attention to her hair. Short: she liked the cut. It made her face longer. A woman bumped against her in the rush for the hand-drier. Loud snorts from one of the cubicles: someone doing a line? Conversations in the toilet queue: off-colour remarks about tonight's talent, who had the nicest bum. Which was preferable: a bulging crotch or a bulging wallet? Sandra had disappeared into one of the cubicles. Clarke folded her arms and waited. Someone stood in front of her.

'Are you the condom attendant or what?'

Laughter from the queue. She saw that she was standing beside the wall dispenser, moved slightly so the woman could drop a couple of coins into the slot. Clarke focused on the woman's right hand. Liver spots, sagging skin. The left hand went to the tray: her wedding finger was still marked from where she'd removed her ring. It was probably in her bag. Her face was machine-tanned, hopeful but hardened by experience. She winked.

'You never know.'

Clarke forced a smile. Back at the station, she'd heard

19

Singles Night at the Marina called all sorts of things: Jurassic Park, Grab-a-Granny. The usual bloke jokes. She found it depressing, but couldn't have said why. She didn't frequent nightclubs, not when she could help it. Even when she'd been younger – school and college years – she'd avoided them. Too noisy, too much smoke and drink and stupidity. But it couldn't just be that. These days, she followed Hibernian football club, and the terraces were full of cigarette smoke and testosterone. But there was a difference between the crowd in a stadium and the crowd at a place like the Marina: not many sexual predators chose to do their hunting in the midst of a football crowd. She felt safe at Easter Road; even attended away matches when she could. Same seat at every home game . . . she knew the faces around her. And afterwards . . . afterwards she melted into the streets, part of the anonymous mass. Nobody'd ever tried to chat her up. That wasn't why they were there, and she knew it, hugging the knowledge to her on cold winter afternoons when the floodlights were needed from kick-off.

The cubicle bolt slid back and Sandra emerged.

'About bleedin' time,' someone called out. 'Thought you'd a fellah in there with you.'

'Only to wipe my backside on,' Sandra said. The voice – all tough, casual humour – was forced. Sandra started fixing her make-up at the mirror. She'd been crying. There were fresh veins of red in the corners of her eyes.

'All right?' Clarke asked quietly.

'Could be worse, I suppose.' Sandra studied her reflection. 'I could always be pregnant, couldn't I?'

Her rapist had worn a condom, leaving no semen for the labs to analyse. They'd run checks on sex offenders, ruled out a slew of interviewees. Sandra had gone through the picture books, a gallery of misogyny. Just looking at their faces was enough to give some women nightmares. Bedraggled, vacuous features, dull eyes, weak jaws. Some victims who'd gone through the process . . . they'd had unasked questions, questions Clarke thought she could phrase along the lines of: *Look at them, how could we let them do this to us? They're the ones who look weak.*

Yes, weak at the moment of photographing, weak with shame or fatigue or the pretence of submission. But strong at the necessary moment, the crackling moment of hate. The thing was, they worked alone, most of them. The second man, the accomplice ... Siobhan was curious about him. What did he get out of it?

'Seen anyone you fancy?' Sandra was asking now. Her lipstick trembled slightly as she applied it.

'No.'

'Got someone at home?'

'You know I haven't.'

Sandra was still watching her in the mirror. 'I only know what you've told me.'

'I told you the truth.'

Long conversations, Clarke setting aside the rule book and opening herself to Sandra, answering her questions, stripping away her police self to reveal the person beneath. It had begun as a trick, a ploy to win Sandra over to the scheme. But it had evolved into something more, something real. Clarke had said more than she'd needed to, much more. And now it seemed Sandra hadn't been convinced. Was it that she didn't trust the detective, or was it that Clarke had become part of the problem, just someone else Sandra could never wholly trust? After all, they hadn't known one another until the rape; would never have met if it hadn't happened. Clarke was here at the Marina, looking like Sandra's friend, but that was another trick. They weren't friends; probably would never be friends. A vicious assault had brought them together. In Sandra's eyes, Clarke would always remind her of that night, a night she wanted to forget.

'How long do we have to stay?' she was asking now.

'That's up to you. We can leave any time you like.'

'But if we do, we might miss him.'

'Not your fault, Sandra. He could be anywhere. I just felt we had to give it a try.'

Sandra turned from the mirror. 'Half an hour more.' She glanced at her watch. 'I promised my mum I'd be home by twelve.'

Clarke nodded, followed Sandra back into a darkness punctuated by lightning, as if the light show could somehow earth all the energy in the room.

Back at the booth, Clarke's seat had been taken by a new arrival. Youngish male, fingers running down the condensation on a tall glass of what looked like straight orange juice. The club members seemed to know him.

'Sorry,' he said, getting to his feet as Clarke and Sandra approached. 'I've nicked your seat.' He stared at Clarke, then put out his hand. When Clarke took it, his grip tightened. He wasn't going to let her go.

'Come and dance,' he said, pulling her in the direction of the dance floor. She could do little but follow him, right into the heart of the storm where arms buffeted her and the dancers squealed and roared. He looked back, saw that they were no longer visible from the table, and kept moving, crossing the floor, leading them past one of the bars and into the foyer.

'Where are we going?' Clarke asked. He looked around, seemed satisfied and leaned towards her.

'I know you,' he said.

Suddenly, she knew that his face was familiar to her. She was thinking: criminal, someone I helped put away? She glanced to left and right.

'You work at St Leonard's,' he went on. She stared towards where his hand still held her wrist. Following her gaze, he let go suddenly. 'Sorry,' he said, 'it's just that . . .'

'Who are you?'

He seemed hurt that she didn't know. 'Derek Linford.'

Her eyes narrowed. 'Fettes?' He nodded. The newsletter, that's where she'd seen his face. And maybe in the canteen at HQ. 'What are you doing here?'

'I could ask you the same thing.'

'I'm with Sandra Carnegie.' Thinking: *no, I'm not; I'm out here with you . . . and I promised her . . .*

'Yes, but I don't . . .' His face crumpled. 'Oh, hell, she was raped, wasn't she?' He ran thumb and forefinger down the slope of his nose. 'You're trying for an ID?'

'That's right.' Clarke smiled. 'You're a member?'

'What if I am?' He seemed to expect an answer, but Clarke just shrugged. 'It's not the kind of information I bandy about, DC Clarke.' Pulling rank, warning her off.

'Your secret's safe with me, DI Linford.'

'Ah, speaking of secrets . . .' He looked at her, head tilted slightly.

'They don't know you're CID?' It was his turn to shrug. 'Christ, what have you told them?'

'Does it matter?'

Clarke was thoughtful. 'Hang on a sec, we talked to the club members. I don't remember seeing your name.'

'I only joined last week.'

Clarke frowned. 'So how do we play this?'

Linford rubbed his nose again. 'We've had our dance. We go back to the table. You sit one side, me the other. We really don't need to talk to one another again.'

'Charming.'

He grinned. 'I didn't mean it like that. Of course we can talk.'

'Gee, thanks.'

'In fact, something incredible happened this afternoon.' He took her arm, guided her back into the club. 'Help me get a round of drinks from the bar, and I'll tell you all about it.'

'He's an arse.'

'Maybe so,' Clarke said, 'but he's rather a sweet arse.'

John Rebus sat in his chair, holding the cordless phone to his ear. His chair was by the window. There were no curtains and the shutters were still open. No lights were on in his living room, just a bare sixty-watt bulb in the hall. But the street lamps bathed the room in an orange glow.

'Where did you say you bumped into him?'

'I didn't.' He could hear the smile in her voice.

'All very mysterious.'

'Not compared to your skeleton.'

'It's not a skeleton. Kind of shrivelled, like a mummy.' He gave a short, mirthless laugh. 'The archaeologist, I thought he was going to jump into my arms.'

'So what's the verdict?'

'SOCOs came in, roped the place off. Gates and Curt can't look at Skelly till Monday morning.'

'Skelly?'

Rebus watched a car cruising past, seeking a parking space. 'Bobby Hogan came up with the name. It'll do for now.'

'Nothing on the body?'

'Just what he was wearing: flared jeans, a Stones T-shirt.'

'Lucky us, having an expert on the premises.'

'If you mean a rock dinosaur, I'll take that as a compliment. Yes, it was the cover of *Some Girls*. Album came out in '78.'

'Nothing else to date the body?'

'Nothing in the pockets. No watch or rings.' He checked his own watch: 2 a.m. But she'd known she could call him, had known he'd be awake.

'What's on the hi-fi?' she asked.

'That tape you gave me.'

'The Blue Nile? There goes your dinosaur image. What do you think?'

'I think you're smitten by Mr Smarty-Pants.'

'I do like it when you come over all fatherly.'

'Watch I don't put you over my knee.'

'Careful, Inspector. These days I could have you off the job for saying something like that.'

24

'Are we going to the game tomorrow?'

'For our sins. I've a spare green and white scarf set aside for you.'

'I must remember to bring my lighter. Two o'clock in Mather's?'

'There'll be a beer waiting for you.'

'Siobhan, whatever it was you were up to tonight . . . ?'

'Yes?'

'Did you get a result?'

'No,' she said, sounding suddenly tired. 'Not even a goalless draw.'

He put the phone down, refilled his whisky glass. 'Refined tonight, John,' he told himself. Oftentimes nowadays he just swigged from the bottle. The weekend stretched ahead of him, one football game the extent of his plans. His living room was wreathed in shadows and cigarette smoke. He kept thinking of selling the flat, finding somewhere with fewer ghosts. Then again, they were the only company he had: dead colleagues, victims, expired relationships. He reached again for the bottle, but it was empty. Stood up and watched the floor sway beneath him. He thought he had a fresh bottle in the carrier bag beneath the window, but the bag was empty and crumpled. He looked out of his window, catching his reflection and its puzzled frown. Had he left a bottle in the car? Had he brought home two bottles or just the one? He thought of a dozen places where he could get a drink, even at two in the morning. The city – his city – was out there waiting for him, waiting to show its dark, shrivelled heart.

'I don't need you,' he said, resting the palms of his hands on the window, as if willing the glass to shatter and take him tumbling with it. A two-storey descent to the street below.

'I don't need you,' he repeated. Then he pushed off from the glass, went to find his coat.

3

Saturday, the clan had lunch at the Witchery.

It was a good restaurant, sited at the top of the Royal Mile. The Castle was a near neighbour. Lots of natural light: it was almost like eating in a conservatory. Roddy had organised it for their mother's 75th. She was a painter, and he reckoned she'd like all the light that poured into the restaurant. But the day was overcast. Squalls of rain drilled at the windows. Low cloud base: standing at the Castle's highest point, you felt you could have touched heaven.

They'd started with a quick walk around the battlements, Mother looking unimpressed. But then she'd first visited the place some seventy years before, had probably been there a hundred times since. And lunch hadn't improved her spirits, though Roddy praised each course, each mouthful of wine.

'You always overdo things!' his mother snapped at him.

To which he said nothing, just stared into his pudding bowl, glancing up eventually to wink at Lorna. When he did so, she was reminded of her brother as a kid, always with that shy, endearing quality – something he mostly reserved for voters and TV interviewers these days.

You always overdo things! Those words hung in the air for a time, as though others at the table wanted to relish them. But then Roddy's wife Seona spoke up.

'I wonder who he gets that from.'

'What did she say? *What did she say?*'

And of course it was Cammo who brokered the peace: 'Now, now, Mother, just because it's your birthday . . .'

'Finish the bloody sentence!'

Cammo sighed, took one of his deep breaths. 'Just because it's your birthday, let's take a walk down towards Holyrood.'

His mother glared at him. She had eyes like a frigate's hull. But then her face cracked into a smile. The others resented Cammo for his ability to bring about this transformation. At that moment, he possessed the powers of a magus.

Six of them at the table. Cammo, the elder son, hair swept back from his forehead, sporting his father's gold cuff links – the one thing the old man had left him in the will. They'd never agreed on politics, Cammo's father a Liberal of the old school. Cammo had joined the Conservative Party while still an undergraduate at St Andrews. Now he had a safe seat in the Home Counties, representing a mainly rural area between Swindon and High Wycombe. He lived in London, loved the nightlife and the sense of being at the core of something. Married, his wife a drunk and serial shopper. They were seldom seen together. He was photographed at balls and parties, always with some new woman on his arm.

That was Cammo.

He'd come north overnight on the sleeper; had complained that the club car hadn't been open – staff shortages.

'Bloody disgrace. You privatise the railways and still can't get a decent whisky and soda.'

'Christ, does anybody still drink soda?'

This was Lorna, back at the house as they prepared to go out to lunch. Lorna had always had the handling of her brother. She was all of eleven months younger than him, had somehow found time in her schedule for this reunion. Lorna was a fashion model – a story she was sticking to despite encroaching age and a shortage of bookings. In her late forties now, she'd been at her earning height in the 1970s. She still got work, cited

Lauren Hutton as an influence. She'd dated MPs in her time, just as Cammo had seen fit to 'walk out' with the occasional model. She'd heard stories about him, and was sure he'd heard stories about her. On the rare occasions when they met, they circled one another like bare-knuckle fighters.

Cammo had made a point of choosing whisky and soda as his aperitif.

Then there was baby Roddy, just touching forty. Always the rebel at heart, but somehow lacking the curriculum vitae. Roddy the one-time Scottish Office boffin, now an investment analyst. He was New Labour. Didn't really possess the ammunition when his big brother came in with all ideological guns blazing. But Roddy sat there with quiet, immutable authority, the shells failing to scratch him. One political commentator had called him Scottish Labour's Mr Fixit, because of his ability to brush away the sand from around the party's many landmines and set about defusing them. Others called him Mr Suck-Up, a lazy explanation of his emergence as a prospective MSP. In fact, Roddy had planned today's lunch as a double celebration, since he'd had official notice just that morning that he would be running in Edinburgh West End as Labour's candidate for the Scottish Parliament.

'Bloody hell,' had been Cammo's rolling-eyed reaction as the champagne was being poured.

Roddy had allowed himself a quiet smile, tucking a stray lock of thick black hair back behind his ear. His wife Seona had squeezed his arm in support. Seona was more than the loyal wife; if anything, she was the more politically active of the two, and history teacher at a city comprehensive.

Billary, Cammo often called them, a reference to Bill and Hillary Clinton. He thought most teachers were a short hop from subversives, which hadn't stopped him flirting with Seona on half a dozen separate, usually drunken occasions. When challenged by Lorna, his defence was always the same: 'Indoctrination by seduction. Bloody cults get away with it, why shouldn't the Tory Party?'

Lorna's husband was there, too, though he'd spent half the meal over by the doorway, head tucked in towards a mobile phone. From the back he looked faintly ridiculous: too paunchy for the cream linen suit, the pointy-toed black shoes. And the greying ponytail – Cammo had laughed out loud when introduced to it.

'Gone New Age on us, Hugh? Or is professional wrestling your new forte?'

'Sod off, Cammo.'

Hugh Cordover had been a rock star of sorts back in the 1970s and '80s. These days he was a record producer and band manager, and got less media attention than his brother Richard, an Edinburgh lawyer. He'd met Lorna at the tail-end of her career, when some adviser had assured her she could sing. She'd turned up late and drunk at Hugh's studio. He'd opened the door to her, thrown a glass of water into her face, and ordered her to come back sober. It had taken her the best part of a fortnight. They'd gone to dinner that night, worked in the studio till dawn.

People still recognised Hugh on the street, but they weren't the people worth knowing. These days, Hugh Cordover lived by his holy book, this being a bulging, black leather personal organiser. He had it open in his hand as he paced the restaurant, phone tucked between shoulder and cheek. He was fixing meetings, always meetings. Lorna watched him over the rim of her glass, while her mother demanded that the lights be turned on.

'So damned awful dark in here. Am I supposed to be reminded of the graveyard?'

'Yes, Roddy,' Cammo drawled, 'do something about it, will you? This was your idea after all.' Looking around the premises with all the disdain he could muster. But then the photographers had arrived – one organised by Roddy, one from a glossy magazine – which brought Cordover back to the table, and fixed authentic-seeming smiles to all the members of the Grieve clan.

Roddy Grieve hadn't meant for them to walk the whole length of the Royal Mile. He'd gone so far as to organise a couple of taxis which were waiting for them outside the Holiday Inn. But his mother wouldn't have it.

'If we're going to walk, then for Christ's sake let's walk!' And off she set, her walking stick seven parts affectation to three parts painful necessity, leaving Roddy to pay off the drivers. Cammo leaned towards him.

'You always overdo things.' A pretty good imitation of their mother.

'Bugger off, Cammo.'

'I wish I could, dear brother. But the next train to civilisation's not for some time yet.' Making show of studying his watch. 'Besides, it's Mother's birthday: she'd be devastated if I suddenly departed.'

Which, Roddy couldn't help feeling, was probably true.

'She'll go over on that ankle,' Seona said, watching her mother-in-law moving downhill with that peculiar shuffling gait which attracted all manner of attention. Sometimes, Seona felt that it was affectation, too. Alicia had always had ways and means of drawing the looks of those around her, and of including her offspring in the spectacle. It hadn't been so bad when Allan Grieve had been alive – he'd kept his wife's eccentricities in check. But now that Roddy's father was dead, Alicia had started compensating for years of enforced normality.

Not that the Grieves were a normal family: Roddy had warned Seona about them the first time they'd gone out together. She'd already known, of course – everyone in Scotland knew at least *something* about the Grieves – but had elected to keep her counsel. Roddy wasn't like them, she'd told herself back then. She still said it to herself sometimes, but without the old conviction.

'We could go look at the parliament site,' she suggested as they reached the St Mary's Street junction.

'Good God, whatever for?' Cammo droned predictably.

Alicia pursed her lips, then, saying nothing, turned towards Holyrood Road. Seona tried not to smile: it had been a small but palpable victory. But then who was she fighting?

Cammo held back. The three women were matching each other for pace. Hugh had stopped by a shop window to take yet another call. Cammo fell into step beside Roddy, pleased to note that he was still immeasurably better groomed and dressed than his younger brother.

'I've had another of those notes,' he said, keeping the tone conversational.

'What notes?'

'Christ, didn't I tell you? They come to my parliamentary office. My secretary opens them, poor girl.'

'Hate mail?'

'How many MPs do you know who get fan letters?' Cammo tapped Roddy's shoulder. 'Something you're going to have to live with if you get elected.'

'If,' Roddy repeated with a smile.

'Look, do you want to hear about these bloody death threats or not?'

Roddy stopped in his tracks, but Cammo kept walking. It took Roddy a moment to catch up.

'Death threats?'

Cammo shrugged. 'Not unknown in our line of work.'

'What do they say?'

'Nothing much. Just that I'm "in for it". One of them had a couple of razor blades inside.'

'What do the police say?'

Cammo looked at him. 'So middle-aged, and yet so naïve. The forces of law and order, Roddy – I offer this lesson gratis and for nothing – are like a leaky sieve, especially when there's a drink in it for them and one or more MPs is involved.'

'They'd talk to the media?'

'Bingo.'

'I still don't see . . .'

'The papers would be all over it, and all over me.' Cammo waited for his words to sink in. 'Wouldn't have a life to call my own.'

'But death threats . . .'

'A crank.' Cammo sniffed. 'Not worth mentioning really, except as a warning. My fate could be yours some day, baby bro.'

'If I get elected.' That shy smile again, the shyness masking a real appetite for the fight.

'If ne'er won fair maiden,' Cammo said. Then he shrugged. 'Something like that anyway.' He looked ahead. 'Mother's fairly shifting, isn't she?'

Alicia Grieve had been born Alicia Rankeillor, and it was under this name that she'd found fame – and a certain fortune – as a painter. The particular nature of Edinburgh light had been her subject. Her best-known painting – duplicated on greetings cards, prints and jigsaws – showed a series of jagged beams breaking through a carapace of cloud to pick out the Castle and the Lawnmarket beyond. Allan Grieve, though only a few years her elder, had been her tutor at the School of Art. They'd married young, but hadn't become parents until their careers were well established. Alicia had the sneaking feeling that Allan had always resented her success. He was a great teacher, but lacked the spark of genius as an artist himself. She'd once told him that his paintings were too accurate, that art needed a measure of artifice. He'd squeezed her hand but said nothing until just before his death, when he'd thrown her words back at her.

'You killed me that day, snuffed out any hope I might have still had.' She'd started to protest but he'd hushed her. 'You did me a good turn, you were right. I lacked the vision.'

Sometimes Alicia wished that she'd lacked the vision,

too. Not that it would have made her a better, more loving mother. But it might have made her a more generous wife, a more pleasing lover.

Now she lived alone in the huge house in Ravelston, surrounded by the paintings of others – including a dozen of Allan's, smartly framed – and a short walk from the Gallery of Modern Art, where they'd recently held a retrospective of her work. She had contrived an illness to excuse her from attending, then had gone in secret one day, only minutes past opening time when the place was dead, and had been shocked to find that thematic order had been placed on her work, an order she didn't recognise.

'They found a body, you know,' Hugh Cordover was saying.

'Hugh!' Cammo piped up with mock cordiality. 'You're back with us!'

'A body?' Lorna asked.

'It was on the news.'

'I heard it was a skeleton actually,' Seona said.

'Found where?' Alicia asked, pausing to take in the skyline of Salisbury Crags.

'Hidden in a wall in Queensberry House.' Seona pointed to the location. They were standing in front of its gates. They all stared at the building. 'It used to be a hospital.'

'Probably some poor old sod from the waiting list,' Hugh Cordover said, but no one was listening.

4

'Who do you think you are?'

'What?'

'You heard me.' Jayne Lister threw a cushion at her husband's head. 'Those dishes have been sitting since last night.' Her head motioned towards the kitchen. 'You said you were going to do them.'

'I *am* going to do them!'

'When?'

'It's Sunday, day of rest.' He was trying to make a joke of it; didn't want his whole day ruined.

'The whole week's a day of rest as far as you're concerned. What time did you get in last night?'

He tried to see past her to where the TV was playing: some kids' morning show; presenter was a bit of all right. He'd told Nic about her. She was there right now, talking on the telephone, waving a card. Imagine waking up of a morning and finding that beside you in the scratcher.

'Move your arse,' he told his wife.

'You've taken the words out of my mouth.' She turned and pushed the off button. Jerry was off the sofa with a speed which surprised her. He liked the look on her face: startled, and with a little bit of fear mixed in. He pushed her aside, reached for the button, but her hands were in his hair, yanking him back.

'Out with that Nic Hughes till all hours,' she was yelling. 'Think you can come and go as you please, fucking pig!'

He grabbed one of her wrists, squeezed. 'Let go!'

'Think I'm going to put up with it?' She seemed

oblivious to the pain. He squeezed harder, wrenching the wrist round. Her grip on his hair tightened. His scalp felt like it was on fire. Threw his head back and caught her just above the nose. That did it. She shrieked and let go, and he half-turned, pushing her hard on to the sofa. Her foot sent the coffee table flying: ashtray, empty cans, Saturday's paper. Whole lot hit the deck. A thumping noise on the ceiling – upstairs neighbours complaining again. Her forehead was reddening where he'd connected. Christ, she'd given him a headache, too: as if the hangover wasn't enough to be going on with.

He'd done his arithmetic this morning: eight pints and two nips. That tallied with the small change in his pockets. Taxi had cost six quid. Nic had paid for the curry: lamb rogan josh, lovely. Nic had wanted to hit the clubs, but Jerry had said he wasn't in the mood.

'What if *I'm* in the mood, though?' Nic had said. But after the curry he hadn't seemed so keen. Two or three pubs . . . then a taxi for Jerry. Nic had said he'd walk. That was the clever thing about living in the middle of town: no need to worry over transport. Out here in the sticks, transport was always a problem. The buses weren't to be relied on, and he could never remember when they stopped running anyway. Even taxi drivers, you had to lie to them, tell them you were bound for Gatehill. When you reached Gatehill, you could either get out and walk across the playing fields, or you could persuade the driver to take you the final half-mile into the Garibaldi Estate. One time, Jerry had been jumped while crossing the football pitch: four or five of them, and him too drunk to do anything but capitulate. Ever since, he would argue to be taken the distance.

'You really are a bastard,' Jayne was saying, rubbing her brow.

'You started it. I'm lying there with a head like blazes. If you'd just held off a few hours . . .' His voice was soothing. 'I was going to do the dishes, cross my heart. I just need a bit of peace first.' Opening his arms to her. Fact was, the little bout of sparring had given him a hard-on. Maybe Nic was right about sex and violence, about how they were pretty much the same thing.

Jayne pounced to her feet, seemed to have seen straight through him. 'Forget it, pal.' Stalked out of the room. Temper on her . . . and always quick to take the huff. Maybe Nic was right, maybe he really *could* do better. But then look at Nic with his good job and his clothes and everything. Mortgage and money, and still Catriona had left him. Jerry snorted: *left him for someone she met at a singles night! Married woman, and off she trots to a singles night . . . and meets someone!* Life could be cruel, all right; Jerry should be thankful for small mercies. Back on with the telly, lying down on the sofa. His beer can was on the floor, untouched. He lifted it. Cartoons now, but that was all right; he liked cartoons. Didn't have any kids, which was just as well: he was still a bit of a kid at heart himself. The ceiling thumpers upstairs, they had three . . . and had the gall to say *he* was noisy! And there it was on the floor, where it had fallen from the coffee table: the letter from the council. Complaints have reached us . . . powers to deal with problem neighbours . . . blah blah. Was it his fault they built the walls so thin? Bloody things would barely hold a Rawlplug. When the buggers upstairs were trying for kid number four, you felt like you were in the bed with them. One night, when they'd stopped he'd given them a round of applause. Deadly silence after, so he knew they'd heard.

He wondered if maybe that was why Jayne had gone off sex: fear of being heard. One day he'd ask her about it. Either that or he'd make her do it anyway. Make her cry out long and hard so they heard her upstairs, give them something to think about. That wee thing on the telly, he'd bet she was a noisy one. You'd have to clamp your hand over her mouth, but making sure she could still breathe.

Like Nic said, that was the important part.

'You like football then?'

Derek Linford had taken Siobhan's number at the Marina. Saturday, he'd left a message on her machine asking if she fancied a Sunday walk. So here they were in the Botanic Gardens, a crisp afternoon, couples all around, strolling just like them. But talking football.

'I go most Saturdays,' Siobhan confessed.

'I thought there was a winter shutdown or something.' Struggling to show some knowledge of the game.

She smiled at the effort he was making. 'Only for the premier league. Last season, Hibs got knocked down to the first.'

'Oh, right.' They were coming to a signpost. 'If you're cold, we could go to the tropical house.'

She shook her head. 'I'm fine. I don't usually do much on a Sunday.'

'No?'

'Maybe a car boot sale. Mostly, I just stay home.'

'No boyfriend then?' She didn't say anything. 'Sorry I asked.'

She shrugged. 'It's not a sin, is it?'

'Career we're in, how are we supposed to meet people?'

She looked at him. 'Hence the singles club?'

He reddened. 'I suppose so.'

'Don't worry, I'm not about to tell anyone.'

He tried a smile. 'Thanks.'

'You're right anyway,' she went on, 'when *do* we ever meet anyone? Apart from other cops, that is.'

'And villains.'

The way he said it made her suspect he'd not met too many 'villains'. But she nodded anyway.

'I think the tea room'll be open,' he said. 'If you're ready . . . ?'

'Tea and a scone.' She took his arm. 'A perfect Sunday afternoon.'

Except that the family at the table next to them had one hyperactive child and a squealing infant in a pushchair. Linford turned to glower at the infant, as though it would instantly recognise his authority and start behaving.

'What's so funny?' he said, turning back to Clarke.

'Nothing,' she said.

'Must be something.' He started attacking the contents of his coffee cup with a spoon.

She lowered her voice so the family wouldn't hear. 'I was just wondering if you were going to take him into custody.'

'Chance would be a fine thing.' He sounded serious.

They sat in silence for a minute or two, then Linford started telling her about Fettes. When she got a chance, she asked him: 'And what do you like to do when you're not working?'

'Well, there's always a lot of reading to do: textbooks and journals. I keep pretty busy.'

'Sounds fascinating.'

'It is, that's what most people . . .' His voice died away, and he looked at her. 'You were being ironic, right?'

She nodded, smiling. He cleared his throat, got to work with the spoon again.

'Change of subject,' he said at last. 'What's John Rebus like? You work with him at St Leonard's, don't you?'

She was about to say that he hadn't exactly changed the subject, but nodded instead. 'Why do you ask?'

He shrugged. 'The committee, he doesn't seem to take it seriously.'

'Maybe he'd rather be doing something else.'

'From what I've seen of him, that would involve sitting in a pub with a cigarette in his mouth. Got a drink problem, has he?'

She stared at him. 'No,' she said coldly.

He was shaking his head. 'Sorry, shouldn't have asked. Got to stick up for him, haven't you? Same division and all that.'

She bit back a reply. He let the spoon clatter back on to its saucer.

'I'm being an idiot,' he said. The infant was screaming again. 'It's this place . . . Can't think straight.' He risked a look at her. 'Can we go?'

5

Monday morning, Rebus headed for the city mortuary. Normally, when an autopsy was being carried out, he would enter by the side door, which led directly to the viewing area. But the building's air filtering wasn't up to scratch, so all autopsies were now carried out at a hospital, and the mortuary was for storage only. There were none of the distinctive grey Bedford vans in the parking area – unlike most cities, the Edinburgh mortuary picked up every dead body; only later did undertakers enter the equation. He entered by the staff door. There was no one in the 'card room' – so called because employees spent their spare time playing cards there – so he wandered into the storage area. Dougie, who ran the place, was standing there in his white coat, clipboard in hand.

'Dougie,' Rebus said, announcing himself.

Dougie peered at him through wire-rimmed glasses. 'Morning, John.' His eyes twinkled with good humour. He always joked that he worked in the dead centre of Edinburgh.

Rebus twitched his nostrils, letting Dougie know he could smell the faint but noticeable smell.

'Aye,' Dougie said. 'A bad one. Elderly lady, probably dead a week.' He nodded towards the Decomposing Room, where the worst-smelling corpses were stored.

'Well, my one's been dead a sight longer than that.'

Dougie nodded. 'You're too late though. He's already gone.'

'Gone?' Rebus checked his watch.

'Two of my boys took him off to the Western General about an hour ago.'

'I thought the autopsy was scheduled for eleven.'

Dougie shrugged. 'Your man was keen – keen and persuasive. It takes a lot to get the Two Musketeers to change their diaries.'

The Two Musketeers: Dougie's name for Professor Gates and Dr Curt. Rebus frowned.

'My man?'

Dougie looked down at his clipboard, found the name. 'DI Linford.'

When Rebus got to the hospital, the autopsy was in full swing, and with it the double act of Gates and Curt. Professor Gates liked to describe himself as big-boned. Certainly as he leaned over the remains he seemed the antithesis of his colleague, who was tall and gaunt. Curt, Gates' junior by a decade, kept clearing his throat, something newcomers took as a comment on Gates' handiwork. They didn't know about the smoking habit, which was up to thirty a day now. Every moment Curt spent in the autopsy suite was precious time away from his fix. Rebus, whose mind had been on other things during the journey, suddenly craved a cigarette.

'Morning, John,' Gates said, glancing up from his work. Under his rubberised full-length apron he was wearing a crisp white shirt and red-and-yellow striped tie. Somehow his ties always stood out against the grey colours of the suite.

'Been jogging?' Curt asked. Rebus was aware that he was breathing heavily. He ran his hand over his forehead.

'No, I just . . .'

'If he keeps that up,' Gates said, his eyes on Curt, 'he'll be next on the slab.'

'Won't that be fun?' Curt responded. 'Digestive tract full of bridies and beetroot.'

'And the man's so thick-skinned, we'll need hatchets

rather than scalpels.' The pair shared a laugh. Not for the first time, Rebus cursed the rule of corroboration, which necessitated two pathologists at each autopsy.

The corpse – literally skin and bone, though some of the skin had been removed already – lay on a shallow stainless-steel trolley, the surface of which was moulded so as to catch any spilled blood. The corpse, however, had dust and cobwebs to spare, but no life fluid. Its skull lay on an angled wooden plinth which, in another context, might have been taken for a curio cheeseboard.

'There's a time and a place for banter, gentlemen.' The voice was Linford's. He was younger than either pathologist, but something about his tone quietened them. Then his eyes were on Rebus. 'Good morning, John.'

Rebus walked over towards him. 'Good of you to tell me about the change of schedule.'

Linford blinked. 'Is there a problem?'

Rebus stared him out. 'No, no problem.' There were others in the room: two hospital technicians, a police photographer, someone from Scene of Crimes, and a suited and queasy-looking man from the Advocate Depute's office. Autopsies were always crowded, everyone either getting on with their work, or else fidgeting nervously.

'I did a bit of boning up over the weekend,' Gates was saying, addressing the room. 'So I can tell you that, judging by the deterioration, our friend here probably died some time in the late nineteen seventies or early eighties.'

'Have his clothes gone for analysis?' Linford asked.

Gates nodded. 'Howdenhall got them this morning.'

'A young man's clothes,' Curt added.

'Or an old one trying to look trendy,' the photographer said.

'Well, the hair shows no signs of grey. Doesn't necessarily mean anything.' Gates looked at the photographer, letting him know his theories weren't welcome. 'The lab will give us a better date of death.'

'How did he die?' This from Linford. Normally Gates would punish such impatience, but he didn't so much as glance at the young DI.

'Skull fracture.' Curt pointed to the area with a pen. 'Could be a post-mortem injury, of course. Might not be the cause of death.' He caught Rebus's eye. 'A lot depends on the Scene of Crime results.'

The SOCO was scribbling into a thick notepad. 'We're working on it.'

Rebus knew what they'd be looking for – murder weapon to start with, and then trace evidence such as blood. Blood had a way of sticking around.

'How did he end up in the fireplace anyway?' he asked.

'Not our problem,' Gates said, smiling towards Curt.

'I take it we're noting this as a suspicious death?' the Fiscal Depute asked, his bass baritone belying the lack of height and brittle frame.

'I'd say so, wouldn't you?' Gates had straightened up, clattering one of his tools back on to its metal tray. It took a moment for Rebus to realise that the pathologist was holding something in his gloved hand. Something shrivelled and the size of a large peach.

'Tough old organ, the heart,' Gates said, examining the specimen.

'You missed the beginning,' Curt explained to Rebus. 'Gash in the skin over the ribcage. Could have been rats . . .'

'Aye,' Gates admitted, 'rats carrying knives.' He showed the organ to his colleague. 'Inch-wide incision. Maybe a kitchen knife, eh?'

'Suspicious death,' the Fiscal Depute muttered to himself, writing it down in his notebook.

'I should have been told,' Rebus hissed. He was in the hospital car park, not about to let Derek Linford drive back to the Big House.

'I know about you, John. You're not a team player.'

43

'And that was your idea of team playing? Leaving me out?'

'Look, maybe you've got a point. I just don't think it's anything to get het up about.'

'But it's our case, right?'

Linford had opened the driver's door of his shiny new BMW. It was a 3-Series, but would do him for now. 'In what way?'

'The PPLC. We found him.'

'It's not in our brief.'

'Come on. Who else is going to want it? Do you think the parliament really wants an unsolved murder on the premises?'

'A murder from twenty-odd years ago: I hardly think it'll cost them any sleep.'

'Maybe not, but the press won't let it go. Any whiff of scandal, they'll be able to point back to it: Holyrood's murky past, a parliament tainted with blood.'

Linford snorted, but then was thoughtful, finally producing a smile. 'Are you always like this?'

'I think Skelly is ours.'

Linford folded his arms. Rebus knew what he was thinking: the investigation would touch the parliament; it was a route to meeting the movers and shakers. 'How do we play it?'

Rebus rested a hand on the BMW's wing, saw Linford's look and removed it. 'How did he end up there? A couple of decades back, the place was a hospital. I'm guessing you couldn't just walk in, tear down a wall and stuff a body behind it.'

'You think the patients might have noticed?'

It was Rebus's turn to smile. 'It will mean a bit of digging.'

'Your forte, I believe?'

Rebus shook his head. 'I've had enough of all that.'

'What do you mean?'

He meant ghosts, but wasn't about to try to explain.

'What about Grant Hood and Ellen Wylie?' he said instead.

'Will they want it?'

'They won't have any choice. Ever heard the phrase pulling rank?'

Linford nodded thoughtfully, then got into his car, but Rebus's hand stopped him pulling the door closed.

'Just one other thing. Siobhan Clarke is a friend of mine. Anyone makes her unhappy makes *me* unhappy.'

'Don't tell me: I wouldn't like you when you're angry?' Linford smiled again, but coldly this time. 'I get the feeling Siobhan wouldn't thank you for fighting her battles for her. Especially when they're all in your head. Goodbye, John.'

Linford started the engine, then let it idle as he took a call on his mobile. After listening for a few seconds, he stared out at Rebus and slid his window down.

'Where's your car?'

'Two rows back.'

'You'd better follow me then.' Linford terminated the call and tossed the mobile on to his passenger seat.

'Why? What's happened?'

Linford slid both hands around the steering wheel. 'Another body at Queensberry House.' He stared through the windscreen. 'Only a bit fresher this time.'

6

They'd passed the summer house the previous Friday. It was a flimsy wooden affair which had belonged to the hospital and stood inside the grounds, next to Her Majesty's cherry tree. Like the tree, the summer house was for the chop. But for now it was a handy storage area; nothing valuable, there was no lock on the door. And even a lock would have been ineffective, since most of the windows were broken.

This was where the body had been found, lying amidst old paint tins, bags of rubble and broken tools.

'Probably not the way he'd have chosen to go,' Linford muttered, looking around him at the chaos of the site. Uniforms were erecting a cordon around the summer house and its vicinity. Workers in hard hats were being told to disperse. A crowd of them had gathered on the roof of one of the buildings under demolition, from where they had a grandstand view of proceedings. Maybe their fellow workers would join them. Maybe the roof would cave in. Not yet midday and Rebus was conjuring up worst-case scenarios, while praying this would be as bad as it got. The site manager was being interviewed in the security hut, complaining that all the police officers needed to be issued with hard hats. Rebus and Linford had filched a couple from the hut. SOCOs were unpacking the arcana of their craft. A doctor had pronounced death; the call had gone out to the available pathologists. All the building work on Holyrood Road had reduced it to a single lane, controlled by traffic lights. Now, with police cars and vans on the scene (including a grey one from the mortuary,

46

Dougie behind the wheel) queues were forming and tempers fraying. The sound of horns was growing into a chorus, rising into the bruised-looking sky.

'Snow's on the way,' Rebus commented. 'It's cold enough for it.' Yet the previous day had started mild, and even the rain had been like an April shower. Twelve degrees.

'The weather's not exactly a consideration,' Linford snapped. He wanted to get closer to the body, wanted to be inside the summer house, but the *locus* had to be secured. He knew the rules: barging in meant leaving traces.

'Doctor says the back of the skull was cracked open.' He nodded to himself, looked towards Rebus. 'Coincidence?'

Hands in pockets, Rebus shrugged. He was sucking on only his second cigarette of the morning. He knew Linford was tasting something: he was tasting fast-track. Not content with his own momentum, he was seeing a case, a big case. He was seeing himself at its heart, with media attention, the public clamouring for a result. A result he thought *he* could deliver.

'He was running in my constituency,' Linford was saying. 'I've got a flat in Dean Village.'

'Very nice.'

Linford stifled an embarrassed laugh.

'It's okay,' Rebus assured him. 'Times like this, we all tend to talk crap. It fills the spaces.'

Linford nodded.

'Tell me,' Rebus went on, 'just how many murders have you worked?'

'Is this where you pull the old I've-seen-more-corpses-than-you've-had-hot-dinners routine?'

Rebus shrugged again. 'Just interested.'

'I wasn't always at Fettes, you know.' Linford shuffled his feet. 'Christ, I wish they'd get on with it.' The body was still *in situ*, the body of Roddy Grieve. They knew his identity because a gentle search of his pockets had

47

produced a wallet. But they knew, too, because his face was recognisable, even though the light had gone from its eyes. They knew because Roddy Grieve was *somebody*, and seemed so even in death.

He was a Grieve, part of 'the clan', as they'd come to be called. Once, a keen interviewer had gone so far as to name them Scotland's first family. Which was nonsense.

Everyone knew Scotland's first family was the Broons.

'What are you smiling at?'

'Nothing.' Rebus nipped his cigarette and returned it to the packet. He couldn't know for sure whether stubbing it out would have contaminated the crime scene. But he knew the importance of Scene of Crime work. And he felt the sudden pang of desire for a drink, the drink he'd arranged with Bobby Hogan just before Friday's discovery. A long bar-room session of reminiscence and tall tales, with no bodies buried in walls or dumped in summer houses. A drink in some parallel universe where people had stopped being cruel to each other.

And speaking of mental torture, here came Chief Superintendent Farmer Watson. He had Rebus in his sights, and his eyes had narrowed, as though taking aim.

'Don't blame me, sir,' Rebus said, getting his retaliation in first.

'Christ, John, can't you stay out of trouble for one minute?' It was only half a joke. Watson's retirement was a couple of months away. He'd already warned Rebus that he wanted a quiet canter downhill. Rebus held up his hands in surrender and introduced his boss to Derek Linford.

'Ah, Derek.' The Chief Super held out a hand. 'Heard of you, of course.' The two men shook; kept shaking as they sized one another up.

'Sir,' Rebus interrupted, 'DI Linford and I . . . we feel this should be our case. We're looking at parliamentary security, and this is a prospective MSP who's been killed.'

Watson seemed to ignore him. 'Do we know how he died?'

'Not yet, sir,' Linford was quick to answer. Rebus was impressed at the way he had changed. He was all fawning inferior now, eager to please the Big Chief. It was calculated, of course, but Rebus doubted Watson would notice, or even want to notice.

'Doctor mentioned head trauma,' Linford added. 'Curiously, we're getting a similar result from the body in the fireplace. Skull fracture and stab wound.'

Watson nodded slowly. 'No stab wounds here, though.'

'No, sir,' Rebus said. 'But all the same.'

Watson looked at him. 'You think I'd let you *near* a case like this?'

Rebus shrugged.

'I can show you the fireplace,' Linford told Watson. Rebus wondered if he was trying to defuse the situation. Linford could get the case only through the PPLC, which meant not without Rebus.

'Maybe later, Derek,' the Farmer was saying. 'Nobody's going to bother much about a mouldy old skeleton when we've got Roddy Grieve on our hands.'

'It wasn't that mouldy, sir,' Rebus felt bound to say. 'And it'll still need investigating.'

'Naturally,' Watson snapped. 'But there are priorities, John. Even you've got to see that.' Watson held a hand out, palm upwards. 'Hell, is it starting to snow?'

'Might persuade some of the audience to head indoors,' Rebus said.

The Farmer grunted in agreement. 'Well, if it's going to start snowing, Derek, you might as well show me this fireplace of yours.'

Derek Linford looked as though he'd melt with pleasure, and started leading the Farmer indoors, leaving Rebus out in the cold, where he allowed himself a cigarette and a little smile. Let Linford work on the Farmer . . . that way they might get both cases, a workload to keep Rebus busy through the winter's darkest weeks, and the perfect excuse to ignore Christmas for another year.

7

Identification was a formality, albeit a necessary one. The public entered the mortuary by a door in High School Wynd, and were immediately faced by a door marked Viewing Room. There were chairs for them to sit in. If they chose to wander, they'd come across a desk with a department store mannequin seated behind it. The mannequin was dressed in a white lab coat and had a moustache pencilled below its nose – a rare, if bizarre, example of humour, given the surroundings.

It would be some time before Gates and Curt could get round to doing an autopsy, but, as Dougie reassured Rebus, there was 'plenty of room in the fridge'. There wasn't nearly so much space in the reception area outside the Viewing Room. Roddy Grieve's widow was there. So were his mother and sister. His brother Cammo was flying up from London. An unwritten rule stated that the media kept clear of the mortuary, no matter how juicy the story. But a few of the most rapacious vultures had gathered on the pavement across the road. Rebus, stepping outside for a cigarette, approached them. Two journalists, one photographer. They were young and lean and had little or no respect for old rules. They knew him, shuffled their feet but made no attempt to move.

'I'm going to ask nicely,' Rebus said, shaking a cigarette from its pack. He lit it, then offered the pack around. The three shook their heads. One was fiddling with his mobile phone, checking messages on its tiny screen.

'Anything for us, DI Rebus?' the other reporter asked.

Rebus stared at him, seeing immediately that it was no good appealing to reason.

'Off the record, if you like,' the reporter persisted.

'I don't mind being quoted,' Rebus said quietly. The reporter lifted a tape-recorder from his jacket pocket.

'Bit closer, please.'

The reporter obliged, switched the machine on.

Rebus was careful to enunciate slowly and clearly. After eight or nine words, the reporter flicked the machine off, the look on his face somewhere between a sneer and a grudging smile. Behind him, his colleagues were staring at their shoes.

'Need a spell-check for any of that?' Rebus asked. Then he crossed the road and headed back into the mortuary.

The ID was over, the paperwork complete. The family members looked numb. Even Linford looked a bit shaken: maybe it was another of his acts. Rebus approached the widow.

'We can arrange for a couple of cars . . .'

She sniffed back tears. 'No, that's all right. Thanks anyway.' She blinked, eyes finally focusing on him. 'A taxi should be coming.' The deceased's sister came across, leaving her mother stony-faced and straight-backed on one of the chairs.

'Mum has a funeral home she wants to use, if that's all right with you.' Lorna Cordover was speaking to the widow, but it was Rebus who answered.

'You realise we can't release the body just yet.'

She stared at him with eyes he'd stared at a thousand times in newspapers and magazines. Lorna Grieve: her modelling name. She wasn't yet fifty, but was closing in on it fast. Rebus had first come across her towards the end of the sixties, when she'd have been in her late teens. She'd dated rock stars, was rumoured to have caused the break-up of at least one successful band. She'd been in *Melody Maker* and *NME*. Long straw-blond hair back then, and thin to the point of emaciation. She'd filled out quite a bit, and her hair was shorter, darker. But there was still something about her, even in this place, at this time.

'We're his bloody family,' she snapped.

'Please, Lorna,' her sister-in-law cautioned.

'Well, we are, aren't we? Last thing we need is some jumped-up little squirt with a clipboard telling us—'

'I think maybe you're confusing me with the staff here,' Rebus cut in.

She looked at him again, eyes narrowing. 'Then just who the hell are you?'

'He's the policeman,' Seona Grieve explained. 'He'll be the one who looks into . . .' But she couldn't find the words, and the sentence died softly with an exhalation.

Lorna Grieve snorted, pointed towards Derek Linford, who had seated himself next to the mother, Alicia. He was leaning towards her, his hand touching the back of hers. 'That', Lorna informed them, 'is the officer who'll be investigating Roddy's murder.' She squeezed Seona's shoulder. '*He*'s the one we should be talking to,' she said. Then, with a final glance towards Rebus, 'Not his monkey.'

Rebus watched her move back towards the chairs. Beside him, the widow spoke so softly he didn't catch it.

'Sorry,' she repeated.

He smiled, nodded. There were a dozen platitudes scrawled and waiting in his head. He rubbed a hand across his forehead to erase them.

'You'll want to ask us questions,' she said.

'When you're ready.'

'He didn't have any enemies . . . not really.' She seemed to be speaking to herself. 'That's what they always ask on TV, isn't it?'

'We'll get round to it.' He was watching Lorna Grieve, who was crouched in front of her mother. Linford was looking at her, drinking her in. The main door opened, a head appearing.

'Somebody order a taxi?'

Rebus watched as Derek Linford escorted Alicia Grieve all the way out. It was a shrewd move: not the widow, but the matriarch. Linford knew power when he saw it.

They gave the family a few hours, then drove to Ravelston Dykes.

'What do you reckon then?' Linford asked. From his tone, he might have been asking what Rebus thought of the BMW.

Rebus just shrugged. Between them, they'd managed to sort out a Murder Room at St Leonard's, it being the closest station to the *locus*. Not that it was a murder inquiry yet, but they knew it would be, just as soon as the autopsy was finished. Calls had gone out to Joe Dickie and Bobby Hogan. Rebus had also hooked up with Grant Hood and Ellen Wylie, neither of whom objected to the idea of working together on the Skelly case.

'It'll be a challenge,' both had said, independently of one another. Their bosses would have the final say, but Rebus didn't foresee problems. He'd told Hood and Wylie to get together, thrash out a plan of attack.

'And who do we report to?' Wylie had asked.

'Me,' he'd told her, making sure Linford wasn't in earshot.

The BMW eased down into second as they approached an amber light. Had Rebus been driving, he'd have accelerated, probably just missing red. Maybe not on his own, but with a passenger – he'd have done it to impress. He'd have laid money on Linford doing it, too. The BMW stopped at the lights. Linford applied the handbrake and turned towards him.

'Investment analyst, Labour candidate, high-profile family. What do you think?'

Rebus shrugged again. 'I've seen the newspaper stories, same as you. Some people haven't always liked the way candidates were selected.'

Linford was nodding. 'Maybe some bad blood there?'

'We'll ask. Could just be a mugging gone wrong.'

'Or a liaison.'

Rebus glanced at him. Linford was staring at the lights, fingers poised on the handbrake. 'Maybe the SOCOs will work their magic.'

'Fingerprints and fibres?' Linford sounded sceptical.

'Lot of mud around. Could be we'll find footprints.'

The light turned green. With an empty road ahead, the BMW quickly changed up through its gears.

'The boss has already been on to me,' Linford told his passenger. Rebus knew that by boss he didn't mean anything as middle-management as a chief super. 'The ACC,' Linford explained: Colin Carswell, Assistant Chief Constable (Crime). 'He wanted to bring in a special team, something as high profile as this.'

'Crime Squad?'

It was Linford's turn to shrug. 'Hand picked. I don't know who he had in mind.'

'What did you tell him?'

'I said with me in charge, he didn't have to worry.' Linford couldn't help it, had to turn towards Rebus to enjoy his reaction. Rebus was trying to look unmoved by it all. All his years on the force, he'd probably spoken with the ACC no more than two or three times.

Linford smiled, knew he'd hit some soft, fleshy part beneath Rebus's shell-like exterior.

'Of course,' he went on, 'when I mentioned that DI Rebus would be assisting . . .'

'Assisting?' Rebus bristled, and only now recollected that Linford had also spoken of being in charge.

'He was a bit more dubious,' Linford went on, ignoring the outburst. 'But I told him you'd be fine, said we were working well together. That's what I mean by assisting – you helping me, me helping you.'

'But with you in charge?'

Hearing his own phrase thrown back at him seemed to

please Linford: another palpable hit. 'Your own chief super doesn't want you on the case, John. Why is that?'

'None of your business.'

'Everyone knows about you, John. I could say that your reputation precedes you.'

'But it'll be different with you in charge?' Rebus guessed.

Linford shrugged and was silent for a moment, then shifted in his seat. 'While we're enjoying this time together,' he said, 'maybe I should throw in that I'm seeing Siobhan tonight. But don't worry, I'll have her home by eleven.'

Roddy Grieve and his wife had lived together somewhere in Cramond, but Seona Grieve had intimated that she would be with Roddy's mother. Situated at the end of a short narrow street, the huge detached house had a jagged feel to it. Maybe it was to do with the several crow-step gables, or the stone relief thistle set into the wall above the front door. There were no cars in the drive, and curtains had been drawn closed in every window – a sensible precaution: the reporters and cameraman were back, parked kerbside in a silver Audi 80. TV crews were probably on their way. Rebus had no doubt the Grieves would cope with the attention.

Grieve: the resonance of the name hit him for the first time. The grieving Grieves.

Linford rang the doorbell. 'Nice place,' he said.

'I was brought up in something similar,' Rebus told him. Then, after a pause: 'Well, we lived in a cul-de-sac.'

'And there', Linford guessed, 'the comparison ends.'

The door was opened by a man dressed in a camel-hair coat with dark brown lapels. The coat was unbuttoned. Beneath it could be glimpsed a tailored pinstripe suit and white shirt. The shirt was unbuttoned at the neck. In his left hand, the man carried a plain black tie.

'Mr Grieve?' Rebus guessed. He'd seen Cammo Grieve

on TV many times. In the flesh he seemed taller and more distinguished, even in his present confused-looking state. His cheeks were red, either from cold or a few airline drinks. A couple of strands of silver and black hair were out of place.

'You the police? Come inside.'

Linford followed Rebus into the hallway. There were paintings and drawings everywhere, not just covering the wood-panelled walls, but resting against the skirting boards, too. Books were piled high on the bottom step of the stone staircase. Several pairs of dusty-looking rubber wellington boots – men's and women's, and all of them black – sat at the foot of an overloaded coat rack. There were walking sticks protruding from an umbrella stand, and umbrellas hooked over the banister. An open jar of honey sat on a telephone table, as did an answering machine. The machine wasn't plugged in, and there was no sign of a phone. Cammo Grieve seemed to take in his surroundings.

'Sorry,' he said. 'In a bit of a . . . well, you understand.' He stroked the stray hairs back into place.

'Of course, sir,' Linford said, his voice deferential.

'A bit of advice, though,' Rebus added, waiting till he had the MP's attention. 'Anyone at all could turn up claiming to be police officers. Make sure you ask for ID before letting them in.'

Cammo Grieve nodded. 'Ah yes, the fourth estate. Bastards for the most part.' He looked at Rebus. 'Off the record.'

Rebus merely nodded; it was Linford who smiled too brightly at the attempted levity.

'I still can't . . .' Grieve's face hardened. 'I trust the police will be working flat-out on this case. If I so much as hear of any corners being cut . . . I know what it's like these days, tightened budgets, all of that. Labour government, you see.'

It was in danger of turning into a speech. Rebus

interrupted. 'Well, standing around here isn't exactly helping matters, sir.'

'I'm not sure I like you,' Grieve said, narrowing his eyes. 'What's your name?'

'His name's Monkey Man,' a voice called from a doorway. Lorna Grieve was carrying two glasses of whisky. She handed one to her brother, clinked her own against it before taking a gulp. 'And this one', she said, meaning Linford, 'is the Organ Grinder.'

'I'm DI Rebus,' Rebus informed Cammo Grieve. 'This is DI Linford.'

Linford turned from the wall. He'd been studying one of the framed prints. It was unusual in that it was a series of handwritten lines.

'A poem to our mother,' Lorna Grieve explained. 'From Christopher Murray Grieve. He wasn't any relation, in case you're wondering.'

'Hugh MacDiarmid,' Rebus said, seeing the blank look on Linford's face. The look didn't change.

'The Monkey Man has a brain,' Lorna cooed. Then she noticed the honey. 'Oh, there it is. Mother thought she'd put it down somewhere.' She turned back to Rebus. 'I'll let you into a secret, Monkey Man.' She was standing right in front of him. He stared at lips he had kissed as a young man, tasting printer's ink and cheap paper in his mouth. She smelt of good whisky, a perfume he could savour. Her voice was harsh but her eyes were numb. 'Nobody knows about that poem. He gave it to our mother. No other copy exists.'

'Lorna . . .' Cammo Grieve laid a hand against the back of his sister's neck, but she twisted away from him. 'It's a sin beyond redeeming to stand here drinking while our guests go without.' He ushered them into the morning room. It was wood-panelled like the hall, but boasted only a few small paintings hanging from a picture rail. There were two sofas and two armchairs, a TV and hi-fi. Apart from that, the room was all books, piled on the floor, squeezed into shelves, filling all the spaces between the potted plants on the window sill. With the curtains closed, the lights were on. The ceiling candelabrum could accommodate three bulbs, but only one was working. Rebus lifted a pile of birthday cards from the sofa: someone had decided the celebrations were over.

'How is Mrs Grieve?' Linford asked.

'My mother's resting,' Cammo Grieve said.

'I meant Mr Grieve's . . . um, your brother's . . .'

'He means Seona,' Lorna said, dropping on to one of the sofas.

'Resting also,' Cammo Grieve explained. He walked over to the marble fireplace, gestured towards the grate, which had become a repository for whisky bottles. 'No longer a working fire,' he said, 'but it can still—'

'Put fire in our bellies,' his sister groaned, rolling her eyes. 'Christ, Cammo, that one wore out long ago.'

Red had risen again in her brother's cheeks – anger this time. Maybe he'd been angry when he'd answered the door, too. Lorna Grieve could have that effect on a man, no doubt about it.

'I'll have a Macallan,' Rebus said.

'A man with sharp eyes,' Cammo Grieve said, making it sound like praise. 'And yourself, DI Linford?'

Linford surprised Rebus, asked for a Springbank. Grieve produced tumblers from a small cupboard and poured a couple of decent measures.

'I won't insult you by offering to dilute them.' He handed the drinks over. 'Sit down, why don't you?'

Rebus took one armchair, Linford the other. Cammo Grieve sat on the sofa beside his sister, who squirmed at the intrusion. They drank their drinks and were silent for a moment. Then there was a trilling sound from Cammo's coat pocket. He lifted out a mobile phone and got to his feet, making for the door.

'Hello, yes, sorry about that, but I'm sure you understand . . .' He closed the door after him.

'Well,' Lorna Grieve said, 'what have I done to deserve this?'

'Deserve what, Mrs Cordover?' Linford asked.

She snorted.

'I think, DI Linford,' Rebus said slowly, 'she means what has she done to deserve being left alone here with two complete duds like us. Would that be accurate, Mrs Cordover?'

'It's Grieve, Lorna Grieve.' There was some venom in her eyes, but not enough to kill her prey, merely stun it. But at least she was focused again – focused on Rebus. 'Do we know one another?' she asked.

'I don't think so,' he admitted.

'It's just the way you keep staring at me.'

'And how's that?'

'Like a lot of photographers I've met along the way. Sleazeballs with no film in the camera.'

Rebus hid his smile behind the whisky glass. 'I used to be a big fan of Obscura.'

Her eyes widened a little, and her voice softened. 'Hugh's band?'

Rebus was nodding. 'You were on one of their album sleeves.'

'God, so I was. It seems like a lifetime ago. What was it called . . . ?'

'*Continuous Repercussions.*'

'My God, I think you're right. It was their last record, wasn't it? I never really liked their stuff, you know.'

'Really?'

They were talking now, having a conversation. Linford was on the periphery of Rebus's vision, and if Rebus concentrated on Lorna Grieve, the younger man faded away until he could have been a trick of the light.

'Obscura,' Lorna reminisced. 'That name was Hugh's idea.'

'It's up near the Castle, isn't it, the Camera Obscura?'

'Yes, but I'm not sure Hugh ever went there. He chose

60

the name for another reason. You know Donald Cammell?'

Rebus was stumped.

'He was a film director. He made *Performance*.'

'Yes, of course.'

'He was born there.'

'In the Camera Obscura?'

Lorna nodded, smiled across the room at him with something approaching warmth.

Linford cleared his throat. 'I've been to the Camera Obscura,' he said. 'It's quite amazing, the view.'

There was silence for a moment. Then Lorna Grieve smiled again at Rebus. 'He doesn't have a clue, does he, Monkey Man? Not the slightest clue what we've been talking about.'

Rebus was shaking his head in agreement as Cammo walked back into the room. He'd removed his coat, but not the jacket. Now that Rebus thought of it, the house was none too warm. These big old places, you put in central heating but not double glazing. High ceilings and draughts. Maybe it was time to turn the makeshift drinks cabinet back to its original use.

'Sorry about that,' Cammo said. 'Blair was saddened by the news, apparently.'

Lorna snorted, back to her old self. 'Tony Blair: I'd trust him as far as I could throw him.' She looked at her brother. 'Bet he's never heard of you either. Roddy would have made twice the MP you'll ever be. What's more, at least he had the guts to stand for the *Scottish* parliament, somewhere he felt he could do some good!'

Her voice had risen, and with it the colour in her brother's cheeks.

'Lorna,' he said quietly, 'you're distraught.'

'Don't you dare patronise me!'

The MP looked at his two guests, his smile attempting to reassure them that there was nothing here to worry about, nothing to take to the outside world.

'Lorna, I really think—'

'All the crap this family's been through over the years, it's all down to you!' Lorna was growing hysterical. 'Dad tried his damnedest to hate you!'

'That's enough!'

'And Roddy, poor bastard, actually wanted to *be* you! And everything with Alasdair—'

Cammo Grieve raised his hand to slap his sister. She reared back from him, shrieking. And then there was someone in the doorway, shaking slightly, leaning heavily on a black walking cane. And someone else in the hall, hand clutching at the neck of her dressing-gown.

'Stop this at once!' Alicia Grieve shouted, stamping down hard with her cane. Behind her, Seona Grieve looked almost ghostly, as if alabaster had replaced the blood in her veins.

8

'I didn't even know this place had a restaurant.' Siobhan looked around her. 'You can smell the paint.'

'It's only been open a week,' Derek Linford said, sitting down opposite her. They were in the Tower restaurant at the top of the Museum of Scotland on Chambers Street. There was a terrace outside, but no one was eating alfresco this December night. Their window table gave a view of the Sheriff's Court and the Castle. The rooftops shone with frost. 'I hear it's pretty good,' he added. 'Same owner as the Witchery.'

'Busy enough.' Siobhan was studying the other diners. 'I recognise that woman over there. Doesn't she do restaurant reviews for one of the papers?'

'I never read them.'

She looked at him. 'How did you hear about it?'

'What?'

'This place.'

'Oh.' He was already studying the menu. 'Some guy from Historic Scotland mentioned it.'

She smiled at 'guy', reminded that Linford was her own age, maybe even a year or two younger. His dress sense was so conservative – dark wool suit, white shirt, blue tie – that he seemed older. It might help explain his popularity with the 'high hiedyins' at the Big House. When he'd asked her to dinner, her first instinct had been to refuse. It wasn't as if they'd exactly hit it off in the Botanics. But at the same time she wondered if she could learn anything from him. Her own mentor, Chief Inspector Gill Templer, didn't seem to be helping much – too busy proving to her male colleagues that she was every bit their equal. Which wasn't the truth. Truth was, she was better than most male CIs Siobhan had worked for. But Gill Templer didn't seem to know that.

'Would this be the guy who discovered the body in Queensberry House?'

'That's him,' Linford said. 'See anything you fancy?'

With some men, it would have come out as a chat-up line, trying to hook the expected response from her. But Linford was checking the menu like it was evidence.

'I'm not much of a meat-eater,' she told him. 'Any news on Roddy Grieve?'

The waitress arrived and they ordered. Linford checked that Siobhan wasn't driving before asking for a bottle of white wine.

'Did you walk?' he asked.

She shook her head. 'Taxied it.'

'I should have asked. I could've picked you up.'

'That's all right. You were telling me about Roddy Grieve.'

'God, that sister of his.' Linford shook his head at the memory.

'Lorna? I'd like to meet her.'

'She's a monster.'

'Good-looking monster.' Linford shrugged, as if looks meant nothing to him. 'If I look half as good at her age,' Siobhan went on, 'I'll be doing well.'

He busied himself with his wineglass. Maybe he thought she was fishing for a compliment. Maybe she was.

'She seemed to hit it off with your bodyguard,' he said at last.

'My what?'

'Rebus. The one who doesn't want me seeing you.'

'I'm sure he—'

Linford leaned back suddenly in his chair. 'Oh, let's forget it. Sorry I said anything.'

Siobhan was confused now. She didn't know what kind

of signals her dinner partner was giving off. She brushed non-existent crumbs from her red crushed-velvet dress, checked the knees of her black tights for runs that weren't there. With her coat off, her arms and shoulders were bare. Was she making him nervous?

'Is there something wrong?' she asked.

He shook his head, eyes everywhere but on her. 'It's just . . . I've never dated anyone from work before.'

'Dated?'

'You know, gone out for a meal with them. I mean, I've been to official functions, but never . . .' His eyes finally rested on hers. 'Just two people, me and one other. Like this.'

She smiled. 'We're having dinner, Derek, that's all.' She swallowed the sentence back, but too late. *Was* that all they were going to do, have dinner? Was he expecting anything more?

But he seemed to relax a little. 'Bloody strange house, too,' he said, as though his mind had been on the Grieves all along. 'Paintings and newspapers and books spread everywhere. Deceased's mother lives alone, should probably be in a home, someone to look after her.'

'She's a painter, isn't she?'

'Was. Not sure she still is.'

'Her stuff fetches a small fortune. It was in the papers.'

'Bit gaga if you ask me, but then she'd just lost a son. Not really for me to say, is it?' He looked at her to see how he was doing. Her eyes told him to go on. 'Cammo Grieve was there, too.'

'He's supposed to be a rake.'

Linford seemed surprised. 'Bit fat to be a rake.'

'Not a garden rake. You know, a bit of a ladies' man, not to be trusted.'

She was grinning, but he took her at her word. 'Not to be trusted? Hmm.' He went thoughtful again. 'God knows what they were talking about.'

'Who?'

'Rebus and Lorna Grieve.'

'Rock music,' Siobhan stated, leaning back so the waitress could pour the wine.

'Some of the time, yes.' Linford studied her. 'How did you know?'

'She's married to a record producer, and John loves all that. Immediate connection.'

'I can see why you're in CID.'

She shrugged. 'He's probably the only man I know who plays Wishbone Ash on surveillance.'

'Who are Wishbone Ash?'

'Exactly.'

Later, when they'd finished their starters, Siobhan asked again about Roddy Grieve. 'I mean, we are talking suspicious death here, aren't we?'

'Autopsy's not been done yet, but it's a racing certainty. He didn't kill himself and it doesn't look like an accident.'

'Killing a politician.' Siobhan tutted.

'Ah, but he wasn't, was he? He was a financial analyst who just happened to be running for parliament.'

'Making it harder to fathom why he was killed?'

Linford nodded. 'Could be a client with a grudge. Maybe Grieve made some bad investments.'

'Then there are the people he beat to the Labour nomination.'

'Agreed: plenty of infighting there.'

'And there's his family.'

'A way of getting at them.' Linford was still nodding.

'Or he was just in the wrong place, et cetera.'

'Goes to take a look at the parliament site, becomes victim of a mugging gone wrong.' Linford puffed out his cheeks. 'Lots of possible motives.'

'And they all have to be looked at.'

'Yes.' Linford didn't look too happy at the prospect. 'Some hard work ahead. No easy answers.'

It sounded like he was trying to convince himself the whole thing was worth the candle. 'John's reliable, is he? Just between you and me.'

She thought it over, nodded slowly. 'Once he gets his teeth in, he doesn't let go.'

'That's what I'd heard. Doesn't know when to let go.' He made it sound like something less than praise. 'The ACC wants me running the show. How do you think John will take it?'

'I don't know.'

He attempted a laugh. 'It's all right, I won't tell him we've spoken.'

'It's not that,' she said, though partly it was. 'I genuinely don't know.'

Linford looked disappointed in her. 'Doesn't matter,' he said.

But Siobhan knew that it did.

Nic Hughes was driving his friend Jerry through the city streets. Jerry kept asking him where they were headed.

'Christ almighty, Jerry, you're like a broken record.'

'I just like to know.'

'What if I say we're not going anywhere?'

'That's what you said before.'

'And have we reached a destination?' Jerry didn't seem to understand. 'No, we have not.' Nic told him. 'Because we're driving aimlessly, and sometimes that can be fun.'

'Eh?'

'Just shut up, will you?'

Jerry Lister stared from his passenger window. They'd been south as far as the bypass, taken it to the Gyle and headed back towards Queensferry Road. But then instead of heading back into the centre, Nic had forked off towards Muirhouse and Pilton. They saw some guy urinating against a lamp-post and Jerry said to watch; pressed the button so his window slid down, and as they passed he let out a blood-curdling scream, laughing afterwards, checking the result in the rearview. You could hear the guy swearing.

'They're dogs out here, Jerry,' Nic had warned him, as if Jerry needed telling.

Jerry liked Nic's car. It was a shiny black Sierra Cosworth. When they passed a group of lads, Nic sounded the horn, waved as if he knew them. They stared, watching the car, watching its driver watching them.

'Car like this, Jer, those kids would kill for it. I'm not joking, they'd do their granny in just for the chance of a test drive.'

'Better not run out of petrol then.'

Nic looked at him. 'We could take them, pal.' All bravado with some speed in his system and wearing his blue suede jacket. 'You don't think so?' Slowing the car, his foot all the way off the accelerator. 'We could go back there and . . .'

'Just keep driving, eh?'

A few moments of silence after that, Nic caressing the steering wheel round all the roundabouts they came to.

'Are we going to Granton?'

'Do you want to?'

'What's there?' Jerry asked.

'I don't know. You're the one who brought it up.' A sly glance at his friend. 'Ladies of the night, Jer, is that it? You want to try another?' Tongue lolling from his mouth. 'They won't get in the car with two of us, you know. Too sussed for that, the night ladies. Maybe you could hide in the boot. I'd pick one up, take her to the car park . . . There'd be two of us, Jer.'

Jerry Lister licked his lips. 'I thought we'd decided?'

'Decided what?'

Jerry sounding worried. 'You know.'

'Memory's shot, pal.' Nic Hughes tapped his head. 'It's the drink. I drink to forget, and it seems to work.' His face hardened, left hand twisting the gear stick. 'Only I forget all the wrong things.'

Jerry turned to him. 'Let her go, Nic.'

'Easy for you to say.' He bared his teeth as he spoke. There were flecks of white at the corners of his mouth. 'Know what she told me, pal? Know what she said?'

Jerry didn't want to hear. James Bond's car had an ejector seat; all the Cosworth boasted was a sunroof. Jerry looked around anyway, as if seeking the ejector button.

'She said this was a crap car. Said everyone laughed at it.'

'They don't.'

'These kids out here, they'd tear this car up for an hour and then get bored. That's all it would mean to them, which is a hundred per cent more than it meant to Cat.'

Some men got sad, emotional; they cried. Jerry had cried himself once or twice – a few cans of beer in him and watching *Animal Hospital*; and at Christmas when *Bambi* or *The Wizard of Oz* was on. But he'd never seen Nic cry. Instead, Nic turned it all into anger. Even when he was smiling, like now, Jerry knew he was angry, close to blowing. Not everyone knew, but Jerry did.

'Come on, Nic,' he said. 'Let's head into town, do Lothian Road or the Bridges.'

'Maybe you're right,' Nic said at last. He was stopped at lights. A motorbike drew up alongside, revving. Not a big engine, but those things had no weight either. Kid on it, maybe seventeen. His eyes on them, face masked by the crash helmet. Nic's foot went hard on clutch and accelerator, but when the lights changed the bike left them squashed like a hedgehog.

'See that?' Nic asked quietly. 'That's Cat waving me and my crap car bye-bye.'

Back in town they stopped for a breather, burger and chips, ate from the box, standing roadside, leaning against the car. Jerry's jacket was cheap nylon. He had it zipped but was still shivering. Nic had his jacket open, didn't look to be feeling the cold at all. There were kids in the restaurant, girls in their teens sat at a window table. Nic smiled at them, tried to catch their eyes. They sipped milk shakes, ignored him.

'They think they're in control, Jer,' Nic said. 'That's what's so funny about the whole thing. Here we are, standing out here in the cold, but it's *us* that have the power. Their world's forgotten that, but it would take us ten seconds to haul them into *our* world.' He turned to his friend. 'Wouldn't it?'

'If you say so.'

'No, *you've* got to say it. That way, it becomes true.' Nic dropped his burger box on to the pavement. Jerry hadn't finished his, but Nic was getting back into the car, and he knew Jerry didn't like smells in the Cosworth. There was a bin near by. He dropped his meal into it. One minute it's food, the next it's rubbish. The car was already moving as he pulled himself inside.

'We're not going to do one tonight, are we?' The food seemed to have calmed Nic.

'Don't think so, no.'

Jerry relaxed as they cruised Princes Street – wasn't the same since the council had made it one-way for cars. Headed up Lothian Road. Then down into the Grassmarket and up Victoria Street. Big buildings at the top. Jerry had no idea what any of them were. George IV Bridge: he recognised the old Sheriff Court, which was now the High Court, Deacon Brodie's pub opposite. They took a right at the lights, tyres rippling over the setts as they cruised the High Street. Bitter outside, not many people walking. But Nic was pressing a button, lowering the passenger-side window. Jerry saw her: three-quarter-length coat; black stockings; short dark hair. Good height, trim figure. Nic slowed the car beside her.

'Cold night to be out,' he called. She ignored him. 'You can catch a taxi outside the Holiday Inn if you're lucky. It's just down there.'

'I know where it is,' she snapped.

'You English? On holiday?'

'I live here.'

'Just trying to be friendly. We're always accused of being rude to English people.'

'Just piss off, will you?'

Nic pushed the car forwards, then stopped, so he could turn round and see her face properly. She had a scarf around her neck, chin and mouth tucked into it. As she walked past, for all the world as if they didn't exist, Nic caught Jerry's eye and started nodding.

'Lesbian, Jerry,' he confirmed loudly, closing the window and moving off again.

Siobhan didn't know quite why she was walking. But, entering Waverley Station by the back way, seeing it as a shortcut of sorts, she knew why she was shaking.

Lesbian.

Sod them all. The whole lot of them. She'd turned down Derek Linford's offer of a lift. Said she felt like a walk; unsure straight away why she'd said it. They'd parted amicably enough. No handshake or peck on the cheek, that wasn't the Edinburgh way, not on a first dinner-date. Just smiles and a promise to do it again some time: a promise she was pretty sure she'd be breaking. It was strange, taking the lift down from the restaurant through the museum. Workmen were still busy, even at that hour. Cables and ladders, the sound of an electric drill.

'I thought this place was open for business,' Linford had said.

'It is,' she'd told him. 'It's just not ready yet, that's all.'

She'd walked up George IV Bridge, decided to head down the High Street. But that car, those men . . . she'd wanted off that street. A long flight of dark steps, shadows all around, shouts and music from still-open pubs. Then Waverley. She would cut through, back up on to Princes

71

Street, then down Broughton Street, the city's so-called gay village.

Which was where she lived. It was where a lot of people lived.

Lesbian.

Sod them all.

She thought back on the evening, trying to calm herself. Derek had been nervous, but then who was she to talk? The sex crimes secondment, it had put her off men. The register of offenders . . . all those hungry faces . . . the details of their crimes. And then her time with Sandra Carnegie, swapping stories and feelings. One officer who'd worked sex crimes for the best part of four years had warned her: 'It's a passion-basher, puts you right off.' Three tramps had attacked a student, another student had been assaulted on one of the South Side's richest streets. A car cruising past, an attempted chat-up and stinging punchline; small beer by comparison. All the same, she'd remember that name – Jerry – and the shiny black Sierra.

From the pedestrian bridge, she could look down on to the railway tracks and the concourse. Above her was the station's leaky glass roof. When something plummeted, just on the edge of her vision, she thought she was imagining it. She looked across and saw snow falling. No, not snow: big flakes of glass. There was a hole in the roof, and below on one of the platforms someone was yelling. A couple of taxi drivers had opened their doors, were making for the scene.

Another leaper: that's what it was. An area of darkness on the platform: it was like staring into a black hole. But really it was a long coat, the coat the leaper had been wearing. Siobhan made for the steps down to the concourse. Passengers were waiting for the sleeper to London. A woman was crying. One of the taxi drivers had taken off his jacket and laid it over the top half of the body. Siobhan moved forward. The other taxi driver put a hand out to stop her.

'I wouldn't, love,' he said. For a moment she misheard him: *I wouldn't love. I wouldn't love because love makes you weak. I wouldn't love because your job will kill it dead.*

'I'm a police officer,' she told him, reaching for her warrant card.

So many people had jumped from North Bridge, the Samaritans had bolted a sign to the parapet. North Bridge connected Old Town Edinburgh to the New Town and passed over the deep gully which housed Waverley Station. By the time Siobhan got there, no one was around. Distant shapes and voices: drinkers heading home. Taxis and cars. If anyone had seen the fall, they hadn't bothered stopping. Siobhan leaned over the parapet, looked down on Waverley's roof. Almost directly below was the hole. Through it, she could glimpse movement on the platform. She'd called for assistance, told them to alert the mortuary. She was off duty; let one of the uniforms – Rebus called them woolly suits – deal with it. From the dead man's clothes, she was assuming he was a tramp. Only you didn't call them tramps these days, did you? Problem was, she couldn't think of the right word. Already in her head she was writing her report. Looking around at the empty street, she realised she could just walk away. Leave it to others. Her foot touched something. A plastic carrier bag. She nudged it and felt resistance. Stooping, she picked it up. It was one of the oversized bags you carried skirts or dresses home in. A Jenners bag, no less. The upmarket department store was a couple of minutes' walk away. She doubted the leaper had ever shopped there. But she guessed his whole life was contained in the bag, so she took it with her back down to Waverley.

She'd dealt with suicides before. People who turned on the gas and sat down next to the fire. Cars left running in locked garages. Pill bottles by the bed, blue lips flecked with white. A CID officer had jumped from Salisbury Crags not so long ago. Plenty of places like that in Edinburgh; no shortage of suicide spots.

'You could go home, you know,' a uniform told her. She nodded. The woman officer smiled. 'So what's keeping you?'

A good question. It was as if she knew, knew there was so little to go home to.

'You're one of DI Rebus's, aren't you?' the uniform asked.

Siobhan glared at her. 'What's that supposed to mean?'

The woman shrugged. 'Sorry I spoke.' Then she turned and walked away. They'd cordoned off the section of platform where the body lay. A doctor had confirmed death, and one of the mortuary vans was getting ready to remove the remains. Station staff were in search of a hose, wanted to get a jet-spray on to the platform. Blood and brains would be washed on to the tracks.

The sleeper passengers had departed, the station readying to close for the night. No taxis now. Siobhan wandered over to the left-luggage lockers. There was a desk there, and a male uniform was emptying the Jenners bag on to it, picking out each item gingerly, as if dealing with contamination.

'Anything?' Siobhan asked.

'Just what you see.'

There had been no form of ID on the deceased, nothing in his pockets but a handkerchief and some coins. Siobhan studied the items on the table. A polythene bread bag seemed to contain a rudimentary wash-kit. There were a few articles of clothing, an old copy of *Reader's Digest*. A small transistor radio, its back held on with sticking tape. The day's evening paper, folded and crumpled . . .

You're one of DI Rebus's. Meaning what? Meaning she'd grown to be like him: a loner, a drifter? Were there just the two types of cop: John Rebus or Derek Linford? And did she have to choose?

A sandwich wrapped in greaseproof paper; a child's

lemonade bottle, half-filled with water. More clothing was appearing from the bag, which was all but empty now. The uniform tipped the remnants out. They looked like things the deceased had collected on his travels: a few pebbles, a cheap ring, shoelaces and buttons. A small, thin cardboard box which, from the faded picture on it, had once contained the radio. Siobhan picked it up and shook it, pulled it open and shook out a little book which at first she took for a passport.

'It's a passbook,' the uniform said. 'Building society.'

'So it'll have a name on it,' Siobhan said.

The uniform opened the book. 'Mr C. Mackie. There's an address in the Grassmarket.'

'And how was Mr Mackie's investment portfolio doing?'

The uniform turned a couple of pages, angling the passbook as if he was having trouble focusing.

'Not bad,' he said at last. 'Just over four hundred grand in credit.'

'Four hundred thousand? Looks like the drinks are on him then.'

But the uniform turned the passbook towards her. She reached out and took it. He hadn't been joking. The tramp being scraped and hosed off platform 11 was worth four hundred thousand pounds.

9

Tuesday, Rebus was back at St Leonard's. Chief Superintendent Watson wanted a meeting with him. When he arrived, Derek Linford was already seated, a mug of oily-looking coffee untouched in one hand.

'Help yourself,' Watson said.

Rebus raised the beaker he was holding. 'Already got some, sir.' Whenever he remembered, he tried to bring half a cup of coffee with him. There was a sign you saw above some bars – 'Do not ask for credit as a refusal can often offend'. The beaker was Rebus's way of not giving offence to his senior officer.

When they were all seated, the Chief Super got straight to the point.

'*Everyone*'s interested in this case: reporters, public, government . . .'

'In that order, sir?' Rebus asked.

Watson ignored him. '. . . which means I'm going to be keeping closer tabs on you than usual.' He turned to Linford. 'John here can be like a bull in a china shop. I'm looking to you to be on matador duty.'

Linford smiled. 'As long as the bull's okay about it.' He looked to Rebus, who stayed quiet.

'Reporters are foaming at the mouth. The parliament, the elections . . . dry as dust. Now at last they've got a story.' Watson held up thumb and forefinger. 'Two stories actually. Couldn't be any connection, could there?'

'Between Grieve and the skeleton?' Linford seemed to consider it, glanced towards Rebus who was busy checking the crease in his left trouser leg. 'Shouldn't think so, sir. Not unless Grieve was killed by a ghost.'

Watson wagged a finger. 'That's just the sort of thing the journalists are after. Joking's fine in here, but not outside, understood?'

'Yes, sir.' Linford looked suitably abashed.

'So what have we got?'

'We've conducted preliminary interviews with the family,' Rebus answered. 'Further interviews to follow. Next step is to talk to the deceased's political agent, then maybe to the local Labour Party.'

'No known enemies?'

'Widow didn't seem to think so, sir,' Linford said quickly, leaning forward in his chair. He didn't want Rebus hogging the stage. 'Still, there are things wives don't always know.'

The Chief Super nodded. To Rebus, his face looked even more florid than usual. Run-up to the golden cheerio and he gets landed with this.

'Friends? Business acquaintances?'

Linford nodded back, catching Watson's rhythm. 'We'll speak to them all.'

'Did the autopsy throw up anything?'

'Blow to the base of the skull. It caused immediate haemorrhaging. Seems he died pretty much where he fell. Two more blows after that, producing fractures.'

'These two blows were post-mortem?'

Linford looked to Rebus for confirmation. 'Pathologist seems to think so,' Rebus obliged. 'They were to the top of the skull. Grieve was pretty tall –'

'Six-one,' Linford interrupted.

'– so to render a blow like that, the attacker had to be hellish tall or standing on something.'

'Or Grieve was already prone when the blows arrived,' Watson said, mopping his forehead with a handkerchief. ' Yes, makes sense, I suppose. How the devil did he get in there?'

'Either he climbed the fence,' Linford guessed, 'or else

someone had keys. The gates are kept padlocked at night: too much stuff in there worth nicking.'

'There's a security guard,' Rebus continued. 'He says he was there all night, kept a regular patrol, but didn't see anything.'

'What do you think?'

'I think he was kipping in the office. Nice and warm in there. Radio and kettle, all mod cons. Either that or he'd bunked off home.'

'He says he checked the summer house?' Watson asked.

'He says he *thinks* he did.' Linford quoted from memory: ' "I always shine my torch inside, just in case. No reason I wouldn't have that night." '

The Chief Super leaned forward, rested his elbows on the desk. 'What do you think?' He had eyes only for Linford.

'I think we need to concentrate on the motive, sir. Was this a chance encounter? Prospective MSP wants to take a midnight look at his future workplace, happens across someone who decides to bludgeon him to death?' Linford shook his head persuasively, his eyes dodging Rebus, who was glaring, having said almost exactly the same thing to him about an hour before.

'I'm not sure,' Watson said. 'Say someone was in there stealing tools. Grieve interrupts them, so they whack him.'

'And after he's laid out,' Rebus interrupted, 'they hit him twice more for luck?'

Watson grunted, acknowledging the point. 'And the murder weapon?'

'Not recovered yet, sir,' Linford said. 'Lot of building sites around there, places you could conceal something. We've got officers out looking.'

'The contractors are carrying out an inventory,' Rebus added. 'Just in case anything's missing. If your theory about it being a theft is right, maybe the inventory will throw up something.'

'One more thing, sir. Recent scuff marks on the shoes

and traces of dirt and dust on the inside legs of Grieve's trousers.'

Watson smiled. 'God bless forensics. What does it mean?'

'Means he probably did climb the fence or the gate.'

'All the same, rule nothing out and everything in. Talk to all the keyholders. *All* of them, understood?'

'Very good, sir,' Linford said.

Rebus just nodded, though no one was paying attention.

'And our friend Skelly?' the Chief Super asked.

'Two other members of the PPLC are on it, sir,' Rebus said.

Watson grunted again, then looked at Linford. 'Something wrong with your coffee, Derek?'

Linford's gaze went to the surface of the drink. 'No, sir, not at all. Just don't like it too hot.'

'And how is it now?'

Linford put the mug to his lips, drained it in two swallows. 'It's very good, sir. Thank you.'

Rebus suddenly had no doubts: Linford would go far in the force.

When the meeting was over, Rebus told Linford he'd catch him up, and knocked again on Watson's door.

'I thought we'd finished?' The Farmer was busy with paperwork.

'I'm being sidelined,' Rebus said, 'and I don't like it.'

'Then do something about it.'

'Such as?'

The Farmer looked up. 'Derek's in charge. Accept the fact.' He paused. 'Either that or ask for a transfer.'

'Wouldn't want to miss your retirement do, sir.'

The Farmer put down his pen. 'This is probably the last case I'll handle, and I can't think of one with a higher profile.'

'You saying you don't trust me with it, sir?'

'You always think you know better, John. That's the problem.'

'All Linford knows are his desk at Fettes and which arses to lick.'

'The ACC says different.' The Farmer sat back in his chair. 'Bit of jealousy there, John? Younger man speeding through the ranks . . . ?'

'Oh aye, I've always been gasping for a promotion.' Rebus turned to leave.

'Just this once, John, play for the team. It's that or the sideline . . .'

Rebus closed the door on his boss's words. Linford was waiting for him at the end of the corridor, mobile pressed to his ear.

'Yes, sir, we're headed there next.' He listened, raised a hand to let Rebus know he'd only be a minute. Rebus ignored him, stalked past and down the stairs. Linford's voice carried down a few moments later.

'I think he'll be fine, sir, but if not . . .'

Rebus dismissed the nightwatchman, but the man stayed in his seat, eyes shifting nervously between Rebus and Linford.

'I said you can go.'

'Go where?' the watchman asked at last, voice trembling. 'This is my office.'

Which was true: the three men were seated in the gatehouse of the parliament site. There was a thick register lying on the table, being pored over by Linford. It listed all the visitors to the site since work had begun. Linford had his notebook out, but hadn't jotted a single name into it.

'I thought you might want to go home,' Rebus told the watchman. 'Shouldn't you be asleep or something?'

'Aye, sure,' the man mumbled. He probably reckoned he wouldn't have the job much longer. Bad PR for the security firm, a body finding its way on to the premises. It was a low-pay job, being a security guard, and the hours tended to suit loners and the desperate. Rebus had told the man that they'd be checking up on him – you found a lot of ex-cons in his line of work. The man had admitted to spending some time at what he called the Windsor Hotel Group, meaning in jail. But he swore no one had asked him for copies of his keys. He wasn't protecting anybody.

'On you go then,' Rebus said. The guard left. Rebus let out a long whistle of breath and stretched his vertebrae. 'Anything?'

'A few suspicious names,' Linford announced. He turned the ledger so Rebus could see. The names were their own, along with Ellen Wylie, Grant Hood, Bobby Hogan and Joe Dickie: the group who'd toured Queensberry House. 'Or how about the Scottish Secretary and the Catalan President?'

Rebus blew his nose. There was a one-bar electric fire in the room, but the heat was having no difficulty escaping through the cracks in the door and window. 'What did you reckon to our nightwatchman?'

Linford closed the register. 'I think if my two-year-old nephew asked for the gate keys, he'd hand them over rather than risk a bite to the ankles.'

Rebus went to the window. It was crusted with dirt. Outside, everyone was busy knocking things down and putting things up. An investigation was like that, too: sometimes you were demolishing an alibi or story, sometimes building up the case, each new piece of information another brick in the often unlovely edifice.

'But is that what happened?' he asked.

'I don't know. Let's see what the background check digs up.'

'I think we're wasting our time. I don't think he knows anything.'

'Oh?'

'I don't even think he was here. Remember how vague

he was about the weather that night? He couldn't even be sure which route he took when he patrolled.'

'He's not the brightest of specimens, John. We still have to do the check.'

'Because it's procedure?'

Linford nodded. Outside, something was making a noise: *rugga rugga rugga rugga rugga*.

'Has that thing been going all the time?' Rebus asked.

'What thing?'

'That noise, the cement mixer or whatever it is.'

'I don't know.'

There was a knock at the door. The site manager came in, holding his yellow hard hat by its rim. He wore a yellow oilskin jacket over brown cord trousers. His walking boots were covered in glaur.

'Just a few follow-up questions,' Linford informed him, gesturing for the man to sit.

'I've inventoried the tools,' the site manager said, unfolding a sheet of paper. 'Of course, things *do* go walkabout on any job.'

Rebus looked at Linford. ' You take this one. I need some fresh air.'

He stepped out into the cold and breathed deeply, then searched his pockets for cigarettes. He'd been going off his head in there. Christ, and a drink would go down too well. There was a mobile van parked outside the gates, selling burgers and tea to the construction workers.

'Double malt,' Rebus said to the woman.

'And do you take water with that?'

He smiled. 'Just a tea, thanks. Milk, no sugar.'

'Right, love.' She kept rubbing her hands together between tasks.

'Must get pretty cold, working here.'

'Perishing,' she admitted. 'I could do with a tot now and again myself.'

'What sort of hours are you open?'

'Andy opens at eight, does breakfasts and things. I

usually take over at two, so he can hit the cash and carry.'

Rebus checked his watch. 'It's just gone eleven.'

'Sure you don't want anything else? I've just cooked a couple of burgers.'

'Go on then. Just the one.' He patted his midriff.

'You need feeding up, you do,' she told him, winking as she spoke.

Rebus took the tea from her, then the burger. There were sauce bottles on a ledge. He spiralled some brown on to the contents of the roll.

'Andy's not been too good,' she said. 'So it's down to me just now.'

'Nothing serious?' Rebus took a bite of scalding meat and melting onions.

'Just flu, and maybe not even that. You men are all hypochondriacs.'

'Can't blame him for trying, this weather.'

'Don't see me complaining, do you?'

'Women are made of stronger stuff.'

She laughed, rolled her eyes.

'What time do you finish?'

She laughed again. 'You chatting me up?'

He shrugged. 'I might want another of these later.' He held up the burger.

'Well, I'm here till five. But they go quick, come lunchtime.'

'I'll risk it,' Rebus said. It was his turn to wink, as he headed back through the gate. He drank the tea as he walked. When the roof workers started to winch another load of slates down towards the waiting skip, he remembered he wasn't wearing a hard hat. There were some in the gatehouse, but he didn't want to go back there. Instead, he headed into Queensberry House. The stairs down to the basement were unlit. He could hear voices echoing at the end of the hall. Shadows were moving in the old kitchen. When he stepped into the room, Ellen

Wylie glanced towards him and nodded a greeting. She was listening to an elderly woman speak. They'd found a chair for her to sit in. It was one of those director's chairs with a canvas seat and back, and it complained every time its occupant moved, which she did often and in animated fashion. Grant Hood was standing by a side wall, taking notes. He was keeping out of the woman's eyeline, so as not to distract her.

'It was always covered in wood,' the woman was saying. 'That's my recollection.' She had one of those high-pitched, authoritative accents.

'This sort of stuff?' Wylie asked. She pointed to a section of tongue-and-groove, still fixed to the wall near the door.

'I believe so, yes.' The woman noticed Rebus, gave him a smile.

'This is Detective Inspector Rebus,' Wylie said.

'Good morning, Inspector. My name is Marcia Templewhite.'

Rebus stepped forward, took her hand for a moment.

'Miss Templewhite worked for the Health Board back in the seventies,' Wylie explained.

'And for many years before that, too,' Miss Templewhite added.

'She remembers some building work,' Wylie went on.

'*Lots* of work,' Miss Templewhite corrected. 'The whole basement was gutted. New heating system, floor repairs, pipework ... It was quite a guddle, I can tell you. Everything had to be moved upstairs, and then we didn't know where to put it. Went on for weeks.'

'And the wooden sections were removed?' Rebus asked.

'Well, I was just telling ...'

'DS Wylie,' Wylie reminded her.

'I was just telling DS Wylie, if they'd found these fireplaces, surely they'd have said something?'

' You didn't know about them?'

'Not until DS Wylie told me.'

'But the building work', Grant Hood said, 'coincides fairly well with the skeleton's age.'

'You don't suppose one of the workers could have got himself bricked up?' Miss Templewhite asked.

'I think he'd have been noticed,' Rebus told her. All the same, he knew they'd be asking the builders that very question. 'Who were the contractors?'

Miss Templewhite threw up her hands. 'Contractors, subcontractors ... I could never really keep up with them.'

Wylie looked at Rebus. 'Miss Templewhite thinks there'll be records somewhere.'

'Oh yes, most definitely.' She looked around her at her surroundings. 'And now Roddy Grieve's dead, too. It was never a lucky place this. Never was, never will be.' She nodded at all three of them, her confident words accompanied by a solemn, knowing face, as if she took no comfort from the truth.

Back at the snack van, he paid for the teas.

'Guilty conscience?' Wylie said, accepting hers. A patrol car had arrived to take Miss Templewhite home. Grant Hood was seeing her safely into the back of it, waving her off.

'Why should I feel guilty?' Rebus asked.

'Story is, it was you that put our names down for this.'

'Who told you that?'

She shrugged. 'Word gets around.'

'Then you should be thanking me,' Rebus said. 'High-profile case like this could make your career.'

'Not as high profile as Roddy Grieve.' She was staring at him.

'Spit it out,' he said. But she shook her head. He handed the spare styrofoam beaker to Grant Hood. 'Seemed like a nice old sort.'

'Grant likes the more mature woman,' Wylie said.

'Get lost, Ellen.'

'Him and his pals go to Grab-a-Granny night at the Marina.'

Rebus looked at Hood, who was blushing. 'That right, Grant?'

Hood just looked at Wylie, concentrated on his tea.

Seemed to Rebus they were getting on okay, felt comfortable enough to talk about their private lives, then to joke about it. 'So,' he said, 'getting back to business . . .' He moved away from the van, where workers were queuing for lunchtime treats of crisps and chocolate bars, their eyes roving towards Ellen Wylie. Wylie and Hood were both wearing hard hats, but didn't look right in them. The line of workers knew they were just visiting. 'What have we got so far?'

'Skelly's gone to some specialist lab down south,' Wylie said. 'They reckon they can give us a more accurate date of death. But meantime the thinking is '79 to '81.'

'And we know building work was going on down there in 1979,' Hood added. 'Which I'd say is our best bet.'

'Based on what?' Rebus asked.

'Based on the fact that if you're going to hide a body down there, you need the means and the opportunity. Most of the time, the basement was off-limits. And who'd dump a body there unless they knew about the fireplace? They knew it was going to be blocked up again, probably thought it would stay that way for a few more hundred years.'

Wylie was nodding agreement. 'Has to be tied in to the refit work.'

'So we need to know which companies were involved, and who was working for them at the time.' The two junior officers shared a look. 'I know, it's a big job. Firms could have gone to the wall. Maybe they're not as good at keeping old paperwork as Miss Templewhite. But they're all we've got.'

'Personnel records will be a nightmare,' Wylie said. 'A lot of the building trade, they take people on for a job, lay them off again afterwards. Builders move on, don't always stay in the business.'

Rebus was nodding. 'You're going to have to depend on goodwill a lot of the time.'

'Meaning what, sir?' Hood asked.

'Meaning you have to be nice and polite. That's why I chose you. Someone like Bobby Hogan or Joe Dickie, they'd go barging in demanding answers. Play it like that, suddenly the person you're talking to could become forgetful. Like the song says, nice and easy does it.' He was looking at Wylie.

Through the gate behind her, he glimpsed the site manager emerging from the gatehouse, slipping his hard hat back on. Linford came out, hard hat in hand, and looked around, seeking Rebus. Saw him and came out of the gate.

'Missing tools?' Rebus asked.

'A few bits and pieces.' Linford nodded across the road. 'Any news from the search parties?' Two groups of uniforms were checking the area for the murder weapon.

'I don't know,' Rebus said. 'I haven't seen them.'

Linford looked at him. 'But you've got time to stop for tea?'

'Just keeping my junior officers happy.'

Linford was still staring. 'You think this is a waste of time, don't you?'

'Yes.'

'Mind if I ask why?' He folded his arms.

'Because it's all arse-backwards,' Rebus said. 'Does it really matter how he got into the site or what he was killed with? We should be looking at the who and why. You're like one of those office managers who worries about paperclips when the case-files are ten feet high on everybody's desk.'

Linford glanced at his watch. 'Bit early in the day for character assassination.' Trying to make a joke of it, aware that others were listening.

'You can interview the site manager as much as you like,' Rebus went on, 'but even if you narrow it down to a missing claw hammer, how much further on will you be? Let's face it, whoever killed Roddy Grieve knew what they were doing. If they'd been caught nicking slates, they might have thumped him, but more likely they'd just have run off. They certainly wouldn't have kept hitting him after he was down. He *knew* his killer, and it wasn't by chance that he was here. It's to do with what he was or who he was. That's what we should be concentrating on.' He paused, aware that the line of workers was watching the performance.

'Here endeth the lesson,' Ellen Wylie said, smiling into her cup.

10

Roddy Grieve's election agent was called Josephine Banks. Sitting in one of the interview rooms at St Leonard's, she explained that she'd known Grieve for about five years.

'We were pretty active in New Labour, right from the start. I did some canvassing for John Smith, too.' Her eyes lost their focus for a moment. 'He's still missed.'

Rebus sat across from her, fingers busy exploring a cheap pen. 'When did you last see Mr Grieve?'

'The day he died. We met in the afternoon. Only five months till the election, there was a lot of work to get through.'

She was five and a half feet tall and carried most of her weight at the stomach and hips. Her face was small and round with the beginnings of a double chin. She'd pulled back her thick black hair and tied it at the nape of her neck. She wore half-moon glasses with Dalmatian-spotted frames.

'You never thought of standing?' Rebus asked.

'What? As an MSP?' She smiled at the suggestion. 'Maybe next time.'

'You've ambitions that way?'

'Of course.'

'So what made you want to help Roddy Grieve, as opposed to any other candidate?'

She wore black mascara and eyeshadow. Her eyes were green. They seemed to sparkle when she moved them.

'I liked him,' she said, 'and I trusted him. He still had ideals, unlike his brother, say.'

'Cammo?'

'Yes.'

'You don't get on?'

'No reason why we should.'

'What about Cammo and Roddy?'

'Oh, they argued politics whenever they could, but that wasn't often. They only met at family occasions, and then they had Alicia and Lorna to stop them.'

'What about Mr Grieve's wife?'

'Which one?'

'Roddy's.'

'Yes, but which one? He had two, you know.'

Rebus was confused momentarily.

'First one didn't last long,' Josephine Banks said, crossing her legs. 'It was a teenage thing.'

Rebus turned his pen the right way round and opened his notebook. 'What was her name?'

'Billie.' She spelled it for him. 'Her maiden name's Collins. But maybe she's remarried.'

'Is she still around?'

'Last I heard she was teaching somewhere in Fife.'

'Did you ever meet her?'

'God no, she was long gone by the time I met Roddy.' She looked at him. ' You know there's a son?'

None of the family had mentioned it. Rebus shook his head. Banks looked disappointed in him.

'His name's Peter. He uses the surname Grief. Ring any bells?'

Rebus was busy writing. 'Should it?'

She shrugged. 'He's in a pop group. The Robinson Crusoes.'

'Never heard of them.'

'Some of your younger colleagues may have.'

'Ouch.' Rebus winced; it made her smile.

'But Peter's almost beyond the pale.'

'Because of what he does?'

'Oh no, not that. I think his grandmother's thrilled to have a pop star in the family.'

'What then?'

'Well, he chooses to make his home in Glasgow.' She paused. 'You *have* spoken to the family, haven't you?' He nodded. 'Only I'd have thought Hugh would have mentioned him.'

'I haven't actually met Mr Cordover yet. He's the band's producer, is he?'

'He's their manager. Dear me, do I have to tell you everything? Hugh's got this thing about young bands now – Vain Shadows, Change and Decay . . .' She smiled at his lack of recognition.

'I'll ask one of my younger colleagues,' he said, causing her to laugh.

He went to the canteen, fetched them coffee. The burger had given him indigestion, so he stopped at his desk and downed a couple of Rennies. At one time, he could have eaten anything, any time of day. But his guts seemed to have taken early retirement. He picked up his phone and called Lorna Grieve, thinking: so far Josephine Banks hadn't mentioned Seona Grieve. She'd managed to sidetrack him by bringing the first Mrs Grieve, Billie Collins, into play. There was no answer at the Cordover residence. He took the drinks back to the interview room. 'There you go, Ms Banks.'

'Thank you.' She looked as if she hadn't moved all the time he'd been away.

'I keep wondering', she said, 'when you'll get round to me. I mean, all this other stuff *is* just a roundabout way of getting there, isn't it?'

'You've lost me.' Rebus took the notebook and pen from his pocket, laid them on the desk.

'Roddy and me,' she said, leaning towards him. 'The affair we were having. Is it time to talk about that now?'

Right hand reaching for the pen, Rebus agreed that it was.

'It's like that in politics.' She paused. 'Well, any profession

91

really. Two people working closely together.' She sipped the coffee. 'Politicians are nothing if not gossips. I think it's down to a lack of self-confidence. Bad-mouthing everyone else is such a simple option.'

'So you weren't actually having an affair?'

She looked at him, smiled. 'Did I give that impression?' Bowed her head slightly in apology. 'What I should have said was, the rumoured affair. And that's as far as it got. You didn't know?'

He shook his head.

'All these interviews . . . I thought someone would have . . .' She straightened in her chair. 'Well, maybe I've misjudged them.'

'You're really the first person we've spoken to.'

'But you've talked to the clan?'

'You mean Mr Grieve's family?'

'Yes.'

'They knew?'

'Seona knew. I'm assuming she didn't keep it to herself.'

'Did Mr Grieve tell her?'

She smiled again. 'Why should he? There wasn't any truth in it. If someone here made a sly reference about you, would you report it to your wife?'

'So how did Mrs Grieve find out?'

'The usual way. Our old friend, Anonymous.'

'A letter?'

'Yes.'

'Just the one?'

'You'll have to ask her.' She placed her beaker on the table. 'You're dying for a cigarette, aren't you?' Rebus looked at her. She nodded towards his pen, which was raised to his mouth. 'You keep doing that,' she said. 'And I wish you wouldn't.'

'Why's that, Ms Banks?'

'Because I'm gasping for one myself.'

Smoking at St Leonard's was restricted to the rear car

park. Since this was off-limits to the public, he stood with Josephine Banks on the pavement out front, the pair of them shuffling their feet as they enjoyed their individual fixes.

Nearing the end of his cigarette, perhaps to defer the moment when he would have to finish it, he asked her if she'd any idea who had written the letter.

'Not a clue.'

'It had to be someone who knew you both.'

'Oh, yes. I'm guessing it was someone in the local party. Or maybe a sore loser. The selection process for candidates, it was pretty rough at times.'

'How so?'

'Old Labour versus New. Ancient grievances given fresh momentum.'

'Who stood against Mr Grieve?'

'There were three others: Gwen Mollison, Archie Ure and Sara Bone.'

'Was it a fair fight?'

A mixture of smoke and chilled breath billowed from her mouth. 'As these things go, yes. I mean, there weren't any dirty tricks.'

Something in her tone made him ask: 'But?'

'There was a certain amount of bad feeling when Roddy won the vote. Mostly from Ure. You must have seen it in the papers.'

'Only if it reached the sports pages.'

She looked at him. 'You *are* going to vote?'

He shrugged, examined what was left of his cigarette. 'Why was Archie Ure so upset?'

'Archie's been in the Labour Party for donkey's. And he believes in devolution. Back in '79, he canvassed half of Edinburgh. Then along comes Roddy, snatches his birthright from under his nose. Tell me, did you vote in '79?'

March 1, 1979: the failed devolution referendum. 'I don't remember,' Rebus lied.

'You didn't, did you?' She watched him shrug. 'Why-ever not?'

'I wasn't the only one.'

'I'm just curious. It was bitter cold that day, maybe the snow put you off.'

'Are you poking fun at me, Ms Banks?'

She flicked her cigarette stub into the road. 'I wouldn't dare, Inspector.'

1979.

He remembered Rhona, his wife at the time, with her roll of 'Vote Yes' stickers. He kept finding them on his jackets, the car windscreen, even on the flask he some-times took with him to work. The winter had been hell: dark and freezing and with strikes breaking out all over. The Winter of Discontent, the papers called it, and he wasn't about to disagree. His daughter Sammy was four. When he and Rhona had arguments, they kept their voices down so as not to wake her. His work was a problem: not enough hours in the day. And recently Rhona had been becoming active politically, campaigning for the SNP. For her, devolution meant a step towards independence. For Jim Callaghan and his Labour govern-ment, it meant . . . well, Rebus was never sure exactly. A sop to the Nationalists? Or to the nation as a whole? Would it really strengthen the Union?

They argued politics at the kitchen table until Rebus became bored by it all. He would fall on to the sofa and tell Rhona he didn't care. At first she would stand in front of him, blocking his view of the TV screen. Her arguments were cogent as well as passionate.

'I really can't be scunnered,' he'd say when she finished, and she'd start hitting him with a cushion until he wrestled her down on to the carpet, the pair of them laughing.

Maybe it was because he was getting a reaction. Whatever, his intransigence grew. He wore a 'Scotland

Says NO' badge home one night. They were at the kitchen table again, eating supper. Rhona looked tired: day job and childcare and out canvassing. She didn't say anything about his badge, even when he unpinned it from his coat and fixed it to his shirt. She just stared at him with deadened eyes, and wouldn't talk the rest of the evening. In bed, she turned her back on him.

'I thought you wanted me to get more political,' he joked. She stayed silent. 'I'm serious,' he said. 'I've thought through the issues like you said, and I've decided to vote No.'

'You do what you want,' she said coldly.

'I will then,' he answered, his eyes on her hunched form.

But on the day, 1 March, he did something worse than voting No. He didn't vote at all. He could blame work, the weather, any number of things. But really, it was to make Rhona suffer. He knew this as he watched the office clock, watched the hands pass the referendum's close. With minutes left, he almost dashed for his car, but told himself it was too late. It was too late.

Felt like hell on the drive home. She wasn't there; was off somewhere to watch ballot boxes being emptied, or with like-minded people in the back room of a pub, awaiting news of exit polls.

The babysitter left him to it. He looked in on Sammy, who was fast asleep, one arm cradling Pa Broon, her favoured teddy bear. It was late when Rhona returned. She was a little bit drunk, and so was he: four cans of Tartan Special in front of the TV. He had the picture on but the sound down, listening to the hi-fi. He was about to tell her that he'd voted No, but knew she'd see through the lie. Instead, he asked how she was feeling.

'Numb,' she said, standing in the doorway, as if reluctant to enter the room. 'But then,' she said, turning back into the hall, 'that's almost an improvement.'

March 1, 1979. The referendum had a clause attached,

40 per cent of the electorate had to vote Yes. The rumour was the Labour government down in London wanted obstacles put in the way of devolution. They feared that Scottish Westminster MPs would be lost, and that the Conservatives would be gifted a permanent majority in the Commons. Forty per cent had to vote Yes.

It wasn't even close. Thirty-three said Yes, 31 No. The turnout was just under 64 per cent. The result, as one paper put it, was 'a nation divided'. The SNP withdrew their support for the Callaghan government – he called them 'turkeys voting for Christmas' – an election had to be called, and the Conservatives came back into power, led by Margaret Thatcher.

'Your SNP did that,' Rebus told Rhona. 'Now where's your devolution?'

She just shrugged a response, beyond goading. They'd come a long way since the cushion fights on the floor. He turned to his work instead, immersing himself in other people's lives, other people's problems and miseries.

And hadn't voted in an election since.

After Josephine Banks had gone, he returned to the Murder Room. DS 'Hi-Ho' Silvers was making telephone calls. So were a couple of DCs who'd been brought in from other divisions. Chief Inspector Gill Templer was having a confab with the Farmer. A WPC walked past and handed the Farmer a sheaf of telephone messages – so many they were held by a bulldog clip. The Farmer frowned at them, went on listening to Templer. The Farmer's jacket was off and the sleeves of his white shirt were rolled up. All around Rebus people were moving, and computer keyboards were being hammered, and ringing phones were being answered. On his desk were copies of inquiry transcripts, initial interviews with the members of the clan. Cammo Grieve had drawn the short straw, ended up under the inquisitorial gaze of Bobby Hogan and Joe Dickie.

Cammo Grieve: Any idea how long this will take?

Hogan: Sorry, sir. Don't mean to inconvenience you.

Grieve: My brother's been murdered, you know!

Hogan: Why else would we be talking to you, sir?

(Rebus had to smile: Bobby Hogan had a way of saying 'sir' that made it sound like an insult.)

Dickie: You went back down to London on the Saturday, Mr Grieve?

Grieve: First bloody chance I could.

Dickie: You don't get on with your family?

Grieve: None of your bloody business.

Hogan: (To Dickie) Put down that Mr Grieve refused to answer.

Grieve: For Christ's sake!

Hogan: No need to take Our Lord's name in vain, sir.

(Rebus laughed out loud this time. Apart from the usual trinity – weddings, funerals and christenings – he doubted Bobby Hogan had ever seen the inside of a church.)

Grieve: Look, let's just get on with it, shall we?

Dickie: Couldn't agree more, sir.

Grieve: I was back in London Saturday night. You can check with my wife. We spent Sunday together, except when I had some constituency business to discuss with my agent. Couple of friends joined us for dinner. Monday morning, I was on my way to the House when I got the call on my mobile to say Roddy was dead.

Hogan: And how did you feel, sir . . . ?

On it went, Cammo Grieve combative, Hogan and Dickie soaking up his hostility like a sponge, hitting back with questions and comments that illustrated their feelings towards him.

As Hogan had commented afterwards – strictly off the record – 'Only time that shite would get a cross from me was if he had fangs.'

Lorna Grieve and her partner had, individually, faced up to the easier pairing of DI Bill Pryde and DS Roy Frazer. Neither had seen Roddy on the Sunday. Lorna had gone to visit friends in North Berwick, while Hugh Cordover had busied himself in his home-based studio, with an engineer and various band members as witnesses.

There were still no sightings of Roddy Grieve on the Sunday night, when he'd supposedly been out for a drink with friends. No friends seemed to have seen him. The implication was: Roddy had enjoyed a secret life, something apart from his marriage. And this, by its very nature, would give the investigation all sorts of problems.

Because no matter how hard you tried, some secrets were bound to stay unrevealed.

11

The building society was on George Street. When Siobhan Clarke had first arrived in Edinburgh, George Street had seemed a windy ghetto of stunning architecture and sluggish business. Half the office space seemed to be empty, with To Let notices strung like pennants from the buildings. Now the street was changing, upmarket shops being joined by a string of bars and restaurants, most of them housed in what had been banks.

That C. Mackie's building society was still trading seemed, under the circumstances, a minor miracle. Clarke sat in the manager's office while he found the relevant paperwork. Mr Robertson was a small, rotund man with a large, polished head and beaming smile. The half-moon glasses gave him the appearance of a Dickensian clerk. Clarke tied not to imagine him in period clothes, but failed. He took her smile as one of approbation – either of his character in general or his efficiency – and sat back down at his modern desk in his modern office. The manila file was slim.

'The C stands for Christopher,' he remarked.

'Mystery solved,' Clarke said, opening her notebook. Mr Robertson beamed at her.

'The account was opened in the March of 1980. The fifteenth, to be precise, a Saturday. I'm afraid I wasn't the manager then.'

'Who was?'

'My predecessor, George Samuels. I wasn't even at this branch, prior to my elevation.'

Clarke flipped through Christopher Mackie's passbook. 'The opening balance was £430,000?'

Robertson checked the figures. 'That is correct. Thereafter, we have a history of occasional minor withdrawals and annual interest.'

'You knew Mr Mackie?'

'No, I don't believe so. I took the liberty of asking the staff.' He ran his fingers down the columns of figures. 'You say he was a tramp?'

'His clothing would suggest he was homeless.'

'Well, I know house prices are extortionate, but all the same . . .'

'With four hundred thousand to spare, he might have found himself something?'

'With that sort of money, he might have found just about anything.' He paused. 'But then there *is* this address in the Grassmarket.'

'I'll be going there later, sir.'

Robertson nodded distractedly. 'One of the staff, our Mrs Briggs. He seemed to deal with her when he made a withdrawal.'

'I'd like to talk to her.'

He nodded again. 'I presumed as much. She's ready for you.'

Clarke looked at her pad. 'Has his address changed at all, while he's been a customer here?'

Robertson peered at the paperwork. 'It would seem not,' he said at last.

'Didn't it seem unusual to you, sir: that amount of money in the one account?'

'We did write to Mr Mackie from time to time, asking if he'd like to discuss other options. Thing is, you can't be too pushy.'

'Or the customer might take umbrage?'

Mr Robertson nodded. 'This is a wealthy place, you know. Mr Mackie wasn't the only one with that kind of cash at his disposal.'

'Thing is, sir, he didn't dispose of it.'

'Which brings me to another point . . .'

'We haven't found anything resembling a will, if that's what you're getting at.'

'And no next of kin?'

'Mr Robertson, I didn't even have a first name till you gave me one.' Clarke closed her notebook. 'I'll talk to Mrs Briggs now, if I may.'

Valerie Briggs was a middle-aged woman who'd recently had her hair restyled. Clarke guessed as much from the way Mrs Briggs kept touching a hand to her head, as if not quite believing the shape and texture.

'The very first time he came in here, it was me he talked to.' A cup of tea had been provided for Mrs Briggs. She looked at it uncertainly: tea in her boss's office was, like her hairstyle, a new and challenging experience. 'Said he wanted to open an account and who should he speak to. So I gave him the form and off he went. Came back with it filled in and asked if he could open the account with cash. I thought he'd made a mistake, put down too many noughts.'

'He had the money with him?'

Mrs Briggs nodded, wide-eyed at the memory. 'Showed me it, all in a smart-looking briefcase.'

'A briefcase?'

'Lovely and shiny it was.'

Siobhan scribbled a note to herself. 'And what happened?' she asked.

'Well, I had to fetch the manager. I mean, that amount of cash . . .' She shivered at the thought.

'This was Mr Samuels?'

'The manager, yes. Lovely man, old George.'

'You keep in touch?'

'Oh, yes.'

'So what happened?'

'Well, George . . . Mr Samuels, that is, took Mr Mackie

into the office. The old office.' She nodded at where they were sitting. 'It used to be over by the front door. Don't know why they moved it. And when Mr Mackie came out, that was it, we had a new customer. And every time he came in, he'd wait until I could deal with him.' She shook her head slowly. 'Such a shame to see him go like that.'

'Go?'

'You know, let himself go. I mean, the day he opened the account . . . well, he wasn't dressed to the nines but he was presentable. Suit and what have you. Hair might have needed a wash and trim . . .' She patted her own hair again. '. . . but nicely spoken and everything.'

'Then he started going downhill?'

'Pretty much straight away. I mentioned it to Mr Samuels.'

'What did he say?'

She smiled at the memory, recited the reply: ' "Valerie, dear, there are probably more eccentric rich people out there than normal ones." He had a point, I suppose. But he said something else I remember: "Money brings with it a responsibility some of us are unable to handle." '

'He could have a point.'

'Maybe so, dear, but I told him I'd be willing to take my chances any time he felt like emptying the safe.'

They shared a laugh at this, before Clarke asked Mrs Briggs how she might find Mr Samuels.

'That's an easy one. He's a demon for the bowls. It's like a religion with him.'

'In this weather?'

'Do you give up churchgoing because it's snowing outside?'

It was a good point, and one Clarke was willing to concede in exchange for an address.

She walked past the bowling green and pushed open the door to the social club. She hadn't been to Blackhall before, and the maze of streets had defeated her, twice

102

misleading her back on to the busy Queensferry Road. This was Bungalow Land, an area of the city that seemed to have stepped straight out of the 1930s. It seemed a world away from Broughton Street. Here, you appeared to have left the city. There was precious little commerce, precious few people about. The bowling green had a careworn look, its grass a dull emulsion. The clubhouse behind it was a single-storey affair of brown wooden slats, probably thirty years old and showing its age. She stepped inside to a furnace-blast from the ceiling-mounted heater. There was a bar ahead of her, where an elderly woman was humming some show tune as she dusted the bottles of spirits.

'Bowls?' Clarke called.

'Through the doors, hen.' Nodding in the general direction without losing her beat. Clarke pushed open the double doors and was in a long narrow room. A green baize mat, twelve feet wide and about fifty long, took up most of the available space. A few plastic chairs were scattered around the periphery, but there were no spectators, just the four players, who looked towards the interruption with all the ire they could muster until, noting her sex and youth, their faces melted and backs straightened.

'One of yours, I'll bet,' one man said, nudging his neighbour.

'Away to hell.'

'Jimmy likes them with a bit more meat on their bones,' the third player added.

'And a few more miles on the clock, too,' said player four. They were laughing now, laughing with the confidence of old men, immune from penalty.

'Wouldn't you give your left one to be forty years younger?' The speaker stooped to pick up one of his bowls. The jack had been dispatched to the far end of the carpet. Two bowls sat either side of it.

'Sorry to interrupt your game,' Clarke said, deciding

immediately on her approach. 'I'm Detective Constable Clarke.' She showed them her warrant card. 'I'm looking for George Samuels.'

'Told you they'd catch up with you, Dod.'

'It was only a matter of time.'

'I'm George Samuels.' The man who stepped forward was tall and slender and wore a burgundy tie under his sleeveless V-neck jumper. His hand when she shook it had a firm grip and was warm and dry. His hair was snowy white and plentiful, like cotton wadding.

'Mr Samuels, I'm from St Leonard's police station. Would you mind if I had a word?'

'I've been expecting you.' His eyes were the blue of summer water. 'It's about Christopher Mackie, isn't it?' He saw the look of surprise on her face and broke into a smile, pleased that he still had some force in the world.

They sat in a corner of the bar. An elderly couple sat in the other corner: the man had drifted off to sleep and the woman was knitting. A half-pint of beer sat in front of the man, a sherry in front of his companion.

George Samuels had ordered a whisky, doubling its volume with water. He'd signed Clarke in so that she could drink as his guest, but she'd only wanted coffee. Now, after the first sip, she was wishing she hadn't bothered. The catering-sized tin of instant behind the bar should have given her the first clue. The second should have been when the barmaid started chipping away at the contents.

'How did you know?' she asked.

Samuels ran a hand over his forehead. 'I always knew there was something wrong with it ... with him. You don't just walk into a building society with that amount of money.' He looked up from his drink. 'You don't, do you?'

'I'd like the chance to try,' she said.

He smiled. 'You've been talking to Val Briggs. She said much the same thing. We always joked about it.'

'If you thought there was something odd about it, why take the money?'

He opened his arms. 'If I hadn't, someone else would. This was twenty years ago. We weren't under any obligation to tell the police if something like that happened. That one deposit made me Branch Manager of the Month.'

'Did he say anything about the money?'

Samuels was nodding. There was something Christmasy about his hair; Clarke imagined playing with it, like playing with fresh snow. 'Oh, I asked,' he told her. 'I came straight out.'

'And?' A couple of biscuits had arrived with the coffee. She bit into one. It was soft, felt greasy in her mouth.

'He asked if I needed to know. I said I'd *like* to know, which wasn't quite the same thing. He told me it was from a bank robbery.' Her look pleased him all over again. 'Of course, we both laughed. I mean, he was joking. The notes . . . their serial numbers . . . I'd have known if they'd been stolen.'

Clarke nodded. There was a paste in her mouth. The only way she could swallow it was with the help of a drink, and the only drink available was the coffee. She took a swig, held her breath and swallowed.

'So what else did he say?'

'Oh, he said something about the money coming to him in a will. Him having cashed the cheque to see what that amount of cash looked like.'

'He didn't say where he cashed the cheque?'

Samuels shrugged. 'I'm not sure I'd have believed him, even if he had.'

She looked at him. 'You thought the money was . . . ?'

'Tainted in some way.' He was nodding. 'But no matter what I thought, there he was, offering to place it in an account at *my* branch.'

'No qualms?'

'Not at the time.'

'But you always knew someone would be coming to speak with you about Mr Mackie?'

Another shrug. 'I'm beyond the point of giving excuses, Miss Clarke. But I'm guessing you know where the money came from.'

Clarke shook her head. 'Haven't a clue, sir.'

Samuels sat back in his chair. 'Then why are you here?'

'Mr Mackie committed suicide, sir. Lived like a tramp, then threw himself off North Bridge. I'm trying to find out why.'

Samuels couldn't help. He'd spoken with Mackie only on that one occasion. As Clarke drove back into the city, heading for the Grassmarket, she considered her options. The process took all of three seconds. She had this one slender trail, that was all. To find out the what and why, she had to find out *who* Christopher Mackie had been. She'd already phoned a search request to the records people. He wasn't in any phone book, and, just as she'd suspected, when she arrived at the Grassmarket address she found herself at a hostel for the homeless.

Grassmarket was an odd little world all of its own. Centuries back, they'd held executions here, a fact commemorated by the name of one of the pubs: The Last Drop. Until the 1970s, the area had borne the reputation of being a haven for the destitute and the wandering. But then gentrification became the model. Small specialist shops opened, the bars were spruced up, and tourists began their hesitant, steep descent down Victoria Street and Candlemaker Row.

The hostel wasn't exactly publicising its existence. Two grimy windows and a solid-looking door. Outside, a couple of men were crouched beside the wall. One of them asked if she had a light. She shook her head.

'Probably means you've no fags on you either,' he said, resuming his conversation with his friend.

Clarke turned the door handle, but the door was locked. There was a buzzer on the wall. She pressed it twice and waited. A scrawny young man yanked open the door, took one look at her and retreated back inside, saying to no one in particular, 'Surprise, surprise, it's the polis.' He fell into a chair and got back to the serious business of daytime TV. There were a couple of beaten-up armchairs in the room, plus a long wooden bench and two that looked like bar stools. The TV and a coffee table more or less completed the furnishings. There was a tin ashtray on the table, but the linoleum floor looked to be the more popular destination for stubbed cigarettes. One elderly man was asleep in an armchair, his face speckled with bits of white paper. Clarke was about to investigate, when her meeter and greeter tore a scrap from an old newspaper, moistened it in his mouth, then spat it towards the sleeping figure.

'Two points for the face,' he explained. 'One for the hair or beard.'

'What's your record?'

He grinned, showing a mouth missing half its teeth. 'Eighty-five.'

A door opened at the far end of the room. 'Can I help you?'

Clarke walked over, shook the woman's hand. Behind her, the record-holder made siren noises. 'I'm DC Clarke, St Leonard's police station.'

'Yes?'

'Do you know a man called Christopher Mackie?'

A protective look. 'I might do. What has he done?'

'I'm afraid Mr Mackie's dead. Suicide, it looks like.'

The woman closed her eyes for a second. 'Was he the one who jumped from North Bridge? All it said in the papers was that he was homeless.'

'You knew him then?'

'Let's talk about it in the store.'

*

Her name was Rachel Drew and she'd been in charge of the hostel for a dozen years.

'Not that it's really a hostel,' she said. 'It's a day centre. But to be honest, when there's no place else for them to go, they do use the front room for bedding down in. I mean, it's winter, what else are you going to do?'

Clarke nodded. The room they sat in was pretty much as Rachel Drew had said: a store. There was a desk and a couple of chairs, but the rest of the space was taken up with boxes of tinned foods. Drew had explained that there was a tiny kitchen annexe, and that she and a couple of helpers rustled up three meals a day.

'It's not *haute cuisine*, but I don't get many complaints.'

Drew was a large, homely woman, maybe mid-forties, with shoulder-length brown hair which looked naturally frizzy. She had dark eyes and a sallow face, but there was warmth and humour in her voice, fighting what Clarke reckoned was near-permanent tiredness.

'What can you tell me about Mr Mackie?'

'He was a lovely, gentle man. Didn't make friends easily, but that was his choice. It took me a long time to get to know him. He was already a feature here when I arrived. I don't mean he was always hanging about the place, but you'd see him regularly.'

'You kept his mail for him?'

Drew nodded. 'There was never much. His DSS cheque was about it . . . Maybe two or three letters a year.'

His building society statements, Clarke guessed. 'How well did you know him?'

'Why do you ask?'

Clarke stared her out. Drew managed a wry smile. 'Sorry, I'm pretty protective about my boys and girls. You're wondering if Chris was suicidal.' She shook her head slowly. 'I wouldn't have said so.'

'When did you last see him?'

'A week or so back.'

'Do you know where he went when he wasn't here?'

'I make it a rule never to ask.'

'Why's that?' Clarke was genuinely interested.

'You never know which question will hit a nerve.'

'He didn't tell you anything about his past?'

'A few stories. He said he'd been in the forces. Another time, he told me he'd been a chef. Said his wife ran off with one of the waiters.'

Clarke caught Drew's tone. 'You didn't believe him?'

Drew sat back in her chair, her face and shoulders framed by tinned goods. Every day she opened some tins and did some cooking, feeding people so the rest of the world could forget about them. 'I get told a lot of stories. I'm a good listener.'

'Did Chris have any close friends?'

'Not here, not that I noticed. But maybe outside . . .' Drew narrowed her eyes. 'Don't get me wrong or anything, but just why the hell are you so interested in a down and out.'

'Because he wasn't. Chris had a building society account. He was in credit to the tune of four hundred thousand pounds.'

'Lucky him,' Drew snorted. Then she saw the look on Clarke's face. 'Oh, Christ, you're serious.' Now she sat forward in her chair, toes on the ground, elbows on her knees. 'Where did he get . . . ?'

'We don't know.'

'Goes some way to explaining your interest. Who gets the money?'

Clarke shrugged. 'Next of kin . . . relatives.'

'Always supposing he has any.'

'Yes.'

'And supposing you can find them.' Drew chewed at her bottom lip. 'You know, there were times when this place was struggling. Christ, we're struggling now. And he never so much as . . .' She laughed suddenly and harshly, clapping her hands together. 'The sneaky little sod. What was he playing at?'

'That's what I'm wondering.'

'If you can't trace his family, where does the money go?'

'I think the Treasury.'

'The government? Christ, there's no justice, is there?'

'Careful who you say that to,' Clarke said with a smile.

Drew was shaking her head and chuckling. 'Four hundred grand. And he jumped and left it all behind.'

'Yes.'

'Knowing you'd find out about it.' Drew stared at Clarke. 'It's like he was setting you a puzzle, isn't it?' She was thoughtful for a moment. 'You should take it to the papers. Once the story's out, the family will come to *you*.'

'Along with every shyster and fraud in the game. That's why I need to find out about him: so I can weed out the con artists.'

'True enough. You've got a head on your shoulders, haven't you?' She exhaled loudly. 'Things I could do with that money.'

'Like hire a cook?'

'I was thinking more of a year in Barbados.'

Clarke smiled again. 'One last thing: I don't suppose you've a picture of Chris?'

Drew raised an eyebrow. 'You know, I think you might be in luck.' She opened a drawer of the desk and began pulling out sheets of paper and raffle tickets, pens and cassette tapes. Finally she found what she was looking for: a packet of photographs. She flicked through them, picked one out and handed it over.

'Taken last Christmas, but Chris hasn't really changed much since. That's him next to the Bearded Wonder.'

Clarke recognised the sleeping man from the other room. In the photo, he was in his armchair but very much awake, mouth agape in almost a parody of joy. On the arm of the chair sat the man called Christopher Mackie. Medium height, the beginnings of a paunch. Black hair swept back from a prominent forehead. His smile was mischievous, as though he was in on some secret. Yes, and wasn't he just? It was the first time she'd been face to face with him. It felt strange. So far, she'd only known him in death . . .

'Here he is on his own,' Drew said.

The second photo showed Mackie washing a sinkful of dishes. He'd been caught unawares by the photographer, and his face was determined, focused on the job at hand. The flash made his face ghostly white, red dots for eyes.

'Mind if I take these?'

'Go ahead.'

Clarke tucked the pictures into her jacket pocket. 'I'd also appreciate it if you'd keep what I've told you to yourself for the moment.'

'Don't want to be snowed under with cranks?'

'Wouldn't make my job any easier.'

Drew seemed to make her mind up about something. She opened a red plastic card index, flicked through the contents and lifted out one of the cards.

'Chris's personal details,' she said, handing the card over. 'Date of birth and his doctor's name and phone number. Maybe they'll help.'

'Thanks,' Clarke said. She drew a banknote from her pocket. 'This isn't a bribe or anything, I'd just like to put something towards the hostel.'

Drew stared at the money. 'Fair enough,' she said at last, accepting it. 'If it helps your conscience, how can I refuse?'

'I'm a police officer, Ms Drew. The conscience is removed during training.'

'Well,' Rachel Drew said, getting to her feet, 'looks to me like you've maybe grown a new one.'

12

Rebus gave Derek Linford the choice: Roddy Grieve's workplace, or Hugh Cordover's studio. Knowing full well which one Linford would go for.

'I might pick up a few tips for my portfolio while I'm at it,' Linford said, leaving Rebus to head out towards Roslin and the baronial home of Hugh Cordover and Lorna Grieve. Roslin was the home of the ancient and extraordinary Rosslyn Chapel, which in recent years had become the target of a range of millennialist nutters. They said the Ark of the Covenant was buried beneath its floor. Or it was an alien mothership. The village itself was quiet, nondescript. High Manor sat a quarter-mile further on, behind a low stone wall. There were stone gateposts but no gates, just a sign saying 'Private'. It was called High Manor because in his days as a member of Obscura, Hugh had been 'High Chord'. Rebus had one of their albums with him: *Continuous Repercussions*. Lorna was on the sleeve, seated high-priestess style on a throne, diaphanous white dress, a snake coiled around her head. Laser lights shone from her eyes. Around the edges of the album sleeve were rows of hieroglyphs.

He parked his Saab beside a Fiat Punto and a Land-Rover. A couple of other cars stood off to one side: a beaten-up old Merc and an open-topped American classic. He left the album in the car and made for the front door. Lorna Grieve herself opened it. Ice rattled in the glass she was holding.

'My little Monkey Man,' she cooed. 'In here with you.

Hugh's down in the bowels. You have to be quiet till he's finished.'

What she meant was that Hugh Cordover was in his studio. It took up the whole lower ground floor of the house. Cordover himself sat in the production suite with an engineer. The equipment around them seemed about to swamp them. Through the thickened window, Rebus could see into the studio proper. Three young men, shoulders slumped with exhaustion. The drummer was pacing behind his kit, a bottle of Jack Daniels hanging from one hand. The guitarist and bassist seemed to be concentrating on the sound from their headphones. Empty beer cans lay strewn around them, along with cigarette packets, wine bottles and guitar strings.

'See what I mean?' Cordover said into a microphone. The musicians nodded. He glanced towards Rebus. 'All right, guys, the police are here to talk to me, so don't go chopping lines in there, okay?'

Sneers, V-signs towards the window. Rock and roll, Rebus thought, had never been so dangerous.

Cordover gave the engineer some instructions, then rose stifflly from his chair. He ran a hand over his unshaven face, shaking his head slowly. Motioned for Rebus to precede him from the production suite.

'Who are they?' Rebus asked.

'The next big thing,' Cordover told him, 'if I get my way. They're called The Crusoes.'

'The Robinson Crusoes?'

'You've heard of them?'

'Someone mentioned you were their manager.'

'Manager, arranger, producer. All-round general father figure.' Cordover pushed open a door. 'This is the Rec Room.'

More mess on the floor. Music magazines lying on chairs. A portable TV, portable hi-fi. A pool table.

'All mod cons,' Cordover said, pulling open the fridge and reaching in for a soft drink. 'Want something?'

Lorna Grieve, seated on a red sofa, closed the newspaper she'd been skimming. 'If I'm any judge of character, my Monkey Man will be wanting something stronger than that.' She rattled her own glass to make the point. She was dressed in a swirling green silk trousersuit. Barefoot, with a red chiffon scarf around her neck.

'A soft drink will be fine actually,' Rebus said, nodding when Cordover brought out two bottles of flavoured mineral water.

'Is it okay to talk here?' Cordover said. 'Or would you prefer upstairs?'

'Mind you,' Lorna added, 'it's no tidier up there than down here.'

'This is fine,' Rebus said, settling himself on one of the chairs. Cordover hauled himself up on to the pool table, legs swinging over the side. His wife rolled her eyes, as if in wonder at his inability to use a chair.

'Which one was Peter Grief?' Rebus asked.

'The bassist,' Cordover answered.

'He knows about his father?'

'Of course he knows,' Lorna Grieve snapped back.

'They were never close,' Cordover added.

'The Monkey Man', Grieve said to her husband, 'is shocked that so soon after Roddy's brutal murder, the pair of you can be back at work as though nothing's happened.'

'Yes,' Cordover shot back. 'So much more useful to hit the bottle.'

'When did I ever need the excuse of a death in the family?' She smiled at Cordover, eyes heavy-lidded. Then, turning to Rebus: 'You've a lot to learn about the clan, Monkey Man.'

'Why do you keep calling him that?' Cordover sounding irritated.

'It's a Rolling Stones song,' Rebus said. He watched Lorna Grieve toast him on this response. Smiled at her, couldn't help himself. She was drinking brandy; even from this distance he could all but taste it.

'I knew Stew,' Cordover said.

'Stew?' Lorna narrowed her eyes.

'Ian Stewart,' Rebus explained. 'The sixth Stone.'

Cordover nodded. 'His face didn't fit the image, so he couldn't be in the band. Played session for them instead.' He turned to Rebus. 'You know he came from Fife? And Stu Sutcliffe was born in Edinburgh.'

'And Jack Bruce was Glaswegian.'

Cordover smiled. 'You know your stuff.'

'I know *some* stuff. For example, I know that Peter's mother is called Billie Collins. Has anyone been in touch with her?'

'Why the hell should we care?' Lorna said. 'She can buy a paper, can't she?'

'I think Peter's spoken with her,' Cordover added.

'Where does she live?'

'St Andrews, I think.' Cordover looked to his wife for confirmation. 'She teaches at a school there.'

'Haugh Academy,' Lorna said. 'Is she a suspect?'

Rebus was writing in his notebook. 'Do you want her to be?' Asked casually, not looking up.

'The more the merrier.'

Cordover leapt from his perch. 'For Christ's sake, Lorna!'

'Oh, yes,' his wife spat back, 'you always did have a soft spot for her. Or should that be a hard spot?' She looked at Rebus. 'Hugh always excused his rutting by saying he was an artist. Only he's never been much of a sack artist, have you, sweetie?'

'Stories, that's all they were.' Cordover was pacing now.

'Speaking of stories,' Rebus said, 'had you heard anything about Josephine Banks?'

Lorna Grieve chuckled, cupped her hands in mock prayer. 'Oh yes, let it be her. That would be *too* perfect.'

'Roddy was a public figure, Inspector,' Cordover said,

his eyes on his wife. 'You get all sorts of rumours. It goes with the territory.'

'Does it?' Lorna said. 'How fascinating. And tell me, what rumours have you heard about *me*?'

Cordover stayed silent. Rebus could tell the man had some reply formed, something wounding: *none, which just proves how far you've fallen.* Something like that. But he stayed silent.

It seemed as good a time as any to toss a grenade into the room. 'Who's Alasdair?'

There was silence. Lorna gulped at her drink. Cordover rested against the pool table. Rebus was content to let the silence do its work.

'Lorna's brother,' Cordover said at last. 'Not that I ever knew him.'

'Alasdair was the best of us,' Lorna said quietly. 'That's why he couldn't bear to stay.'

'What happened to him?' Rebus asked.

'He ran off into the wild blue yonder.' She made a sweeping motion with her glass. It was all ice now, nothing left to drink.

'When?'

'Ancient history, Monkey Man. He's in warm climes now, and good luck to him.' She turned towards Rebus, pointed to his left hand. 'No wedding ring. Would I make a good detective, do you think? And you're a drinker, too. You've been eyeing up my glass.' She pouted. 'Or is there something else you're interested in?'

'Please ignore her, Inspector.'

She flung the tumbler at her husband. 'Nobody ignores me! I'm not the has-been here.'

'That's right, the agencies are clamouring at your door. The phone never stops ringing.' The tumbler had missed him; he brushed ice-water from his arm.

Lorna pushed herself off the sofa. Rebus got the idea the pair were used to arguing in public, that they considered it their inalienable right as *artists*.

'Hey, you two.' A voice of reason from the doorway. 'We can't hear ourselves think in there. So much for soundproofing.' It was a drawl, easy, relaxed. Peter Grief reached into the fridge for a bottle of water. 'Besides, it's the rock star who should be having the tantrums, not his aunt and uncle.'

Rebus and Peter Grief sat in the control room. Everyone else was upstairs in the dining room. A baker's van had arrived, bearing trays of sandwiches and patisserie. Rebus had a little paper plate in his hand, just the one triangle of bread on it: chicken tikka filling. Peter Grief was using a finger to remove the cream from a wedge of sponge cake. It was all he'd eaten so far. He'd asked if it was all right to have music on in the background. Music helped him to think.

'Even when it's a rough mix of one of my own songs.'

Which is what they were listening to. Rebus said he considered three-piece bands a rarity. Grief corrected him by mentioning Manic Street Preachers, Massive Attack, Supergrass, and half a dozen others, then added: 'And Cream, of course.'

'Not forgetting Jimi Hendrix.'

Grief bowed his head. 'Noel Redding: not many bassists could keep up with James Marshall.'

Niceties dispensed with, Rebus put down his plate. 'You know why I'm here, Peter?'

'Hugh told me.'

'I'm sorry about your father.'

Grief shrugged. 'Bad career move for a politician. Now if he'd only been in *my* business . . .' It had the sound of a rehearsed line, something to be used over and again as self-protection.

'How old were you when your parents separated?'

'Too young to remember.'

'You were brought up by your mother?'

117

Grief nodded. 'But they stayed close. You know, "for the sake of the child".'

'Something like that still hurts though, doesn't it?'

Grief glanced up. There was a seam of anger in his voice. 'How would you know?'

'I left my wife. She had to bring up our daughter.'

'And how's your daughter doing?' The anger quickly replaced by curiosity.

'She's okay.' Rebus paused. 'Now, that is. Back then . . . I'm not so sure.'

'You *are* a cop, right? I mean, this isn't some cheap trick to get me discussing my feelings with a counsellor?'

Rebus smiled. 'If I was a counsellor, Peter, my next question would be, "Do you think you need to discuss your feelings?" '

Grief smiled, bowed his head. 'Sometimes I wish I was like Hugh and Lorna.'

'They don't exactly keep things bottled up, do they?'

'Not exactly.' Another smile, dying slowly on his lips. Grief was tall and slender with black hair, possibly dyed, and slicked back from a semi-quiff. His face was long and angular, prominent cheekbones and dark, haunted eyes. He looked right for the part: soiled white T-shirt baggy at the sleeves. Black drainpipe denims and biker boots. Thin leather braids around both wrists and a pentangle hanging from his throat. If Rebus had been casting for bassist in a rock band, he'd have told the other applicants to head for home.

'You know we're trying to figure out who might have wanted to kill your father?'

'Yes.'

'When you spoke with him, did he ever . . . ? Did you get the feeling he had enemies, anyone he was worried about?'

Grief was shaking his head. 'He wouldn't have told me.'

'Who would he have told?'

'Maybe Uncle Cammo.' Grief paused. 'Or Grandma.' His

fingers were busy imitating the loudspeaker bass-line. 'I wanted you to hear this song. It's about the last time Dad and I spoke.'

Rebus listened; the rhythm wasn't exactly funereal.

'We had this big falling-out. He thought I was wasting my time, blamed Uncle Hugh for stringing me along.'

Rebus couldn't make out the words. 'So what's the song called?'

'Here's the chorus coming.' Grief began to sing along, and now Rebus could make out the words only too well.

> Your heart could never conceive of beauty,
> Your head could never receive the truth
> And now at last I feel it's my duty
> To deliver the final reproof
> Oh yes, this is the final reproof.

Hugh Cordover and Lorna Grieve walked Rebus out to his car.

'Yes,' Cordover said, 'that's probably their best song.' He carried a cordless phone with him.

'You know it's about his father?'

'I know they argued, and Peter got a song out of it.' Cordover shrugged. 'Does that mean it's about his father? I think you're being a bit too literal, Inspector.'

'Maybe.'

Lorna Grieve was showing no ill-effects from the drink she'd consumed. She examined Rebus's Saab as though it was a museum piece. 'Do they still make these?'

'The new models don't come with gas lamps,' Rebus told her. She smiled at him.

'A sense of humour, how refreshing.'

'Just one more thing . . .' Rebus leaned into the car, came out with the Obscura album.

'My God,' Cordover said. 'You don't see many of these around.'

'Wonder why,' his wife muttered, staring at her photo on the cover.

'I was going to ask if you'd sign it?' Rebus said, bringing out a pen.

Cordover took the pen from him. 'With pleasure. But hang on, do you want me or High Chord?'

Rebus smiled. 'It's got to be High Chord, hasn't it?'

Cordover scrawled the name across the cover and made to hand the album back.

'And the model . . . ?' Rebus asked. She looked at him and he thought she was going to refuse. But then she took the pen and added her name, studying the cover afterwards.

'The hieroglyphs,' Rebus asked, 'any idea what they mean?'

Cordover laughed. 'Not a clue. Some guy I knew, he was into that stuff.' Rebus was noticing that some of the hieroglyphs were actually pentangles, like the pendant Peter Grief had worn.

Lorna laughed. 'Come on, Hugh. You were into that stuff.' She looked at Rebus. 'He still is. Not quite Jimmy Page's league, but it's why we moved to Roslin, to be near the chapel. Bloody New Age mumbo-jumbo, growing a ponytail and everything.'

'I think the Inspector has heard enough character assassination for one day,' Cordover said, his face growing ugly. Then the phone rang, and he turned away to answer it, sounding suddenly excited. His voice took on a transatlantic twang, forgetting all about Lorna, all about Rebus. Leaving the two of them together. She folded her arms.

'He's pathetic, isn't he? What do I see in him?'

'Not for me to say.'

She studied him. 'So was I right? Do you drink?'

'Only socially.'

'You mean as opposed to antisocially?' She laughed. 'I can be social when I want to. It's just that I seldom want

120

to be when Hugh's around.' She glanced back to where her husband was making for the house. He was talking numbers – money or record pressings, Rebus couldn't tell.

'So where do you drink?' she asked.

'A few places.'

'Name them.'

'The Oxford Bar. Swany's. The Malting.'

She wrinkled her nose. 'Why is it I'm seeing bare floorboards and cigarette smoke, swearing and bluster and not many women?'

He couldn't help smiling. 'You know them then?'

'I feel I do. Maybe we'll bump into one another.'

'Maybe.'

'I feel like kissing you. That's probably not allowed, right?'

'Right,' Rebus agreed.

'Maybe I'll do it anyway.' Cordover had disappeared into the house. 'Or would that be classed as assault?'

'Not if no charges were brought.'

She leaned forward, pecked him on the cheek. When she stepped back, Rebus saw a face at a window. Not Cordover: Peter Grief.

'Peter's song,' Rebus said. 'The one about his father. I didn't catch the title.'

' "The Final Reproof",' Lorna Grieve told him. 'As in condemning.'

In his car, Rebus got on his mobile and asked Derek Linford how things had gone at The Exchange.

'Roddy Grieve was whiter than white,' Linford said. 'No bad deals, no cock-ups, no unhappy punters. Also, none of his colleagues were out drinking with him on Sunday night.'

'Which tells us what exactly?'

'I'm not sure.'

'A dead end then?'

'Not quite: I did get a hot tip for an investment. How about you?'

Rebus glanced at the album on the passenger seat. 'I'm not sure what I got, Derek. Talk to you later.' He made another call, this time to a vinyl dealer in the city.

'Paul? It's John Rebus. Obscura's *Continuous Repercussions*, signed by High Chord and Lorna Grieve.' He listened for a moment. 'It's not mint, but it's not bad.' Listened again. 'Get back to me if you can go any higher, eh? Cheers.'

He slowed the car so he could search in the glove compartment, found a Hendrix tape and slotted it home. 'Love or Confusion'. Sometimes, you couldn't be sure what the difference was.

Howdenhall was home to the city's forensic science lab. Rebus wasn't sure why Grant Hood and Ellen Wylie wanted to meet him there. Their message had been vague, hinting at some surprise. Rebus hated surprises. That kiss from Lorna Grieve ... it hadn't been a surprise exactly, but all the same. And if he hadn't angled his head at the last moment, bottling out of some mouth-to-mouth ... Jesus, and with Peter Grief watching from the window. Grief: Rebus had meant to ask about the name change. Grieve to Grief; verb to noun. But then he'd been brought up by his mother, so maybe his surname had been Collins. In which case, the change of name was still resonant, the young man laying claim to the missing half of his identity, his missed past.

Howdenhall: full of brainboxes, some of them looking barely out of their teens. People who knew about DNA and computer data. These days at St Leonard's, you didn't roll ink over a suspect's fingers, you merely placed their palm to a computer pad. The prints flashed up on the screen, and Criminal Records came back to you immediately if there was a match. The process still amazed him, even after all these months.

Hood and Wylie were waiting for him in one of the meeting rooms. Howdenhall was still fairly new, and had a clean no-nonsense smell and feel to it. The large oval desk, made up of three movable sections, hadn't had time to get scuffed or scored. The chairs were still comfortably padded. The two junior officers made to get up, but he waved them back down and seated himself across the table from them.

'No ashtray,' he remarked.

'There's no smoking, sir,' Wylie explained.

'I know that well enough. I just keep thinking I'll wake up and it'll all have been a bad dream.' He looked around. 'No coffee or tea either, eh?'

Hood sprang to his feet. 'I can get you . . .'

Rebus shook his head. Still, it was good to see Hood so keen. Two empty polystyrene beakers on the table: he wondered who'd fetched them. Even money on Hood; Wylie at three to one.

'Latest news?' he asked.

'Very little blood in the fireplace,' Wylie said. 'Chances are, Skelly was killed elsewhere.'

'Which means less chance of the SOCOs coming up with anything useful.' Rebus was thoughtful for a moment. 'So why the secrecy?' he asked.

'No secrecy, sir. It's just that when we found out Professor Sendak was going to be here this afternoon for a meeting . . .'

'Seemed too good to miss, sir,' Hood concluded.

'And who's Professor Sendak when he's at home?'

'Glasgow University, sir. Head of Forensic Pathology.'

Rebus raised an eyebrow. 'Glasgow? Listen, if Gates and Curt find out, it's your heads, not mine, okay?'

'We cleared it with the Procurator Fiscal's office.'

'So what can this Sendak do that our own boffins can't?'

There was a knock at the door.

'Maybe we'll let the professor explain,' Hood said, not quite disguising the relief in his voice.

Professor Ross Sendak was approaching sixty, but still boasted a head of thick black hair. The shortest person in the room, he carried himself with weight and confidence, demanding respect. Introductions complete, he settled himself on a chair and spread his hands out on the table.

'You think I can help you,' he stated, 'and perhaps you're right. I'll need the skull brought to Glasgow. Can that be arranged?'

Wylie and Hood shared a look. Rebus cleared his throat.

'I'm afraid the Time Team here haven't had time to brief me, Professor.'

Sendak nodded, took a deep breath. 'Laser technology, Inspector.' He reached into his briefcase, slid out a laptop computer and switched it on. 'Forensic facial reconstruction. Your forensic colleagues here have already ascertained that the decedent's hair was brown. That's a start. What we would do in Glasgow is place the skull on a revolving plinth. We then aim a laser at the skull, feeding the information into a computer, building up details. From these, the facial contours are formed. Other information – the decedent's general physique; his age at date of death – help with the final image.' He turned the computer around so it was facing Rebus. 'And what you get is something like this.'

Rebus had to get up. From where he was sitting, the screen seemed blank. Hood and Wylie did likewise, until all three of them were jockeying for position, the better to make out the face which flickered at them. By moving a few inches to right or left, the image faded, disappeared, but when in focus it was clearly the face of a young man. There was something of the mannequin about it, a deadness to the eyes, the one visible ear not quite right and the hair clearly an afterthought.

'This poor devil rotted on a hillside in the Highlands. He

was past normal means of ID by the time he was found. Animals and the elements had taken their toll.'

'But you think this is what he looked like in life?'

'I'd say it's close. Eyes and hairstyle are speculative, but the overall structure of the face is true.'

'Amazing,' Hood said.

'Using the inset screen,' Sendak went on, 'we can reconfigure the face – change hairstyle, add a moustache or beard, even change eye colour. The variations can be printed out and used for a public appeal.' Sendak pointed to the small grey square in the top right corner of the screen. It contained what looked like a children's version of an identikit: the rough outline of a head, plus hats, facial hairstyles, glasses.

Rebus looked to Hood and Wylie. They were looking at him now, seeking his okay.

'So how much is this going to cost?' he asked, turning back to the screen.

'It's not an expensive process,' Sendak said. 'I appreciate that funds are being soaked up by the Grieve case.'

Rebus glanced towards Wylie. 'Someone's been whispering.'

'It's not like we're spending money on anything else,' Wylie argued. Rebus saw anger in her eyes. She was beginning to feel sidelined. Any other time of year, Skelly would have been big news, but not with Roddy Grieve as competition.

In the end, Rebus gave the nod.

Afterwards, there was just time for a coffee. Sendak explained that his Human Identification Centre had helped with war crimes cases in Rwanda and the former Yugoslavia. In fact, he was flying out to The Hague at the end of the week to testify in a war crimes trial.

'Thirty Serb victims buried in a mass grave. We helped identify the victims and prove they were shot at close range.'

'Sort of puts things into perspective, doesn't it?' Rebus

said afterwards, eyes on Wylie. Hood was off finding a phone. He needed to talk to the Procurator Fiscal's office again, tell them what was happening.

'You'll have to tell Prof. Gates what's happening,' Rebus went on.

'Yes, sir. Will that be a problem?'

Rebus shook his head. 'I'll have a word. He won't like the fact that Glasgow have got something he hasn't . . . but he'll live with it.' He winked at her. 'After all, we've got everything else.'

13

The Murder Room at St Leonard's was fully operational – computers, civilian support, extra phone lines – with an additional Portakabin parked on the pavement outside Queensberry House. Chief Superintendent Watson was kept busy in a series of meetings with Fettes brass and politicians. He'd lost the head at one of the junior officers, shouting the odds before marching off to his office and slamming the door. Nobody'd seen him like that before. DS Frazer's comment: 'Get Rebus back here, we need to offer a sacrifice.' Joe Dickie had nudged him: 'Any news on overtime?' He had a blank expenses form ready on his desk.

Gill Templer had been put in charge of press briefings. Her background was in liaison work. So far she'd managed to tamp down a couple of the wilder conspiracy theories. ACC Carswell had come to inspect the troops, given the tour by Derek Linford. Space at the station was cramped, and Linford didn't even have his own office. Twelve CID officers were attached to the case, along with a further dozen uniforms. The uniforms were there to search the area around the *locus* and help with door-to-door. Secretarial support came extra, and Linford was still waiting to hear what budget the case would merit. He wasn't stinting, not yet: he reckoned this was a flier, meaning it would justify any amount of staffing and overtime.

All the same, he liked to keep an eye on the money side. It didn't help that he was playing away from home. He ignored the looks and comments, but they got to him all the same. *Fettes bastard . . . thinks he can tell us how to run our station.* It was all about territory. Not that Rebus seemed to mind. Rebus had given him the run of the place, had admitted that Linford was the better administrator. His exact words: 'Derek, to be honest, no one's ever accused me of being able to mind the store.'

Linford made a circuit of the room now: wall charts; staff rotas; crime scene photographs; telephone numbers. Three officers sat silently at their computers, tapping the latest gen into the database. An investigation like this was all about information, its gathering and cross-referencing. Detection lay in making connections, and it could be a painstaking business. He wondered if anyone else in the room felt the same electricity he did. Back to the rota: DS Roy Frazer was in charge of the Holyrood operation, managing the house-to-house inquiries, interviewing the demolition teams and builders. Another DS, George Silvers, was plotting the deceased's final movements. Roddy Grieve had lived in Cramond, had told his wife he was going out for a drink. Nothing unusual in that, and he'd acted naturally. Had taken his mobile with him. Not that there'd been any reason to check up on him. At midnight she'd turned in for the night. Next morning when he wasn't there, she'd begun to worry, but had decided to leave it an hour or two; might be some rational explanation . . . Sleeping it off somewhere.

'Did that often happen?' Silvers had asked.

'Once or twice.'

'And where did he end up sleeping?'

Answer: at his mother's; or on a friend's sofa.

Silvers didn't look like he put much effort into anything. You couldn't imagine him in a hurry. But he gave himself time to form questions and strategies.

Time, too, for the interviewee to start twitching.

Grieve's press officer was a young man called Hamish Hall, and Linford had interviewed him. Playing it back in his head afterwards, Linford reckoned he'd come off

128

second best in the encounter. Hall, in his sharp suit and with a sharp, bright face, had snapped out his answers, as if dismissing the questions. Linford had snapped another question back at him, taking him on rather than playing to his own strengths.

'How did you get on with Mr Grieve?'

'Fine.'

'Never any problems?'

'Never.'

'And Ms Banks?'

'Do you mean how did I get along with her, or how did she get along with Roddy?' Light glinting from the circular chrome frames of his spectacles.

'Both, I suppose.'

'Fine.'

'Yes?'

'That's my answer to both questions: we got along fine.'

'Right.'

And on it went, like machine-gun fire. Hall's background: party man, single-minded, economics degree. Economy his strong point when speaking, too.

'Press agent . . . Is that like a spin doctor?'

A bending of the mouth. 'That's a cheap shot, Inspector Linford.'

'Who else was in Mr Grieve's retinue? I'm assuming there'd be local volunteers . . . ?'

'Not yet. Electioneering proper doesn't start until April. That's when we'd have needed canvassers.'

' You had people in mind?'

'Not my bailiwick. Ask Jo.'

'Jo?'

'Josephine Banks, his election agent. That's what we called her: Jo.' A glance at his watch, loud exhalation.

'So what will you do now, Mr Hall?'

'You mean when I leave here?'

'I mean now your employer's dead.'

'Find another one.' A genuine smile this time. 'There'll be no shortage of takers.'

Linford could see Hall five or ten years down the line, standing just behind some dignitary, maybe even the Prime Minister, murmuring something which the PM would utter aloud mere seconds later. Always in shot; always close to the power.

When the two men stood up, Linford shook Hall's hand warmly, offered him a grin and a cup of tea or coffee.

'Really appreciate . . . sorry to have . . . wish you all the best . . .'

Because you never knew. Five, ten years on, you just never could tell . . .

'Tell me this is a joke.'

Ellen Wylie was examining the dimly lit interior of one of the downstairs interview rooms. It was half-filled with broken equipment: chairs with missing castors; golf-ball typewriters.

'It's been used for storage, as you can see.'

She turned to the desk sergeant, who'd unlocked the door for her and turned on the light. 'I'd never have guessed.'

'So where do we put all this stuff?' Grant Hood asked.

'Maybe you can work around it?' the desk sergeant offered.

'We're working a *murder* inquiry,' Wylie hissed at him. Then she looked around the room again, before turning to her partner. 'And this is how they treat us, Grant.'

'Well, it's all yours,' the desk sergeant said, removing the key from the lock and handing it to Hood. 'Have fun.'

Hood watched him retreat, then held the key up in front of Wylie. 'It's all ours, he says.'

'Can we complain to the management?' Wylie kicked at one of the chairs, whose arm promptly fell off.

'I know the brochure said sea view,' her partner said,

'but with any luck, we won't be spending much time here.'

'Those bastards upstairs have got a coffee-maker,' Wylie said. Then she burst out laughing. 'What am I saying? We haven't even got any phones!'

'Maybe so,' Hood informed her, 'but if I'm not mistaken, we've just cornered the global market in electric typewriters.'

Siobhan Clarke had insisted on somewhere 'a bit fancy' for their drink, and when she told him about her day, Derek Linford thought he understood. Her last couple of working hours had been spent questioning dossers.

'Not easy,' he said. 'You were all right, though?' She looked at him. 'I mean, they didn't bite?'

'No, they were just . . .' She tipped her neck back, inspecting the spectacular ceiling of The Dome Bar and Grill as if expecting the rest of the sentence to be painted there. 'I mean, they weren't even smelly for the most part. But it was the past.' Now she nodded to herself.

'How do you mean?' He was using his swizzle-stick to chase a sliver of lime around his glass.

'I mean the stories, all the tragedies and tiny mishaps and wrong turns that had brought them there. Nobody's *born* homeless, not that I know of.'

'I know what you mean. They needn't be homeless, the majority of them. The support system's out there.' She was looking at him, but he didn't notice. 'I never give them money, it's a sort of principle with me. Some of them probably make more a week than we do. You can make two hundred a day, just begging on Princes Street.' He shook his head slowly, saw the look on her face. 'What?'

She studied her own drink, a large gin and tonic to his lime juice and soda. 'Nothing.'

'What did I say?'

'Maybe it's just . . .'

'Been a rough day?'

131

She glowered. 'I was going to say, maybe it's just your attitude.'

They sat in silence for a while after that. Not that anyone in The Dome minded. It was the cocktail hour: George Street suits; black two-pieces with matching tights. Everyone focused on their own little group: office blather. Clarke took a long swallow. There was never enough gin; you could order a double and still not feel the kick. At home, she poured half and half, gin to tonic. Lots of ice, and a wedge of lemon rather than something that looked like it had been pared with a razor blade.

'Your accent changes,' Linford said at last. 'Modulates to suit the occasion. It's a clever trick.'

'How do you mean?'

'Well, you've got an English accent, right? But in some company, at the station for example, you manage to bring in some Scots.'

It was true: she knew she did it. She'd been a bit of a mimic even at school and college, knowing she did it so she'd fit in with whoever she was talking to, whichever peer group. Used to be, she could hear herself switching, but not now. The question she'd asked herself was: why the need to change, just to fit in? Was she that desperate, that lonely as a girl?

Was she?

'Where were you born?'

'Liverpool,' she said. 'My parents were lecturers. The week after I was born, they moved to Edinburgh.'

'Mid-seventies?'

'Late sixties, and flattery will get you nowhere.' But she managed a smile. 'We only stayed a couple of years, then it was Nottingham. I got most of my schooling there, finished off in London.'

'Is that where your parents live now?'

'Yes.'

'Lecturers, eh? What do they make of you?'

It was a perceptive question, but she didn't know him

132

well enough to answer it. Just as she'd always let people assume that her New Town flat was a rental. When she'd eventually sold it and got her own mortgage on a place half the size, she'd put the money back into her parents' bank account. She'd never explained to them why she'd done it. They'd only asked the once.

'I came back here to go to college,' she told Linford. 'Fell in love with the city.'

'And chose a career where you'd always see its mucky underwear?'

She chose to ignore this question, too.

'So that makes you a settler . . . one of the New Scots. I think that's what the Nationalists call them. You *will* be voting Scot Nat, I trust?'

'Oh, are you SNP?'

'No.' He laughed. 'I just wondered if you were.'

'It's a pretty underhand way of finding out.'

He shrugged, finished his drink. 'Another?'

She was still studying him, feeling suddenly enervated. All the other drinkers, the nine-to-fives, were winding down, a few drinks before home. Why did people do that? They could get a drink at home, couldn't they? Feet up in front of the telly. Instead of which, they stuck close to their office building and had a drink with their work-mates. Was it so hard to let go? Or was home something less than a refuge? You needed a drink before facing it, courage to confront the evening's redundancy? Was that what she was doing here?

'I think I'll head off,' she said suddenly. Her jacket was on the back of her chair. A while back, someone had been stabbed outside this place. She'd worked the case. Just another act of violence, another life wasted.

'Got plans?' He looked expectant, nervous, childlike in his ignorance and egotism. What could she tell him? Belle and Sebastian on the hi-fi; another gin and tonic; the last third of an Isla Dewar novel. Tough competition for any man.

133

'What are you smiling at?'

'Nothing,' she said.

'Must be something.'

'Women have to have some secrets, Derek.' She had her jacket on now, was wrapping her scarf around her neck.

'I thought a bite to eat,' he blurted out. 'You know, make an evening of it.'

She looked at him. 'I don't think so.' Hoping her tone would alert him to the missing final word: *ever*.

And she walked.

He'd offered to see her home, but she'd declined. Offered to call her a cab, but she lived a stone's throw away. It wasn't even seven thirty, and he was all at once alone. The noise around him was suddenly deafening, skull-crushing. Voices, laughter, chiming glasses. She hadn't asked about his day. Hadn't said much at all, really, except when prompted. His drink looked fake yellow, the colour of children's sweets. Sticky-tasting and souring his stomach, corroding his teeth. He walked to the bar, ordered a whisky. Didn't put any water in it. Looking around, he saw that another couple had already taken his table. Well, that was fine. He didn't stand out so much here at the bar. Could belong to one of the office parties either side of him. But he didn't, and he knew he didn't. He was an outsider in this place, same as in St Leonard's. When you worked as hard as he did, that was what happened: you got the promotions, but lost the intimacy. People steered a course past you, either out of fear or jealousy. The ACC had pulled him aside at the end of the St Leonard's tour.

'You're doing good work, Derek. Keep at it. Few years down the road, who knows? Maybe you'll look back at this one as the inquiry that made your name.' And the ACC had winked and patted his arm.

'Yes, sir. Thank you, sir.'

But then had come the postscript, the ACC readying to

leave but half-turning towards him. 'Family men, Derek, that's what the public should see when they look at us. People they can respect, because we're no different from them.'

Family men. He meant wife and kids. Linford had gone straight to his phone and called Siobhan's mobile . . .

Balls to it. He left, nodded to the doorman even though he didn't know him. Out into the horizontal wind, the night seizing him and taking a bite. His lungs complained when he breathed in. Left turn: he'd be home in ten minutes. Left turn, he'd be going home.

He turned right, heading for Queen Street, the top of Leith Walk. The Barony Bar on Broughton Street, he liked it there. Good beer, an old-fashioned place. You wouldn't stand out in a place like that, drinking alone.

And afterwards, it only took him a couple of minutes to find Siobhan Clarke's building. Addresses: no problem in CID. First time they'd met, he'd gone to the office next day, checked up on her. Her flat was on a quiet street, a terrace of four-storey Victorian tenements. Second floor: that was where she lived. 2FL: second floor, left side. He went to the terrace opposite. The main door was unlocked. Climbed the stairs, until he reached the half-landing between second and third floors. There was a window, looking out on to the street and the flats opposite. Lights burning in her windows, curtains open. Yes, there she was: briefest of glimpses as she walked across the room. Carrying something, reading it: a CD cover? Hard to tell. He wrapped his jacket around him. Temperature wasn't much above freezing. The skylight above had a hole in it; cold gusts assailing him.

But still he watched.

14

'When will his body be released?'

'I'm not sure.'

'It's awful, to have someone die and not be able to bury them.'

Rebus nodded. He was in the sitting room of the house in Ravelston. Derek Linford was seated beside him on the sofa. Alicia Grieve looked small and frail in the armchair opposite. Her daughter-in-law, who'd just been speaking, was perched on the arm. Seona Grieve was dressed in black, but Alicia wore a flowery dress, the splashes of colour contrasting with her ash-grey face. To Rebus, her skin seemed like an elephant's, the way the folds fell from her face and neck.

'You have to understand, Mrs Grieve,' Linford said, his voice pouring like treacle, 'in a case like this, there's a need to keep the body. The pathologist may be called on to—'

Alicia Grieve was rising to her feet. 'I can't listen any more!' she trilled. 'Not here, not now. You're going to have to go.'

Seona helped her up. 'It's all right, Alicia. I'll talk to them. Would you like to go upstairs?'

'The garden . . . I'm going into the garden.'

'Mind you don't slip.'

'I'm not helpless, Seona!'

'Of course not. I'm just saying . . .'

But the old woman was making for the door. She didn't say anything, didn't look back. Closed the door after her. They could hear her feet shuffling away.

Seona slipped into the chair her mother-in-law had vacated. 'Sorry about that.'

'No need to apologise,' Linford said.

'But we *will* need to talk to her,' Rebus cautioned.

'Is that absolutely necessary?'

'I'm afraid so.' He couldn't tell her: because your husband might have confided in his mother; because maybe she knows things we don't.

'How about you, Mrs Grieve?' Linford asked. 'How are you managing?'

'Like an alcoholic,' Seona Grieve said with a sigh.

'Well, a drink often helps—'

'She means', Rebus interrupted, 'she's taking things one day at a time.'

Linford nodded, as though he'd known this all along.

'Incidentally,' Rebus added, 'does anyone in the family have a drink problem?'

Seona Grieve looked at him. 'You mean Lorna?'

He stayed silent.

'Roddy didn't drink much,' she went on. 'The odd glass of red wine, maybe a whisky before dinner. Cammo . . . well, Cammo seems unaffected by drink, unless you know him well. It's not that he slurs or starts singing.'

'What then?'

'His behaviour changes, just ever so slightly.' She looked down at her lap. 'Let's say his morals become hazy.'

'Has he ever . . . ?'

She looked at Rebus. 'He tried once or twice.'

Linford, no subtlety on display, glanced meaningfully towards Rebus. Seona Grieve caught the look and snorted.

'Clutching at straws, Inspector Linford?'

He flinched. 'How do you mean?'

'Crime of passion, Cammo killing Roddy so he can get to me.' She shook her head.

'Are we being too simplistic, Mrs Grieve?'

She considered Rebus's question. Took her time over it. So he lobbed in another.

'You say he didn't drink much, your husband, and yet he went out drinking with friends?'

'Yes.'

'Sometimes stayed out overnight?'

'What are you trying to say?'

'It's just that we can't find anyone who was out drinking with him the night he died.'

Linford checked his notebook. 'So far, we've found one bar in the West End, they think he was there early on in the evening, drinking by himself.'

Seona Grieve didn't have anything to say to that. Rebus sat forward. 'Did Alasdair drink?'

'Alasdair?' Caught unawares. 'What's he got to do with this?'

'Any idea where he might be?'

'Why?'

'I'm wondering if he knows about your husband. Surely he'd want to be here for the funeral.'

'He hasn't phoned ...' She turned thoughtful again. 'Alicia misses him.'

'Does he ever get in touch?'

'A card now and then: Alicia's birthday, never misses that.'

'But no address?'

'No.'

'Postmarks?'

She shrugged. 'All over, mostly abroad.'

There was something in the way she said it that made Rebus state: 'There's something else.'

'I just ... I think he gets people to post them for him, when they're on the move.'

'Why would he do that?'

'In case we're trying to find him.'

Rebus sat forward a little further, cutting down the

distance between himself and the widow. 'What happened? Why did he leave?'

She shrugged again. 'It was before my time. Roddy was still married to Billie.'

'Had that marriage broken up before you met Mr Grieve?' Linford asked.

Her eyes narrowed. 'What exactly are you implying?'

'To get back to Alasdair,' Rebus said, hoping his tone would dissuade Linford from further queries, 'you've no idea why he left?'

'Roddy talked about him now and again, usually when a card arrived.'

'Cards to him?'

'No, to Alicia.'

Rebus looked around him, but someone had removed Alicia Grieve's birthday cards. 'Did he send one this year?'

'He's always late. It'll arrive in a week or two.' She looked towards the door. 'Poor Alicia. She thinks I'm staying here as a sort of sanctuary.'

'Whereas, in reality, you're looking after her?'

She shook her head. 'Not looking after exactly, but I *am* worried about her. She's grown fragile. This is the only room you've been in. That's because it's practically the only room left that's habitable. The rest, they fill with old papers and magazines – she won't let them be thrown out. All sorts of rubbish, and when the room gets full, she moves into another. This room will go the same way, I suppose.'

'Can't her children do anything?' Linford again.

'She won't let them. Refuses even to have a cleaner. "Everything's in its place for a reason," that's what she says.'

'Maybe she has a point,' Rebus said. Everything in its place – the body in the fireplace; Roddy Grieve in the summer house – for a reason. There had to be an explanation; it was just that they couldn't see it yet. 'Does she still paint?' he asked.

'Not really. She tinkers. Her studio is at the bottom of the garden, that's probably where she's gone.' Seona looked at her watch. 'God, and I need to buy some food . . .'

'You'd heard the rumours about your husband and Josephine Banks?'

The question had come from Linford. Rebus turned towards him, eyes burning, but Linford was concentrating on the widow.

'Someone sent me a letter.' She tugged the sleeve of her blouse down over her watch; suddenly defensive, where before she'd been opening up.

'You trusted your husband?'

'Completely. I know what it's like in politics.'

'Any idea who might have sent the letter?'

'I threw it straight in the bin. We agreed that was the best place for it.'

'How did Ms Banks react?'

'She thought about hiring a detective. We talked her out of it. Anything we did would have made it all seem legitimate. We'd have been playing his game.'

'Whose game?'

'Whoever was spreading the rumour.'

'You're sure it was a he?'

'A question of probability, Inspector Linford. Most of the people in politics are male. It's sad but it's true.'

'I notice', Rebus said, 'there were two women standing against your husband in the selection process.'

'Labour policy.'

'Did you know any of the other candidates?'

'Of course. The Labour Party's one big happy family, Inspector.'

He smiled, as was expected. 'I hear Archie Ure wasn't best pleased with the result.'

'Well, Archie's been in politics a hell of a sight longer than Roddy. He thought it was his birthright.'

Jo Banks had used the selfsame word: birthright.

'And the two women on the shortlist?'

'Young and intelligent . . . they'll get what they want eventually.'

'So what happens now, Mrs Grieve?'

'Now?' She was staring at the pattern in the carpet. 'Archie Ure was the runner-up. I suppose they'll go with him.' Staring hard at the carpet, as if some message were imprinted there.

Linford cleared his throat and turned towards Rebus, indicating that for him the interview was complete. Rebus tried to think of some brilliant final question, but came up empty.

'Just give me back my husband,' Seona Grieve said, leading them into the hall. Alicia was standing there at the foot of the stairs, a china cup in her hand. She'd folded a slice of bread into the cup and squashed it down.

'I wanted something,' she told her daughter-in-law. 'But I'm not sure now why.'

As they left, Roddy Grieve's widow was leading his mother up the stairs like a parent with a sleepy child.

Back at the car, Rebus told Linford: 'You go on ahead.'

'What?'

'I want to stick around, do the Good Samaritan bit.'

'Babysitting?' Linford got in, started the engine. 'Something tells me that's not the whole story.'

'I might have a word with the old woman while I'm at it.'

'Just tell me you're not playing Grab-a-Granny.'

Rebus winked. 'We don't all have young ladies lusting after us.'

The look on Linford's face changed. He put the car into gear and drove off.

A grin spread over Rebus's face. 'Good on you, Siobhan, you went and dumped him.'

He went back up the path, rang the doorbell. Explained to Seona Grieve that he could spare twenty minutes or so if she wanted to pop out. She hesitated.

'It's just milk and bread, Inspector. We can probably manage till—'

'Well, I'm here now, and my driver's gone.' He waved back towards the empty roadway. 'Besides, the way Mrs Grieve is getting through that bread . . .'

He made himself comfy in the sitting room. She told him he was welcome to make tea or coffee, as long as he didn't take milk. 'But fair warning,' she added, 'the kitchen's a bomb-site.'

'I'll be fine,' he said, picking up a Sunday supplement from six months before. He heard the door close – she hadn't bothered telling her mother-in-law, hadn't seen the point. There was a newsagent's a quarter of a mile away. She wouldn't be long. Rebus waited a couple of minutes, then climbed the stairs. Alicia Grieve was standing in her bedroom doorway. She was still dressed, but wore a dressing-gown over her clothes.

'Oh,' she said. 'I thought I heard someone leaving.'

'Nothing wrong with your ears, Mrs Grieve. Seona's just nipped out to the shop.'

'Then why are you still here?' She peered at him. 'You *are* the policeman?'

'That's right.'

She shuffled past him, one hand reaching out to steady herself against the wall. 'I'm looking for something,' she told him. 'It's not in my bedroom.'

He could see into her room through the open door. It was chaotic. Clothes were piled on chairs and the floor, more spilling from the wardrobe and chest of drawers. Books and magazines, paintings stacked against the walls. There was a large patch of damp on the ceiling by the window.

She'd pushed open another door. The patterned carpet inside was faded to an almost uniform grey, where it wasn't threadbare. Rebus followed her in. Was it a living room? An office? Impossible to tell. Cardboard boxes filled with memories and rubbish. Old letters, some not yet opened. Photograph albums spilling loose pictures across the floor. More magazines and newspapers, more paintings. Children's toys and games from ages past. A collection of mirrors on one wall. A wigwam propped up against the far corner, its yellow canvas patched and crumbling. A child's doll, sporting tunic and kilt, lay headless under a chair. Rebus picked it up, found the head resting in an open biscuit tin along with loose dominoes, playing cards, empty cotton reels. He fixed the head back on. The doll's blue eyes looked neither pleased nor displeased.

'What is it you're looking for?'

She looked round. 'What are you doing with Lorna's doll?'

'Its head had come off. I just—'

'No, no, no.' She grabbed the doll from him. 'Its head didn't *come* off, the little madam yanked it off.' Which was what Alicia Grieve did now. 'It was her way of telling us she'd broken with childhood.'

Rebus smiled. 'How old was she?' Expecting to hear nine or ten.

'Twenty-five, twenty-six, something like that.' Her mind was half on her visitor, half on the search.

'What did you think when she took up modelling?'

'I've always supported my children.' It had the sound of a prepared line, a titbit she offered to journalists and the curious.

'How about Cammo and Roddy? Were you political, Mrs Grieve?'

'In my younger days I was. Labour, mostly. Allan was a Liberal, we had many a debate . . .'

'Yet one of your sons is a Tory.'

'Oh, Cammo could always be difficult.'

'And Roddy?'

'Roddy needs to step out from his brother's shadow. You haven't seen the way he runs after Cammo. Always

143

watching, studying him. But Cammo has his own chums. Boys that age can be cruel, can't they?'

She was drifting away from him, the years dancing in her eyes.

'They're grown men now, Alicia.'

'They'll always be boys to me.' She started taking things out of a box, studying each item – binoculars, marmalade jar, football pennant – as though it might reveal itself to her.

'Are you close to Roddy?'

'Roddy's a dear.'

'He talks to you? Comes to you with problems?'

'He's . . .' She broke off, looked confused. 'He's dead, isn't he?' Rebus nodded. 'I told him, warned him often enough. Climbing over railings at his age.' She shook her head. 'Bound to be accidents.'

'He'd done it before? Climbed the railings?'

'Oh yes. It was a shortcut to school, you see.'

Rebus slid his hands into his pockets. She was travelling elsewhere now. 'I did dally with the Nationalists in the fifties. They were a strange lot, maybe they still are. Kilts and Gaelic and a chip on the shoulder. We attended some good parties, though, lots of dancing. Sword and Shield . . .'

Rebus frowned. 'I've heard of that. An offshoot of the Nationalists?'

'It didn't last long. Very little did in those days. An idea would blossom, then you'd have a few drinks and that would be the end of that.'

'Did you know Matthew Vanderhyde?'

'Oh, yes. Everyone knew Matthew. Is he still with us?'

'I see him occasionally. Maybe not as often as I should.'

'Matthew and Allan would argue politics with Chris Grieve . . .' She broke off. 'You know he's not related?' Rebus nodded, remembering the framed poem in the downstairs hall. 'Allan would be doing Chris's portrait, only the man wouldn't sit still. Always moving, flinging out his arms to make a point.' She flung out her own arms in imitation. The marmalade jar was in one hand, a roll of Christmas parcel-tape in the other. 'Edwin Muir was a great foil for him. Then there was dear Naomi Mitchison. Do you know her work?' Rebus was silent, as if speech might break the spell.

'And the painters – Gillies, McTaggart, Maxwell.' She smiled. 'Sparks always flew. We were lucky with the Festival, it brought visitors to the galleries. The Edinburgh School, we called ourselves. It was a different country then, you know. Trapped between one world war and the threat of another. Hard to bring up children with the A-bomb hanging over your head. It affected my work, I think.'

'Were your children interested in art?'

'Lorna dabbled, maybe she still does. But not the boys. Cammo always had his cronies around him, almost like a Praetorian Guard. Roddy liked the company of grown-ups, always so deferential and willing to listen.'

'And Alasdair?'

She angled her head. 'Alasdair was a painter's nightmare, an angelic tearaway. I never captured that. You always knew he was up to something, but you didn't mind because it was Alasdair. Do you see?'

'I think so.' Rebus knew a few young villains like that: charming and cheeky, but always on the make and take. 'He keeps in touch, doesn't he?'

'Oh, yes.'

'Why did he leave home?'

'He wasn't strictly *at* home. He had a flat of his own near the foot of the Canongate. When he'd gone, we found out it was a furnished rental, practically none of it was his. He took a suitcase of clothes, some books, and that was it.'

'He didn't say why he was leaving?'

'No, just phoned out of the blue. Told me he'd be in touch.'

Rebus heard the front door open and close, the words 'I'm back' drifting up the stairs.

'I'd better be going,' he said.

Alicia Grieve looked as though she'd already dismissed him. 'I wish I knew where it was,' she said to herself, replacing the marmalade jar in its box. 'Dear me, if only I knew . . .'

Seona Grieve was halfway up the stairs when he met her.

'Is everything all right?'

'Everything's fine,' he assured her. 'Mrs Grieve's just lost something, that's all.'

Seona stared up towards the landing. 'Inspector, she's lost practically *everything*. It's just that she doesn't know it yet . . .'

15

It was an office much like any other.

Grant Hood and Ellen Wylie shared a look. They'd been expecting a builder's yard – glaur and breeze-blocks, an Alsatian tethered and barking. Wylie even had wellies in the car, just in case. But this was the third floor of a 1960s office block halfway down Leith Walk. Wylie had asked Hood, would it be all right to nip into Valvona and Crolla's after? He'd told her yes, no problem, but wasn't it expensive?

'Quality costs.' That's what she'd said, like an advertising slogan.

They were doing the rounds of Edinburgh's building contractors, starting with the largest and longest established. Phone calls first, and if there was anyone in the firm who could help, then it was time for a visit.

Wylie: 'Maybe John's right when he calls us the Time Team. Never saw myself as an archaeologist.'

'Twenty years, it's hardly prehistory.'

Hood had found that their conversation flowed. No awkward pauses or slips of the tongue. They'd had one disagreement, over whether they were on a dead-end case.

Wylie: 'We should be working the Grieve inquiry. That's where all the attention is.'

Hood: 'But if we get a result here, it's something special, isn't it? And it's all ours.'

Wylie: 'Any leads we get, I'll bet we end up relegated. We're DCs, Grant. That's too low in the league to get any medals that might be going.'

'You like football?'

'I might.'

'Who do you support?'

'You first.'

Hood: 'I've always been Rangers. You?'

Grinning: 'Celtic.'

Sharing a laugh. Then Wylie again: 'What is it they say about opposites attracting?'

A line Grant Hood carried with him as they sat in the waiting room. *Opposites attracting.*

Peter Kirkwall of Kirkwall Construction was in his early thirties and wore an immaculate pinstripe suit. It was impossible to picture him with a shovel in one of his smooth hands, yet there he was in a series of framed photographs around the walls of his office.

'The first one', he said, leading them as if through an exhibition, 'is me at seven, mixing concrete in Dad's yard.' Dad being Jack Kirkwall, who'd founded the company back in the 1950s. He was in some of the photos, too. But the focus was on Peter: Peter bricklaying during a summer break from college; Peter with the plans of one of the city's office blocks, his first Kirkwall project; Peter meeting dignitaries ... and behind the wheel of a Mercedes CLK ... and on the day of Jack Kirkwall's retirement.

'If you want it first-hand,' he said, easing into his chair and business both, 'you need to talk to Dad.' He paused. 'Coffee? Tea?' Seemed pleased when they shook their heads: his was a busy schedule.

'We appreciate you taking the trouble, sir,' Wylie said, not above a bit of soft-soap. 'Business good, is it?'

'Phenomenal. What with the Holyrood redevelopment and the Western Approach corridor, Gyle, Wester Hailes, and now the plans for Granton ...' He shook his head. 'We can hardly keep up. Every week we're making bids on some project or other.' He waved towards where some plans lay on the room's conference table. 'Know how my dad started? He built garages and extensions. Now it looks like we might get a finger in a pie as big as London Docklands.' He rubbed his hands with what looked to Hood like glee.

'But in the seventies, the firm worked on Queensberry House?' Wylie was first with the question. It pulled Kirkwall back down to earth.

'Yes, sorry. Once you get me started, I don't know when to stop.' He cleared his throat, composed himself. 'I did look up our records . . .' Reaching into a drawer, bringing out an old ledger, some notebooks and a card index. 'Late in '78, we were one of the firms renovating the hospital. Not me, of course, I was still at school. And now you've found a skeleton, eh?'

Hood handed over photographs of the two fireplaces. 'The room to the far end of the basement. It was originally the kitchen.'

'And that's where the body was?'

'We estimate it's been there twenty years,' Wylie said, easing into her role: talker to Hood's silent type. 'Which would coincide with the building works.'

'Well, I've had my secretary dig up what she can.' He smiled to let them know the pun was deliberate. Kirkwall – striped shirt, oval glasses, groomed black hair – was, Wylie presumed, trying for the sophisticated look. But there was something uncomfortable and ill-defined about him. She'd seen footballers turned TV pundits: they could wear the clothes but failed to carry the style.

'It's not much, I'm afraid,' Kirkwall was saying, reaching into a drawer. He unrolled the plan so it faced them, weighting its corners with pieces of polished stone. 'I collect one from each job I do,' he explained. 'Get it cleaned and varnished.' Then: 'This is Queensberry House. The blue shaded areas were our project, plus the red lines.'

'It looks like exterior work.'

'It was. Downpipes, cracks in the masonry, and one summer house to be built from scratch. It's like that

149

sometimes with public works, they like to spread the contract around.'

'You obviously weren't greasing enough palms at the council,' Hood muttered.

Kirkwall glared at him.

'So another firm was doing the internal work?' Wylie was studying the plan.

'Firm or firms. I've no record. Like I say, you'd have to ask Dad.'

'Then that's what we'll do, Mr Kirkwall,' Ellen Wylie said.

But first they hit Valvona's, where Wylie did her shopping before asking if Hood fancied a bite to eat. He made show of checking his watch.

'Come on,' she said. 'There's an empty table, and I've been here often enough to know that must be a sign.'

So they ate salad and pizza and shared a bottle of mineral water. Around them, couples were doing the same thing. Hood smiled.

'We don't stick out,' he commented.

She looked at his stomach. 'Well, I don't.'

He sucked in some gut and decided to leave the last slice of pizza. 'You know what I mean,' he said.

Yes, she knew. Being a cop, being around people who knew cops, you always felt they could spot you, and you came to think everyone had the knack.

'Bit of a shock to find you're not a social leper?'

Hood looked at his plate. 'More of a shock to find I can actually leave food.'

Afterwards, they headed out to the house Jack Kirkwall had built for his retirement. It sat in countryside on the edge of South Queensferry, with both bridges visible in the distance. The house was angular with tall windows. When Wylie stated that it was like a scaled-down cathedral, Hood knew what she meant.

Jack Kirkwall welcomed them by insisting that he be remembered to John Rebus.

'You know Inspector Rebus?' Wylie asked.

'He did me a good turn once.' Kirkwall chuckled.

'You might be able to return the favour, sir,' Hood said. 'Depending on how good your memory is.'

'Nothing wrong with the napper,' Kirkwall grumbled.

Wylie shot her partner a warning look. 'What DC Hood meant, Mr Kirkwall, is that we're in the dark and you're our one ray of light.'

Kirkwall perked up, settled into an easy chair and motioned for them to be seated.

The sofa was cream leather and smelt brand new. The lounge was large and bright with inch-thick white shag pile and a whole wall of French windows. To Wylie's eye, there seemed very little of Kirkwall's past on display: no photos or old-looking ornaments or furniture. It was as though, in later life, he had decided to reinvent himself. There was something anonymous about it all. Then Wylie realised: it was a show house. Prospective clients could be shown around, Kirkwall Construction workmanship evident everywhere.

And no place for individual personality.

She wondered if that explained the sad depths to Jack Kirkwall's face. No way was this his idea of retirement: in the choice of fabrics and furnishings she saw the son, Peter.

'Your firm', she said, 'did some work at Queensberry House in 1979.'

'The hospital?' She nodded. 'Started work in '78, finished it in '79. What a hellish time that was.' He peered at them. 'Likely you're too young to remember. That winter there was a rubbish strike, teachers' strike, even the mortuary was on strike.' He snorted at the memory, looked to Hood. Tapping his head, he said: 'See, son? Nothing wrong with the napper. Remember it like it was yesterday. We started in December, finished in March. The eighth, to be precise.'

Wylie smiled. 'That's incredible.'

Kirkwall accepted her praise. He was a big man, broad-shouldered, chisel-jawed. He'd probably never been handsome, but she could imagine him having power and presence.

'Know why I remember?' He shook his head. 'You'll be too young.'

'The referendum?' Hood guessed.

Kirkwall looked deflated. Wylie gave another warning look: they needed him on their side.

'It was March first, wasn't it?' Hood continued.

'Aye, it was. And we won the vote but lost the war.'

'A temporary setback,' Wylie felt bound to add.

He glared at her. 'If you can call twenty years temporary. We had dreams . . .' Wylie thought he was turning wistful, but he surprised her. 'Just think what it would have meant: inward investment, new homes and businesses.'

'A building boom?'

Kirkwall was shaking his head at the thought of so much opportunity wasted.

'The boom's happening now, according to your son,' Wylie said.

'Aye.'

She doubted she'd ever heard so much bitterness in a single syllable. Had Jack Kirkwall gone willingly, or had he been pushed?

'We're interested in the hospital's interior,' Hood said. 'Which firms had the contracts?'

'Roofing was Caspian,' Kirkwall said tonelessly, still lost in thought. 'Scaffolding was Macgregor. Coghill's did a lot of the inside work: replastering, a few new partition walls.'

'Was this in the basement?'

Kirkwall nodded. 'A new laundry room and a boiler.'

'Do you remember any of the original walls being

exposed?' Wylie handed over the photo of the fireplaces. 'Like this?' Kirkwall looked, shook his head. 'But the work in the basement was done by a firm called Coghill's?'

Kirkwall nodded again. 'Gone now. Firm went bust.'

'Is Mr Coghill still around?'

Kirkwall shrugged. 'Shouldn't have gone bust really. Good firm. Dean knew his stuff.'

'The building trade's a tough game,' Wylie agreed.

'It's not that.' He looked at her.

'What then?'

'I might be speaking out of turn.' He considered this. 'But at my age, who cares?' Took a deep, noisy breath. 'It's just that, way I heard it, Dean fell foul of Mr Big.'

Wylie and Hood responded as one voice. 'Mr Big?'

The Oxford Bar was busy when Rebus arrived. He'd already had one drink at The Maltings, leaving before the evening influx of students, and two drinks at Swany's on Causewayside. In Swany's he'd bumped into an old colleague, recently retired.

'You look too young,' Rebus had chided him.

'Same age as you, John,' had been the reply.

But Rebus didn't have thirty years in; had joined the force in his mid-twenties. Two or three more years, he could be a gentleman of leisure. Rebus got a round in, then sneaked out into the cold blast of winter. Headlamps piercing the darkness; recent rainfall threatening ice. A fifteen-minute walk home. Across the street, a taxi filling up at the petrol station.

Retirement. The word bouncing around in his skull. Jesus, but what would he do with himself? One man's retirement was another's redundancy. He thought of the Farmer, then waved down the taxi, asked to be taken to the Oxford Bar.

No sign of Doc and Salty, Rebus's usual drinking partners, but plenty of faces he knew. The place was buzzing, bodies crammed in the front room. Football on the TV: a game from down south. A regular called Muir was standing close by the door. He nodded a greeting.

'Your wife has a gallery, doesn't she?' Rebus asked. Muir nodded again. 'Ever sell any stuff by Alicia Rankeillor?'

Muir snorted. 'If only. Rankeillor's stuff, as you call it, fetches tens of thousands. Every city in the western world wants something of hers in its collection – preferably something from the forties or fifties. Even her limited prints fetch a grand or two apiece.' Muir looked up. 'Don't know anyone who wants to sell, do you?'

'I'll let you know.'

The Two Margarets were behind the bar, busy in their confinement. Rebus's IPA arrived, and he ordered a whisky to go with it. Music from the back room. He could just make it out: acoustic guitar, young woman on vocals. But here was his favourite duet: a pint and a dram. He added water to the whisky, removing the edge. A deep swallow, coating his throat. One of the Margarets was back with his change.

'Friend of yours through the back.'

Rebus frowned. 'Singing?'

She smiled, shook her head. 'Up by the cigarette machine.'

He looked. Saw a wall of bodies. The ciggie machine was in an alcove, up three steps and next to the toilets. Fruit machine there, too. But all he could see were men's backs, meaning someone had an audience.

'Who is it?'

Margaret shrugged. 'Said she knew you.'

'Siobhan?'

Another shrug. He craned his neck. A new round was being got in. The backs half-turned. Rebus saw faces he knew: regulars. Glazed smiles and cigarette smoke. And behind them, relaxed, leaning against the fruit machine, Lorna Grieve. A tall drink was raised to her lips. It looked like neat whisky or brandy, three measures at least. She

154

smacked her lips; her eyes met his and she smiled, raising her glass. He smiled back, raised his own glass to her. A sudden flash of memory: as a kid, he'd been coming home from school. Passing a street corner by the sweet shop, a crowd of older boys hemming in a girl from his class. He couldn't see what was going on. Her eyes, suddenly catching his between the heads of two of the boys. Not panicked, but not enjoying herself either . . .

Lorna Grieve touched one of her suitors on the arm, said something to him. His name was Gordon, a Fifer like Rebus. Probably young enough to be her son.

Now she was walking forwards, negotiating the steps. Squeezing through the crowd, touching arms and shoulders and backs; each touch enough to aid her progress.

'Well, well,' she said, 'fancy seeing you here.'

'Yes,' he said, 'just fancy.' He'd finished the whisky. She asked if he wanted another. He shook his head, lifted the pint.

'I don't think I've ever been here,' she said, leaning into the bar. 'I've just been hearing about the old owner, how he wouldn't serve women or people with English accents. I think I might have liked him.'

'He was an acquired taste.'

'The best kind, don't you think?' Her eyes were on him. 'I've been hearing about you, too. I may have to stop calling you Monkey Man.'

'Why's that?'

'Because from what I've been told, not many people make a monkey out of you.'

He smiled. 'Bars are great places for tall stories.'

'There you go, Lorna.' It was Gordon, presenting her with another drink. Armagnac: Rebus had watched Margaret pouring. 'All right, John? You never told us you knew famous people.'

Lorna Grieve accepted the compliment; Rebus stayed quiet.

'And if I'd known there were honeys like you in

Edinburgh,' she told Gordon, 'I wouldn't have moved out to the sticks. And I certainly wouldn't have married a grim old beast like Hugh Cordover.'

'Don't knock High Chord,' Gordon said. 'I saw Obscura supporting Barclay James Harvest at the Usher Hall.'

'Were you still at school?'

Gordon considered the question. 'I think I was fourteen.'

Lorna Grieve looked at Rebus. 'We're dinosaurs,' she informed him.

'We were dinosaurs when Gordon here was just primordial soup,' he agreed.

But she wasn't at all like a dinosaur. Her clothes were colourful and flowing, her hair immaculate, and her make-up striking. Surrounded by men in work suits, she was a butterfly in the company of fluttering grey moths.

'What are you doing here?' he asked.

'Drinking.'

'Did you drive in?'

'The band gave me a lift.' She peered at him. 'I didn't just come here to see you, you know.'

'No?'

'Don't flatter yourself.' She brushed invisible flecks from her scarlet jacket. Beneath was an orange silk blouse, and on her legs faded denims, frayed where they touched her ankles. Black suede moccasins on her feet. No jewellery anywhere.

Not even a wedding ring.

'I like new things, that's all,' she was explaining. 'And currently my life is so dreary', looking at her surroundings, 'that this counts as new.'

'Poor you.'

Her glance was arch and wry at the same time. Gordon shuffled his feet and said he'd see her upstairs. She nodded unconvincingly.

'Have you been drinking all day?' he asked.

'Jealous?'

He shrugged. 'I've been there often enough.' He turned so he was facing her. 'How does the Ox measure up?'

Her nose wrinkled. 'It's very *you*,' she said.

'Is that good or bad?'

'I haven't decided yet.' She studied him. 'There's a darkness in you.'

'Probably all the beer.'

'I'm serious. We all come from darkness, you have to remember that, and we sleep during the night to escape the fact. I'll bet you have trouble sleeping at night, don't you?' He didn't say anything. Her face grew less animated. 'We'll all return to darkness one day, when the sun burns out.' A sudden smile lit her eyes. ' "Though my soul may set in darkness, It will rise in perfect light." '

'A poem?' he guessed.

She nodded. 'I forget the rest.'

The door creaked open. Two expectant faces: Grant Hood and Ellen Wylie. Hood looked ready for a drink, but he wasn't coming in. Wylie spotted Rebus, motioned for him to step outside.

'Back in a minute,' he told Lorna Grieve, touching her arm before squeezing his way past the other drinkers. The night air was fresh after the pub fug. Rebus took in several deep gulps.

'Sorry to bother you, sir,' Wylie said.

'You wouldn't be here if there wasn't a good reason.' He slipped his hands into his pockets. There was ice in the gutters now. The narrow street was badly lit. Cars were parked down one side, windscreens rimed with frost. Sudden clouds in the air when the three detectives spoke.

'We went to see Jack Kirkwall,' Hood explained.

'And?'

'You two know each other?' Wylie asked.

'A case few years back.'

Hood and Wylie exchanged a look. 'You tell him,' Hood said. So Wylie told the story, and at the end Rebus was thoughtful.

'He's flattering me,' he said at last.

'He said you'd tell us about Mr Big,' she repeated.

Rebus nodded. 'That's what some in CID called him. Not very original.'

Hood: 'But the name fitted?'

Rebus nodded, moved aside to let a couple into the bar. The singer had started up again: he could hear her through the back room's closed window.

My mind returns, she sang, *to things I should have left behind.*

'His name was Callan, first name Bryce.'

'I thought Big Ger Cafferty ran Edinburgh?'

Rebus nodded. 'But only after Callan retired, moved to the Costa del Sol or somewhere. He's never been away, though.'

Wylie: 'How do you mean?'

'You still hear stories, how a piece of Cafferty's action heads out to Spain. Bryce Callan's almost grown . . .' He sought the word. More lyrics from the back room:

My mind returns, to things best left unsaid.

'Mythical?' Wylie suggested.

He nodded, stared at the window of the barber's shop across the lane. 'Because we never put him away, I suppose.'

'How would Dean Coghill have fallen foul of him?'

Rebus shrugged. 'Protection maybe. There's a lot can go wrong on a building site, and those projects . . . even then they'd be worth thousands. A few days lost could mean everything.'

Hood was nodding. 'So we need to find Coghill.'

'Always supposing he'll speak to us,' Wylie warned.

'Let me do some checking on Bryce Callan,' Rebus said.

The past is here now, insistent, carved from darkness,
So please beware, take care now where you tread . . .

'Meantime,' he went on, 'you better try to get hold of Coghill's employee files. We need to know who was working on the site.'

'And if any of them disappeared,' Hood added.

'I'm assuming you've made a start on MisPer records.'

Wylie and Hood shared a look, said nothing.

'It's shit work,' Rebus acknowledged, 'but it's got to be done. Two of you on it, takes half the time.'

Wylie: 'Can we limit the search to late '78, first three months of '79?'

'To start with, yes.' He looked towards the pub. 'Buy the pair of you a drink?'

Wylie was quick to shake her head. 'I think we'll head for the Cambridge, bit quieter there.'

'Fair enough.'

'In there', nodding towards the door of the Ox, 'looks too much like the broom cupboard we're having to work out of.'

'I'd heard,' Rebus said. Wylie's look was accusatory.

'Sir,' she said, 'the woman in there . . .' Wylie looked down at her feet. 'Was it who I thought it was?'

Rebus nodded. 'Just a coincidence,' he said.

'Of course.' She nodded slowly, began to move off. She still hadn't made eye contact. Hood made to catch up with her. Rebus pushed open the door a crack but waited. Wylie and Hood with their heads together, Hood asking who the woman had been. If the story got around St Leonard's, Rebus would know who'd started it.

And that would be the end of the Time Team.

He woke at 4 a.m. The bedside lamp was still on. The duvet had been kicked to the foot of the bed. The sound of an engine turning over outside. He stumbled to the window, just in time to see a dark shape disappearing into the back of a taxi. He weaved naked into the living room, reaching for handholds, his balance shot. She'd left him a gift: a four-track demo by the Robinson Crusoes. It was titled *Shipwrecked Heart*. Made sense, band having the name they did. 'Final Reproof' was the last song on it. He stuck it on the hi-fi, listened for a minute or two with the volume down low. Empty bottle and two tumblers on the floor by the sofa. There was still half an inch of whisky in one of them. He sniffed it, took it into the kitchen. Poured it down the sink and filled the glass with cold water, gulped it down. Then another, and another after that. No way he was getting away from this one without a hangover, but he'd do his best. Three paracetamol tablets and more water, then another glassful to take through to the bathroom with him. She'd showered: there was a wet towel hanging from the rail. Showered first, then called the taxi. Had he woken her with his snoring? Had she ever been asleep? He ran a bath, looked at himself in the shaving mirror. Slack skin covered his face, looking for somewhere else to go. He bent down, dry-retched into the sink, almost bringing the tablets back up. How much had they drunk? He couldn't begin to count. Had they come back here straight from the Ox? He didn't think so. Back in the bedroom, he searched his pockets for clues. Nothing. But the fifty quid he'd gone out with had been reduced to pennies.

'Dear Christ.' He squeezed shut his eyes. His neck felt stiff; so did his back. In front of the bathroom mirror again he stared into his eyes. 'Did we do it?' he asked himself. The answer came back: definitely maybe. Screwed shut his eyes again. 'Oh, for Christ's sake, John, what have you done?'

Answer: slept with Lorna Grieve. Twenty years ago, he'd have been doing cartwheels. But then twenty years ago, she hadn't been part of a murder inquiry.

He turned off the taps, eased himself into the water and slid down, knees bent, so that his whole head went under. Maybe, he thought, if I just lie here like this it'll all go away. His first mistake on booze had been over thirty years before, outside a school dance.

A bloody long apprenticeship, he thought, coming up

for air. Whatever happened now, he felt tied to the Grieves, one more thread of their history.

And if Lorna put the story around, he'd be history, too.

Part Two

Fitful
and
Dark

16

Jerry had this morning routine, soon as Jayne had gone off to work. Tea, toast and the paper, and then into the living room to play a few records. Old stuff, punk 45s from his teens. Really set him up for the day. There might be thumps from upstairs, but he'd flick the Vs at the ceiling and dance on regardless. He had a few favourites – Generation X, 'Your Generation'; Klark Kent, 'Don't Care'; Spizzenergi, 'Where's Captain Kirk?' Their picture sleeves were dog-eared, and the vinyl was scratched to hell – too many lendings and parties. He still remembered gate-crashing a Ramones gig at the uni: October '78. The Spizz single was May '79: date of purchase scrawled on the back of the sleeve. He was like that back then. He'd time all his singles, make notes. A top five every week – best things he'd heard, not necessarily bought. The Virgin on Frederick Street had been shoplifting heaven for a while. Hadn't been so easy at Bruce's. The guy who ran Bruce's had gone on to manage Simple Minds. Jerry'd seen them when they'd been called Johnny and the Self Abusers.

It all used to matter, to mean something. Weekends, the adrenaline could make you dizzy.

These days, dancing did that for him. He fell on to the sofa. Three records and he was knackered. Rolled himself a joint and switched on the TV, knowing there'd be nothing worth watching. Jayne was working a double shift, wouldn't be home till nine, maybe ten. That gave him twelve hours to wash the dishes. Some days he itched to be working again, sitting in an office maybe with suit and tie on, making decisions and fielding phone calls. Nic said he had a secretary. A *secretary*. Who'd have thought it? He remembered the pair of them at school, kicking a football across the cul-de-sac, pogoing to punk in their bedrooms. Well, Jerry's bedroom mostly. Nic's mum had been funny about visitors; always a frown on her face when she opened her door and saw Jerry standing there. Dead now though, the old cow. Her living room had smelt of the Hamlet cigars Nic's dad smoked. He was the only person Jerry knew who didn't smoke cigarettes, had to be a cigar. Jerry, TV remote busy in his hand, chuckled now at the thought. *Cigars! Who did the old sod think he was?* Nic's dad had worn ties and cardigans . . . Jerry's dad had worn a vest most of the time, and a trouser-belt that came off whenever there was justice to dispense. But Jerry's mum, she'd been a treasure: no way he'd have swapped his parents for Nic's.

'No bloody way,' he said out loud.

He switched off the TV. The joint was down to the hot bit near the roach. He took a last draw and went to flush it down the bog. Not that he was worried about the pigs; it was Jayne didn't like him doing the wacky bac. Way Jerry looked at it, the wacko kept him sane. Government should put the stuff on the National Health, way it kept the likes of him from going off the rails.

He went to the bathroom to have a shave: little treat for Jayne when she came home. Still humming 'Captain Kirk'. Brilliant record, one of the best. He was thinking about Nic, how the two of them had become pals. You could never tell, could you, people you'd end up liking. They'd been in the same class since age five, but it was only when they went up to secondary that they started hanging around together, listening to Alex Harvey and Status Quo, trying to work out which lyrics were about sex. Nic had written a poem, hundreds of lines long, all about an orgy. Jerry had reminded him about it recently, and they'd had a good laugh. That was what it was about, at the end of the day: having a laugh.

166

He realised he was staring into the bathroom mirror; foam on his face and the razor in his hand. He had bags and lines under his eyes. It was catching up with him. Jayne kept talking about kids and ticking clocks; he kept telling her he'd think about it. Fact was, he didn't fancy himself as a dad, and Nic kept talking about how it ruined a relationship. Guys in the office who hadn't had sex since their nipper was born – months, sometimes years. And the mothers letting themselves go, gravity working against them. Nic would wrinkle his nose in disgust.

'Not a pretty outlook, is it?' Nic would say.

And Jerry would be bound to agree.

After school, Jerry had assumed they'd get jobs in the same place, maybe a factory or something. But Nic had dropped a bombshell: he was staying on an extra year, doing his Highers. It hadn't stopped them seeing one another, but there were all these books in Nic's room now – stuff Jerry couldn't make head or tail of. And after that there was Napier for three years, and more books, essays to hand in. They saw one another some weekends, but almost never through the week – maybe Friday night for a disco or a gig. Iggy Pop . . . Gang of Four . . . the Stones at the Playhouse. Nic hardly ever introduced Jerry to his student pals, unless they met them at a gig. Once or twice they ended up in the pub. Jerry had chatted up one of the girls, then Nic had grabbed him.

'What would Jayne say?'

Because he was seeing Jayne by then. They worked in the same factory: semiconductors. Jerry drove the fork-lift, got really good with it. He'd show off, do circuits around the women. They'd laugh, say he was daft, he'd get someone killed. Then Jayne came along and that was that.

Fifteen years they'd been married. Fifteen years and no kids. How could she expect them to have kids now, with him on the dole? His only letter this morning: dole people wanted him in for an interview. He knew what that

167

meant. They wanted to know what he was doing to find himself a job. Answer: sweet FA. And now Jayne was at him again, 'The clock's ticking, Jerry.' A double meaning there: her body clock, plus the threat that she might walk out if she didn't get what she wanted. She'd done it before, packed her bags and off to her mum's three streets away. Be as well bloody living there anyway . . .

He'd go mad if he stayed in the flat. He wiped the foam from his face and put his shirt back on, grabbed his jacket and was out. Walked the streets, looking for people to talk to, then into the bookies for half an hour, warming himself by the heater, pretending to study form. They knew him in there: highly unlikely he'd place a bet, but he sometimes did, always losing. When the lunchtime paper came in, he took a look. Page three, there was a story about a sexual assault. He read it closely. Nineteen-year-old student, grabbed in the Commonwealth Pool car park. Jerry flung the paper down and headed out to find a phone box.

He had Nic's office number in his pocket, called him there sometimes when he was bored, holding the receiver to the stereo so Nic could hear some song they used to dance to. He got the receptionist and asked for Mr Hughes.

'Nic, man, it's Jerry.'

'Hiya, pal. What can I do you for?'

'Just saw the paper. There was a student attacked last night.'

'The world's a terrible place.'

'Tell me it wasn't you.'

A nervous laugh. 'That's a sick kind of joke, Jerry.'

'Just tell me.'

'Where are you? Got any mates *listening in*?'

The way he said it made Jerry stop. Nic was telling him something, telling him someone could be listening in – maybe the receptionist.

'I'll talk to you later,' Nic said.

'Listen, man, I'm sorry—' But the phone was dead.

Jerry was shaking when he left the phone box. Jogged all the way home, fixed another joint. Put the TV on and sat there, trying to get his heartbeat down. Safer here; wasn't anything could touch him here. This was the only place to be.

Until Jayne got home.

Siobhan Clarke had asked Register House to run a search for Chris Mackie's birth certificate. She'd also begun asking around about Mackie, concentrating on Grassmarket and the Cowgate, but spreading out to take in the Meadows, Princes Street and Hunter Square.

But this Thursday morning she sat in a doctor's waiting room, surrounded by pale and sickly sufferers, until her name was called and she could put aside the women's magazine with its alien articles on cookery, clothes and kids.

Where, she wondered, was the magazine for her, one that concentrated on Hibs FC, hashed relationships and homicide?

Dr Talbot was in his mid-fifties and wore a weary smile below his half-moon glasses. He already had Chris Mackie's medical records laid out on his desk, but checked that Clarke's own paperwork – death certificate; authorisation – was in order before beckoning for her to move her chair in towards the desk.

It took her a couple of minutes to substantiate that the records only went back as far as 1980. When Mackie had registered with the surgery, he'd given a previous address in London and had stated that his records were held by a Dr Mason in Crouch End. But a letter from Dr Talbot to Dr Mason's address had been returned 'No Such Street'.

'You didn't pursue this?' Clarke asked.

'I'm a doctor, not a detective.'

Mackie's Edinburgh address was the hostel. Date of birth was different from that on Drew's filing-card. Clarke had the uneasy feeling that Mackie had laid a false trail all the way along. She went back to the records. Once or twice a year he'd attended the surgery, usually with some minor complaint: a facial cut turned septic; influenza; a boil requiring to be lanced.

'He was in pretty good health, considering his circumstances,' Dr Talbot said. 'I don't think he drank or smoked, which helped.'

'Drugs?'

The doctor shook his head.

'Is that unusual in someone who's homeless?'

'I've known people with stronger constitutions than Mr Mackie.'

'Yes, but someone homeless, not doing drink or drugs . . . ?'

'I'm no expert.'

'But in your opinion . . . ?'

'In my opinion, Mr Mackie gave me very little trouble.'

'Thank you, Dr Talbot.'

She left the surgery and headed for the Department of Social Security office, where a Miss Stanley sat her down in a lifeless cubicle usually reserved for claimant interviews.

'Looks like he didn't have a National Insurance number,' she said, going through the file. 'We had to issue an emergency one at the start.'

'When was this?'

It was 1980, of course: the year of Christopher Mackie's invention.

'I wasn't here at the time, but there are some notes from whoever it was interviewed him initially.' Miss Stanley read from these. ' "Filthy, not sure of where he is, no NI number or tax reference." Previous address is given as London.'

Clarke dutifully jotted it all down.

'Does it answer your questions?'

'Pretty much,' she admitted. The night he'd died, that was as close to 'Chris Mackie' as she was going to get.

Since then she'd been moving away from him, because he didn't exist. He was a figment, imagined by someone with something to hide.

The who and what she might never discover.

Because Mackie had been clever. Everyone else had said he kept himself clean, but for the DSS he'd camouflaged himself with filth. Why? Because it made his act the more believable: bumbling, forgetful, unhelpful. The sort of person a hard-pressed official would want rid of pronto. No NI number? Never mind, issue an emergency one. Vague address in London? Fine, leave it be. Just sign your name to his claim and get him out of the cubicle.

A call on her mobile to Register House confirmed that there was no birth record of a Christopher Mackie on the date she'd given. She could try the other date she had, or spread the net wider, ask Register House in London ... But she knew she was chasing shadows. She sat in a cramped café, drinking her drink, staring into space, and wondered if it was time to write up her report and call an end to the hunt.

She could think of half a dozen reasons for doing so.

And just four hundred thousand for not.

Back at her desk, she found over a dozen messages waiting for her. A couple of the names she recognised: local journalists. They'd tried calling three times apiece. She screwed shut her eyes and mouthed a word her grandmother would have clapped her ear for using. Then she headed downstairs to the Coms Room, knowing someone there would have the latest edition of the *News*. Front page: TRAGIC MYSTERY OF MILLIONAIRE TRAMP. As they didn't have a photograph of Mackie, they'd opted for one of the spot where he'd jumped. There wasn't much to the piece: well-known face around city centre ... bank account well into six figures ... police trying to establish who might have 'a claim on the cash'.

Siobhan Clarke's worst nightmare.

When she got upstairs, her phone was ringing again. Hi-Ho Silvers came across the floor on his knees, hands held in mock prayer.

'I'm his love child,' he said. 'Give me a DNA test, but for God's sake give me the dosh!'

Laughter in the CID suite. 'It's for yoo-ou,' someone else said, pointing to her phone. Every nutter and chancer in the kingdom would be getting ready. They'd call 999 or Fettes, and to get them off the line, someone would eventually admit that it was a St Leonard's matter.

They all belonged to Siobhan now. They were her children.

So she turned on her heels and left, ignoring the pleas from behind her.

And headed back on to the streets, finding new people to ask about Mackie. She knew she had to be quick: news travelled. Soon they'd all claim to have known him, to have been his best pal, his nephew, his executor. The street people knew her now, called her 'doll' and 'hen'. One old man had even christened her 'Diana, the Huntress'. She was wise to some of the younger beggars, too; not the ones who sold the *Big Issue*, but the ones who sat in doorways, blankets around them. She'd been sheltering from a downpour when one had come into Thin's Bookshop, blanket discarded and a mobile phone to his ear, complaining because his taxi hadn't turned up. He'd seen her, recognised her, but kept the diatribe going.

The foot of the Mound was quiet. Two young guys with ponytails and cross-breeds; the dogs licking themselves while their owners shared a can of headnip.

'Don't know the guy, sorry. Got a fag on you?'

She had learned to carry a packet with her, offered them each a cigarette, smiling when they took two. Then it was back up the Mound. John Rebus had told her something: the steep hill had been constructed from New Town rubble. The man whose idea it had been had owned a business at the top. Construction had meant the demolition of his shop. John Rebus hadn't found the story amusing; he'd told her it was a lesson.

'In what?' she'd asked.

'Scots history,' he'd replied, failing to explain.

She wondered now if it had been a reference to independence, to self-made, self-destructing schemes. It did seem to amuse him that, when pushed, she would defend independence. He wound her up, telling her it was a trick and she was an English spy, sent to undermine the process. Then he'd call her a 'New Scot', a 'settler'. She never knew when he was being serious. People in Edinburgh were like that: obtuse, thrawn. Sometimes she thought he was flirting, that the jibes and jokes were part of some mating ritual made all the more complex because it consisted of baiting the subject rather than wooing them.

She'd known John Rebus for several years now, and still they weren't close friends. Rebus, so far as she could tell, saw none of his colleagues outside work hours, apart from when she invited him to Hibs matches. His only hobby was drinking, and he tended to indulge where few women did, his chosen pubs museum pieces in a gallery marked prehistoric.

He'd been living on and off for years with Dr Patience Aitken, but that seemed to be over, not that he was saying anything about it. At first she'd thought him shy, awkward, but now she wasn't so sure. It seemed more like a strategy, a wilfulness. She couldn't imagine him joining a singles club the way Derek Linford had done. Linford . . . another of her little mistakes. She hadn't spoken to him since The Dome. He'd left precisely one message on her answerphone: 'Hope you've got over whatever it was.' As if it was her fault! She'd almost called him back, forced an apology, but maybe that was his game: get her to make the move; contact of any kind the prelude to a rematch.

Maybe there was method in John Rebus's madness. Certainly there was a lot to be said for quiet nights in, a video rental, the gin, and a box of Pringle's. Not trying to impress anyone; putting on some music and dancing by yourself. At parties and in clubs there was always that self-consciousness, that sense of being watched and graded by anonymous eyes.

But next morning at the office it would be: 'What did you get up to last night then?' Asked innocently enough, but she never felt comfortable saying more than, 'Not much, how about you?' Because to utter the word alone implied that you were lonely.

Or available. Or had something to hide.

Hunter Square was empty save for a tourist couple poring over a map. The coffee she'd drunk was asking permission to leave, so she headed for the public toilet. When she came out of her cubicle, a woman was standing by the sinks, hunting through a series of carrier bags. Bag lady was an American term, but it suddenly seemed right. The woman's padded jacket was grubby, the stitching loose at the neck and shoulders. Her hair was short and greasy, cheeks red from exposure. She was talking to herself as she found what she'd been looking for: a half-eaten burger, still in its greaseproof wrapper. The woman held the comestible under the hand-dryer and let hot air play on it, turning it in her fingers. Clarke watched in fascination, unsure whether to be appalled or impressed. The woman knew she was being watched, but stuck to her task. When the dryer had finished its cycle, she pushed it on again with her finger. Then she spoke.

'Nosy little beggar, aren't you?' She glanced towards Clarke. 'You laughing at me?'

' "Beggar",' Clarke quoted.

The woman snorted. 'Easy amused then. And I'm no beggar, by the way.'

Clarke took a step forward. 'Wouldn't it heat up quicker if you opened it?'

'Eh?'

'Heat the inside rather than the outside.'

'You saying I'm cack-handed?'

'No, I just . . .'

'I mean, you're the world expert, are you? Lucky for me you just happened to be passing. Got fifty pence on you?'

'Yes, thanks.'

The woman snorted again. 'I make the jokes around here.' She took an exploratory bite of the burger, spoke with her mouth full.

'I didn't catch that,' Clarke said.

The woman swallowed. 'I was asking if you were a lesbian. Men who hang around toilets are poofs, aren't they?'

'You're hanging around a toilet.'

'I'm no lesbian, by the way.' She took another bite.

'Ever come across a guy called Mackie? Chris Mackie?'

'Who's asking?'

Clarke produced her warrant card. ' You know Chris is dead?'

The woman stopped chewing. Tried swallowing but couldn't, ended up coughing the mouthful out on to the floor. She went to one of the sinks, cupped water to her mouth. Clarke followed her.

'He jumped from North Bridge. I'm assuming you knew him?'

The woman was staring into the soap-flecked mirror. The eyes, though dark and knowing, were so much younger and less worn than the face. Clarke placed the woman in her mid-thirties, but knew that on a bad day she could pass for fifty.

'Everybody knew Mackie.'

'Not everybody's reacted the way you just did.'

The woman was still holding her burger. She stared at it, seemed about to ditch it, but finally wrapped it up again and placed it at the top of one of her bags.

'I shouldn't be so surprised,' she said. 'People die all the time.'

'But he was your friend?'

The woman looked at her. 'Gonny buy me a cup of tea?'

Clarke nodded.

The nearest café wouldn't take them. When pressed, the manager pointed to the woman and said she'd caused trouble, trying to beg at the tables. There was another café further along.

'I'm barred there as well,' the woman admitted. So Clarke went in, fetched two beakers of tea and a couple of sticky buns. They sat in Hunter Square, stared at by passengers on the top decks of the passing buses. The woman flicked the Vs from time to time, dissuading the spectators.

'I'm a bad bugger, me,' she confided.

Clarke had her name now: Dezzi. Short for Desiderata. Not her real name: 'Left that behind when I left home.'

'And when was that, Dezzi?'

'I don't remember. A lot of years now, I suppose.'

'You always been in Edinburgh?'

A shake of the head. 'All over. Last summer I ended up on a bus to some commune in Wales. Christ knows how that happened. Got a fag?'

Clarke handed one over. 'Why did you leave home?'

'Like I said, nosy little beggar.'

'All right, what about Chris?'

'I always called him Mackie.'

'What did he call you?'

'Dezzi.' She stared at Clarke. 'Is that you trying to find out my last name?'

Clarke shook her head. 'Cross my heart.'

'Oh aye, a cop's as honest as the day is long.'

'It's true.'

'Only, this time of year the days are awfy short.'

Clarke laughed. 'I walked into that one.' She'd been trying to work out if Dezzi knew about Mackie, knew about the detective who was asking about him. Knew about the story in the *News*. 'So what can you tell me about Mackie?'

176

'He was my boyfriend, just for a few weeks.' The sudden, unexpected smile lit up her face. 'Wild weeks they were, mind.'

'How wild?'

An arch look. 'Enough to get us arrested. I'm saying no more than that.' She bit into her bun. She was alternating: mouthful of bun, puff on the cigarette.

'Did he tell you anything about himself?'

'He's dead now, what does it matter?'

'It matters to me. Why would he kill himself?'

'Why does anyone?'

'You tell me.'

A slurp of tea. 'Because you give in.'

'Is that what he did, give in?'

'All the shite out here . . .' Dezzi shook her head. 'I tried it once, cut my wrists with a bit of glass. Eight stitches.' She turned one wrist as if to show it, but Clarke couldn't see any scars. 'Couldn't have been serious, could I?'

Clarke was well aware that a great many homeless people were ill; not physically, but mentally. She had a sudden thought: could she trust any stories Dezzi told her?

'When did you last see Mackie?'

'Maybe a couple of weeks back.'

'How did he seem?'

'Fine.' She pushed the last morsel of bun into her mouth. Washed it down with tea, before concentrating on the cigarette.

'Dezzi, did you really know him?'

'What?'

'You haven't told me one thing about him.'

Dezzi prickled. Clarke feared she would walk off. 'If he meant something to you,' Clarke went on, 'help me get to know him.'

'Nobody knew Mackie, not really. Too many defences.'

'But you got past them?'

'I don't think so. He told me a few stories . . . but I think that's all they were.'

'What sort of stories?'

'Oh, all about places he'd been – America, Singapore, Australia. I thought maybe he'd been in the navy or something, but he said he hadn't.'

'Was he well educated?'

'He knew things. I'm positive he'd been to America, not sure about the others. He knew London, though, all the tourist places and the underground stations. When I first met him . . .'

'Yes?' Clarke was shivering; couldn't feel her toes.

'I don't know, I got the feeling he was just passing through. Like, there was somewhere else he could go.'

'But he didn't?'

'No.'

'Are you saying he was homeless by choice rather than necessity?'

'Maybe.' Dezzi's eyes widened a little.

'What is it?'

'I can prove I knew him.'

'How's that?'

'The present he gave me.'

'What present?'

'Only, I didn't have much use for it, so I . . . I gave it to someone.'

'Gave it to someone?'

'Well, sold it. A second-hand shop on Nicolson Street.'

'What was it?'

'A briefcase sort of thing. Didn't hold enough stuff, but it was made of leather.'

Mackie had carried his cash to the building society in a briefcase. 'So now it'll have been sold on to someone else?' Clarke guessed.

But Dezzi was shaking her head. 'The shopkeeper's still got it. I've seen him walking about with it. Leather it was, and the bastard only gave me five quid.'

It wasn't far from Hunter Square to Nicolson Street. The shop was an Aladdin's cave of tat, narrow aisles leading them past teetering pillars of used goods: books, cassettes, music centres, crockery. Vacuum cleaners had been draped with feather boas; picture cards and old comics lay underfoot. Electrical goods and board games and jigsaw puzzles; pots and pans, guitars, music-stands. The shop-keeper, an Asian, didn't seem to recognise Dezzi. Clarke showed her warrant card and asked to see the briefcase.

'Five measly quid he gave me,' Dezzi grumbled. 'Genuine leather.'

The man was reluctant, until Clarke mentioned that St Leonard's was just around the corner. He reached down and placed a scuffed black briefcase on the counter. Clarke asked him to open it. Inside: a newspaper, packed lunch and a thick roll of banknotes. Dezzi seemed to want a closer look, but he snapped shut the case.

'Satisfied?' he asked.

Clarke pointed to a corner of the case where the scuffing was worst.

'What happened?'

'The initials were not my initials. I attempted to erase them.'

Clarke looked more closely. She was wondering if Valerie Briggs could identify the case. 'Do you remember the initials?' she asked Dezzi.

Dezzi shook her head; she was looking, too.

The shop was badly lit. The faintest indents remained.

'ADC?' she guessed.

'I believe so,' the shopkeeper said. Then he wagged a finger at Dezzi. 'And I paid you a fair price.'

'You as good as robbed me, you sod.' She nudged Clarke. 'Stick the handcuffs on him, girl.'

ADC, Clarke was thinking, *was Mackie really ADC?*

Or would it prove another dead end?

Back at St Leonard's, she kicked herself for not checking Mackie's criminal record sooner. August 1997, Christopher Mackie and 'a Ms Desiderata' (she refused to give the police her full name) were apprehended while involved in a 'lewd exhibition' on the steps of a parish church in Bruntsfield.

August: Festival time. Clarke was surprised they hadn't been mistaken for an experimental theatre group.

The arresting officer was a uniform called Rod Harken, and he remembered the incident well.

'She got a fine,' he told Clarke by telephone from Torphichen police station. 'And a few days in clink for refusing to tell us her name.'

'What about her partner?'

'I think he got off with a caution.'

'Why?'

'Because the poor sod was nearly comatose.'

'I still don't get it.'

'Then I'll spell it out. She was straddling him, knickers off and skirt up, trying to haul his pants down. We had to wake him up to take him to the station.' Harken chuckled.

'Were they photographed?'

'You mean on the steps?' Harken was still chuckling.

Clarke heaped more ice into her voice. 'No, I do not mean on the steps. I mean at Torphichen.'

'Oh aye, we took some snaps.'

'Would you still have them?'

'Depends.'

'Well, could you take a look.' Clarke paused. 'Please.'

'Suppose so,' the uniform said grudgingly.

'Thank you.'

She put the phone down. An hour later, the photos arrived by patrol car. The ones of Mackie were better than the hostel pictures. She stared into his unfocused eyes. His hair was thick and dark, brushed back from the forehead. His face was either tanned or weather-beaten. He hadn't shaved for a day or two, but looked no worse than many a summertime backpacker. His eyes looked heavy, as though no amount of sleep could compensate for what they'd seen. Clarke had to smile at the photos of

Dezzi: she was grinning like a Cheshire cat, not a care in her world.

Harken had put a note in the envelope: *One other thing. We asked Mackie about the incident and he told us he wasn't a 'sexual beast' any more. Something got lost in the translation and we kept him locked up while we checked if he'd had previous as a sex offender. Turned out he hadn't.*

Her phone rang again. It was the front desk. There was someone downstairs for her.

Her visitor was short and round with a red face. He wore a Prince of Wales check three-piece suit and was mopping his brow with a handkerchief the size of a small tablecloth. The top of his head was bald and shiny, but hair grew copiously to either side, combed back over his ears. He introduced himself as Gerald Sithing.

'I read about Chris Mackie in the newspaper this morning, gave me quite a turn.' His beady eyes were on her, voice high and quavering.

Clarke folded her arms. 'You knew him, sir?'

'Oh, yes. Known him for years.'

'Could you describe him for me?'

Sithing studied her, then clapped his hands. 'Oh, of course. You think I'm a crank.' His laughter was sibilant. 'Come here to claim his fortune.'

'Aren't you?'

He drew himself up, recited a good description of Mackie. Clarke unfolded her arms, scratched her nose. 'In here, please, Mr Sithing.'

There was an interview room just to the side of the front desk. She unlocked it and looked in. Sometimes it was used for storage, but today it was empty. Desk and two chairs. Nothing on the walls. No ashtray or waste bin.

Sithing sat down, looked around as though intrigued by his surroundings. Clarke had gone from scratching her nose to pinching it. She had a headache coming on, felt dead beat.

'How did you come to know Mr Mackie?'

'Complete accident really. Daily constitutional, back then I took it in the Meadows.'

'Back when?'

'Oh, seven, eight years ago. Bright summer's day, so I sat myself down on one of the benches. There was a man already seated there, scruffy . . . you know, gentleman of the road. We got talking. I think I broke the ice, said something about how lovely the day was.'

'And this was Mr Mackie?'

'That's right.'

'Where was he living at the time?'

Sithing laughed again. 'You're still testing me, aren't you?' He wagged a finger like a fat sausage. 'He was in a hostel sort of place, Grassmarket. I met him the very next day, and the day after that. It got to be a routine with us, and one I enjoyed very much.'

'What did you talk about?'

'The world, the mess we've made of it. He was interested in Edinburgh, in all the architectural changes. He was very anti.'

'Anti?'

'You know, against all the new buildings. Maybe in the end it got too much for him.'

'He killed himself in protest at ugly architecture?'

'Despair can come from many quarters.' His tone was admonishing.

'I'm sorry if I sounded . . .'

'Oh, I'm sure it's not your fault. You're just tired.'

'Is it that obvious?'

'And maybe Chris was tired, too. That's the point I was making.'

'Did he ever talk about himself?'

'A little. He told me about the hostel, about people he'd met . . .'

'I meant his past. Did he talk about his life before he went on the street?'

Sithing was shaking his head. 'He was more of a good listener, fascinated by Rosslyn.'

Clarke thought she'd misheard. 'Rosalind?'

'*Rosslyn*. The chapel.'

'What about it?'

Sithing leaned forward. 'My whole life's devoted to the place. You may have heard of the Knights of Rosslyn?'

Clarke was getting a bad feeling. She shook her head. The stems of her eyes ached.

'But you know that in the year 2000, the secret of Rosslyn will reveal itself?'

'Is this some New Age thing?'

Sithing snorted. 'It's very much an *ancient* thing.'

'You believe Rosslyn's some sort of . . . special place?'

'It's the reason Rudolf Hess flew to Scotland. Hitler was obsessed with the Ark of the Covenant.'

'I know. I saw *Raiders of the Lost Ark* three times. You're saying Harrison Ford was looking in the wrong place?'

'Laugh all you like,' Sithing sneered.

'And that's what you talked about with Chris Mackie?'

'He was an acolyte!' Sithing slapped the desk. 'He was a believer.'

Clarke was getting to her feet. 'Did you know he had money?'

'He'd have wanted it to go to the Knights!'

'Did you know anything about him?'

'He gave us a hundred pounds to carry on our researches. Beneath the floor of the chapel, that's where it's buried.'

'What?'

'The portal! The gateway!'

Clarke had the door open. She grabbed Sithing's arm. It felt soft, as if there were no bones beneath the flesh.

'Out,' she commanded.

'The money belongs to the Knights! We were his family!'

'Out.'

He wasn't resisting, not really. She swung him into the revolving door and gave it a push, propelling him out on to St Leonard's Street, where he turned to glare at her. His face was redder than ever. Strands of hair had fallen forwards over his eyes. He began talking again, but she turned away. The desk sergeant was grinning.

'Don't,' she warned.

'I hear my Uncle Chris passed away,' he said, ignoring her raised finger. As she made for the stairs, she could hear his voice. 'He said he'd leave me a little something when he went. Any chance, Siobhan? Come on, just a few quid from my old Uncle Chris!'

Her phone was ringing when she reached it. She picked up the receiver, rubbing at her temples with her free hand.

'What?' she snapped.

'Hello?' A woman's voice.

'You'll be the mystery tramp's sister then?' Clarke slipped into her chair.

'It's Sandra here. Sandra Carnegie.'

The name meant nothing to her for a moment.

'We went to the Marina that night,' the voice explained.

Clarke screwed her eyes shut. 'Oh, hell, yes. Sorry, Sandra.'

'I was just phoning to see if . . .'

'It's been a hellish day, that's all,' Clarke was saying.

'. . . there'd been any progress. Only no one's telling me anything.'

Clarke sighed. 'I'm sorry, Sandra. It's not my case any more. Who's your contact at Sex Crimes?'

Sandra Carnegie mumbled something inaudible.

'I didn't catch that.'

A burst of fury: 'I said you're all the same! You look like you're concerned, but you're not doing anything to catch him! I can't go out now without wondering, is he

184

watching me? Is that him on the bus, or crossing the road?' The anger melting to tears. 'And I thought you . . . that night we . . .'

'I'm sorry, Sandra.'

'Stop saying that! Jesus, just stop, will you?'

'Maybe if I talked to the officers at Sex Crimes . . .' But the phone had gone dead. Siobhan put down the receiver, then lifted it off the hook, sat it on the desktop. She had Sandra's number somewhere, but looking at the chaos of papers on her desk, she knew it might take hours to find.

And her headache was getting worse.

And the frauds and lunatics would keep hammering at her.

And what kind of job was it that could make you feel so bad about yourself . . . ?

17

The kind of morning just made for a long drive: sky a pale wash of blue, thin strings of clouds, almost no traffic and Page/Plant on the radio-cassette. A long drive might help clear his head. The bonus ball: he was missing the morning briefing. Linford could have the stage all to himself.

Rebus headed out of town against the tide of the rush hour. Crawling queues on Queensferry Road, the usual tailback at the Barnton roundabout. Snow on the roofs of some cars: the gritting lorries had been out at dawn. He stopped for petrol and downed two more paracetamol with a can of Irn-Bru. Crossing the Forth Bridge, he saw that they'd put up the Millennium Clock on the Rail Bridge, providing a reminder he didn't need. He remembered a trip to Paris with his ex-wife . . . was it twenty years ago? A similar clock was set up outside the Beaubourg, only it had stopped.

And here he was time travelling, back to the haunt of childhood holidays. When he came off the M90, he was surprised to see he still had over twenty miles to go. Was St Andrews really so isolated? A neighbour had usually given the family a lift: Mum and Dad, and Rebus and his brother. Three of them crushed against each other on the back seat, bags squashed by their knees and legs, beach balls and towels resting on their laps. The trip would take all morning. Neighbours would have waved them off, as though an expedition were being undertaken. Into the dark continent of north-east Fife, final destination a caravan site, where their four-berth rental awaited, smelling of mothballs and gas mantles. At night there'd be the toilet block with its skittering insect life, moths and jenny-long-legs casting huge shadows on the white-washed walls. Then back to the caravan for games of cards and dominoes, their father usually winning except when their mother persuaded him not to cheat.

Two weeks of summer. It was called the Glasgow Fair Fortnight. He was never sure if 'fair' was as in festival or not raining. He never saw a festival in St Andrews and it seemed to rain often, sometimes for a whole week. Plastic macs and long bleak walks. When the sun broke through, it could still be cold; the brothers turning blue as they splashed in the North Sea, waving at ships on the horizon, the ships their father told them were Russian spies. There was an RAF base near by; the Russians were after their secrets.

As he approached the town, the first thing he saw was the golf course, and heading into the centre he noticed that St Andrews seemed not to have changed. Had time really stood still here? Where were the High Street shoe shops and bargain outlets, the fast-food chains? St Andrews could afford to be without them. He recognised the spot where a toy shop had once stood. It now sold ice cream. A tearoom, an antique emporium . . . and students. Students everywhere, looking bright and cheerful in keeping with the day. He checked his directions. It was a small town, six or seven main streets. Even so, he made a couple of mistakes before driving through an ancient stone archway. He stopped by the side of a cemetery. Across the road were gates which led to a Gothic-style building, looking more like a church than a school. But the sign on the wall was clear enough: Haugh Academy.

He wondered if he needed to lock the car, but did so anyway: too old to change his ways.

Teenage girls were heading into the building. They all wore grey blazers and skirts, crisp white blouses with school ties knotted tight at the throat. A woman was

187

standing in the doorway, donning a long black woollen coat.

'Inspector Rebus?' she asked as he approached. He nodded. 'Billie Collins,' she said, a hand shooting out towards him. Her grip was brisk and firm. As a girl, head bowed, made to pass them, she tutted and gripped her by the shoulder.

'Millie Jenkins, have you finished that homework yet?'

'Yes, Miss Collins.'

'And has Miss McCallister seen it?'

'Yes, Miss Collins.'

'Then along you go.'

The shoulder was released, the girl fairly flew through the door.

'Walk, Millie! No running!' She kept her head turned, checking the girl's progress, then brought her attention back to Rebus.

'The day being a fine one, I thought we might walk.'

Rebus nodded his agreement. He wondered, the day apart, whether there might be some other reason she didn't want him in the school . . .

'I remember this place,' he said.

They'd descended the hill and were crossing a bridge over a burn, harbour and pier to the left of them, sea views ahead. Rebus pointed far to the right, then brought his arm down, lest the teacher scold him: *John Rebus, no pointing!*

'We came here on holiday . . . that caravan site up there.'

'Kinkell Braes,' Billie Collins said.

'That's right. There used to be a putting green just there.' Nodding with his head, a safer option. 'You can still see the outline.'

And the beach falling away just yards below them. The promenade was empty, save for a Labrador being walked by its owner. As the man passed them, he smiled, bowed his head. A typically Scots greeting: more evasion than anything else. The dog's hair hung wetly from its belly, where it had enjoyed a trip into the water. A wind was whipping off the sea, icy-smelling and abrasive. He got the feeling his companion would call it bracing.

'You know,' she said, 'I think you're only the second policeman I've had dealings with since I came here.'

'Not much crime, eh?'

'The usual student boisterousness.'

'What was the other time?'

'I'm sorry?'

'The other policeman.'

'Oh, it was last month. The severed hand.'

Rebus nodded, remembered reading about it. Some student joke, bits going missing from the medical lab, turning up around the town.

'Raisin Day, it's called,' Billie Collins informed him. She was tall, bony. Prominent cheekbones and black brittle-looking hair. Seona Grieve was a teacher, too. Roddy Grieve had married two teachers. Her profile showed a jutting forehead, hooded eyes. Her nose fell to a point. Masculine features married to a strong, deep voice. Low-heeled black shoes, the navy-blue skirt falling way past her knees. Blue woollen jumper with decoration provided by a large Celtic brooch.

'Some sort of initiation?' Rebus asked.

'The third-year students throw out challenges to the first years. There's a lot of dressing up, and far too much drinking.'

'Plus body parts.'

She glanced at him. 'That was a first, so far as I'm aware. An anatomy prank. The hand was found on the school wall. Several of my girls had to be treated for shock.'

'Dear me.'

Their walk had slowed. Rebus gestured towards a

bench and they sat a decent distance apart. Billie Collins tugged at the hem of her skirt.

'You came here on holidays, did you say?'

'Most years. Played on the beach down there, went to the castle . . . There was a kind of dungeon there.'

'The bottle dungeon.'

'That's it. And a haunted tower . . .'

'St Rule's. It's just over the cathedral wall.'

'Where my car's parked?' She nodded and he laughed. 'Everything seemed a lot further apart when I was a boy.'

'You'd have sworn St Rule's was a distance from your putting green?' She seemed to consider this. 'Who's to say it wasn't?'

He nodded slowly, almost understanding her. She was saying that the past was a different place, that it could not be revisited. The town had tricked him by seeming unchanged. But *he* had changed: that was what mattered.

She took a deep breath, spread her hands out across her lap. 'You want to talk to me about my past, Inspector, and that's a painful subject. Given the choice, it's something I'd avoid. Few happy memories, and those aren't what interest you anyway.'

'I can appreciate—'

'I wonder if you can, I really do. Roddy and I met when we were too young. Second-year undergraduates, right here. We were happy here, maybe that's why I've been able to stay. But when Roddy got his job in the Scottish Office . . .' She reached into a sleeve for her handkerchief. Not that she was about to cry, but it helped her to work at the cotton with her fingers, her eyes fixed on the embroidered edges. Rebus looked out to sea, imagining spy ships – probably fishing boats, transformed by imagination.

'When Peter was born,' she went on, 'it was at the worst time. Roddy was snowed under at work. We were living at his parents' place. It didn't help that his father was ailing. With my post-natal depression . . . well, it was a kind of living hell.' Now she looked up. In front of her lay the beach, and the Labrador bounding across it to fetch a stick. But she was seeing a different picture altogether. 'Roddy seemed to immerse himself in his work; his way of escaping it all, I suppose.'

And now Rebus had his own pictures: working ever longer hours, keeping clear of the flat. No arguments about politics; no cushion fights. Nothing any more but the knowledge of failure. Sammy had to be protected: the unspoken agreement; the last pact of husband and wife. Until Rhona told him he was a stranger to her, and walked away, taking their daughter . . .

He couldn't recall his own parents ever arguing. Money had always been an issue: every week they put a little aside, saving for the boys' holiday. They scrimped, but Johnny and Mike never went without: patched clothes and hand-me-downs, but hot meals, Christmas treats and the annual holiday. Ice cream and deckchairs, bags of chips on the walk back to the caravan. Games of putting, trips to Craigtoun Park. There was a miniature train there, you sat on it and ended up in some woods with little elfin houses.

It had all seemed so easy, so innocent.

'And the drinking got worse,' she was saying, 'so I ran back here, bringing Peter with me.'

'How bad did the drinking get?'

'He did it in secret. Bottles hidden in his study.'

'Seona says he wasn't much of a drinker.'

'She would, wouldn't she?'

'Protecting his good name?'

Billie Collins sighed. 'I'm not sure I really blame Roddy. It was his family, the way they can suffocate you.' She looked at him. 'All his life, I think he dreamed of parliament. And just when it was within his reach . . .'

Rebus shifted on the bench. 'I've heard he worshipped Cammo.'

'Not quite the right word, but I suppose he did want at least some of what Cammo appeared to have.'

'Meaning?'

'Cammo can be charming and ruthless. Sometimes never more ruthless than when he's being charming to your face. Roddy was attracted to that side of his brother: the ability to scheme.'

'He had more than one brother, though.'

'Oh, you mean Alasdair?'

'Did you know him?'

'I liked Alasdair, but I can't say I blame him for leaving.'

'When did he leave?'

'Late seventies. Seventy-nine, I think.'

'Do you know why he left?'

'Not really. He had a business partner, Frankie or Freddy . . . a name like that. Story was, they went off together.'

'Lovers?'

She shrugged. 'I didn't believe it; nor did Alicia, though I don't think she'd have been against a homosexual in the family.'

'What did Alasdair do?'

'All sorts. He owned a restaurant at one time: Mercurio's on Dundas Street. I should think it's changed names a dozen times since. He was hopeless with the staff. He dabbled in property – I think that was Frankie or Freddy's line of work also – and put money into a couple of bars. As I say, Inspector, all sorts.'

'No arts or politics then?'

She snorted. 'Lord, no. Alasdair was far too down-to-earth.' She paused. 'What has Alasdair got to do with Roddy?'

Rebus slid his hands into his pockets. 'I'm trying to get to know Roddy. Alasdair's just another piece of the puzzle.'

'Bit late to get to know him, isn't it?'

'By getting to know him, it's possible I may see who his enemies were.'

'But we don't always know who our enemies are, do we? The wolf in sheep's clothing, et cetera.'

He nodded agreement, stretched out his legs and crossed them at the ankles. But Billie Collins was getting to her feet. 'We can be at Kinkell Braes in five minutes. Might be interesting for you.'

He doubted it, but as they began to climb the steep path to the caravan site, he remembered something else from his childhood: a hole, deep and manmade, sided with concrete. It had sat to one side of the path, and he'd had to shuffle past it, fearful of falling in. Some sort of sluice? He recalled water trickling through it.

'Christ, it's still here!' He stood looking down. The hole had been fenced off from the path; didn't seem half as deep. But this was definitely the same hole. He looked to Billie Collins. 'This thing scared me half to death when I was a kid. Cliffs to one side and this on the other, I could hardly bring myself to come down this path. I had nightmares about this hole.'

'Hard to believe.' She was thoughtful. 'Or maybe not so hard.' She walked on.

He caught her up. 'How did Peter get on with his father?'

'How do fathers and sons usually get on?'

'Did they see much of one another?'

'I didn't dissuade Peter from visiting Roddy.'

'That doesn't exactly answer my question.'

'It's the only answer I can give.'

'How did Peter react when he heard his father was dead?'

She stopped, swung towards him. 'What is it you're trying to say?'

'Funny, I'm wondering what it is you're trying *not* to say.'

193

She folded her arms. 'Well, that puts us at somewhat of an impasse, wouldn't you agree?'

'I'm just asking if they got on, that's all. Because Peter's last song about his father is called "The Final Reproof", and that doesn't exactly conjure up harmony and good humour.'

They were at the top of the path. Ahead of them stood the rows of caravans, vacant windows awaiting warmer weather, the arrival of bottled gas and released spirits.

'You spent your holidays here?' Billie Collins asked, looking around. 'Poor you.' She was seeing uniformity and the brutal North Sea, cold facts separated from anecdote.

' "The Final Reproof",' she said to herself. 'It's a powerful line, isn't it?' She looked at him. 'I spent years trying to understand the clan, Inspector. Don't vex yourself. Try something feasible.'

'Such as?'

'Conjure up the past and make it work this time.'

'I might have a round table in my living room,' he said. 'That doesn't necessarily mean I'm Merlin.'

He took the coastal road south to Kirkcaldy. Stopped for lunch in Lundin Links. One of the regulars at the Oxford Bar, his father owned the Old Manor Hotel. Rebus had been promising a visit for a while. He ate East Neuk fish soup followed by the catch of the day: local fish, simply cooked, washed down with mineral water, and tried not to dwell on the past – anyone's past. Afterwards, George gave him the tour. From the main bar, the scenery was stunning: a golf links with the sea and horizon beyond. In a sudden shaft of sunlight, Bass Rock looked like a nugget of white gold.

'Do you play?' George asked.

'What?' Rebus still gazing out of the window.

'Golf.'

Rebus shook his head. 'Tried it when I was a kid.

Hopeless.' He managed to turn his head away from the view. 'How can you drink in the Ox with this as the alternative?'

'I only drink at night, John. And after dark, you can't see any of this.'

It was a fair point. Darkness could make you forget what was in front of your face. Darkness would swallow the caravan site, the old putting green, and St Rule's Tower. It would swallow crimes and grieving and remorse. If you gave yourself to the darkness, you might start to make out shapes invisible to others, but without being able to define them: the movement behind a curtain, the shadows in an alleyway.

'See how Bass Rock is shining?' George said.

'Yes.'

'It's the sun reflecting off all the bird shit.' He got up. 'Sit there and I'll fetch us some coffee.'

So Rebus sat by the window, the glorious winter's day set out before him – bird shit and all – while his thoughts churned and churned in the dark. What was waiting for him in Edinburgh? Would Lorna want to see him? When George came back with the coffee, he told Rebus there was a bedroom vacant upstairs.

'Only you look like you could use a few hours off.'

'Christ, man, don't tempt me,' Rebus said. He took his coffee black.

18

The hospital corridors were all rubber-soled efficiency. Nurses darted in and out of doorways. Doctors consulted clipboards as they made their rounds. No beds here, just waiting rooms, examination rooms, offices. Derek Linford disliked hospitals. He'd watched his mother die in one. His father was still alive, but they didn't talk much; the occasional phone call. The first time Derek had owned up to voting Tory, his father had disowned him. That was the kind of man he was: headstrong, full of erroneous grievances. His son had sneered at him: 'How can you be working class? You haven't worked in twenty years.' It was true: disability benefit for a mining accident. A limp that would appear at convenient times, but never when he was on his way to meet old pals at the pub. And Derek's mother, slogging her guts out in a factory until the final illness took her.

Derek Linford had succeeded not in spite of his background but because of it, each rung he climbed another jibe at his father, another way of letting his mother know he was all right. The old man – not so old really; fifty-eight – still lived in the council semi. Linford would drive past it occasionally, slowing to a crawl, not really caring if he was seen. A neighbour might wave, half-recognising the face. Would they pass the news on to his father? *I see young Derek was round the other day. He still keeps in touch then . . . ?* He wondered how his father would react: with a grunt most likely, turning back to his sports pages, his quick crossword. When Derek was a teenager, doing well in all his subjects, his father would make show of asking him for the answers to crossword clues. He'd rack his brains, get them wrong . . . It took Derek a while to realise the old man was making them up. Seven letters, umbrella, c something p. Derek would have a go, then his father would sigh and say something like, 'No, you looper, it's capulet.'

No such word in the dictionary.

Derek's mother hadn't died in this hospital. She'd held his hand, her breathing ragged. She couldn't speak, but her eyes told him she wasn't sorry to go. Worn out, like some machine run to death. And like a machine she'd lacked care, lacked maintenance. The old man standing at the foot of the bed, flowers in his arms: carnations picked from a neighbour's garden. And books he'd brought from the library, books she could no longer read.

Was it any wonder he hated hospitals? Yet in his early days on the force he'd been made to spend long hours in them, waiting for victims and aggressors to be treated, waiting to take statements from patients and staff. Blood and dressings, swollen faces, twisted limbs. He'd watched an ear being stitched, had witnessed grey-white bone protruding from a shattered leg. Crash victims; muggings; rapes.

Was it any wonder?

Finally, he found the family room. It was supposed to be a quiet space for families who were 'awaiting news of a loved one', as the receptionist had put it. But as he pushed open the door, he was assailed by the death rattle of vending machines, a cloud of cigarette smoke, and the glare of daytime TV. Two middle-aged women were puffing away. Their eyes fixed on him for a moment, then returned to the chat show.

'Mrs Ure?'

The women looked up again. 'You don't look like a doctor.'

'I'm not,' he told the speaker. 'Are you Mrs Ure?'

'We're both Mrs Ure. Sisters-in-law.'

'Mrs Archie Ure?'

The other woman, who hadn't spoken yet, stood up. 'That's me.' She saw she was holding a cigarette, stubbed it out.

'My name's Detective Inspector Derek Linford. I'd been hoping to have a word with your husband.'

'Get in the queue,' the sister-in-law said.

'I was sorry to hear . . . Is it serious?'

'He's had trouble with his heart before,' Archie Ure's wife said. 'Never stopped him working for what he believed in.'

Linford nodded. He'd done his reading, knew all about Archie Ure. Head of the council's planning executive, a councillor for more than two decades. He was Old Labour, popular with those who knew him, a thorn in the side of some 'reformers'. A year or so back he'd written several bitter articles for the *Scotsman*, had got into trouble with the party as a result. Chastened, he'd applied for an MSP post, the first to do so. He probably hadn't allowed for the possibility of an upstart like Roddy Grieve beating him for the nomination. He'd worked ceaselessly during the '79 campaign. Twenty years later, his reward was a runner-up spot for a constituency, and the promise of a place near the top of Labour's top-up list.

'Are they operating?' Linford asked.

'Christ, listen to him,' the sister-in-law said, glowering at him. 'How the hell would we know if they're operating? We're only the family, last to be told.' She stood up, too. Linford felt himself shrink back. Big women they were, addicted to Scotland's pantry: cigarettes and lard. Training shoes, elasticated waistbands. Matching YSL tops, probably knock-off if not fake.

'I just wanted to know—'

'What did you want to know?' This from the wife, rising to her friend's ire. She folded her arms. 'What d'you want Archie for?'

To ask questions . . . because he's a possible suspect in a murder. No, he couldn't tell her that. So he shook his head instead. 'It can wait.'

'Is it to do with Roddy Grieve?' she asked. He couldn't answer. 'Bloody thought it might be. *He's* the reason Archie's in here. Tell that slut of a widow of his to remember that. And if my Archie . . . if he . . .' She bowed her head, words choking. An arm went around her shoulder.

'Come on now, Isla. It'll be fine.' The sister-in-law looked at Linford. 'Got what you came for?'

He turned away, but then stopped. 'What did she mean? About Roddy Grieve being to blame?'

'With Grieve dead, it should have been Archie standing.'

'Yes?'

'Only now the widow's put her name forward, and knowing those bastards on the selection committee, she'll be the one. Oh aye, shafted again, Isla. As it was, so shall it be. Shafted all the way to the grave.'

'Frankly, they'd be lunatics not to.'

After the hospital, the wine bar on the High Street came as some relief. Linford sipped his chilled Chardonnay and asked Gwen Mollison why that should be. Mollison was tall with long fair hair, probably mid-thirties. She wore steel-rimmed glasses which magnified her long-lashed eyes, and toyed with her mobile phone as it sat on the table between them, just next to a bulging Filofax. She kept looking around, as though expecting to be able to greet a friend or acquaintance. Here, Linford had done his reading, too. Mollison was number three in the council's housing department. She didn't quite have Roddy Grieve's pedigree, or Archie Ure's longevity, which was why she'd lost to them, but great things were expected of her. Good working-class roots; New Labour to her core. She spoke well in public, presented well. Today she was wearing a cream linen trouser suit, maybe Armani. Linford recognised a kindred spirit and had laid his own mobile a foot and a half from hers.

'It's a PR coup,' Mollison explained. She had a glass of Zinfandel in front of her, but had asked for mineral water as an accompaniment, and had concentrated on that so far. Linford appreciated the tactic: you were a drinker, not an abstainer, but somehow you contrived to drink only water.

'I mean,' Mollison went on, 'the sympathy vote's out there. And Seona has friends in the party: she's been every bit as active as Roddy ever was.'

'Do you know her?'

Mollison shook her head – not in answer to the question but to dismiss it as irrelevant. 'I don't think the party would have gone to her; might've looked like bad taste. But when she phoned them, they weren't slow to see the possibilities.' She angled her phone, testing the signal strength. There was jazz music in the background. Only half a dozen other people in the place: mid-afternoon hiatus. Linford had skipped lunch. He'd finished one bowl of rice crackers; they weren't about to bring another.

'Are you disappointed?' he asked.

Mollison shrugged. 'There'll be other chances.' So confident; so controlled. No telling where she'd be in a few years. Linford had already handed over one of his business cards, the good ones, embossed. He'd added his home phone number on the back, smiled at her: 'Just in case.' A little later, she'd caught him stifling a yawn, had asked if she was boring him.

'Just a late night,' he'd explained.

'It's Archie I feel sorry for,' she went on now. 'This might've been his last chance.'

'But he's going on the regional list, isn't he?'

'Well, they have to, or else it looks like they're snubbing him. But you don't understand, that list is weighted

200

against whichever party gets most first-past-the-post seats.'

'I think you've lost me.'

'Even if Archie was top of the list, he probably wouldn't get in.'

Linford mulled that over; decided he still didn't get it. 'You're being very magnanimous,' he said instead.

'Am I?' She smiled at him. 'You don't understand politics. If I'm graceful in defeat, that counts for me next time. You have to learn to lose.' She shrugged again. Padded shoulders, giving some bulk to her thin frame. 'Anyway, shouldn't we be talking about Roddy Grieve?'

Linford smiled. 'You're not a suspect, Ms Mollison.'

'That's good to hear.'

'Not unless *Mrs* Grieve meets with some accident.'

Mollison laughed, a sudden trill which had the other drinkers looking at them. She clamped a hand over her mouth, took it away. 'God, I shouldn't laugh, should I? What if something did happen to her?'

'Such as?'

'I don't know . . . Say she gets hit by a car.'

'Then I'll want to talk to you again.' He opened his notebook, reached for his pen. It was a Mont Blanc; she'd commented on it earlier, looking impressed. 'Maybe I should take down your number,' he said with a smile.

The final candidate on the shortlist, Sara Bone, was a social worker in south Edinburgh. He caught up with her at a daycare centre for the elderly. They sat in the conservatory, surrounded by potted plants wilting from neglect. Linford said as much.

'Quite the opposite,' she informed him. 'They're suffering from over-attention. Everybody thinks they need a drop of water. Too much is as bad as not enough.'

She was a small woman – a shade over five feet – with a mother's face framed by a youthful haircut, short and feathered.

'Horrible,' was what she said when he asked her about Roddy Grieve's death. 'The world just seems to get worse and worse.'

'Could an MSP do anything to help?'

'I'd hope so,' she said.

'But now you're not going to get the chance?'

'Much to the relief of my clients.' She nodded towards the building's interior. 'They were all saying how much they would miss me.'

'It's nice to be wanted,' Linford said, feeling that he was wasting his time with this woman . . .

He called Rebus. The two met at Cramond. The normally leafy suburb had a grey, pinched look to it: winter wasn't welcome here. They stood on the pavement by Linford's BMW. Rebus, having listened to Linford's report, was thoughtful.

'How about you?' Linford asked. 'How was St Andrews?'

'Fine. I took a walk down by the seashore.'

'And?'

'And what?'

'And did you talk to Billie Collins?'

'That's why I was there.'

'And?'

'And she shed about as much light as an asbestos candle.'

Linford stared at him. 'You wouldn't tell me anyway, would you? She could confess, and I'd be the last to know.'

'It's how I work.'

'Keeping things to yourself?' Linford's voice was rising.

'You're awfully tense, Derek. Not been getting any lately?'

Linford's face flushed. 'Sod you.'

'Come on, you can do better than that.'

'I don't need to. You're not worth it.'

202

'Now that's a comeback.'

Rebus lit a cigarette, smoked in the uncompanionable silence. He could still see St Andrews as it had been to him nearly half a century before. He knew it represented something extraordinary, but couldn't have said what. The words didn't quite exist. It was as though loss and permanence had mingled and become some new entity, the one tasting of the other.

'Should we talk to her?'

Rebus sighed, sucked again on the cigarette. The smoke was blowing back into Linford's face. The wind, Rebus thought, is on my side. 'I suppose so,' he said at last. 'Now we're here.'

'It's good to hear such enthusiasm. I'm sure our respective bosses would be thrilled.'

'Oh, I've always cared what the brass think.' He looked at Linford. 'You don't get it, do you? I'm the best thing that could have happened to you.' Linford hooted. 'Think about it,' Rebus went on. 'Case solved, you take the credit. Case unsolved, you lay the blame on me. Either way, your boss and mine will go for it. You're their blue-eyed boy.' He flicked the cigarette on to the road. 'Every time I refuse to share information with you, you should make a note. Gives you ammo for later. Every time I piss you off or head off on my own tangent, same thing.'

'Why are you telling me this? Does pariah status give you some kind of thrill?'

'I'm not the pariah here, son. Think about it.' Rebus unbuttoned his jacket, affected a Wild West drawl. 'Now let's go visit the widow lady.'

Left Linford lurching in his wake.

The door was opened by Hamish Hall, Roddy Grieve's press officer.

'Oh, hello again,' he said, ushering them inside. It was a neat semi-detached, brick-built and of 1930s vintage. Lots of doors seemed to lead off the entrance hall. Hamish squeezed past them and they followed, through the dining room and into a recent addition, a conservatory, much smarter, Linford noted, than the one out at the daycare centre. An electric fan-heater was humming briskly in one corner. Cane furniture, including a glass-topped table, and seated at the table Seona Grieve and Jo Banks, a mound of paperwork before them. The few pot plants looked expertly tended.

'Oh, hello,' Seona Grieve said.

'Coffee?' Hamish asked. Both detectives nodded, and he headed into the kitchen.

'Sit down if you can find a space,' Seona Grieve said. Jo Banks got up and scooped newspapers and folders from a couple of the chairs. Rebus picked up one folder, examined it: *In Prospect – A Briefing Pack on the Scottish Parliament for Prospective Candidates*. Notes had been scribbled in most of the margins; Roddy Grieve's writing, most probably.

'And to what do we owe this pleasure?' Seona Grieve asked.

'Just a few follow-up questions,' Linford told her, easing his notebook out of his pocket.

'We heard you were stepping into your husband's shoes,' Rebus added.

'My feet are much smaller than Roddy's,' the widow said.

'Maybe so,' Rebus went on, 'but we've not got a motive yet for his death. DI Linford here thinks maybe you've just supplied us with one.'

Linford looked ready to remonstrate, but Jo Banks beat him to it. 'You think Seona would kill Roddy, just to become an MSP? That's ludicrous!'

'Is it?' Rebus scratched his nose.. 'I don't know, I tend to agree with DI Linford. It *is* a motive. Had you thought of running before?'

Seona Grieve straightened her back. 'You mean before Roddy was killed?'

'Yes.'

She thought about it, then nodded. 'I suppose I had, yes.'

'What stopped you?'

'I'm not sure.'

'This is totally out of order,' Jo Banks said. Seona Grieve touched her arm.

'It's all right, Jo. Best just put their minds at rest.' She glared at Rebus. 'It was when I realised that one of them, Ure, Mollison or Bone, would take Roddy's place . . . I thought: I could do it, maybe better than any of them, so why not ask?'

'Good for you,' Jo Banks said. 'It's in memory of Roddy. It's what he would have wanted.'

They had the sound of words used previously. Rebus wondered: maybe Jo Banks had come to the widow with the idea. Just maybe . . .

'I can see your point, Inspector,' Seona Grieve informed Rebus. 'But if I'd wanted to, I could have stood. Roddy wouldn't have minded. I didn't need him dead for me to stand.'

'And yet he's dead, and here you are.'

'Here I am,' she agreed.

'With the whole of the party behind her,' Jo Banks cautioned. 'So if you're thinking of making any accusations . . .'

'They just want to find Roddy's killer,' Seona Grieve told her. 'Isn't that right, Inspector?'

Rebus nodded.

'Then we're still on the same side, aren't we?'

Rebus nodded again, but judging from the look on Jo Banks' face, he wasn't so sure she'd agree.

By the time Hamish arrived with a tray bearing coffee pot and cups, Seona Grieve was asking for a progress report and Linford was hauling out the usual flannel about 'pursuing leads' and 'inquiries still to make'. None of which looked to be convincing the two women, despite the effort he was putting in. Seona Grieve met Rebus's eyes and inclined her head a little, telling him she knew what he was thinking. Then she turned to Linford, interrupting him.

'It's an American phrase, I think. Never kid a kidder . . . Or is it never shit a shitter?' She looked to Hamish as if for help, but he merely shrugged and went on handing out the coffees. 'Sounds to me, DI Linford, as though you've made precious little progress.'

'Clutching at straws, more like,' Jo Banks muttered.

'We still have every confidence . . .' Linford began.

'Oh, I can see that. I can see you're positively brimming with the stuff. Because that's what's got you where you are today. I'm a teacher, DI Linford. I've seen plenty of boys like you. They leave school and feel it in their bones that they can do anything they set their minds to. With most of them, it doesn't last long. But you . . .' She wagged a finger, then turned towards Rebus, who was blowing on the scalding coffee. 'DI Rebus, on the other hand . . .'

'What?' The question coming from Linford.

'DI Rebus has no confidence in anything very much any more. An accurate assessment?' Rebus blew on the coffee, said nothing. 'DI Rebus is jaded and cynical about most things. *Weltschmerz*, do you know that word, Inspector?'

'I think I ate some last time I was abroad,' Rebus said.

She smiled at him; a smile without happiness. 'World-weariness.'

'Pessimism,' Hamish agreed.

'You won't be voting, will you, Inspector?' Seona Grieve asked. 'Because you don't see the point.'

'I'm all for job creation schemes,' Rebus said. Jo Banks let out a hiss of air; Hamish snorted good-naturedly. 'But there's something I can't figure out. If I've got a problem, who do I go to – my MSP, my list MSP, or my MP? Maybe my MEP or councillor? That's what I mean about job creation.'

'Then why am I doing this?' Seona Grieve said quietly, her hands in her lap. Jo Banks reached out and touched her hand.

'Because it makes sense,' she said.

When Seona Grieve looked up at Rebus, there were tears in her eyes. Rebus looked away.

'This may not seem like the time,' he said, 'but you told us your husband didn't drink. I believe at one time his drinking may have been a problem.'

'For heaven's sake,' Jo Banks hissed.

Seona Grieve blew her nose, sniffed. 'You've been talking to Billie.'

'Yes,' he acknowledged.

'Trying to blacken a dead man's name,' Jo Banks muttered.

Rebus looked at her. 'See, there's a problem, Ms Banks. We don't know what Roddy Grieve was doing in the hours prior to his death. So far we've a sighting of him in one pub, just the one, drinking on his own. We need to know if that's the kind of man he was: a solitary drinker. Then maybe we can stop wasting our time trying to locate the friends we've been told he would be out drinking with.'

'It's all right, Jo,' Seona Grieve said quietly. Then, to Rebus: 'He said he felt he sometimes had to get out of himself.'

'Where would he have gone?'

She shook her head. 'He never said.'

'The times he stayed out all night . . . ?'

'I think maybe he went to hotels, or slept in the car.'

Rebus nodded, and she seemed to read his thoughts. 'Maybe he wasn't alone in doing that, Inspector?'

'Maybe,' he conceded. Some mornings, he'd woken in his car and didn't even know where he was . . . country roads, the middle of nowhere . . . 'Is there anything else we should know?'

She shook her head slowly.

'I'm sorry,' he said. 'I really am. I'm sorry.'

Rebus laid his coffee cup on the table, got up, and left the room.

By the time Linford caught up with him, Rebus was seated in his Saab, window down, smoking. Linford leaned down so their faces were almost touching. Rebus blew some smoke past his ear.

'So what do you think?' Linford asked.

Rebus considered his answer. Late afternoon; light had died from the sky. 'I think we're in the dark,' he said, 'swiping at things we think might be bats.'

'What does that mean?' The young man sounding genuinely annoyed.

'It means we'll never understand one another,' Rebus answered, starting his engine.

Linford stood at the kerbside, watching the Saab move off. He reached into his pocket for his mobile, put in a call to ACC Carswell at Fettes. He had the words formed and waiting in his head: *I think maybe Rebus is going to be a problem after all.* But as he waited to be put through, he had another thought: in saying as much to Carswell, he'd be admitting defeat, showing weakness. Carswell might understand, but that didn't mean he wouldn't see it as such: defeat; weakness. Linford cut the call, switched the phone off. This was his problem. It was up to him to think of a way round it.

19

Dean Coghill was dead. His building firm had been wound up, the company office now a design consultancy, the builders' yard turned into a three-storey block of flats. Hood and Wylie eventually tracked down an address for Coghill's widow.

'All these dead guys . . .' Grant Hood had commented.

Ellen Wylie's reply: 'The male of the species doesn't live as long as the female.'

They couldn't get a phone number for the widow, so went to the last known address.

'Probably died or retired to Benidorm,' Wylie said.

'Is there a difference then?'

Wylie smiled, brought the car in to the kerbside and pulled on the handbrake. Hood opened his door a fraction and peered down.

'No,' he said, 'this is fine. I can walk to the kerb from here.'

Wylie gave his arm a thump. He suspected it would bruise.

Meg Coghill was a short, spry woman in her early seventies. Though it didn't look like she was going out or ready for visitors, she was dressed immaculately and had made up her face. As she led them into the sitting room, there were noises from the kitchen.

'My cleaner,' Mrs Coghill explained. Hood felt like asking if she always dressed up for the cleaner, but thought he probably knew the answer already.

'Do you want a cup of tea or something?'

'No, thank you, Mrs Coghill.' Ellen Wylie sat on the

sofa. Hood remained standing, while Mrs Coghill sank into an armchair big enough to accommodate someone three times her size. Hood was looking at some framed photographs on a wall unit.

'Is this Mr Coghill?'

'That's Dean. I still miss him, you know.'

Hood guessed that the chair the widow now sat in had been her husband's. The photos showed a bear of a man, thick arms and neck, back held straight, the chest prominent and gut sucked in. His face told you he'd be fair as long as you didn't muck him around. Cropped silver hair. Jewellery around his neck and on his left wrist, a fat Rolex on the right.

'When did he pass away?' Wylie was asking, her voice trained in dealing with the bereaved.

'Best part of a decade ago.'

'Was it a medical condition?'

'He'd had problems with his heart before. Hospitals, specialists. He couldn't slow down, you see. Had to keep working.'

Wylie nodded slowly. 'It's hard for some people.'

'Were there any partners in the business, Mrs Coghill?' Hood had rested his backside on the arm of the sofa.

'No.' Mrs Coghill paused. 'Dean had hopes for Alexander.'

Hood turned to look again at the photos: family groups, a boy and girl from their pre-teens through to their twenties. 'Your son?' he asked.

'But Alex had other ideas. He's in America, married. He works in a car showroom, only over there they call them automobiles.'

'Mrs Coghill,' Wylie said, 'did your husband know a man called Bryce Callan?'

'Is that why you're here?'

'You know the name then?'

'He was some kind of gangster, wasn't he?'

'He had that reputation, certainly.'

Meg Coghill got up, fussed with some ornaments on the mantelpiece. Little china animals: cats playing with balls of wool; spaniels with floppy ears.

'Is there something you want to tell us, Mrs Coghill?' Hood spoke quietly, his eyes meeting Wylie's.

'It's too late now, isn't it?' There was a tremor in Meg Coghill's voice. She kept her back to her visitors. Wylie wondered if she took any tablets for nerves.

'You tell us, Mrs Coghill,' she suggested.

The widow's hands kept busy with the ornaments as she spoke.

'Bryce Callan was a thug, wasn't he? You paid up, or you got in trouble. Tools would disappear, or the tyres on the van would be slashed. The job you were working on might end up vandalised, only they weren't just vandals, they were Bryce Callan's men.'

'Your husband paid protection to Bryce Callan?'

She turned towards them. 'You didn't know my Dean. He was the only one who stood up to Callan. And I think it killed him. All the extra work and worry . . . Bryce Callan as good as stuck his hand into Dean's chest and squeezed his heart dry.'

'Your husband told you this?'

'Lord, no. He never said a word, liked to keep me separate from anything to do with the business. Family on one hand, work on the other, he'd say. That's why he needed an office, didn't want work coming home with him.'

'He wanted his family kept separate,' Wylie said, 'yet he thought maybe Alex would help in the business?'

'That was in the early days, before Callan.'

'Mrs Coghill, you heard about the body in the fireplace at Queensberry House?'

'Yes.'

'Your husband's firm worked there twenty years ago. Would there be any records, or anyone who worked for your husband that we could talk to?'

'You think it has something to do with Callan?'

'The first thing we need', Hood said, 'is to identify the body.'

'Do you remember your husband working there, Mrs Coghill?' Wylie asked. 'Maybe he mentioned someone disappearing from the job. . . ?'

When Mrs Coghill started shaking her head, Wylie looked to Hood, who smiled. Yes, that would have been too easy. She got the feeling this would be one of those cases where you never got a lucky break.

'His business came here in the end,' Mrs Coghill said. 'Maybe that will help you.'

And when Ellen Wylie asked what she meant, Meg Coghill said it might be easier if she showed them.

'I can't drive,' the widow explained. 'I sold Dean's cars. He had two of them, one for work and one for pleasure.' She smiled at some private memory. They were walking across the mono-blocked drive in front of the house. It was an elongated bungalow on Frogston Road, with views to the snowcapped Pentland Hills to the south.

'He had his men build this double garage,' Mrs Coghill went on. 'They extended the house, too, added a couple of rooms to either side of the original.'

The two CID officers nodded, still unsure why they were headed for the twin garage. There was a door to the side. Mrs Coghill unlocked it and reached in to turn on a light. The large space had been almost completely filled with tea chests, office furniture and tools. There were pickaxes and crowbars, hammers and boxes filled with screws and nails. Industrial drills, a couple of pneumatics, even steel pails splashed with mortar. Mrs Coghill rested her hand on one of the tea chests.

'All the paperwork. There's a filing-cabinet somewhere, too . . .'

'Under that blanket maybe?' Wylie suggested, pointing towards the far corner.

'If you want to know anything about Queensberry House, it'll be here somewhere.'

Wylie and Hood shared a look. Hood puffed out his cheeks.

'Another job for the Time Team,' Ellen Wylie said.

Hood nodded, looked around. 'Any heating in here, Mrs Coghill?'

'I could bring you out an electric fire.'

'Show me where it is,' Hood said, 'I'll fetch it.'

'And something tells me you wouldn't say no to that cup of tea now,' said Mrs Coghill, seeming delighted by the thought of their company.

Siobhan Clarke sat at her desk with 'Supertramp''s effects spread before her. To wit: the contents of his carrier bag, his building society passbook, the briefcase (which its most recent owner hadn't given up without a fight) and the photographs. She also had a pile of crank letters and telephone messages, including three from Gerald Sithing.

It was one of the tabloids who had coined the name Supertramp. They'd also dragged up the sex-on-church-steps story, with an archive photo of Dezzi. Siobhan knew the vultures would be out there, trying to track Dezzi down for an interview, for some juicy morsel. Maybe Dezzi would tell them about the briefcase. It wouldn't be chequebook journalism – she doubted Dezzi had a bank account. Call it cashpoint journalism then. Maybe they'd talk to Rachel Drew, too. She wouldn't say no to a cheque. A few more titbits for the readers and gold-diggers.

And as long as the story ran, the letters and calls would keep coming.

She rose from the desk, pushed at her spine until the vertebrae clicked. It was gone six, and the office was empty. She'd had to move desks – the Grieve murder had taken priority – and was squeezed into a corner of the long, narrow room. No window near by. Mind you, Hood and Wylie had it even worse: no natural light at all in the shoebox they'd been given. The Chief Super had been blunt with her this afternoon: take a few more days, but if there was no ID on Supertramp by then, that was an end of it. The cash went to the Treasury; the suicide, Mackie's whole prehistory, would remain unexplained.

'We've got real work to be getting on with,' her boss had said. He looked like a candidate for a stroke. 'Dossers kill themselves every day.'

'No suspicious circumstances, sir?' she'd dared to ask.

'The money doesn't make for suspicious circumstances, Siobhan. It's a mystery, that's all. Life's full of them.'

'Yes, sir.'

'You've been too close to John Rebus for too long.'

She'd looked up, frowning. 'Meaning?'

'Meaning you're looking for something here that probably doesn't exist.'

'The money exists. He walked into a building society, all of it in cash. Next thing he's living as a down and out.'

'A rich eccentric; money does strange things to some people.'

'He erased his past. It's like he was in hiding.'

'You think the money was stolen? Then why didn't he spend it?'

'That's just one other question, sir.'

A sigh; a scratch of the nose. 'A few more days, Siobhan. All right?'

She'd nodded. 'Yes, sir,' she'd said . . .

'Evening all.'

John Rebus was standing in the doorway.

She glanced at her watch. 'How long have you been there?'

'How long have you been staring at that wall?'

She realised she was halfway down the office, and had been gazing at photos of the Grieve *locus*. 'I was dreaming. What are you doing here?'

214

'Working, same as you.' He came into the office, leaned against one of the desks with his arms folded.

You've been too close to John Rebus for too long.

'How's the Grieve case?' she asked.

He shrugged. 'Shouldn't your first question be "How's Derek?"'

She half-turned from him, cheeks reddening slightly.

'Sorry,' he said. 'That was bad taste, even for me.'

'We just didn't hit it off,' she told him.

'I'm having the selfsame problem.'

She turned to him. 'Is Derek the problem though, or is it you?'

He feigned a pained look, then winked and walked up the central aisle between the rows of desks. 'Is this your man's stuff?' he asked. She followed him back to her desk. She could smell whisky.

'They're calling him Supertramp.'

'Who are?'

'The media.'

He was smiling. She asked him why.

'Supertramp: I saw them in concert once. Usher Hall, I think it was.'

'Before my time.'

'So what's the story with Mr Supertramp anyway?'

'He had all this money he either couldn't spend or didn't want to. He took on a new identity. My theory is that he was hiding.'

'Maybe.' He was rifling through the scraps on the desk. She folded her arms, gave him a hard look which he failed to notice. He opened the bread bag and shook out the contents: disposable razor, a sliver of soap, toothbrush. 'An organised mind,' he said. 'Makes himself a washbag. Doesn't like being dirty.'

'It's like he was acting the part,' she said.

He caught her tone, looked up. 'What is it?' he asked.

215

'Nothing.' She couldn't say the words: *my* case, *my* pitch.

Rebus lifted the arrest photograph. 'What did he do?' She told him and he laughed.

'I've tracked him back as far as 1980. That was when "Chris Mackie" was born.'

'You should talk to Hood and Wylie. They're checking MisPers from '78 and '79.'

'Maybe I'll do that.'

'You sound tired. What if I offered to buy you dinner?'

'And we talk shop all through the meal? Yes, that would be a real break from routine.'

'I happen to have a wide range of conversational topics.'

'Name three.'

'Pubs, progressive rock, and . . .'

'And you're struggling.'

'Scottish history: I've been reading up on it lately.'

'How thrilling. Besides, pubs are where you have conversations; they're not what you talk about.'

'*I* talk about them.'

'That's because you're obsessed.'

He was sorting through her messages. 'Who's G. Sithing?'

She rolled her eyes. 'His first name's Gerald. He came to see me this morning: the first of many, no doubt.'

'He's keen to talk to you.'

'Once was enough.'

'Woodwork creaks and out come the freaks, eh?'

'I've a feeling that's a line from a song.'

'Not a song, a *classic*. So who is he?'

'He runs some bunch of nutters called the Knights of Rosslyn.'

'As in Rosslyn Chapel?'

'The same. He says Supertramp was a member.'

'Sounds unlikely.'

'Oh, I think they knew one another. I just can't see Mackie leaving all that money to Mr Sithing.'

'So who are these Knights of Rosslyn?'

'They think there's something beneath the chapel floor. Come the millennium, up it pops and they're in the vanguard.'

'I was out there the other day.'

'I didn't know you were interested.'

'I'm not. But Lorna Grieve lives out that way.' Rebus had turned his attention to the newspaper which had been in Mackie's carrier. 'Was this folded like this?'

The newspaper looked filthy, as though it had been fished out of a bin. It had been opened to an inside page, and folded into quarters.

'I think so,' she said. 'Yes, it was crumpled like that.'

'Not crumpled, Siobhan. Look what story it's open at.'

She looked: a follow-up article on the 'body in the fireplace'. She took the paper from Rebus and unfolded it. 'Could be one of these other stories.'

'Which one: traffic congestion or the doctor who's prescribing Viagra?'

'Don't forget the advert for New Year in County Kerry.' She gnawed her bottom lip, turned to the paper's front page: the lead was Roddy Grieve's murder. 'Are you seeing something I'm not?' Thinking of the Chief Super's words: *you're looking for something here that probably doesn't exist.*

'Seems to me maybe Supertramp had some interest in Skelly. You should ask the people who knew him.'

Rachel Drew at the hostel; Dezzi, heating burgers by hand-dryer; Gerald Sithing. Siobhan managed not to look thrilled by Rebus's suggestion.

'We've a body in Queensberry House,' Rebus said, 'dates back to late '78 or early '79. A year later, Supertramp is born.' He held up a finger on his right hand. 'Supertramp suddenly decides to top himself, having read in the paper about the find in the fireplace.' He held up a finger on his left hand, touched the two together.

'Careful,' Siobhan said, 'that means something rude in several countries.'

'You don't see a connection?' He sounded disappointed.

'Sorry to play Scully to your Mulder, but couldn't it be that you're seeing connections here because nothing's happening in your own case?'

'Which translated means: get your nose out of my business, Rebus?'

'No, it's just that I . . .' She rubbed at her forehead. 'I only know one thing.'

'What's that?'

'I haven't eaten since breakfast.' She looked at him. 'The dinner offer still stand?'

20

They ate at Pataka's on Causewayside. She asked how his daughter was doing. Sammy was down south, some specialist physiotherapy place. Rebus told her there wasn't much news.

'She'll get over it though?'

Meaning the hit and run which had left Sammy in a wheelchair. Rebus nodded; didn't say anything for fear of tempting fate.

'And how's Patience?'

Rebus helped himself to more tarka dal, though he'd eaten way too much as it was. Siobhan repeated the question.

'Nosy little beggar, aren't you?'

She smiled: Dezzi had said the selfsame thing. 'Sorry, I thought maybe at your age it was just that your hearing was going.'

'Oh, I heard you all right.' He lifted a forkful of ginger murgh, but put it down again untouched.

'Me, too,' Siobhan said. 'I always eat too much in Indian restaurants.'

'I always eat too much all the time.'

'So the pair of you have split up then?' Siobhan hid behind her glass of wine.

'We parted amicably.'

'I'm sorry.'

'How did you want us to part?'

'No, I just . . . the two of you seemed . . .' She looked down at her plate. 'Sorry, I'm talking rubbish here. I only met her four or five times, and here I am pontificating.'

'You don't look much like a pontiff.'

'Bless you for that.' She glanced at her watch. 'Not bad: eighteen minutes without shop talk.'

'Is that a new record?' He finished his beer. 'I notice we haven't been talking much about *your* private life. Seen anything of Brian Holmes?'

She shook her head, made show of looking around the restaurant. Three other couples in the place, and one family of four. Ethnic music kept low enough that it didn't intrude but ensured a conversation stayed private.

'I saw him a couple of times after he left the force. Then we lost touch.' She shrugged.

'Last I heard,' Rebus said, 'he was in Australia; thinking of staying there.' He pushed some of the food around his plate. 'You don't think it's worth asking around about Supertramp and Queensberry House?'

Siobhan mimicked the noise of a buzzer as she checked her watch again. 'Twenty minutes dead. You've let the side down, John.'

'Come on.'

She sat back. 'You're probably right. Thing is, the boss has only given me a couple more days.'

'Well, what other leads have you got?'

'None,' she admitted. 'Just a slew of cranks and gold-diggers to put out of the frame.'

Their waiter materialised and asked if they wanted any more drinks. Rebus looked at Siobhan. 'I'm driving,' he told her. 'You go ahead.'

'In that case I'll have another glass of white.'

'And another pint for me,' Rebus said, handing the waiter his empty glass. Then, to Siobhan: 'It's only my second. My vision doesn't start blurring till four or five.'

'But you were drinking earlier; I could smell it.'

'So much for the extra-strong mints,' Rebus muttered.

'How long till it starts affecting your job.'

His eyes smouldered. '*Et tu*, Siobhan?'

'Just wondering,' she said, not about to apologise for the question.

He shrugged. 'I could stop drinking tomorrow.'

'But you won't.'

'No, I won't. And I won't stop smoking either, or swearing, or cheating at crosswords.'

'You cheat at crosswords?'

'Doesn't everybody?' He watched as one of the couples got up to leave. They left the restaurant hand in hand. 'Funny,' he said.

'What?'

'Lorna Grieve's husband, he has an interest in Rosslyn, too.'

Siobhan snorted. 'Speaking of changing the subject . . .'

'They bought a house in the village,' Rebus went on, 'that's how serious he is.'

'So?'

'He might know your Mr Sithing. He could even be a member of the Knights.'

'So?'

'So you're beginning to sound like a record with the needle stuck.' He stared at her until, suitably chastened, she mouthed the word 'sorry' before taking another glug of wine. 'An interest in Rosslyn connects your Supertramp to my murder case. And Mr Supertramp also might have had an interest in Queensberry House.'

'You're turning three cases into one?'

'I'm just saying there are—'

'Connections, I know. The old six degrees of separation.'

'The old what?'

She looked at him. 'Okay, maybe it was after your time. It's to do with how anyone on the planet is connected to anyone else by only six links.' She paused. 'I think that's right anyway.'

As her second glass of wine arrived, she drained the first.

'It's at least got to be worth talking to Sithing.'

She wrinkled her nose. 'I didn't like him.'

'I'll sit in with you, if you like.'

'You *are* trying to hijack my case.' She smiled to let him know she was joking. But inside, she wasn't so sure.

After their meal, Rebus asked if she fancied a nightcap in Swany's, but she shook her head.

'I wouldn't want to lead you into temptation,' she said.

'I'll give you a lift home then.' Rebus, heading for the Saab, gave a valedictory wave towards the pub's bright lights. Sleet was blowing horizontally down Causeway-side. They got into the car and he started the engine, making sure the heating was on full.

'Did you notice the weather today?' Siobhan asked.

'What about it?'

'Well, it was cold, raining, windy and sunny – all at the same time. It was like four seasons in one.'

'You can't say you don't get your money's worth in Edinburgh. Here, hang on a sec.' He reached over to open the glove compartment, saw Siobhan stiffen her body, thinking he was going to touch her. He smiled, found the tape he was looking for.

'Little treat for you,' he said, pushing the tape home. She'd flinched; she'd thought he was making a move on her. Jesus. She wasn't much older than Sammy.

'What is it?' she asked. He had the idea she was blushing; hard to tell in the semi-dark interior. He handed her the case. '*Crime of the Century*,' she recited.

'Supertramp's finest moment,' he explained.

'You like all this old music, don't you?'

'And that Blue Nile tape you made for me. I might be a dinosaur in many respects, but I'm open-minded about rock.'

They headed for the New Town. Divided city, Rebus was thinking. Divided between the Old Town to the south and the New Town to the north. And divided again between the east end (Hibs FC) and west (Hearts). A city

222

which seemed defined by its past as much as by its present, and only now, with the parliament coming, looking towards the future.

'*Crime of the Century*,' Siobhan repeated. 'Which one, do you think – your dead MSP or my mystery suicide?'

'Don't forget the body in the fireplace. Where's your flat again?'

'Just off Broughton Street.'

As they drove, they watched the buildings and the pedestrians, were aware of other cars drawing level with them at traffic lights. Cop instinct: always on the lookout. Most people just got on with their lives, but a detective's life was made up of other people's lives. The city seemed quiet enough. Not yet late enough for drunks, and the weather was keeping people off the streets.

'You have to worry about the homeless, this time of year,' Siobhan said.

'You should take a look at the cells on the run-up to Christmas. The woolly suits take in as many as they can.'

She looked at him. 'I didn't know that.'

'You've never worked Christmas.'

'They arrest them?'

Rebus shook his head. 'Ask to be locked up. That way there's a hot meal for them right through to New Year. Then we let them out again.'

She leaned back against the headrest. 'God, Christmas.'

'Do I detect a hint of humbug?'

'My parents always want me to go back home.'

'Tell them you're working.'

'That would be dishonest. What are you doing anyway?'

'For Christmas?' He thought about it. 'If they want me for a shift at St Leonard's, I'll probably clock in. It's a good laugh at the station, Christmas Day.'

She looked at him but didn't say anything, until she told him her street was next left. There were no parking spaces outside her building. Rebus drew up alongside a gleaming black 4×4.

'That's not yours, is it?'

'Hardly.'

He peered up at the flats. 'Nice street though.'

'Do you want some coffee?'

He thought it over, remembering the way she'd flinched: did it say something about what she thought of him, or about Siobhan herself? 'Why not?' he said at last.

'There's a parking space further back.'

So Rebus reversed fifty yards and parked kerbside. Her flat was two floors up. No clutter; everything in its place. It was what he'd have expected, and he was pleased he'd been right. Framed prints on the walls, adverts for art exhibitions. A rack of CDs and a decent hi-fi system. Several shelves of videos: comedies mostly, Steve Martin, Billy Crystal. Books: Kerouac, Kesey, Camus. Lots of law texts. There was a functional-looking green two-seat sofa, plus a couple of unmatching chairs. From the window, he looked on to an identical tenement, curtains closed, windows darkened. He wondered if Siobhan wanted her curtains left open.

She'd gone straight into the kitchen to put the kettle on. His tour of the living room complete, he went to find her. Past two bedrooms, doors open. Clatter of mugs and teaspoons. She was opening the fridge as he came in.

'We should talk about Sithing,' Rebus said. 'How best to tackle him.' Siobhan swore. 'What is it?'

'Out of milk,' she said. 'I thought I'd one of those UHT packets in the cupboard.'

'I'll take it black.'

She turned to the worktop. 'Fine.' Opened a storage jar, peered in. 'Except I'm out of coffee, too.'

Rebus laughed. 'Do much entertaining, do you?'

'Just haven't managed a supermarket run this week.'

'No problem. There's a chippie on Broughton Street. Coffee and milk both, if we're lucky.'

'Let me give you some money.' She was looking for her bag.

'My treat,' he said, heading for the door.

When he was gone, Siobhan rested her head against the cupboard door. She'd hidden the coffee right at the back. She just needed a minute or two. It was so seldom she brought people back here, and John Rebus's first visit. A minute or two to herself, that was all she wanted. In the car, when he'd reached towards her . . . what was he going to think about that? She'd thought he was making a move; not that he ever had before, so why had she flinched? Most of the men she worked with, there was innuendo, the occasional blue joke – looking for her to react. But never John Rebus. She knew he was flawed, had problems, but still he'd brought a certain solidity to her life. He was someone she felt she could trust, come hell or high water.

Something she didn't want to lose.

She turned the kitchen light off, walked into the living room, stood at her window and stared out at the night. Then turned and started doing some tidying.

Rebus buttoned up his jacket, glad to be outdoors. Siobhan hadn't been happy about him being there, that was obvious. He'd felt the same way: uncomfortable. Try to keep your work and social life separate. It was hard in the force: you drank together, telling stories outsiders wouldn't understand. The bond went deeper than desk and office, patrol car and local beat.

But tonight, he felt, was different. And after all, he didn't like visitors either; had never encouraged Siobhan or anyone else to visit his home. Maybe she was more like him than he realised. Maybe that was what made her nervous.

He didn't think he was going to go back. Head home, phone and apologise. He unlocked the car, but didn't start the engine straight away: left the keys hanging from the ignition. Lit a cigarette instead. Maybe he'd fetch the milk and coffee, leave them at her door before heading off. That would be the decent thing. But the main door to the building was locked. He'd have to buzz her to be let in. Leave the stuff on the pavement . . . ?

Just go home.

He heard a sudden noise, watched as someone left the tenement opposite Siobhan's. Sort of jogging their way along the pavement, but then taking the first left into an alley, where they stopped. A jet of urine hitting the wall, steam rising into the frosted air. Rebus sitting in darkness, watching. Someone on their way out, caught short? Maybe a blocked toilet at home . . . ? The man was zipping himself up, jogging back the way he'd come. Rebus caught a glimpse of the face as the man passed beneath a street lamp. Back to the tenement, door opening and closing.

Rebus kept smoking his cigarette, a vertical frown-line appearing in the centre of his brow.

He stubbed the cigarette into his ashtray, removed his keys from the ignition. Opened and closed his door quietly, leaving it unlocked. Crossed the street practically on tiptoe, keeping out of the light. A taxi passed by at speed, Rebus hugging the rails in front of the tenement. Reached the main door. This one, unlike Siobhan's, was unlocked. The block looked less cared-for, the stairwell needing a coat of paint. Faint smell of cat piss. Rebus closed the door slowly, another taxi masking any noise. Made his way to the foot of the stairs and listened. He could hear a television playing somewhere, or maybe it was a radio. He looked at the stone steps, knew he couldn't walk up them without making a noise. His shoes would sound like sandpaper on wood, echoing up four storeys. Shoes off? Not a chance. Besides, he wasn't sure an element of surprise was strictly necessary.

He began to climb.

Reached the first-floor landing. Started up to the second.

Now footsteps could be heard coming down. A man with the collar of his raincoat turned up, face all but obscured. Hands deep in pockets. A grunt, but no eye contact as he made to pass Rebus.

'Hello there, Derek.'

Derek Linford was two steps further on before he seemed to realise. He stopped, turned.

'Thought you lived in Dean Village,' Rebus said.

'I was just visiting a friend.'

'Oh aye? Who's that then?'

'Christie, next floor up.' Said too quickly.

'First name?' Rebus asked, smiling a humourless smile.

'What do you want?' Climbing back up one step, not liking the fact that Rebus was standing so far above him. 'What are you doing here?'

'This Christie, got a blocked toilet or what?'

Now Linford realised. He tried to think of something to say.

'Save it,' Rebus advised him. 'We both know what's going on here. You're a peeping Tom.'

'That's a lie.'

Rebus tutted. 'Try a bit more conviction next time.' He paused. 'Otherwise a conviction's just what you're going to get.'

'And what about you, eh?' Sneering. 'A quickie, was it? I notice it didn't take you long.'

'If you'd been noticing anything, you'd have seen me get into my car.' Rebus shook his head. 'How long's this been going on? Don't you think the neighbours will suss eventually? Strange man shuffling up and down the stairs at all hours . . . ?'

Rebus went down a step to meet Linford at eye level.

'Go away now,' he said quietly. 'And don't come back. If you do, first thing I do is tell Siobhan. And after her, your boss at Fettes. They might like pretty boys there, but they don't go big on perverts.'

'It would be your word against mine.'

Rebus shrugged. 'What have I got to lose? You, on the other hand . . .' He let the sentence drift away. 'One more thing: it's my case now. I want you to stay out of the way; do you understand?'

'The brass won't go for it,' Linford scoffed. 'Without me, they'll take it away from you.'

'Will they?'

'Bet on it.' Derek Linford turned and started down the stairs. Rebus watched him leave, then climbed to the next landing. From the window, he could see Siobhan's living room and one of her bedrooms. Her curtains still weren't closed. She was seated on her sofa, chin resting on one hand, staring into space. She looked utterly miserable, and somehow he didn't think coffee was the answer.

He called her from his mobile as he headed home. She didn't sound too upset. Back at his own flat, he collapsed into the chair with a single measure of Bunnahabhain. 'Westering home', it said on the bottle, and they'd quoted from the ballad: *Light in the eye, and it's goodbye to care.* Yes, he'd known malts that could do that. But it was a sham relief. He got up, added a dribble of water to the drink and put some music on the hi-fi: Siobhan's tape of the Blue Nile. There were messages on his answerphone.

Ellen Wylie: progress report, and reminding him he'd said he'd find out about Bryce Callan.

Cammo Grieve: wanting a meeting; suggesting time and place. 'If it's at all convenient, don't bother getting back to me. I'll see you there.'

Bryce Callan was long gone. Rebus checked his watch. He knew someone he could talk to. Wasn't sure it would help, but he'd made the offer to Wylie and Hood. It didn't do to go crapping on the junior officers.

Remembering how he'd just dumped a bucketload on Derek Linford, Rebus grew thoughtful.

Another ten minutes of the Blue Nile – 'Walk Across the Roofops', 'Tinseltown in the Rain' – and he decided it was time to take his own walk. Not across the rooftops, but down to his car. He was heading for the badlands of Gorgie.

Gorgie was the centre of Big Ger Cafferty's operations. Cafferty had been Edinburgh's biggest player until Rebus had put him in Barlinnie Prison. But Cafferty's empire still existed, maybe even flourished, under the control of a man called the Weasel. Rebus knew that the Weasel operated out of a private cab company in Gorgie. The place had been torched a while back, but had risen from the ashes. There was a small front office, with a compound behind. But the Weasel did his business upstairs, in a room few people knew about. It was nearly ten by the time Rebus got there. He parked the car and left it unlocked: this was probably the safest place in the city.

The front office comprised a counter, with chair and telephone behind, and a bench-seat in front. The bench-seat was where you sat if you were waiting for your cab. The man seated behind the counter eyed Rebus as he walked in. He was on the phone, taking details of a morning booking: Tollcross to the airport. Rebus sat on the bench and picked up a copy of the evening paper from the day before. Fake wood panelling surrounded him. The floor was linoleum. The man finished his call.

'Can I help you?' he asked.

He had black hair so badly cut it looked like an ill-fitting wig, and a nose which hadn't so much been broken in the past as thoroughly dismantled. His eyes were narrow, almond-shaped, and his teeth were crooked where they existed at all.

Rebus took a look around. 'Thought the insurance money might have bought better than this.'

'Eh?'

'I mean it's no better than what was here before Tommy Telford torched the place.'

The eyes became little more than slits. 'What do you want?'

'I want to see the Weasel.'

'Who?'

'Look, if he's not upstairs, just say so. But make sure you're not lying, because I get the feeling I'll be able to tell, and I won't be very happy.' He flipped open his warrant card, then stood up and held it towards the security camera in the far corner. A wall-mounted speaker crackled into life.

'Henry, send Mr Rebus up.'

There were two doors at the top of the stairs, but only one was open. It led to a small, neat office. Fax machine and photocopier, one desk with a laptop and surveillance screen on it, and at the second desk the Weasel. He still looked insignificant, but he was the power in this part of Edinburgh until Big Ger came home. Thinning hair greased back from a protruding forehead; a jawline that was all bones; narrow mouth, so that his face seemed to come to a point.

'Take a seat,' the Weasel said.

'I'll stand,' Rebus answered. He made to close the door.

'Leave it open.'

Rebus took his hand off the door handle, thought for a moment – the room was stuffy, mixed body odours – then crossed the narrow landing to the other door. He knocked three times. 'All right in there, lads?' Pushed the door open. Three of the Weasel's men were standing just inside. 'This won't take long,' he told them, closing the door again. Then he closed the Weasel's door, too, so that it was just the two of them.

Now he sat down. Spotted the carrier bags by one wall, whisky bottles peeping out.

'Sorry to spoil the party,' he said.

'What can I do for you, Rebus?' The Weasel's hands were resting on the arms of his chair, as though he might be about to spring to his feet.

'Were you here in the late seventies? I know your boss was. But he was small beer then: playing a few little games, bedding himself in. Were you with him that far back?'

'What do you want to know?'

'I thought I'd just told you. Bryce Callan was running things then. Don't tell me you didn't know Bryce?'

'I know the name.'

'Cafferty was his muscle for a while.' Rebus cocked his head. 'Any of this jarring your memory? See, I thought I could ask you, save a trip to the Bar-L and me wasting your boss's time.'

'Ask me what?' The hands came off the chair arms. He was relaxing, now that he knew Rebus's subject was ancient history rather than current affairs. But Rebus knew that one false move on his part and the Weasel would squeal, bringing his minders charging in and ensuring Rebus a visit to A&E at the very least.

'I want to know about Bryce Callan. Did he have a spot of bother with a builder called Dean Coghill?'

'Dean Coghill?' The Weasel frowned. 'Never heard of him.'

'Sure?'

The Weasel nodded.

'I heard Callan had been giving him grief.'

'This was twenty years ago?' The Weasel waited till Rebus nodded. 'Then what the hell's it got to do with me? Why should I tell you anything?'

'Because you like me?'

The Weasel snorted. But now his face changed. Rebus turned to look at the monitor, but too late; he'd missed whatever the Weasel had seen. Heavy footsteps, taking the stairs with effort. The door swung open. The Weasel was on his feet, moving from behind the desk. And Rebus was on his feet, too.

'Strawman!' The voice booming. Big Ger Cafferty filled the doorway. He was wearing a blue silk suit, crisp white shirt open a couple of buttons at the neck. 'Just to make my day complete.'

Rebus just stood there, speechless for maybe the second or third time in his life. Cafferty entered the room, so that it suddenly became crowded. He brushed past Rebus, moving with the slow agility of a predator. His skin was as pale and creased as a white rhino's, his hair silver. His bullet-shaped head seemed to disappear into the neck of his shirt as he leaned down, his back to Rebus. When he straightened, he was holding one of the whisky bottles.

'Come on,' he told Rebus, 'you and me are going for a wee ride.' Then he gripped Rebus's arm and steered him to the door.

And Rebus, still numb, did what he was told.

Strawman: Cafferty's nickname for Rebus.

The car was a black 7-Series BMW. Driver in the front, and someone equally large in the passenger seat, which left Rebus and Cafferty in the back.

'Where are we going?'

'Don't panic, Strawman.' Cafferty took a slug of whisky, passed the bottle over, and exhaled noisily. The windows were down a fraction, and cold air slapped at Rebus's ears. 'Bit of a mystery tour, that's all.' Cafferty gazed from his window. 'I've been away a while. I hear the place has changed. Morrison Street and the Western Approach Road,' he told the driver, 'then maybe Holyrood and down to Leith.' He turned to his passenger. 'Regeneration: music to my ears.'

'Don't forget the new museum.'

Cafferty stared at him. 'Why would I be interested in that?' He held out his hand for the bottle. Rebus took a swig and passed it across.

'I get the horrible feeling your being here is legit,' Rebus said at last.

Cafferty just winked.

'How did you swing it?'

'To be honest with you, Strawman, I think the governor didn't like it that I was running the show. I mean, that's what *he's* paid to do, and his own officers were giving Big Ger more respect than they gave him.' He laughed. 'The governor decided I'd be less of a grievance out here.'

Rebus looked at him. 'I don't think so,' he said.

'Well, maybe you're right. I dare say good behaviour and the inoperable cancer swung it for me.' He looked at Rebus. 'You still don't believe me?'

'I want to.'

Cafferty laughed again. 'Knew I could depend on you for sympathy.' He tapped the magazine pouch in front of him. 'The big brown envelope,' he said. 'My X-rays from the hospital.'

Rebus reached across, pulled them out, held them up one at a time to his window.

'The darkish area's the one you're looking for.'

But what he was looking for was Cafferty's name. He found it at the bottom corner of each of the X-rays. Morris Gerald Cafferty. Rebus slid the sheets back into the envelope. It all looked official enough: hospital in Glasgow; radiology department. He handed the envelope to Cafferty.

'I'm sorry,' he said.

Cafferty chuckled quietly, then slapped the front-seat passenger on the shoulder. 'It's not often you'll hear that, Rab: an apology from the Strawman!'

Rab half-turned. Curly black hair with long sideburns.

'Rab got out the week before me,' Cafferty said. 'Best pals inside, we were.' He grabbed Rab's shoulder again. 'One minute you're in the Bar-L, the next you're in a Beamer. Said I'd look after you, didn't I?' Cafferty winked at Rebus. 'Saw me through a few scrapes did Rab.' He rested against the back of his seat, took another gulp of whisky. 'City's certainly changed, Strawman.' His eyes fixed on the passing scene. 'Lots of things have changed.'

'But not you?'

'Prison changes a man, surely you've heard that? In my case, it brought on the big C.' He snorted.

'How long do they say . . . ?'

'Now don't you go getting all maudlin on me. Here.' He passed over the bottle, then pushed the X-rays back into the seat pocket. 'We're going to forget all about these. It's good to be out, and I don't care what got me here. I'm here, and that's that.' He went back to his window-gazing. 'I hear tell there's building work going on all over.'

'See for yourself.'

'I intend to.' He paused. 'You know, it's very nice, just the two of us here, sharing a drink and catching up on old times . . . but what the hell were you doing in my office in the first place?'

'I was asking the Weasel about Bryce Callan.'

'Now there's a name from the crypt.'

'Not quite: he's out in Spain, isn't he?'

'Is he?'

'I must have misheard. I thought you still passed a little percentage on to him.'

'And why would I do that? He's got family, hasn't he? Let them look after him.' Cafferty shifted in his seat, as though made physically uncomfortable by the mere mention of Bryce Callan.

'I don't want to spoil the party,' Rebus said.

'Good.'

'So if you'll tell me what I want to know, we can drop the subject.'

'Christ, man, were you always this irritating?'

'I've been taking lessons while you were away.'

'Your teacher deserves a fucking bonus. Well, if you've a bone stuck in your craw, spit it out.'

'A builder called Dean Coghill.'

Cafferty nodded. 'I knew the man.'

'A body turned up in a fireplace at Queensberry House.'

'The old hospital?'

'They're turning it into part of the parliament.' Rebus

was watching Cafferty carefully. His body felt tired, but his mind was fizzing, still getting over the shock. 'This body had been there twenty-odd years. Turns out there was building work going on in '78 and '79.'

'And Coghill's firm was involved?' Cafferty was nodding. 'Fair play, I can see what you're on about. But what's it got to do with Bryce Callan?'

'It's just that I hear Callan and Coghill might have crossed swords.'

'If they had, Coghill would have gone home minus a couple of hands. Why don't you ask Coghill himself?'

'He's dead.' Cafferty looked round. 'Natural causes,' Rebus assured him.

'People come and go, Strawman. But you're always trying to dig up the corpses. One foot in the past and one in the grave.'

'I can promise you one thing, Cafferty.'

'And what's that?'

'When they bury you, I won't come round after with a shovel. Yours is one corpse I'll be happy to leave rotting.'

Rab turned his head slowly, fixing soulless eyes on Rebus.

'Now you've upset him, Strawman.' Cafferty patted his henchman's shoulder. 'And I know I should take offence myself.' His eyes bored into Rebus's. 'Maybe another time, eh?' He leaned forward. 'Pull over!' he barked. The driver brought them to an immediate skidding halt.

Rebus didn't need to be told. He opened his door, found himself on West Port. The car sped off again, acceleration pulling the door shut. Headed for the Grassmarket . . . and Holyrood after that. Cafferty had said he wanted to see Holyrood, centre of the changing city. Rebus rubbed at his eyes. Cafferty, re-entering his life now of all times. He reminded himself that he didn't believe in coincidence. He lit a cigarette and started in the direction of Lauriston Place. He could cut through the Meadows and be home in fifteen minutes.

But his car was back in Gorgie. Hell, it could stay there till tomorrow; best of British to whoever wanted to steal it.

When he reached Arden Street, however, there it was, waiting for him, double parked and with a note asking him to shift it so the note's author could move his own blocked car. Rebus tried the driver's door. It wasn't locked. No keys: they were in his coat pocket.

Cafferty's men had done it.

They'd done it simply to show that they could.

He headed upstairs, poured himself a malt and sat on the edge of his bed. He'd checked his phone: no messages. Lorna hadn't tried to get in touch. He felt relief, tinged with disappointment. He stared at the bedclothes. Bits and pieces kept coming back to him, making no particular order. And now his nemesis was back in town, ready to reclaim its streets as his own. Rebus went back to his door and put the chain on. He was halfway down the hall when he stopped.

'What are you doing, man?'

He walked back, slid the chain off again. Cafferty would have no intention of going quietly. Doubtless there were scores to be settled. Rebus didn't doubt that he was one of them, which was fine by him.

When Cafferty came, Rebus would be waiting . . .

21

'It'd be easier with the door open,' Ellen Wylie said. She meant that they'd have more room to move, and more light to work by.

'We'd freeze,' Grant Hood reminded her. 'I've lost all feeling in my fingers as it is.'

They were inside the garage at the Coghill house. Another grey winter's morning, bringing chill gusts which shook the metal up-and-over door. The ceiling light was dusty and dim, and only one small frosted window gave any natural light. Wylie held a pocket torch between her teeth as she searched. Hood had brought a plug-in lamp with him, the kind mechanics used in their work bays. But its light was too piercing, and it was awkward to manoeuvre. It sat clipped to a shelf, doing its best to throw shadows over most of the interior.

Wylie thought she'd come prepared: not just the torch, but flasks of hot soup and tea. She was wearing two pairs of wool socks under a pair of walking boots. Her chin was tucked into a scarf. The hood of her olive-green duffel coat was covering her head. Her ears were cold. Her knees were cold. The one-bar electric heater worked to a radius of about six inches.

'We'd get done a lot quicker with the door open,' she argued.

'Can't you hear the wind? Everything would be blown halfway to the Pentlands.'

Mrs Coghill had brought them out a pot of coffee and some biscuits. She seemed worried about them. Loo-breaks came as their only relief. Stepping into the

237

centrally heated house, there was a strong temptation to stay put. Grant had commented on the length of Ellen's last trip to the house. She'd snapped back that she didn't know she was being timed.

Then they'd drifted into this argument about the garage door.

'Anything?' he said now, for about the twentieth time.

'You'll be the first to know,' she replied through gritted teeth. It was no good just ignoring his question: he'd go on asking, same as last time.

'This stuff's all way too recent,' he complained, slapping a pile of paperwork down on to one of the tea chests. Unbalanced, the papers cascaded to the floor.

'Well, that's one way to organise a search,' Wylie muttered. If they put the stuff outside when they'd finished with it, they'd have room to work in, and they'd know which files had been checked . . . And it would all blow away.

'I'm no expert,' Wylie said at last, stopping to pour out some tea from the flask, 'but Coghill's business affairs look pretty disorganised, if this lot's anything to go by.'

'He got in trouble over his VAT returns,' Hood commented.

'And all the casual labour he employed.'

'Doesn't make our job any easier.' Hood came over, accepted a cup from her with a nod of thanks. There was a knock, and someone came in.

'Any left in that?' Rebus asked, nodding towards the flask.

'Half a cup,' Wylie said. Rebus looked at the coffee cups, lifted the cleanest one and held it out while she poured.

'How's it going?' he asked.

Hood made a point of closing the door. 'You mean apart from the wind-chill factor?'

'Cold's healthy,' Rebus said. 'Good for you.' He'd moved to within six inches of the heater.

'It's slow going,' Wylie said. 'Coghill's biggest problem

was he was a one-man band. Tried to run the whole business himself.'

'Now if only he'd employed a nice personnel manager . . .'

Wylie finished the thought: 'We might have what we're looking for by now.'

'Maybe he chucked stuff out,' Rebus said. 'How far back have you found records for?'

'He didn't throw *anything* out, sir: that's the real problem here. He kept every scrap of paper.' She waved a letter at him. It was on paper headed Coghill Builders. He took it from her. The estimate for construction of a one-car garage at an address in Joppa. The estimate was in pounds, shillings and pence. The date was July 1969.

'We're looking for one year out of thirty,' Wylie said. She drained the tea, screwed the cup back on to the Thermos. 'A needle in a bloody haystack.'

Rebus drained his cup. 'Well, sooner I let you get back to it . . .' He checked his watch.

'If you're at a loose end, sir, we can always use another pair of hands.'

Rebus looked at Wylie. She wasn't smiling. 'Another appointment,' he told her. 'Just thought I'd drop by.'

'Much appreciated, sir,' Hood said, catching something of his partner's tone. They went back to work, watched Rebus leave.

Wylie heard an engine start, and flung down her sheaf of papers. 'Do you believe that? Swans in, finishes off the tea, and swans out again. And if we'd found anything, he'd have been off back to the station with it to bag the glory.'

Hood was staring at the door. 'Think so?'

She looked at him. 'Don't you?'

He shrugged. 'Not his style,' he said.

'Then why did he come?'

Hood was still looking at the door. 'Because he can't let go.'

'Another way of saying he doesn't trust us.'

Hood was shaking his head. He picked up another box-file. 'Seventy-one,' he said, looking at it. 'Year I was born.'

'I hope you don't mind the choice of meeting place,' Cammo Grieve said, picking his way over lengths of scaffolding which had either just come down or were just going up.

'No problem,' Rebus said.

'Only I wanted the excuse for a poke around here.'

Here being the temporary home of the Scottish Parliament in the General Assembly building at the top of The Mound. The builders were hard at work. Black metal lighting gantreys had already appeared amidst the wooden ceiling beams. Gyproc walls were being cut to shape, their skeletal wooden frames standing ready to receive them. A new floor was being laid on top of the existing one. It rose amphitheatre-style in a graduated semicircle. The desks and chairs hadn't arrived yet. In the courtyard outside, the statue of John Knox had been boxed in – some said for safekeeping, some so that he could not show his disgust at the renovations to the Church of Scotland's supreme court.

'I hear Glasgow had a building ready and waiting to accommodate the parliament,' Grieve said. He tutted, smiling. 'As if Edinburgh would let them get away with that. All the same . . .' He looked around. 'Shame they couldn't just wait for the permanent site to be ready.'

'We can't wait that long, apparently,' Rebus said.

'Only because Dewar has a bee in his bonnet. Look at the way he banjaxed Calton Hill as a site, all because he worried it was a "Nationalist symbol". Bloody man's an eejit.'

'I'd have preferred Leith myself,' Rebus said.

Grieve looked interested. 'Why's that then?'

'Traffic's bad enough in the city as it is. Besides,' Rebus

went on, 'it would have saved the working girls having to tramp all the way to Holyrood to ply their trade.'

Cammo Grieve's laughter seemed to fill the hall. Around them, carpenters were sawing and hammering. Someone had plugged a radio in. Tinny pop tunes, a couple of the workmen whistling along. Someone hit his thumb with a hammer. His blasphemies echoed off the walls.

Cammo Grieve glanced towards Rebus. 'You don't have a very high opinion of my calling, do you, Inspector?'

'Oh, I think politicians have their uses.'

Grieve laughed again. 'Something tells me I better not ask what those uses might be.'

'You're learning, Mr Grieve.'

They walked on. Rebus, remembering snippets of information from his PPLC tours of the site, kept up a commentary for the English-based MP.

'So this will just be the debating hall?' Grieve said.

'That's right. There are six other buildings, most of them council-owned. Corporate services in one, MSPs and their staff in another. I forget the rest.'

'Committee rooms?'

Rebus nodded. 'Other side of George IV Bridge from the MSP offices. There's a tunnel connecting the two.'

'A tunnel?'

'Saves them crossing the road. We wouldn't want accidents.'

Grieve smiled. Rebus, despite himself, was warming to the man.

'There'll be a media centre, too,' Grieve suggested.

Rebus nodded. 'On the Lawnmarket.'

'Bloody media.'

'Are they still camping outside your mother's house?'

'Yes. Every time I visit, I have to field the same questions.' He looked at Rebus; all the humour had leaked from his features, leaving them pale and tired.

'Have you still no idea who killed Roddy?'

'You know what I'll say, sir.'

'Oh yes: inquiries are proceeding . . . all that guff.'

'It might be guff, but it's also true.'

Cammo Grieve plunged his hands deep into the pockets of his black Crombie-style coat. He looked old and somehow unfulfilled; shared something of Hugh Cordover's solemn disenchantment with life. As crisply dressed as he was, his skin and shoulders were slack. The mandatory white hard hat bothered him; he kept trying to make it fit properly. Rebus had the impression of an ill-fitting life.

They had climbed the stairs to the gallery. Grieve dusted off one of the benches and sat down, arranging his coat around him. Below, in the middle of the amphitheatre, two men were studying plans and pointing in different directions with their fingers.

'A portent?' Grieve asked.

The plan was spread out on a workbench, weighted each end with coffee mugs.

'What can you smell?' Rebus asked, settling himself next to the MP.

Grieve sniffed the air. 'Sawdust.'

'One man's sawdust is another's new wood. That's what I smell.'

'Where I see portents, you see a fresh start?' Grieve looked appraisingly at Rebus, who just shrugged. 'Point taken. Sometimes it's too easy to read meanings into things.' Coils of electric cable sat near them. Grieve rested his feet on one, as though on a footstool. He took off the hard hat and laid it beside him, smoothing his hair back into place.

'We can start any time you're ready,' Rebus said.

'Start what?'

'There's something you want to tell me.'

'Is there? What makes you so sure?'

'If you brought me here as a tour guide, I'll be less than chuffed.'

'Well, yes, there was something, only now I'm not so sure it's relevant.' Grieve stared up at the glass windows in the roof. 'I was getting these letters. I mean, MPs get all sorts of cranks writing to them, so I wasn't too bothered. But I did mention them to Roddy. I suppose I was warning him what he was getting into. As an MSP, he'd probably have to put up with the selfsame thing.'

'He hadn't been getting any then?'

'Well, he didn't *say* he had. But there was something ... When I told him, I got the feeling he already knew about them.'

'What did these letters say?'

'The ones to me? Just that I'd die for being a Tory bastard. There'd be razor blades enclosed, presumably in case I ever felt suicidal.'

'Anonymous, of course?'

'Of course. Various postmarks. Whoever he is, he travels.'

'What did the police say?'

'I didn't tell them.'

'So who knows about them, apart from your brother?'

'My secretary. She opens all my mail.'

'You still have them?'

'No, they were binned the same day. Thing is, I contacted my office, and none have been received since Roddy's death.'

'Respect for the bereaved?'

Cammo Grieve looked sceptical. 'I'd've thought the bastard would want to gloat.'

'I know what you're thinking,' Rebus said. 'You're wondering if the letter writer has something against the whole family, maybe got at Roddy because he or she couldn't get at you.'

'It has to be he surely?'

'Not necessarily.' Rebus was thoughtful. 'If any more letters arrive, let me know. And hang on to them this time.'

'Understood.' He got to his feet. 'I'm off down to London

243

again this afternoon. If you need me, you have the office number.'

'Yes, thanks.' Rebus showed no sign of moving.

'Well, goodbye then, Inspector. And good luck.'

'Goodbye, Mr Grieve. Mind how you go.'

Cammo Grieve stopped for a moment, but then carried on down the stairs. Rebus sat, staring into space, letting the sounds of hammer and saw wash over him.

Back at St Leonard's, he made a couple of phone calls. As he sat at his desk with the receiver at his ear, he sorted through the various messages left for him. Linford communicated only by notes now, and the latest said he was out interviewing people who'd been walking along Holyrood Road on the night of the murder. Hi-Ho Silvers, in his dogged way, had now identified four pubs where Roddy Grieve had been drinking – all alone – on the night he was killed. Two were in the West End, one was in Lawnmarket, and the last was the Holyrood Tavern. There was now a list of Tavern regulars, and these were the men and women Linford was canvassing. Almost certainly a waste of time, but then what was Rebus doing that was so crucial, so wonderful? Following-up hunches.

'Is that Mr Grieve's secretary?' he asked into the mouthpiece. He went on to ask her about the hate mail. From her voice, he had an impression of youth – mid-twenties to early thirties. From what she said, he pictured her as faithful to her boss. But her story didn't sound rehearsed; no reason to think that it was.

Just a hunch.

Next, he spoke to Seona Grieve. He caught her on her mobile. She sounded flustered, and he said as much.

'Not much time to put a campaign together,' she said. 'And my school's not too happy about it. They thought I was taking a bit of time off for bereavement, and now I'm telling them I might not be back ever.'

'If you get elected.'

'Well, yes, there is just that one tiny hurdle.'

She'd mentioned the word bereavement, but she didn't sound recently bereaved. No time to mourn. Maybe it was a good thing, take her mind off the murder. Linford had wondered if Seona Grieve had a motive: kill her husband, step into his shoes, fast-track to parliament. Rebus couldn't see it.

But then right now he couldn't see very much.

'So if this isn't just a social call, Inspector . . . ?'

'Sorry, yes. I was just wondering if your husband ever received any crank letters.'

There was silence for a moment. 'No, not that I'm aware of.'

'Did he tell you that his brother had been receiving them?'

'Really? No, Roddy never mentioned it. Did Cammo tell him?'

'Apparently.'

'Well, it's news to me. Don't you think I might have mentioned it to you before now?'

'You might.'

She was irritated now, sensing that something was being insinuated, but not sure what. 'If there's nothing else, Inspector . . . ?'

'No, just you carry on, Mrs Grieve. Sorry to have bothered you.' He wasn't, of course, and didn't sound it.

She caught the hint. 'Look, I do appreciate what you're doing, all the trouble you're taking.' Suddenly it was a politician's voice, high on effects and low on sincerity. 'And of course you should phone me whenever there's something – anything – that you think I can help with.'

'That's very kind of you, Mrs Grieve.'

She made an effort to ignore the irony in his voice. 'Now, if you've no more questions at this point . . . ?'

Rebus didn't say anything; just put the phone down.

In the office next door, he found Siobhan. She had her

receiver tucked between chin and shoulder while she wrote something down.

'Thank you,' she said. 'I really do appreciate it. I'll see you then.' She glanced up at Rebus. 'And I'll have a colleague with me, if that's all right.' She listened. 'All right, Mr Sithing. Goodbye.'

The receiver fell from her shoulder, clattered home. Rebus looked at the apparatus.

'That's a good trick,' he said.

'It's taken a while to perfect. Tell me it's lunchtime.'

'And I'm buying.' She got her jacket from the back of the chair and slid her arms into it. 'Sithing?' he asked.

'Later this afternoon, if that suits you.' He nodded. 'He's out at the chapel. I said we'd meet him there.'

'How much grovelling did he make you do?'

She smiled, remembering how she'd practically dragged Sithing out of St Leonard's. 'Plenty,' she said. 'But I've got one hell of a carrot.'

'The four hundred thou?'

She nodded. 'So where are you taking me?'

'Well, there's this delightful little place up in Fife . . .'

She smiled. 'Or the canteen does filled rolls.'

'It's a tough choice, but then life's full of them.'

'Fife's too far a drive anyway. Maybe next time.'

'Next time it is,' Rebus said.

They sat at the table in Mrs Coghill's kitchen. Starter was the flask of soup, but for the main course Mrs Coghill had prepared macaroni cheese. They'd been about to demur politely until she'd lifted it from the oven, bubbling and with a crisp golden crust of breadcrumbs.

'Well, maybe just a smidge.'

Having served them, she left them to it, saying she'd already eaten. 'I don't have much of an appetite these days, but a young pair like you . . .' She'd nodded towards the dish. 'I'll expect that to be empty next time I see it.'

Grant Hood leaned his chair back on two legs and

stretched his arms. He'd managed two helpings. There was plenty still left.

Ellen Wylie lifted the serving spoon, gesturing with it towards him.

'God, no,' he said. 'It's all yours.'

'I couldn't,' she said. 'In fact, I'm not sure I can stand up, so it better be you that makes the coffee.'

'Hint taken.' He poured water into the kettle. Outside the window, the sky had darkened. The kitchen lights were on. Leaves and crisp packets were flying past. 'Hellish day,' he commented.

Wylie wasn't listening. She'd opened the black box-file, the one she'd found just before lunch. Business transactions from 6 April 1978 to 5 April 1979. Dean Coghill's tax year. She took out half the documents, slid them across the table. The rest she kept for herself. Hood cleared the plates into the sink, placing the casserole back in the oven. Then he sat down and, waiting for the kettle to boil, picked up the first sheet of paper.

Half an hour later, they got their break. A list of personnel signed up to work at Queensberry House. Eight names. Wylie jotted them into her notebook.

'All we need to do now is track them down and talk to each of them.'

'You make it sound so easy.'

Wylie slid the list towards him. 'Some of them are bound to be still in the building trade.'

Hood read the names. The first seven were typed, the eighth added in pencil. 'Does that say Hutton?' he asked.

'The last one?' Wylie checked her notebook. 'Hutton or Hatton, first name's either Benny or Barry.'

'So we talk to every building firm in Edinburgh? Try out these names on them?'

'It's either that or the phone book.'

The kettle clicked off. Hood went to see if Mrs Coghill wanted a cup. He came back with a copy of Yellow Pages, opened it at the section headed 'Builders'.

'Read the names off to me,' he said. 'We might strike lucky.'

The third name they tried, Hood said, 'Bingo,' his finger stabbing at a display ad. The name on the sheet was John Hicks, and he'd just found J. Hicks. ' "Extensions, Renovations, Conversions",' he recited. 'Got to be worth a call.'

So Wylie got on her mobile, and they celebrated with coffee.

John Hicks' business premises were in Bruntsfield, and the man himself was working on a job in Glengyle Terrace, just off The Links. It was a garden flat, and he was busy converting the large back bedroom into two smaller units.

'Ups the rental income,' he explained. 'Some people don't seem to mind living in a rabbit hutch.'

'Or haven't got the money for anything else.'

'True enough, love.' Hicks was in his late fifties, small and wiry with a tanned dome of a head and thick black eyebrows. His eyes twinkled with humour. 'Way things are in Edinburgh,' he said, 'there won't be a decent building left that hasn't been subdivided.'

'Good for business,' Hood said.

'Oh, I'm not complaining.' He winked at them. 'You said on the phone it was to do with Dean Coghill?'

Somewhere in the flat, a door banged.

'Students,' Hicks explained. 'It pisses them off I'm here at eight, and hammering till four or five.' He picked up his hammer and thumped it a couple of times against a length of two-by-four. Wylie held out the list towards him. He peered at it, took it from her and whistled.

'Now this takes me back,' he said.

'We need to know about the others.'

He looked up. 'Why?'

'Did you read about the body found in Queensberry House?' Hicks nodded. 'It was put there late '78, early '79.'

248

Hicks nodded again. 'While we were working there. You think one of us . . . ?'

'We're just following a line of inquiry, sir. Do you remember the fireplace being open?'

'Oh, yes. We were supposed to be putting in a damp-proof course. Pulled the wall open and there it was.'

'When was it closed up again?'

Hicks shrugged. 'I don't remember. Before we finished the job, but I don't actually recall it happening.'

'Who closed it up?'

'No idea.'

'Can you tell us anything about the other men on this list?'

He looked at it again. 'Well, Bert and Terry, the three of us worked together on a lot of jobs. Eddie and Tam were part-timers, cash in hand. Let's see . . . Harry Connors, he was a bit older, worked with Dean for donkey's. Died a couple of years later. Dod McCarthy moved to Australia.'

'Nobody walked off the job?' Wylie asked.

He shook his head. 'No, we were all present and accounted for at job's end, if that's what you're getting at.' Wylie and Hood shared a look: another theory blown out the water.

Hicks was still studying the list.

'There's one name you haven't mentioned yet,' Hood reminded him.

'Benny Hatton,' Wylie added.

'Barry Hutton,' Hicks corrected her. 'Well, Barry was just with us for a couple of jobs. Bit of a favour to his uncle, or something.'

'But there's something about him?'

'No, not really. It's just, you know . . .'

'What, sir?'

'Well, Barry's made it big, hasn't he? Out of all of us, he's the one who's got to the top.'

Wylie and Hood looked blank.

'You don't know him?' Hicks seemed surprised. 'Hutton Developments.'

Wylie's eyes widened. 'That's *this* Barry Hutton?' She looked to Hood. 'He's a land developer,' she explained.

'One of the biggest,' Hicks added. 'You can never tell with people, eh? When I knew Barry, well, he was nothing really.'

'Mr Hicks,' Hood said, 'you were saying something about his uncle?'

'Well, Barry didn't have much experience in the building game. Seemed to me his uncle must have put a word in with Dean, give the boy a bit of a start.'

'His uncle being . . . ?'

Hicks looked at them again; he couldn't believe they didn't know this either.

'Bryce Callan,' he explained, whacking his hammer against the two-by-four again. 'Barry belongs to Bryce's sister. Friends in high places, eh? No wonder the kid's got where he has.'

22

Rebus took the call on his mobile as Siobhan drove them out to Roslin. When he'd finished, he half-turned in his seat.

'That was Grant Hood. The body in the fireplace; one of the labourers working there at the time was Bryce Callan's nephew. His name's—'

'Barry Hutton,' she interrupted.

'You've heard of him?'

'He's in his thirties, single and a millionaire; of course I've heard of him. I was out with a singles group one night.' She glanced at him. 'Working, I might add. But a couple of the women were talking about eligible bachelors. There was some magazine piece on him. Good-looking, by all accounts.' She looked at Rebus again. 'But he's legit, isn't he? I mean, he runs his own business, nothing to do with his uncle.'

'No.' But Rebus was thoughtful all the same. What was it Cafferty had said about Bryce Callan? *Let his family look after him*, something like that.

As they drove into Roslin and approached Rosslyn Chapel, Siobhan asked why they had different spellings.

'Just another of the chapel's unfathomable mysteries,' Rebus told her. 'Probably with some conspiracy at the bottom of it all.'

'I wanted you to see it,' Gerald Sithing said as he met them in the car park. He was wearing a knee-length blue plastic mac over a tweed jacket and baggy brown cords. The mac made swishing sounds as he moved. He shook Rebus's hand, but kept his distance from Siobhan.

The chapel's exterior didn't look promising, covered as it was by a corrugated structure.

'That's only until the walls dry out,' Sithing explained. 'Then the repairs can be done.'

He led them inside. Prepared as she was, Siobhan Clarke still gave an audible gasp. The interior was as ornate as any cathedral's, its scale serving to heighten the effect of the stonework. The vaulted ceiling boasted carvings of different kinds of flowers. There were intricate pillars and stained-glass windows. The place was chilled, its doors standing open. Green discoloration on the ceiling showed there was a problem with damp.

Rebus stood in the centre aisle and tapped his foot on the stone floor. 'This is where the spaceship is, eh? Under here.'

Sithing wagged a finger, too excited by his surroundings to be annoyed. 'The Ark of the Covenant, the body of Christ . . . yes, I know all the stories. But there are Templar artefacts everywhere you look. Shields and inscriptions . . . some of the carvings. The tomb of William St Clair; he died in Spain in the fourteenth century. He was transporting Robert the Bruce's heart to the Holy Land.'

'Wouldn't it have been easier posting it? Might have got there by now.'

'The Templars', Sithing said patiently, 'were the military wing of the Prieuré de Sion, whose purpose was to find the treasure from the Temple of Solomon.'

'Hence the name?' Siobhan guessed. 'There's a village called Temple near here, isn't there?'

'With a ruined Templar church,' Sithing added quickly. 'Some say that Rosslyn Chapel is a replica of the Temple of Solomon. The Templars came to Scotland to escape persecution in the fourteenth century.'

'When was it built?' Siobhan couldn't take her eyes off the treasures around her.

'Fourteen forty-six, that's when the foundations were laid. It took forty years to complete.'

'Sounds like some builders I know,' Rebus said.

'Can't you feel it?' Sithing was staring at Rebus. 'Right at the core of your cynical heart, can't you feel *something*?'

'It's just indigestion, thanks for asking.' Rebus rubbed his chest. Sithing turned to Siobhan. 'But you can feel it, I know you can.'

'It's an amazing place, I'll grant you that.'

'You could spend a lifetime studying it, and still you wouldn't have learned half its secrets.'

'Who's this ugly mug?' Siobhan pointed to a gargoyle's head.

'That's the Green Man.'

She turned to him. 'Isn't he a pagan symbol?'

'That's the whole point!' Sithing yelped excitedly. He bounded over to her. 'The chapel is almost pantheistic. Not just Christianity, but all belief systems.'

Siobhan nodded.

Rebus shook his head. 'Earth to DC Clarke. Earth to DC Clarke.'

She made a face at him.

'And those carvings on the roof,' Sithing was saying, 'plants from the New World.' He paused for effect. 'Carved a century before Columbus landed in America!'

'Fascinating as this all is, sir,' Rebus said tiredly, 'it isn't why we're here.'

Siobhan pulled her gaze away from the Green Man. 'That's right, Mr Sithing. I told your story to Inspector Rebus, and he felt we should talk.'

'About Chris Mackie?'

'Yes.'

'So you accept I knew him?' He waited till Siobhan nodded. 'And you accept he'd have wanted the Knights to have some sort of financial consideration from his estate?'

'That's not really for us to decide, Mr Sithing,' Rebus said. 'It'll be a case for the lawyers.' He paused. 'But we can always put in a friendly word.' He ignored Siobhan's look, nodded slowly so that Gerald Sithing wouldn't mistake the implication.

'I see,' Sithing said. He sat down on one of the chairs laid out for the congregation. 'What is it you want to know?' he asked quietly. Rebus sat on a chair across the aisle.

'Did Mr Mackie seem at all interested in the Grieve family?'

For a moment, Sithing didn't seem to have understood the question, then he asked, 'How did you know?' And Rebus knew they'd struck gold.

'Is Hugh Cordover a member of your group?'

'Yes,' Sithing said, his eyes widening, as though in the presence of a magus.

'Did Chris Mackie ever come here?'

Sithing shook his head. 'I asked him many times, but he always said no.'

'Didn't that seem strange? I mean, you say he was interested in Rosslyn.'

'I assumed he disliked travelling.'

'So you met him in The Meadows, and talked about . . . ?'

'Lots of things.'

'Among them, the Grieve family?'

Siobhan, aware that she was being excluded, sat herself in the row in front of Sithing, half-facing him.

'Who brought up the Grieves first?' she asked.

Sithing said he wasn't sure.

'My guess is', Rebus said, 'you were telling him about the Knights, and you mentioned Hugh Cordover.'

'Maybe,' Sithing admitted. Then he looked up. 'Actually, that's just how it happened!' His gaze went to Rebus again: magus status confirmed.

Siobhan, even though it was her case, decided to keep quiet. Rebus quite clearly had Gerald Sithing in a kind of trance.

'You mentioned Cordover,' Rebus stated, 'and Mackie wanted to know more?'

'He'd been a fan of the band, said he knew their music. I think he even hummed me one of their songs, not that I was familiar with it. He asked a few questions, I answered where I could.'

'And thereafter, when you met . . . ?'

'He would ask how Hugh and Lorna were.'

'Did he ask about anyone else?'

'They're never out of the news, are they? I told him what stories I had.'

'Ever wonder why he was so interested in the Grieves, Mr Sithing?'

'Please, call me Gerald. Did you know, there's an aura around you, Inspector? I'm sure of it.'

'Probably just my aftershave.' Siobhan snorted, but he ignored her. 'Didn't it seem to you that he was more interested in Hugh Cordover and his family than he was in the Knights of Rosslyn?'

'Oh no, I'm sure that wasn't the case.'

Rebus leaned forward. 'Look into your heart, Gerald,' he intoned.

Sithing did so, swallowed noisily. 'Maybe you're right. Yes, maybe you are. But tell me, why was he so interested in the Grieves?'

Rebus stood up, leaned down over Sithing. 'Now how the hell would I know that?' he said.

Back in the car, Siobhan smiled as she mimicked him. ' "Look into your heart, Gerald." '

'Rum old bugger, wasn't he?' Rebus had the window down, so Siobhan would let him smoke.

'So what have we got?'

'We've got Supertramp feigning an interest in the Knights of Rosslyn while pumping information about the clan. We've got him interested in Hugh Cordover, but unwilling to come down to the chapel. Why? Because he didn't want to meet Cordover.'

'Because Cordover knew him?' Siobhan guessed.

'It's a possibility.'

'So are we any nearer finding out who he was?'

'Maybe. Supertramp's interested in the Grieves *and* in Skelly. Roddy Grieve dies in the grounds of Queensberry House, shortly after Skelly's been uncovered. Around the same time, Supertramp takes the high dive.'

'You want to roll three cases into one?'

Rebus shook his head. 'We don't have enough; the Farmer would never go for it. He'd certainly never let me run it the way it needs to be run.'

'Speaking of which . . .' Siobhan changed up through the gears as she left the village behind. 'Where's your sidekick?'

'You mean Linford?' Rebus shrugged. 'Doing interviews.'

Siobhan looked sceptical. 'Leaving you to your own devices?'

'Derek Linford knows what's good for him,' Rebus said, flicking his cigarette out across the blood-bruised sky.

They had a war meeting: Rebus and Siobhan, Wylie and Hood. The back room at the Oxford Bar. They took the table at the far end, so there'd be no one near enough to overhear the conversation.

'I'm seeing links between the three cases,' Rebus said, having gone through his reasons. 'Tell me now if you think I'm wrong.'

'I'm not saying you're wrong, sir,' Wylie piped up, 'but where's the evidence?'

Rebus nodded. The beer in front of him was almost untouched. In deference to the non-smokers, his cigarette packet was still in its Cellophane. 'Exactly,' he said. 'That's why I want us to ca'canny. At this stage, we need to be aware of each other. That way, when the connections come, we'll see them straight off.'

'What do I tell CI Templer?' Siobhan asked. Gill Templer, Siobhan's boss, the name resonant now.

'You keep her up to snuff. The Chief Super, too, if it comes to that.'

'He's going to close the case on me,' she complained.

'We'll persuade him otherwise,' Rebus promised. 'Now drink up, the next round's on me.'

While Rebus went to the bar, Siobhan stepped outside to call home and check her answering machine messages. There were two of them, both from Derek Linford, making apologies and asking to see her.

'Took you long enough,' she muttered to herself. He'd left his home phone number, but she was only half listening.

Left alone at the table, Wylie and Hood drank in silence for a few moments. Wylie spoke first.

'What do you reckon?'

Hood shook his head. 'The DI has a rep for going out on a limb. Do we want to be out there with him?'

'I don't see it, to be honest with you. What's our case – or Siobhan's, come to that – got to do with this dead MSP?'

'What are you thinking?'

'I think he might be trying to hijack our cases because his own one's hit a wall.'

Hood shook his head. 'I've told you, he's not like that.'

Wylie was thoughtful. 'Mind you, if he's right then we've got a bigger case than we thought.' Her mouth twisted into a smile. 'And if he's wrong, it's not us who'll get carpeted, is it?'

Rebus was coming back with the drinks. Gin, lime and soda for Wylie, half of lager for Hood. He went back to the bar and returned with a whisky for himself, Coke for Siobhan.

'*Slainte*,' he said, as Siobhan settled next to him on the narrow banquette.

'So what's the plan?' Wylie asked.

'You don't need me to tell you,' Rebus said. 'You follow procedure.'

'Talk to Barry Hutton?' Hood guessed.

Rebus nodded. 'You might want to do a little digging, too, just in case there's something about him we should know.'

'And Supertramp?' Siobhan asked.

Rebus turned to her. 'Well, as it happens, I've an idea . . .'

Someone put their head round the corner, as if checking who was in the bar. Rebus recognised the face: Gordon, one of the regulars. He was still in his work suit; probably been out with the office. He saw Rebus, seemed about to retreat but then decided on another course of action. Approached the table, hands in the pockets of his overcoat. Rebus could tell immediately that he'd been celebrating.

'You jammy bastard,' Gordon said. 'You got off with Lorna that night, didn't you?' He was getting ready to make a joke of it: something to embarrass Rebus in front of his friends. 'Sixties supermodel, and you're the best she can do.' He shook his head, missing the look on Rebus's face.

'Thanks, Gordon,' Rebus said. The tone alerted the younger man, who looked at his fellow drinker and slapped his hand to his mouth.

'Sorry I spoke,' he mumbled, heading back towards the bar. Rebus looked at the faces around the table. They all suddenly seemed very interested in their drinks.

'You'll have to excuse Gordon,' he told them. 'Sometimes he gets the wrong end of the stick.'

'I take it he meant Lorna Grieve?' Siobhan said. 'Does she drink in here often?'

Rebus gave her a look; refused to answer.

'She's the sister of the murder victim,' Siobhan went on, her voice low.

'She came in here one night, that's all.' But Rebus knew he was fidgeting too much. He glanced towards Wylie and Hood, remembered that they'd seen her in the Ox that night. He picked up his whisky, found he'd already finished it. 'Gordon doesn't know what he's talking about,' he muttered. Even to his ears, it sounded limp.

23

There were those who said that Edinburgh was an invisible city, hiding its true feelings and intentions, its citizens outwardly respectable, its streets appearing frozen in time. You could visit the place and come away with little sense of having understood what drove it. This was the city of Deacon Brodie, where bridled passions were given free play only at night. The city of John Knox, his rectitude stern and indomitable. You might need half a million pounds to buy one of the better houses, yet outward show was frowned upon; a city of Saabs and Volvos rather than Bentleys and Ferraris. Glaswegians – who considered themselves more passionate, more Celtic – thought Edinburgh staid and conventional to the point of prissiness.

Hidden city. The historical proof: when invading armies advanced, the populace made themselves scarce in the caves and tunnels below the Old Town. Their homes might be ransacked, but the soldiers would leave eventually – it was hard to enjoy victory without the evidence of the vanquished – and the locals would come back into the light to begin the work of rebuilding.

Out of the darkness and into the light.

The Presbyterian ethos swept idolatry from the churches, but left them strangely empty and echoing, filling them with congregations who'd been told that from birth they were doomed. All of this filtering down through the consciousness of the years. The citizens of Edinburgh made good bankers and lawyers perhaps precisely because they held their emotions in check, and were good at keeping secrets. Slowly, the city gained a reputation as a financial centre. At one time, Charlotte Square, where many of the banking and insurance institutions had made their headquarters, was reckoned to be the richest such street in Europe. But now, with the need for purpose-built offices and car-parking facilities, the banks and insurance companies were regrouping in the area around Morrison Street and the Western Approach Road. This was Edinburgh's new financial district, a maze of concrete and glass with the arena-like International Convention Centre at its hub.

Everyone seemed to agree that until the arrival of these new buildings, the area had been a waste ground, an eyesore. But opinion was divided over just how user-unfriendly the maze now was. It was as if humans had been dropped from the planning equation, the buildings existing only to serve themselves. Nobody walked around the financial district for the pleasure of the architecture.

Nobody walked around the financial district at all.

Except, this Monday morning, for Ellen Wylie and Grant Hood. They'd made the mistake of parking too early, in a convenient car park on Morrison Street. Hood's reasoning: the place had to be near by. But the anonymity of the buildings and the fact that walkways were closed due to ongoing construction work meant that they ended up lost somewhere behind the Sheraton on Lothian Road. In the end, Wylie got on her mobile and had a receptionist direct them, until they found themselves entering a twelve-storey building of grey smoked glass and pink facing-stone. The receptionist was smiling as they marched across the floor towards her.

'And here you are,' she said, putting down the phone.

'And here we are,' Wylie agreed, bristling.

Workmen were still busy in Hutton Tower. Electricians in blue overalls fringed with tool belts; painters in white overalls spotted with greys and yellows, whistling as they rested their tins on the floor, awaiting the lift.

'It'll be fine when it's finished,' Hood told the receptionist.

'Top floor,' she said. 'Mr Graham's expecting you.'

They shared their lift with a grey-suited executive, his arms wrestling squid-like with paperwork. He got out three floors below them, almost colliding with a sparky positioning a ladder under some ceiling cables. But when the lift doors opened on the twelfth floor, they entered a calm reception area, with an elegant woman rising from behind her desk to greet them and direct them the eight feet to where two chairs awaited in front of a polished coffee table, arranged with the morning papers.

'Mr Graham will be with you in a moment. Can I get you anything: tea, coffee?'

'It was actually Mr Hutton we were wanting to see,' Wylie said. The woman just kept smiling.

'Mr Graham won't keep you,' she said, turning back to her desk.

'Oh, good,' Hood said, lifting one of the papers. 'My *Financial Times* didn't turn up this morning.'

Wylie looked both ways along the narrow corridor, which disappeared round corners at either end. She got the feeling the corridor made a circuit of this floor of the building, and that the floors below would be identical. There were doors either side, leading either to a window view or to interior space. The windowed offices would be coveted. Working as she presently did from a windowless box in St Leonard's, she herself coveted anything big enough to swing a cat in, even if the cat suffered minor concussion.

A man had rounded the far corner. He was tall, well built, young. His short black hair was professionally styled and gelled, his suit dark grey, immaculately tailored. He wore oval glasses and a gold Rolex. When he introduced himself as John Graham, and put his hand out to shake, Wylie saw a gold cuff link at the end of his pale lemon shirt. It was one of those collarless affairs that wouldn't

262

support a tie. She'd met men before who'd had about them the sheen of success, but for this one she almost needed Ray-Bans.

'We were hoping to speak to Mr Hutton,' Grant Hood said.

'Yes, of course. But you'll appreciate that Barry's an incredibly busy man.' He glanced at his watch. 'He's in a meeting as I speak, and we wondered if perhaps I could be of assistance. Perhaps if we go through what it is you need, I can transmit that to Barry.'

Wylie was about to say that it sounded like a long-winded way of 'assisting', but Graham was already leading them down the corridor, calling back to the receptionist that his calls were to be held for the next fifteen minutes. Wylie shared a look with Hood: *big of him*. Hood's mouth twitched, telling her there was nothing to be gained by riling the emissary – not just yet, at any rate.

'This is the boardroom,' Graham said, leading them into an L-shaped room at one corner of the building. A large rectangular desk filled most of the space. Water glasses, pencils and notepads were laid out, ready for the next meeting. A large marker-board stood unsullied at the head of the table. At the far end, a sofa faced a widescreen TV and video. But what impressed most was the view – east towards the castle, and north towards Princes Street and the New Town, with the Fife coastline just visible beyond.

'Enjoy it while you can,' Graham told them. 'There's a plan to build an even taller tower right next door.'

'A Hutton development?' Wylie guessed.

'Of course,' Graham said. He'd motioned for them to sit, having taken the chair at the top of the table. He brushed non-existent specks from one trouser leg. 'So, if you'd care to give me the background?'

'It's simple enough, sir,' Grant Hood said, pulling his chair in. 'DS Wylie and myself are carrying out a murder inquiry.' Graham raised an eyebrow, and pressed his

263

hands together. 'As part of that inquiry, we need to talk to your boss.'

'Would you care to elaborate?'

Wylie took over. 'Not really, sir. You see, in a case like this, we don't really have the time. We came here out of common courtesy. If Mr Hutton won't see us, then we'll just have to take him down to the station.' She shrugged, her piece said.

Hood glanced at her, then back to Graham. 'What DS Wylie says is correct, sir. We have the powers to question Mr Hutton whether he likes it or not.'

'I can assure you, it's nothing like that.' Graham held both hands up in a pacifying gesture. 'But he does happen to be in a meeting, and these things can take time.'

'We did phone ahead to warn we were coming.'

'And we do appreciate that, DS Wylie. But something came up. This is a multimillion-pound business, and the unexpected does arise from time to time. Decisions sometimes have to made immediately; millions can depend on it. You do see that, don't you?'

'Yes, sir, but as *you* can see, there's nothing you can help us with,' Wylie said. 'You weren't working for a man called Dean Coghill in 1978, were you? I'd guess that twenty years ago, you were still busy in the school playground, trying to look up girls' skirts and comparing plook collections with your pals. So if Mr Hutton would deign to join us . . .' She nodded towards a camera in the corner of the ceiling. 'We'd be very grateful.'

Hood began to apologise for his partner's behaviour. Graham's cheeks had coloured, and he didn't seem to have an answer. Then a voice broke in, coming from a loudspeaker somewhere.

'Show the officers the way.'

Graham rose to his feet, avoiding their eyes. 'If you'll follow me,' he said.

He took them into the corridor, pointed along it.

'Second door on the left.' Then he turned and walked away; his small victory over them.

'Think this corridor's bugged, too?' Wylie asked in an undertone.

'Who knows?'

'He got a fright, didn't he? Wasn't expecting the one in the skirt to play tough.' Hood watched a grin spread across her face. 'And as for you . . .'

'What about me?'

She looked at him. 'Apologising on my behalf.'

'That's what the "good" cop does.'

They knocked at the door, then opened it unasked. An anteroom, with a secretary already rising from her desk. She opened the inner door, and they entered Barry Hutton's office.

The man himself was standing just inside, legs slightly apart and hands behind his back.

'I thought you were a bit rough on John.' He shook Wylie's hand. 'All the same, I admire your style. If you want something, don't let anyone stand in your way.'

It wasn't that big an office, but the walls dripped modern art, and there was a bar in one corner, which is where Hutton was headed.

'Can I get you something?' He pulled a bottle of Lucozade out of the fridge. They shook their heads. He twisted the cap off the bottle and took a swallow. 'I'm addicted,' he said. 'Used to be, when I was a kid you only ever got the stuff when you were ill. Do you remember that? Come on, let's sit here.'

He led them to a cream leather sofa, and took the matching chair opposite. The portable TV in front of them was actually a monitor. It was still showing a view of the boardroom table.

'Cute, isn't it?' Hutton said. He picked up a remote. 'Look, I can move it around, zoom in on faces . . .'

'And it has sound, too?' Wylie guessed. 'So you know what we want to talk to you about.'

'Something about a murder?' Hutton took another swig of his addiction. 'I heard Dean Coghill was dead, but that was natural causes, wasn't it?'

'Queensberry House,' Grant Hood stated.

'Oh, right: the body behind the wall?'

'In a room renovated by Dean Coghill's team between 1978 and '79.'

'And?'

'And that's when the body got walled up.'

Hutton looked from one officer to the other. 'You're kidding?'

Wylie unfolded the list of people who'd worked in the building. 'Recognise these names, sir?'

Hutton ended up smiling. 'Brings back memories.'

'None of them went missing?'

The smile vanished. 'No.'

'Was anyone else working there, casual labour maybe?'

'Not that I remember. Not unless you're counting me.'

'We did notice your name was a late addition.'

Hutton nodded. He was short, maybe five-eight, skinny but with a developing paunch and jowls. His black suit was shiny new, and all three buttons were done up. His black brogues gleamed, the leather not yet broken in. He had small, dark, deep-set eyes, his brown hair cut above the ears but with prominent sideburns. Wylie knew she wouldn't pick him out in a crowd as being especially rich or influential.

'Work experience. I fancied the building trade. Looks like I made the right decision.' His smile invited them to join in his good fortune. Neither detective did so.

'Do you ever have any dealings with Peter Kirkwall?' Wylie asked.

'He's a builder, I'm a developer. Different game.'

'That doesn't quite answer the question.'

Hutton smiled again. 'I'm wondering why you asked it.'

'Just that we talked to him, too. His office was full of plans, photos of his projects . . .'

'And mine isn't? Maybe Peter's got an ego, and I haven't.'

'You do know him then?'

Hutton acknowledged as much with a shrug. 'I've used his firm occasionally. What's that got to do with your body?'

'Nothing,' Wylie conceded. 'Just curious.' All the same, she sensed she'd touched a nerve.

'So,' Grant Hood said, 'getting back to Queensberry House . . .'

'What can I tell you? I was eighteen, nineteen. They had me mixing concrete, all the unskilled jobs. It's called learning from the floor up.'

'You remember that room, though? The fireplaces?'

Hutton nodded. 'Putting in a DPC, yes. I was there when we opened the wall.'

'Was anyone told about the fireplaces?'

'To be honest, I don't think so.'

'Why not?'

'Well, Dean had the feeling they'd want to send in the historians, which would knock our schedule on the head. Something about not getting paid till the work was complete. If we were hanging around waiting for them to do their stuff, it'd be time lost.'

'So you just covered it up again?'

'Must've done. I came to work one morning, and the wall was back up.'

'Do you know who did it?'

'Dean himself maybe, or Harry Connors. Harry was pretty close to Dean, like a right-hand man.' He nodded. 'I see what you're getting at, though: whoever covered that fireplace over had to know there was a body inside.'

'Any theories?' Wylie asked. Hutton shook his head. 'You must have read about the case in the papers, Mr Hutton. Any reason you didn't come forward?'

'I didn't know the body dated from back then. That

fireplace could have been opened and closed again a dozen times since we worked there.'

'Any other reason?'

Hutton looked at her. 'I'm a businessman. Any stories about me get into the press, it can affect how I'm seen in the business community.'

'In other words, not all publicity is good publicity?' Hood asked.

Hutton smiled at him. 'Got it in one.'

'Before we get too cosy,' Wylie interrupted, 'can I just ask how you got your job with Mr Coghill's firm.'

'I applied, same as everyone else.'

'Really?'

Hutton frowned. 'What do you mean?'

'I was just wondering if maybe your uncle put in a word, or maybe more than a word.'

Hutton rolled his eyes. 'I wondered when this would come up. Look, my mum happens to be Bryce Callan's sister, okay? It doesn't make me a criminal.'

'Are you saying your uncle's a criminal?' Wylie asked.

Hutton looked disappointed in her. 'Don't get glib. We all know what the police think of my uncle. All the rumours and insinuations. But nothing's ever been proved, has it? Never even been to a court of law. What does that say, eh? To me, it says you're wrong. It says I've worked to get where I am. Taxes, VAT and the rest: I'm cleaner than anybody. And the idea that you can walk in here and start—'

'I think we get the picture, Mr Hutton,' Hood interrupted. 'Sorry if you thought we were suggesting anything. This is a murder inquiry, which means every angle ends up being considered, no matter how insignificant.'

Hutton stared at Hood, trying to read something into that last word.

'When did you leave Mr Coghill's firm?' Wylie asked.

Hutton had to think about it. 'April, May, something like that.'

'Of '79?' Hutton nodded. 'And you joined . . . ?'

'October, '78.'

'Just the six months then? Not very long.'

'I had a better offer.'

'And what was that, sir?' Hood asked.

'I've got nothing to hide!' Hutton spat.

'We appreciate that, sir,' Wylie said, her voice soothing. Hutton calmed quickly. 'I went to work for my uncle.'

'For Bryce Callan?' Hutton nodded.

'Doing what?' Hood asked.

Hutton took his time finishing the bottle. 'Some land development thing of his.'

'That was your big break then?' Wylie asked.

'It's how I got started, yes. But as soon as I could, I branched off on my own.'

'Yes, sir, of course.' Hood's tone said: *I've worked to get where I am*; but with a helping hand the size of a football field.

As they were leaving, Wylie asked one more question. 'This must be an exciting time for you?'

'We've got plenty of ideas.'

'Sites around Holyrood?'

'The parliament's just the beginning. Out-of-town shopping, marina developments. It's astonishing how much of Edinburgh is still under-developed. And not just Edinburgh. I've got projects in Glasgow, Aberdeen, Dundee . . .'

'And there are enough clients?' Hood asked.

Hutton laughed. 'They're queuing up, pal. All we need is less red tape.'

Wylie nodded. 'Planning permission?'

At mention of the words, Hutton made the sign of the cross with the index fingers of both hands. 'The curse of the developer.'

But he could afford a final laugh as he closed his office door on them.

24

'Fair warning,' Rebus said as they walked up the drive, 'the mother's a bit fragile.'

'Understood,' Siobhan Clarke replied. 'So you'll be your usual charming self?'

'It's Lorna Grieve we want to talk to,' he reminded her. Then he nodded towards the Fiat Punto parked to the right of the front door. 'That's her car.' He'd called High Manor, spoken with Hugh Cordover, listening intently for any new or accusing tone, but all Cordover had done was tell him Lorna was in Edinburgh.

'I'm still not sure this is a good idea,' Siobhan was saying.

'Look,' he said, 'I've told you—'

'John, you can't go getting involved with—'

He grabbed her by the shoulder, turned her so she was facing him. 'I'm not involved!'

'You didn't sleep with her?' Siobhan was trying to keep her voice down.

'What does it matter if I did?'

'We're working a murder case. We're about to question her.'

'I'd never have guessed.'

She stared at him. 'You're hurting my shoulder.'

He released his grip, mumbled an apology.

They rang the doorbell and waited. 'How was your weekend?' Rebus asked. She just glared at him. 'Look,' he said, 'if we go in there spitting at one another, we're not going to get very far.'

She seemed to consider this. 'Hibs won again,' she said at last. 'What did you get up to?'

'I went into the office, can't say I achieved much.'

Alicia Grieve answered the door. She looked older than when Rebus had last seen her, as if she'd lived too long already and was realising the fact. Age could dupe you like that, almost its cruellest trick. You lost a loved one, and time seemed to go into fast forward, so that you withered, sometimes even died. Rebus had seen it before: fit spouses dying in their sleep only days or weeks after burying their partner. It was as if a switch had been flicked, voluntary or involuntary, you could never tell.

'Mrs Grieve,' he said. 'Remember me? DI Rebus?'

'Yes, of course.' Her voice was reedy, parched. 'And who is this?'

'DC Clarke,' Siobhan said by way of introduction. She was smiling the smile of youth when faced with the aged: sympathetic yet not quite understanding. Rebus realised that he was closer to Alicia Grieve's age than Siobhan's. He had to push that thought away.

'Can we bury Roddy? Is that why you've come?' She didn't sound hopeful; she would accept whatever they had to tell her. That was her role now in what was left of the world.

'I'm sorry, Mrs Grieve,' Rebus said. 'Just a little longer.'

She mimicked the final phrase, and added: 'Time is elastic, don't you find?'

'We're actually here to see Mrs Cordover,' Siobhan stressed, trying to draw the woman back from wherever she was headed.

'Lorna,' Rebus added.

'Is she here?' Alicia Grieve asked.

A voice from the interior: 'Of course I'm here, Mother. We were talking not two minutes ago.'

Mrs Grieve stood aside, letting them in. Lorna Grieve stood in the doorway of one of the rooms, a cardboard box in her arms.

271

'Hello again,' she said to Rebus, ignoring Siobhan.

'Could we have a word, do you think?' Rebus asked. He wasn't quite looking at her. She became amused, nodded towards the room she'd just left.

'I'm trying to tidy some of this crap away.'

Mrs Grieve's fingers touched the back of Rebus's hand. They were as cold as a slab. 'She wants to sell my paintings. She needs the money.'

Rebus looked to Lorna, who was shaking her head.

'I want them cleaned and reframed, that's all.'

'She'll sell them,' Mrs Grieve warned. 'I know that's what she's up to.'

'Mother, for Christ's sake. I don't need money.'

'Your husband needs it. He has debts and only the last vestige of anything resembling a career.'

'Thanks for the vote of confidence,' Lorna muttered.

'Don't you get cheeky with me, my girl!' Mrs Grieve's voice was trembling. Her fingers still held Rebus's hand. They were talons; fleshless claws.

Lorna sighed. 'What do you two want anyway? I hope you're here to arrest me; anything would be better than this.'

'You can always go home!' her mother shrieked.

'And leave you here to wallow in self-pity? Oh no, Mummy dearest, we can't have that.'

'Seona looks after me.'

'Seona's too busy with her political career,' Lorna spat. 'She doesn't need you now. She's found a more useful cause.'

'You're a monster.'

'Which must make you Dr Frankenstein, I presume?'

'Vile body.'

'Yes, on you go. You'll be telling us you knew him next.' She turned to Rebus and Siobhan. 'Evelyn Waugh,' she explained. '*Vile Bodies.*'

'Putrid. You threw yourself at every man you ever met.'

'I still do,' Lorna snarled. She didn't so much as glance

at Rebus. 'While you only ever threw yourself at Father, because you knew he'd be useful to you. And once your reputation was established, that was, in a phrase, the end of the affair.'

'How dare you.' Cold rage, the rage of a much younger woman.

Siobhan was touching Rebus's sleeve, edging back towards the door. Lorna saw what she was doing. 'Oh look, we're frightening off the filth! Isn't that precious, Mother? Did you realise we possessed such power?' She started to laugh. A few moments later, Alicia Grieve joined her.

Rebus's thought: it's a fucking mad house. Then he realised that this was normal behaviour for mother and daughter: fighting and spitting the prelude to catharsis. They'd been in the public's eye so long, they'd become actors in their own melodrama; played out their quarrels as though each one had measure and meaning.

Scenes from family life.

Bloody hell.

Lorna was wiping an imaginary tear from her eye, still cradling the paintings. 'I'll put these back,' she said.

'No,' said her mother, 'leave them in the hall with the others.' She pointed to where a dozen or so framed paintings sat against the wall. 'You're right, we'll have them looked at: cleaned up, maybe a few new frames.'

'We should get an insurance quote while we're at it.' Her mother was about to interrupt, so Lorna went on quickly. 'That's not so I can sell them. But if they were stolen . . .'

Alicia seemed about to argue, but sucked in a deep breath and just nodded. The paintings were laid with the others. Lorna stood up again, brushing her hands free of dust.

'Must be forty years since you painted some of these.'

'You're probably right. Maybe even longer.' Alicia

nodded. 'But they'll survive long after I'm gone. It's just that they won't mean the same.'

'How's that?' Siobhan felt compelled to ask.

Alicia looked at her. 'They mean things to me which they never can to anyone else.'

'That's why they're here,' Lorna explained, 'rather than on some collector's walls.'

Alicia Grieve nodded. 'Meaning is precious. The personal is all we have; without it, we're animals, pure and simple.' She suddenly perked up, her hand dropping from Rebus's. 'Tea,' she barked, clapping her hands together. 'We must all have some tea.'

Rebus was wondering if there was any chance of a tot of whisky on the side.

They sat in the sitting room, making small talk while Lorna coped in the kitchen. She brought in a tray, started pouring.

'I'm bound to have forgotten something,' she said. 'Tea's not my strong point.' She looked at Rebus as she spoke, but he was focused on the fireplace. 'Something stronger, Inspector? I seem to remember you enjoy a malt.'

'No, I'm fine, thank you,' he felt compelled to say.

'Sugar,' Lorna said, studying the tray. 'Told you.' She made for the door, but Rebus and Siobhan announced that neither of them took it, so she returned to her seat. There were crumbly digestives on a plate. They turned down the offer, but Alicia took one, dunking it into her tea, where it broke into pieces. They ignored her as she fished the morsels out, popping them into her mouth.

'So,' Lorna said at last, 'what brings you to Happy Acres?'

'It might be something or nothing,' Rebus said. 'DC Clarke has been investigating the suicide of a homeless person. It looks like he was very interested in your family.'

'Oh?'

'And the fact of his suicide, so soon after the murder . . .'

Lorna sat forward in her chair. She was looking at Siobhan. 'This wouldn't be the millionaire tramp by any chance?'

Siobhan nodded. 'Though he wasn't quite a millionaire.'

Lorna turned to her mother. 'You remember me telling you?'

Her mother nodded, but appeared not to have been listening. Lorna turned back to Siobhan. 'But what's it got to do with us?'

'Maybe nothing,' Siobhan conceded. 'The deceased was calling himself Chris Mackie. Does that name mean anything?'

Lorna thought hard, then shook her head.

'We have some photos,' Siobhan said, handing them over. She glanced at Rebus.

Lorna studied the photos. 'Grim-looking creature, isn't he?'

Siobhan was still looking at Rebus, willing him to ask the question.

'Mrs Cordover,' he said, 'there's no easy way to ask this.'

She looked at him. 'Ask what?'

Rebus took a deep breath. 'He's a lot older . . . been living rough.' He dived in. 'It couldn't be Alasdair, could it?'

'*Alasdair?*' Lorna took another look at the top photo. 'What the hell are you talking about?' She looked towards her mother, who seemed to have turned whiter than ever. 'Alasdair's got fair hair, nothing like this.' Alicia's hand was reaching out, but Lorna passed the photos back to Siobhan. 'What are you trying to do? This man's nothing like Alasdair, nothing like him at all.'

'People can change in twenty years,' Rebus said quietly.

'People can change overnight,' she retorted coldly, 'but that's not my brother. What made you think it was?'

Rebus shrugged. 'A hunch.'

'I'll show you Alasdair,' Alicia Grieve said, rising to her feet. She put her cup down on the table. 'Come with me, and I'll show you him.'

They followed her into the kitchen. The glass-fronted china cabinet was full, and piles of clean crockery covered the worktops, awaiting space that would never be there. The sink was full of dirty dishes. An ironing board was piled with clothes. A radio was playing softly: some classical station.

'Bruckner,' Alicia said, unlocking the back door. 'They always seem to be playing Bruckner.'

'Her studio,' Lorna explained as they followed Alicia into the garden. It was overgrown now, untended, but the notion of the garden it had once been was still there. A free-standing swing, its pipework corroded. A stone urn, waiting to be put upright on its plinth. The leaves on the lawn had turned to mulch, making progress difficult. And at the far end of the garden, a stone outhouse.

'The servants' quarters?' Rebus guessed.

'I suppose so,' Lorna said. 'It was our secret place when we were kids. Then Mother turned it into a studio, and we were locked out.' She was watching her mother lead the way, the old woman's back stooped. 'Time was, Father and she painted in the same room – his studio's in the attic.' She pointed back to two skylights in the roof. 'Then Mother decided she needed her own space, her own light. She was locking him out of her life, too.' She looked at Rebus. 'It wasn't easy, growing up a Grieve.'

He almost thought she'd said *growing up aggrieved*.

Alicia took a key from her cardigan pocket, unlocked the door to her studio. It was just one room inside, the stone walls whitewashed and spattered with paint. Paint on the floor, too. Three easels of different sizes. Threads of cobweb hanging from the ceiling. And against one wall, a series of portraits, head and neck only, the canvasses of varying size. The same man, caught at different stages of his life.

'Good God,' Lorna gasped, 'it's Alasdair.' She started sorting through the portraits; there were over a dozen.

'I imagine him growing, ageing,' Alicia said quietly. 'I see him in my mind and then I paint him.'

Fair-haired, sad-eyed. A troubled man, despite the smiles the artist had given him. And nothing at all like Chris Mackie.

'You never said anything.' Lorna had picked up one of the paintings to study it more closely. Her finger brushed the shadowing of cheekbones.

'You'd have been jealous,' her mother said. 'No good denying it.' She turned to Rebus. 'Alasdair was my favourite, you see. And when he ran away . . .' She looked at her own work. 'Maybe this was my way of explaining it.' When she turned back, she saw that Siobhan was still holding the photographs. 'May I?' She took them, held them up to her face.

Recognition lit up her eyes. 'Where is he?'

'You know him?' Siobhan asked.

'I need to know where he is.'

Lorna had put down the portrait. 'He killed himself, Mother. The tramp who left all the money.'

'Who is he, Mrs Grieve?' Rebus asked.

Alicia's hands were shaking as she went through the photos again. 'I've been so wanting to talk to him.' There were tears in her eyes. She wiped them with her wrist. Rebus had taken a step forward.

'Who is it, Alicia? Who's the man in the photographs?'

She looked at him. 'His name's Frederick Hastings.'

'Freddy?' Lorna came over to look. She pried the police photo from her mother's fingers.

'Well?' Rebus asked.

'I suppose it could be. It's twenty years since I last laid eyes on him.'

'But who was he?' Siobhan asked.

Suddenly Rebus remembered. 'Alasdair's business partner?'

Lorna was nodding.

Rebus turned to Siobhan. She looked puzzled.

'You say he's dead?' Alicia asked. Rebus nodded. 'He'd have known where Alasdair is. Those two were inseparable. Maybe there's an address amongst his belongings.'

Lorna was looking at the other photos, the ones of 'Chris Mackie' at the hostel. 'Freddy Hastings a tramp.' Her laughter was a sudden explosion in the room.

'I don't think there was any address,' Siobhan was telling Alicia Grieve. 'I've been through his effects several times.'

'Maybe we'd best go back to the house,' Rebus announced. Suddenly, he had a lot more questions to ask.

Lorna made another pot of tea, but this time fixed herself a drink, half-and-half whisky and spring water. She'd made the offer, but Rebus had turned it down. Her eyes were on him as she took the first sip.

Siobhan had her notebook out, pen ready.

Lorna exhaled; the fumes wafted all the way to where Rebus was sitting. 'We thought they'd gone off together,' she began.

'Utter nonsense,' her mother interrupted.

'Okay, *you* didn't think they were gay.'

'They disappeared at the same time?' Siobhan asked.

'Looked like. After Alasdair had been gone a few days, we tried contacting Freddy. No sign of him.'

'Was he reported as a missing person?'

Lorna shrugged. 'Not by me.'

'Family?'

'I don't think he had any.' She looked to her mother for confirmation.

'He was an only child,' Alicia said. 'Parents died within a year of one another.'

'Left him some money, most of which I thought he'd lost.'

'They *both* lost money,' Alicia added. 'That's why Alasdair ran off, Inspector. Bad debts. He was too proud to ask for help.'

'But not too proud to clear off,' Lorna couldn't help saying. Her mother fixed her with a glare.

'When was this?' Rebus asked.

'Some time in '79.' Lorna looked to her mother for confirmation.

'Halfway through March,' the old woman said.

Rebus and Siobhan locked eyes. March '79: Skelly.

'What sort of business did they have?' Siobhan asked, keeping her voice under control.

'Their last foray was into property.' Lorna shrugged again. 'I don't know much more than that. Probably bought places they couldn't sell on.'

'Land development?' Rebus guessed. 'Would that be it?'

'I don't know.'

Rebus turned to Alicia, who shook her head. 'Alasdair was very private in some ways. He wanted us to think he was so capable . . . so self-sufficient.'

Lorna got up to refill her glass. 'My mother's way of saying he was hopeless at most things.'

'Unlike you, I suppose,' Alicia snapped.

'If they ran off because they were in debt,' Siobhan said, 'how come Mr Hastings had nearly half a million pounds in a briefcase a year or so on?'

'You're the detectives, you tell us.' Lorna sat down again.

Rebus was thoughtful. 'All this stuff about the two men's business failings, is there anything to back it up, or is it another clan myth?'

'What are you suggesting?'

'It's just that we could do with a few solid facts in this case.'

'What case?' The alcohol was kicking in; Lorna's voice

had turned combative, her cheeks tinged with red. 'You're supposed to be investigating Roddy's murder, not Freddy's suicide.'

'The Inspector thinks they may be linked,' Alicia said, nodding at her own deduction.

'What makes you say that, Mrs Grieve?' Rebus asked.

'Freddy was interested in us, you say. Do you think he could have killed Roddy?'

'Why would he do that?'

'I don't know. Something to do with the money, perhaps.'

'Did Roddy and Freddy know one another?'

'They met a few times, when Alasdair brought Freddy to the house. Maybe other times, too.'

'So if Roddy met Freddy again after twenty years, you think he'd have recognised him?'

'Probably.'

'I didn't,' Lorna said, 'when you showed me the photos.'

Rebus looked at her. 'No, you didn't.' He was thinking: *or did you?* Why had she handed the photos back to Siobhan rather than passing them to her mother?

'Did Mr Hastings have an office?'

Alicia nodded. 'In Canongate, not far from Alasdair's flat.'

'Can you remember the address?'

She recited it, seeming pleased that she still had the ability.

'And his home?' Siobhan was writing in her notebook.

'A flat in the New Town,' Lorna said. But again it was her mother who gave the address.

The hotel's downstairs dining room was quiet at lunch-time. Diners either preferred the bistro-style restaurant on the ground floor or else didn't know of this second restaurant's existence. The décor was minimalist, oriental, and the elegantly set tables had plenty of space between them. A discreet place for a conversation. Cafferty got to his feet, shook Barry Hutton's hand.

'Uncle Ger, sorry I'm late.'

Cafferty shrugged, while a flunky helped Hutton into his chair. 'Long time since anyone called me that,' he said with a smile. 'It's not like it's true.'

'It's what I always called you.'

Cafferty nodded, examining the well-dressed young man before him. 'But look at you now, Barry. Doing so well for yourself.'

It was Hutton's turn to shrug. Menus were being handed out.

'Any drinks, gentlemen?' the waiter asked.

'Calls for champagne, I think,' Cafferty said. He winked at Hutton. 'And this is on me, so no arguing.'

'I wasn't about to. It's just that I'll stick to water, if that's all right.'

The smile stuck to Cafferty's face. 'Whatever you want, Barry.'

Hutton turned to the waiter. 'Vittel, if you have it. Evian otherwise.'

The waiter bowed his head, turned to Cafferty. 'And will you still be requiring the champagne, sir?'

'Didn't hear me say otherwise, did you?'

The waiter made his little bow again and headed off.

'Vittel, Evian . . .' Cafferty chuckled and shook his head. 'Christ, if Bryce could see you now.' Hutton was busy adjusting his shirt cuffs. 'Rough morning, was it?'

Hutton looked up, and Cafferty knew something had happened. But the younger man was shaking his head. 'I don't drink at lunchtime, that's all.'

'Then you'll have to let me buy you dinner.'

Hutton looked around the restaurant. There were only two other diners in the place, seated at a far corner and deep in what looked like a business conversation. Hutton studied the faces, but didn't recognise them. He turned back to his host.

'You're staying here?'

Cafferty nodded.

'Did you sell the house?'

Cafferty nodded again.

'And made a fair bit on it, I'd guess.' Hutton looked at him.

'Money's not everything though, is it, Barry? That's one thing I've learned.'

'You mean good health? Happiness?'

Cafferty pressed his palms together. 'You're young still. Wait a few years and maybe you'll see what I mean.'

Hutton nodded, not really sure what the older man was getting at. 'You got out pretty early,' he commented.

'Time off for good behaviour.' Cafferty sat back as one waiter produced a basket of bread rolls, and another asked if he wanted the champagne chilled or served slightly cool.

'Chilled,' Cafferty said, looking at his guest. 'So, Barry, business is good, eh? That's what I hear.'

'I'm not complaining.'

'And how's your uncle?'

'Fine, as far as I know.'

'You ever see him?'

'He won't set foot back here.'

'I know that. I thought maybe you headed out there. Holidays and stuff.'

'I can't remember my last holiday.'

'All work and no play, Barry,' Cafferty counselled.

Hutton looked at him. 'It's not all work.'

'Glad to hear it.'

Their food order was taken, and the drinks arrived. They toasted one another, Hutton refusing the offer of 'just one wee glass'. He took his water neat: no ice, no lemon.

'What about you?' he asked at last. 'Not many people come straight from the Bar-L to a place like this.'

'Let's just say I'm comfortable,' Cafferty said with a wink.

'Of course, you kept a lot of your business interests going while you were away?'

Cafferty heard the quotation marks around business interests. He nodded slowly. 'Lot of people would be disappointed if I hadn't.'

'I don't doubt it.' Hutton tore open one of the tiny, glazed rolls.

'Which brings me to our little lunch here,' Cafferty went on.

'A business lunch then?' Hutton asked. When Cafferty nodded, he felt a little more comfortable. It wasn't just a meal any more; he wasn't wasting his time.

25

Jerry's face recoiled from the slap. He was getting used to slaps recently. But this wasn't Jayne.

This was Nic.

He felt his cheek beginning to sting, knew the imprint of a hand would be forming there, pinkish red against his pale skin. Nic's hand would be stinging, too: small consolation.

They were in Nic's Cosworth. Jerry had just got in. It had been Nic who'd called – Monday night – and Jerry had jumped at the chance of escape. Jayne was in front of the telly, arms folded, eyes drooping. They'd eaten their tea watching the news: sausage, beans and egg. No chips: the freezer was bare, and neither of them felt like taking the trip to the chip shop. That was when the argument had started.

Ya useless lump of . . .

It's you needs to get off your fat arse, no' me . . .

Then the phone call. The phone was Jayne's side of the couch, but she ignored it.

'Two guesses who that'll be,' was all she said. He was hoping she'd be wrong, that it would be her mum. Then he could say, 'That's you quietened,' as he handed over the receiver.

Because if it was Nic . . . Nic on a Monday night, he never usually went out Mondays . . . that could probably mean only one thing.

And now here they were together in the car, and Nic was having a go at him.

'See that stunt you pulled, you ever do something as stupid as that again . . .'

'What stunt?'

'Phoning me at work, ya donkey!'

Jerry thought he was in for another slap, but Nic punched him in the side instead. Not too hard: he was calming down a bit.

'I wasn't thinking.'

Nic snorted. 'When did you ever?' The engine was already turning over. He slammed the car into gear and got a squeal from the tyres as they sped off. No indicator or mirror; a car behind tooted its horn three or four times. Nic checked the rearview, saw an old guy, all by himself. So he gave him the finger and a mouthful of abuse.

When did you ever?

Jerry's mind was working back, forming answers. Hadn't *he* been the one who'd done most of the shoplifting? And the one who bought them their booze when they were under age, because he was that bit taller and older-looking than Nic. Nic: smooth, shiny face, still like a kid's even now; thick dark hair always cut and styled. Nic was the one the girls went for, Jerry hanging back to see if any of them would find him worth talking to.

Nic at college, telling Jerry stories of shagging marathons. Even then, even back then there'd been glimpses: *she didn't fancy that, so I slapped her till she did . . . had her wrists held in one hand and I was pumping away like.*

It was as if the world deserved his violence, and would accept it because in every other way he was just fine, just perfect. The night Nic had met Catriona . . . he'd given Jerry a slap that night, too. They'd been to a couple of bars – Madogs, trendy but pricey, Princess Margaret was supposed to've drunk there, and the Shakespeare, next to the Usher Hall. That's where they'd met Cat and her friends, who were off to see some play at the Lyceum, something to do with horses. Nic knew one of the girls, introduced himself to the group, Jerry mute but keen

285

beside him. And Nic had got talking to this other girl, Cat, short for Catriona. Not a bad looker, but not the best of the bunch either.

'Are you at Napier?' someone asked Jerry.

'Naw,' he said, 'I'm in the electronics business.' That was his line. They were supposed to think he was a games designer, maybe ran his own software company. But it never seemed to work. They asked questions he couldn't answer, until he laughed and admitted he drove a fork-lift. There were smiles at the news, but not much more in the way of conversation.

When the group headed off to their play, Nic nudged Jerry. 'Solid gold, pal,' he said. 'Cat's meeting me after for a drink.'

'Like her then?'

'She's all right.' A wary look. 'She is, eh?'

'Oh aye, she's rare.'

Another nudge. 'And she's related to Bryce Callan. That's her surname: Callan.'

'So?'

Nic going wide-eyed. 'Never heard of Bryce Callan? Fuck me, Jerry, he runs the place.'

Jerry looking around the pub. 'This place?'

'Ya tube, he runs *Edinburgh*.'

Jerry nodding, even though he still didn't understand.

Later, a few more boozers down the road, he'd asked if he could go with Nic when he met Catriona.

'Don't be wet.'

'What am I supposed to do then?'

They were walking along the pavement, and Nic had stopped suddenly, facing him, his eyes glowering.

'I'll tell you what would be a start – you growing up. Everything's changed, we're not kids now.'

'I know that. I'm the one with the job, the one that's getting married.'

And Nic had slapped him. Not hard, but the act itself shocking Jerry rigid.

'Time to grow up, pal. You might have a job but everywhere I take you, you just stand there like a drink of fucking water.' Grabbing Jerry's face. 'Study me, Jer, watch how I do things. You might start growing up.'

Growing up.

Jerry wondered if this was what growing up brought you to: the two of them, in the Cosworth, and, it being a Monday night, out on the hunt. There were Monday-night singles clubs, usually catering to a slightly older clientele. Not that Nic minded what age the women were. He just wanted one of them. Jerry risked a glance at his friend. So good-looking . . . why did he need to do it this way? What was his problem?

But Jerry knew the answer to that. Cat was the problem. The problem of Cat was there at every bloody turn.

'Where we going then?' he asked.

'The van's parked in Lochrin Place.' Nic's voice was cold. Jerry was feeling the boak again in his stomach, like he was breathing bile. But the thing was . . . once they got started, he knew it would be joined by a completely different feeling: he'd get excited, same as Nic. Hunters, the pair of them.

'Treat it like a game,' Nic had said the first time.

Treat it like a game.

And his heart would beat faster, groin tingling. With the gloves and the ski mask, and sitting in the Bedford van, he was a different person. Not Jerry Lister any more, but someone out of a comic book or a film, someone stronger and scarier. Someone you had to fear. It was almost enough to tamp down the dry boak. Almost.

The van belonged to a guy Nic knew. Nic told the bloke he needed it now and again for a bit of moonlighting, helping a friend shift second-hand stuff around. The bloke took two tenners from him and didn't want any other details. Nic had these licence plates, got them from a scrapyard. He'd fix them on with wire, covering the real plates. The van was rusty, a dull white respray. It didn't stand out at all, not when the streets were dark and cold and you were hurrying home, maybe a bit the worse for wear.

The worse for wear was what Nic wanted. They'd park near the nightclub, pay their money and go in. Plenty of guys turning up in pairs, nothing suspicious about them, nothing to mark them out from anyone else. Then Nic would pick out the tables with parties at them. He seemed to be able to tell which ones were singles clubs. One time, he'd even got one of the women up for a dance. Jerry had asked him afterwards, wasn't that risky?

'What's life without a bit of risk?'

Tonight, they drove around a bit first. Nic knew the club would be at its best come ten o'clock. The post-pub drunks wouldn't have arrived yet, but the singles clubs would be in full swing. Most of them had work in the morning, couldn't make too late a night of it. They'd stay till eleven, maybe, then start heading home. And by then, Nic would have picked one or two. He always had a reserve, just in case. Some nights it didn't work out; the women all headed off together or with partners, none of them branching off on her own.

Other nights, it worked to perfection.

Jerry stood at the edge of the dance floor, lager in hand. Already he could feel the surge in him, the dark excited tide. But he was twitchy, too, never knew when some friend of his or Jayne's would come wandering up. *Jayne know you're here, does she?* No, she didn't. Didn't even ask any more. He'd get home at one or two in the morning, and she'd be asleep. Even if he woke her up coming in, she wouldn't say much.

'Hammered again?' Something like that.

He'd go back through to the living room, sit there with the remote in his hand, staring at the TV without switching it on. Sitting in the dark, where nobody could see him, nobody point an accusing finger.

It was you, it was you, it was you.

Not true. It was Nic. It was always Nic.

He stood by the dance floor and held his drink in a hand just barely shaking. And inside he was praying: *Don't let us get lucky tonight!*

But then Nic was coming towards him, a weird gleam in his eyes.

'I don't believe it, Jer. I *do not* believe it!'

'Calm down, man. What's up?'

Nic was running his hands through his hair. '*She's* here!'

'Who?' Looking around, wondering if anyone was listening. No chance: the music was just this side of the pain barrier. Orbital, it sounded like. Jerry kept up with the latest bands.

Nic was shaking his head. 'She didn't see me.' His mind was working now. 'We could do this.' Looking at Jerry. 'We could *do* this.'

'Aw, Jesus, it's not Cat, is it?'

'Don't be dense. It's that slut Yvonne!'

'Yvonne?'

'The one Cat was with that night. The one who took her along.'

Jerry was shaking his head. 'No way. No way, man.'

'But it's perfect!'

'Perfect's just what it isn't, Nic. It's suicide.'

'She could be the last one, Jerry. Think about it.' Nic checked his watch. 'We'll stick around a while, see if she hooks up with anyone.' He slapped Jerry's shoulder. 'I'm telling you, Jer, this'll be wild.'

That's what I'm afraid of, Jerry felt like saying.

Cat had this friend Yvonne who'd split up from her husband. Yvonne had joined a singles club. And one night she'd persuaded Cat to go with her. Jerry wasn't too good on the background. He didn't know why Cat had agreed. Had to mean her own marriage was rocky, but Nic had never said anything. Only things he ever said were along the lines of 'She betrayed me, Jer,' and 'I never saw it coming.' They'd gone to a nightclub – not this one, but a Thursday nighter, same sort of crowd – and one of the singles guys had taken Cat up for a dance, then another. And that was that. Basically, she'd gone off with him.

And now Nic saw his chance for revenge, not on Cat – no way he could touch her; Christ, her uncle was Bryce Callan, her cousin was Barry Hutton – but on her friend Yvonne.

When Nic came over again and nudged him, Jerry knew the singles group was preparing to leave. He finished his pint and followed Nic out of the club. The van was a hundred yards away. What happened was: Nic followed on foot, Jerry driving. Then Nic would find his spot, make a grab, and Jerry would pull up alongside, haul open the back doors. Then it was back on the road till they found a deserted spot, Nic in the back holding down the woman, Jerry taking care not to run any red lights or pull out in front of cop cars. The gloves and ski masks were in the glove box.

Nic unlocked the van, stared at Jerry.

'It's got to be you on foot tonight.'

'What?'

'Yvonne knows me. If she hears something, turns her head, she'd see it was me.'

'Put the mask on then.'

'You thick? Following a woman down the road with a ski mask on?'

'I'm not doing it.'

Nic's teeth were gritted in sudden anger. 'Help me out here!'

'No way, man.' Shaking his head.

Nic made an effort to calm himself. 'Look, maybe she won't be on her own anyway. I'm just asking—'

'And I'm saying no. Whole thing's way too risky, I don't care what you say.' Jerry was moving backwards away from the van.

'Where you going?'

'I need some fresh air.'

'Don't be like that. Christ, Jer, when are you going to grow up?'

'No way.' It was all Jerry could think of to say. Then he turned and ran.

26

Rebus walked from room to room in his flat, waiting for the grill to heat up. Toasted cheese: that most solitary of meals. You never saw it on menus, never invited friends round to share a few slices. It was what you ate when you were alone. A trip to the cupboard revealing a few final slices of bread; marge and cheese in the fridge. You wanted a hot meal this winter evening.

Toasted cheese.

He went back into the kitchen, put the bread under the grill, started slicing the slick wedge of orange Cheddar. A refrain came into his head, something from an old Fringe revue show:

> *Scottish Cheddar, it's our kind of cheese,*
> *Scottish Cheddar, orange, full of grease . . .*

Back into the living room, early Bowie on the hi-fi. 'The Man Who Sold the World.' Life was all about commerce, no doubt about it, daily transactions with friends, enemies and strangers, each one providing a winner and a loser, a sense of something lost or gained. You might not be selling the world, but everyone was selling something, some idea of themselves. When Bowie sang of passing someone on the stairs, Rebus thought again of Derek Linford, caught on the tenement stairwell: voyeur, or just insecure? Rebus himself had done some crazy things in his younger days. One girl, when she'd chucked him he'd phoned her parents to say she was pregnant. Christ, they hadn't even had sex together. He stood beside the window, gazing out at the flats across the way, some still with curtains or shutters open. All those other lives. Opposite him lived a family with two kids, boy and girl. He'd been watching them for so long that one Saturday morning, bumping into them outside the newsagent's, he'd said hello. The kids, no parents to protect them, had edged past him, eyes wary, while he tried to explain that he was one of their neighbours.

Never talk to strangers: it was advice he'd have given them himself. He might be their neighbour, but he was also a stranger. People on the pavement had looked at him oddly, standing there with his bag of rolls, his newspaper and milk, while two kids walked backwards away from him, and him calling out: 'I live across the road from you! You must have seen me!'

Of course, they hadn't seen him. Their minds were elsewhere, fixed on a world entirely separate from his. And from then on, maybe they called him the 'creepy neighbour', the man who lived on his own.

Sell the world? He couldn't even sell himself.

But that was Edinburgh for you. Reserved, self-contained, the kind of place where you might never talk to the person next door. Rebus's stairwell of six flats boasted only three owner-occupiers; the other three were let to students. He couldn't have said who owned them until the statutory notice had come round for roof repairs. Absentee landlords. One of them lived in Hong Kong or somewhere, and the lack of his signature had led the council to make their own estimate of repairs – ten times the original – and pass the work on to a favoured firm.

Not too long ago, one stairwell resident out Dalry way had had a contract taken out on him by someone else in the tenement because he wouldn't sign his name to a repair estimate. That was Edinburgh for you: reserved, self-contained, and lethal when crossed.

Bowie was singing 'Changes' now. Black Sabbath had a song with the same title, a ballad of sorts. Ozzy Osbourne singing, '*I'm going through changes*'. Me too, pal, Rebus felt like telling him.

Back into the kitchen: turning the toast and arranging the cheese slices, then back under the grill. He put the kettle on.

Changes: like with his drinking. A hundred pubs he could name in Edinburgh, yet here he was at home, no beer in the cupboard, and just the one bottle of malt whisky on top of the fridge, half of it gone. He would allow himself a single glass before bed, maybe top it up with water. Then under the duvet with a book. He had all these Edinburgh histories to get through, though he'd already given up on Sir Walter Scott's *Journals*. Plenty of pubs in the city named after Scott's works; probably more than he realised, seeing as how he hadn't read any of the novels.

Smoke from the grill told him the edges of the toast were burning. He tossed both slices on to a plate, took it back through to his chair. The TV was on with the sound muted. His chair was by the window, cordless phone and TV remote on the floor next to it. Some nights the ghosts came, settling themselves on the sofa or cross-legged on the floor. Not enough to fill the room, but more than he'd have liked. Villains, dead colleagues. And now Cafferty was back in his life, as if resurrected. Rebus, chewing, looked to the ceiling, asking God what he'd done to deserve it all. He liked a bit of a laugh, God, even if it was the laughter of cruelty.

Toasted cheese: sometimes at weekends, when Rebus's father had been alive and the son had headed back to Fife to visit, the old boy would be sitting at the table, munching the selfsame meal, washing down each mouthful with swilled tea. When Rebus had been a kid, they'd eaten as a family in the kitchen, bringing out the fold-down table. But in later years, Rebus senior had hauled the table into the living room, so he could eat near the fire and the television. A two-bar electric heater warming his back. There was a Calor gas heater, too. It always steamed up the windows. And then overnight in winter the condensation would freeze, so you had to scrape it off in the morning, or mop it with the kitchen flannel once the heating got going.

A grunt from his father, Rebus settling into what had been his mother's chair. He would say he'd eaten; no intention of joining his father at the table set for one. His mother had always laid a tablecloth, his father never did. Same plates and cutlery, but that one telling difference.

And now, Rebus thought, I don't even use a table.

The ghosts of his parents never visited. Maybe they were at rest, unlike the others. No ghosts tonight, though, just shadows cast by the television screen, street light and the halogen glow of passing cars, the world presented not in terms of colour so much as of light and shade. And Cafferty's shadow looming larger than any. What was he up to? When would he make his move, his real move, the last one of whatever game he was playing?

Christ, he wanted a drink. But he wouldn't have one just yet – to prove it to himself. Siobhan was right about him; he'd made a big mistake with Lorna Grieve. He didn't think it was just the drink to blame – he'd been under the spell of the past, a past of album covers and newspaper photos – but it had played its part. Siobhan had asked when the booze would start affecting his work. He could have told her: it already has.

He picked up his phone, thought about calling Sammy. Then he checked his watch, angling it towards the window. Gone ten. No, it was too late; it was always too late by the time he remembered. And then she'd end up calling him, and he'd apologise, and she'd say he should call anyway, no matter how late. Even so ... he told himself it was too late. There'd be someone in the room next to hers, what if his call woke them up? And Sammy needed her sleep; it was rigorous, all the stuff she was doing: the tests, the exercises. She'd told him she was 'getting there', her way of saying that progress was slow.

Slow progress: he knew all about it. But things were moving now, definitely moving. He felt as if he was in the driving seat, but blindfolded, taking directions from anyone in the car. There were probably lots of Give Way and No Entry signs ahead on the route, but he was pretty good at ignoring those. Problem was, the car had no seat belts, and Rebus's instinct was always to go faster.

He got up, swapped Bowie for Tom Waits. *Blue Valentine*, recorded just before he went 'junkyard'. Bluesy and seamy and seamless. Waits knew the soul's rotten marrow: the vocals might be an affectation, but the lyrics were from the heart. Rebus had seen him in concert, the actorliness all too apparent, the words still failing to ring false. Selling a version of himself, something packaged for public consumption. Pop stars and politicians did it all the time. These days the successful politicians lacked opinion and colour. They were ventriloquists' dummies, their clothes chosen for them by others, colour-coordinated and 'on message'. He wondered if Seona Grieve would be any different; somehow doubted it. The renegades never found progress easy, and he felt Seona Grieve was too ambitious to take that road. No blindfold for her, just careful hard work in between the mourning. He'd joked with Linford about the widow's motives. Motive, means and opportunity: the Holy Trinity of murder. Rebus's real problem was with the means: he didn't see Seona Grieve as the clawhammer type. But then, if she was being clever, that's exactly the weapon she'd have used: something people would find hard to associate with her.

While Linford had stuck to the main road, following the signposts marked Investigative Procedure, Rebus had managed to find himself on a rutted track. What if the suicide of Freddy Hastings was unconnected to Roddy Grieve? Maybe it was even unconnected to the find in Queensberry House. Was he really chasing shadows, every bit as worthwhile as following the trail of headlamp shadows across his ceiling? His phone rang just as a track ended, startling him.

'It's me,' Siobhan Clarke said. 'I think somebody's spying on me.'

Rebus rang her buzzer. She checked it was him before letting him into the stairwell. Her door was open by the time he reached her floor.

'What's happened?' he asked. She led him into the living room, looking a lot calmer than he felt. There was a bottle of wine on the coffee table: a third of it gone, a little left in the single glass. She'd eaten Indian food: he could smell it. But there were no signs of dishes, everything tidied away.

'I've been getting these calls.'

'What sort of calls?'

'Hang-ups. Two or three times a day. If I'm not in, the answering machine picks them up. Whoever's calling, they wait till the thing's recording before putting the phone down.'

'And if you're here?'

'Same thing: the line goes dead. I tried 1471, but they always withhold their number. And then tonight . . .'

'What?'

'I just got this feeling I was being watched.' She nodded towards her window. 'From across there.'

He looked to where she'd closed her curtains. He walked over and opened them, stared out at the tenement opposite. 'Wait here,' he said.

'I could have confronted them myself,' she said, 'but . . .'

'I won't be a tick.'

She stood by her window, arms folded. Heard the main door close, watched Rebus cross the road. He'd been out of breath. Was he just out of condition, or had he arrived in such a rush? Maybe afraid for her . . . She wondered now why she'd called him. Gayfield Square was five minutes away; any officer from there would have responded. Or she could have investigated for herself. It wasn't that she was scared. But things like this . . . creeping feelings . . . once they were shared, they tended to evaporate. He'd pushed open the main door, gone straight in. She saw him pass the first-floor window, and now he was at the second. Standing there, then pressing himself to the glass and waving to let her know it was okay. Up a further flight, checking no one was hiding there, and straight back down again.

By the time he arrived back, he was breathing harder than ever.

'I know,' he said, falling on to her sofa, 'I should join a gym.' He reached into his pocket for his cigarettes, then remembered that she wouldn't let him smoke, not here. She'd fetched a tall-stemmed glass from the kitchen.

'Least I can do,' she said, pouring in some red.

'Cheers.' He took a long swallow, exhaled. 'This your first bottle tonight?' Trying to make a joke of it.

'I'm not seeing things,' she said. She was kneeling by the coffee table, turning the glass in her hand.

'It's just that when you're on your own . . . I don't mean you personally, it goes for me, too.'

'What does? Imagining things?' There was a hint of colour to either cheekbone. 'How come you knew?'

He looked at her. 'Knew what?'

'Tell me you've not been watching me.'

His mouth opened, but he couldn't find the words.

'You pushed open the door,' she explained. 'Didn't check to see if it was locked or anything. Because you already knew it wasn't. Then you stopped two floors up. Just taking a breather?' She widened her eyes. 'That was where he was watching from. Not the tenement either side, and *that* landing.'

Rebus cast his eyes down into his drink. 'It wasn't me,' he said.

'But you know who it is.' She paused. 'Is it Derek?' His

silence was answer enough. She bounded to her feet, began pacing. 'When I get my hands on him . . .'

'Look, Siobhan—'

She turned on him. 'How did you know?'

So then he had to explain it, and as he finished she reached for her phone, punched in Linford's number. When the call was answered, she cut the connection. She was the one breathing hard now.

'Can I ask a question?' Rebus asked.

'What?'

'Did you put 141 first?' She looked at him blankly. 'That's the prefix if you don't want the caller knowing your number.'

She was still wincing when the phone rang.

'I'm not answering,' she said.

'It might not be Derek.'

'Let the machine take it.'

Seven rings, and the machine clicked into life. Her message first, then the sound of a receiver being replaced.

'Bastard!' she hissed. She picked up her receiver again, hit 1471, listened and slammed the phone down.

'Number withheld?' Rebus guessed.

'What's he playing at, John?'

'He's been jilted, Siobhan. We can turn strange when that happens.'

'You sound like you're on his side.'

'No way. I'm just trying to explain it.'

'Someone jilts you, you start stalking them?' She picked up her wineglass, took gulps from it as she paced. Then she noticed the curtains were still open, hurried over and closed them.

'Come and sit down,' Rebus said. 'We'll talk to him in the morning.'

She ran out of floor eventually, dropped on to the sofa next to him. He tried pouring more wine into her glass, but she didn't want any.

'Shame to waste it,' he said.

'You have it.'

'I don't want it.' She stared at him, and he offered a smile. 'I've spent half of this evening avoiding going out for a drink,' he explained.

'Why?'

He just shrugged, and she took the bottle from him. 'Then let's put it out of harm's way.'

When he caught up with her, she was pouring the contents down the kitchen sink.

'Bit radical,' he said. 'The fridge would have done.'

'You don't chill red wine.'

'You know what I mean, though.' He saw the clean dishes on the draining board. Her supper things had already been washed up. The kitchen was white-tiled and spotless. 'We're chalk and cheese,' he said.

'How's that?'

'I only wash up when I run out of mugs.'

She smiled. 'I've always wanted to be a hygiene slut.'

'But?'

She shrugged, surveying the room. 'Must be my upbringing or something. I suppose some people would call me neurotically tidy.'

'They just call me a slob,' Rebus said.

He watched her rinse the bottle and place it beside a few others which, along with empty jars, sat in an orange-box beside the swingbin.

'Don't tell me,' he said: 'recycling?'

She nodded, laughed. Then her face crumpled into seriousness. 'Jesus, John, I only went out with him three times.'

'Sometimes that's all it takes.'

'You know where I met him?'

'You wouldn't tell me, remember?'

'I'll tell you now: it was at a singles club.'

'That night you were out with the rape victim?'

'He goes to this singles club. They don't know he's a cop.'

'Well, it shows he has trouble meeting women.'

'He meets them every day, John.' She paused. 'I don't know, maybe it shows something else.'

'What?'

'I'm not sure. A different side to him.' She leaned back against the sink, folded her arms. 'Remember what you said?'

'I say so many memorable things.'

'You said about jilted guys, what they do sometimes.'

'You think Linford's been jilted one time too many?'

'Maybe.' She was thoughtful. 'But I was thinking more of the rapist, why he seems to focus on singles nights.'

Rebus was concentrating now. 'He went along to one, got the cold shoulder?'

'Or his wife or girlfriend went to one . . .'

Rebus was nodding. 'And got a nice warm shoulder?'

Siobhan was nodding, too. 'It's not my case, of course . . .'

'But whoever's running it, Siobhan, they'll have been asking around all the singles clubs.'

'Yes, but they won't have been asking the female members about jealous partners.'

'Good point. Another job for the morning.'

'Yes,' she said, turning to fill the kettle, 'just as soon as I've had a word with dear old Derek.'

'And if he denies it?'

'I've got corroboration, John.' She looked at him over her shoulder. 'I've got you.'

'No, you've got me and a few suspicions of your own. Not exactly the same thing.'

'What are you getting at?'

'People know Linford and me haven't been getting on like a house on fire. Now I come along and say I've seen him playing peeping Tom. You don't know Fettes, Siobhan.'

'They look after their own?'

'Maybe, maybe not. But they definitely would think

301

more than twice about taking the word of John Rebus over that of a future chief constable.'

'Is that why you wouldn't tell me about Linford?'

'Maybe.'

She turned away from him again. 'How do you want your coffee?'

'Black.'

Derek Linford's flat looked down on to Dean Valley and the Water of Leith. He'd got a good deal on the mortgage – playing the Fettes card for all it was worth – but even so he was making hefty repayments. And with the BMW on top. He had so much to lose.

He'd stripped off his coat and his shirt, sweating after the drive home. She'd seen him at the window, then made a phone call. And he'd run for it, driving like a maniac, taking the stairs to his own flat two at a time . . . and his own phone was ringing. He'd snatched at it, thinking: it's Siobhan! She's seen someone and decided to call me, wanting my help! But the phone had gone dead, and when he'd checked, it *had* been her on the phone. He'd called straight back and she hadn't answered.

Standing shaking by his window, ignoring the rooftop view . . . *She knows it was me!* It was all he could think of. She wouldn't have been calling him for help; she'd have called Rebus. And of course Rebus had told her. Of course he had.

'She knows,' he said aloud. 'She knows, she knows, she knows.'

He walked across the living room, turned and walked back. His right fist was slapping into his open left hand.

He had so much to lose.

'No,' he said, shaking his head, getting his breathing back under control. He wasn't going to lose any of this. Not for anyone or anything. This was all he had to show for the years of work, the long nights, the weekends, the courses and the studying.

'No,' he said again. 'Nobody's taking this away.'

Not if he could help it.

Not without one hell of a fight.

They rang up to Cafferty's room, told him there was a problem in the bar. He got dressed, went down there, and found Rab being pinned to the floor by two of the barmen and a couple of customers. Another man was seated on the floor near by, legs splayed, his nose bust open but holding his ear, blood seeping out between the fingers. He was yelling out for someone to call the police, while his girlfriend knelt beside him.

Cafferty looked at him. 'What you need is an ambulance,' he said.

'Bastard bit my ear!'

Cafferty crouched in front of the man, held two fifties out, and then tucked them into the man's breast pocket. 'An ambulance,' he repeated. The girlfriend took the hint, got up to find the phone. Then Cafferty walked over to Rab, squatted down and took hold of him by the hair.

'Rab,' he said, 'what the fuck are you doing?'

'I was just enjoying masel, Big Ger.' There was a smear of blood on his lips; blood from the wounded man's ear.

'No fun for anyone else,' Cafferty told him.

'What's life if ye can't enjoy yirsel?'

Cafferty stared at him but didn't answer. 'See when you go getting like this,' he said quietly, 'I don't know what I'm going to do with you.'

'Does it matter?' Rab said.

Cafferty didn't answer this either. He told the men they could let go, and they did, cautiously. Rab didn't seem inclined to get up. 'Maybe you could help him,' Cafferty told the men. He had a bundle of notes out, peeled off several and handed them round.

'For your help, and to keep this on the q.t.' The bar hadn't been damaged, but he insisted on paying up anyway. 'Sometimes it takes a while for the damage to show,' he told the barman. Then he bought a round of drinks and clapped a hand on Rab's neck.

'Time you were in bed, son.' Rab's room key was on the bar. The staff all knew he was with Big Ger. 'Next time you want a rammy, try playing away from home, eh?'

'Sorry, Big Ger.'

'Got to look out for one another, eh, Rab? Sometimes that means using the brain as well as the brawn.'

'I'll be fine, Big Ger. Sorry again.'

'Off you go now. There's a mirror in the lift, so don't you go swinging a punch at it.'

Rab tried to smile. He looked sleepy after all the excitement. Cafferty watched him slouch out of the bar. He felt like a drink, but not here, not with these people. Leave them be, let them get it out of their systems with gossip and retelling. There was a minibar in his room, and that would do him for tonight. He apologised with a wave of his arms, then followed Rab to the lift, stood with him in its close confines all the way to the third floor. It was like being back in a cell. Rab's eyes were closed. He was leaning against the mirror. Cafferty kept his eyes on him and didn't blink once.

Does it matter? That had been Rab's question. Cafferty was beginning to wonder.

27

As Rebus walked into St Leonard's next morning, two uniforms were discussing a film from the previous night's TV.

'*When Harry Met Sally*, you must've seen it, sir.'

'Not last night. Some of us have got better things to do.'

'We're just talking about whether men can be friends with women without wanting to sleep with them. That's the plot, you see.'

'I reckon,' the second uniform said, 'as soon as a bloke claps eyes on a woman, first thing he wonders is what she'd be like in the scratcher.'

Rebus could hear raised voices in the CID suite. 'If you'll excuse me, gents, more urgent business . . .'

'Lovers' tiff,' one of the uniforms said.

Rebus turned back towards him. 'Pal, you couldn't be further from the truth.'

Siobhan had Derek Linford backed into a corner of the room. She also had an audience: DI Bill Pryde, DS Roy Frazer and DS George Hi-Ho Silvers. They were seated at their desks, enjoying the spectacle. Rebus gave all three a withering glance as he waded in. Siobhan had Linford by the throat, her face close to his – by dint of standing on tiptoe. He had paperwork in one hand, turned into a crumpled wad by the involuntary tightening of his fist. He was holding his other hand up in a gesture of surrender.

'And if you so much as *think* my telephone number, never mind calling it,' Siobhan was yelling, 'I'll twist your balls so hard they'll drop off!'

From behind, Rebus brought his hands down hard on

hers, pulling them off Linford. Her head snapped round, face flushed with anger. Linford was coughing.

'This what you call a word?' Rebus asked her.

'Knew you'd be involved somewhere,' Linford spat.

Siobhan turned back to him. 'This is you and me, arsehole, nobody else!'

'Think you're God's gift, don't you?'

Rebus: 'Shut up, Linford. Don't make it any worse than you have.'

'I haven't done anything.'

Siobhan tried pulling away from Rebus. 'You fucking snake!'

And then a voice behind them, booming with authority: 'What the hell's going on here?' All three looked towards the open doorway. Chief Superintendent Watson was standing there. And he had a visitor: Colin Carswell, the Assistant Chief Constable.

Rebus was the last to be 'invited' to give the Chief Super his side of the story. There were just the two of them in the office. The Farmer – nicknamed for his ruddy-coloured face and north-east agricultural background – sat with hands pressed together, a sharpened pencil resting between them.

'Am I supposed to fall on that?' Rebus asked, pointing to the pencil. 'Ritual hara-kiri?'

'You're supposed to tell me what was happening back there. The one day the ACC comes calling . . .'

'He'll be taking Linford's side, of course?'

The Farmer glared at him. 'Don't start. Just give me your version, for what it's worth.'

'What's the point? I know what the other two will have told you.'

'What exactly?'

'Siobhan will have told the truth, and Linford will have come up with a pack of lies to save his arse.' Rebus shrugged as the Farmer's face grew darker.

306

'Humour me,' he said.

'Siobhan went out a couple of times with Linford,' Rebus recited. 'Nothing serious. Then she sent him packing. I was round her place one evening discussing her case. Came out and was sitting in my car, saw someone from the opposite tenement come out, go for a pee round the corner, and head back again. I went to investigate, and it was Linford, spying on her from the tenement stairwell. Then last night, she phones me, says she thinks she's being watched. So I told her about Linford.'

'Why didn't you tell her before?'

'Didn't want to upset her. Besides, I thought I'd scared him off.' Rebus shrugged again. 'I'm obviously not the hard case I think I am.'

The Farmer leaned back in his chair. 'And what does Linford say?'

'I'm betting he's told you it's a pile of shite concocted by DI John Rebus. Siobhan was mistaken, I made up this story, and she swallowed it.'

'And why would you do that?'

'So he'd push off and let me work the case the way I want to work it.'

The Farmer looked down at the pencil he was still holding. 'Actually, that's not the reason he gave.'

'What then?'

'He says you want Siobhan for yourself.'

Rebus screwed his face into a sneer. 'Well, that's his fantasy, not mine.'

'No?'

'Absolutely not.'

'I can't let this go, you know. Not with Carswell as witness.'

'Yes, sir.'

'What do you think I should do?'

'If it were me, sir, pack Linford off back to Fettes where he can continue to be their desk-bound blue-eyed boy, far from the hurly-burly of actual policing.'

'Mr Linford doesn't want that.'

Rebus couldn't help reacting. 'He wants to stay here?' The Farmer nodded. 'Why?'

'He says he holds no grudge. Puts it down to the "hothouse conditions" on the case.'

'I don't get it.'

'Frankly, neither do I.' The Farmer rose, made for his coffee machine. Pointedly, he poured just the one mug. Rebus tried not to let his relief show. 'If I was him, I'd want to be shot of the lot of you.' The Farmer paused, sat down again. 'But what DI Linford wants, DI Linford gets.'

'It's going to be ugly.'

'Why?'

'Seen the CID suite lately? We're swamped. Hard enough to keep Siobhan and him apart under normal conditions, but the cases we're working on could be connected.'

'So DS Clarke tells me.'

'She said you were thinking of pulling the Supertramp inquiry.'

'There never really was an inquiry. But I was as curious as the next man about that four hundred thou. To be honest, I didn't give her much chance.'

'She's a good detective, sir.'

Watson nodded. 'Despite the role model,' he said.

'Look,' Rebus said, 'I know the score here. You're coasting to retirement, would rather this was someone else's shit-pile.'

'Rebus, don't think you can—'

'Linford belongs to Carswell, so you're not about to rub his nose in it. That just leaves the rest of us.'

'Careful what you're saying.'

'I'm not saying anything you don't know yourself.'

The Farmer rose to his feet, rested his knuckles on the desk and leaned towards Rebus. 'And what about you? Building your own private little police force – meetings in the Oxford Bar, running around like it's *you* that runs this station.'

'I'm trying to solve a case.'

'And get into Clarke's knickers at the same time?'

Rebus jumped to his feet. Their faces were inches apart. Neither man said anything, as if the next word could prove a hair-trigger. The Farmer's phone started ringing. He moved a hand, picked it up and held it to his ear.

'Yes?' he said. Rebus was so close, he could hear Gill Templer in the earpiece:

'Press briefing, sir. You want to see my notes?'

'Bring them in, Gill.'

Rebus pushed away from the desk. He heard the Farmer calling behind him:

'Had we finished, Inspector?'

'I think so, sir.' Managed to close the door without slamming it.

And went to find Linford. Not in the office. He was told that Siobhan was in the ladies' loo, being calmed by a WPC. Canteen? No. The front desk said he'd left the station five minutes earlier. Rebus looked at his watch: it wasn't opening time yet. Linford's BMW wasn't in the car park. He stood on the pavement, took out his mobile, and called Linford's.

'Yes?'

'Where the hell are you?'

'Parked in the Engine Shed car park.'

Rebus turned and looked down St Leonard's Lane: the Engine Shed was at the end. 'What are you doing there?'

'Some thinking.'

'Don't strain yourself.' Rebus was walking along the lane.

'Great. I really appreciate you calling my mobile to hurl insults at me.'

'Always happy to oblige.' He turned into the car park. And there was the Beamer, parked in a disabled spot beside the front door. Rebus switched off his phone and opened the passenger door, got in.

'What an unexpected pleasure,' Linford said, putting his own phone away and resting his hands on the steering wheel, eyes focused on the windshield.

'I like surprises myself,' Rebus said. 'Like being told by my chief super that I'm chasing DC Clarke.'

'Well, aren't you?'

'You know bloody fine I'm not.'

'You seem to be round her flat often enough.'

'Yeah, with you peeking in the windows.'

'Look, okay, when she dumped me I got a bit . . . It doesn't happen to me very often.'

'Being chucked? I find that hard to believe.'

Linford gave the ghost of a smile. 'Believe what you like.'

'You lied to Watson.'

Linford turned to him. 'You'd have done the same in my shoes. That was my career on the line, right there!'

'Should have thought of that first.'

'Easy to say now,' Linford said quietly. He bit his bottom lip. 'What if I apologise to Siobhan? Went off the rails a bit . . . won't happen again . . . that sort of thing?'

'Better put it in writing.'

'In case I make a mess of it?'

Rebus shook his head. 'It's hard to apologise when there's one hand round your throat and another round your balls.'

'Christ, man, I thought a blood vessel was going to burst.'

Rebus was stony faced. 'You could always have fought back.'

'That would have looked good, three other men in the room watching.'

Rebus studied him. 'You're bloody smooth, aren't you? Every step calculated before you take it.'

'Watching Siobhan wasn't calculated.'

310

'No, I don't suppose it was.' But, despite his words, Rebus wasn't so sure.

Linford turned in his seat, reached for something in the back. Papers: the same crushed bundle he'd been holding in the CID suite.

'Do you think we can talk shop for a minute?'

'Maybe.'

'I know you've been sidetracking me, running your own show and not letting me in. Fine, that's your decision. But all the interviews I've done, there might just be a nugget . . .' He handed the lot over to Rebus. Pages and pages of meticulous interview notes. The Holyrood Tavern, Jennie Ha's . . . and not just pubs but flats and businesses in the vicinity of Queensberry House. Cheekily, he'd even gone asking at Holyrood Palace.

'You've been busy,' Rebus grudgingly admitted.

'Shoe leather: it's an old standby, but sometimes it works.'

'So where's the nugget? Or do I have to sift this lot and be impressed by the number of rocks and stones along the way?'

Linford smiled. 'I saved the best for last.'

Meaning the last few pages, stapled together. Two interviews with the same man, conducted over a single day. One casual chat in the Holyrood Tavern itself, the other conducted at St Leonard's, with Hi-Ho Silvers in tow.

The interviewee's name was Bob Cowan and he gave his address as Royal Park Terrace. He was a university lecturer, Economic and Social History. Once a week, he met a friend for a drink at the Holyrood Tavern. The friend lived in the Grassmarket, and the Tavern made for a convenient halfway house. Cowan enjoyed his walk back through Holyrood Park, past St Margaret's Loch with its colony of swans.

The moon was nearly full that night – the night Roddy Grieve met his end – *and I left the Tavern about quarter* to midnight. Most nights, I never meet a soul on that walk. Precious few dwellings around there. I suppose some people would get a bit nervous. I mean, you read all sorts of stories. But I've never had any bother the three years I've been making that trip. Now, this may not be relevant. I thought about it hard for days after the murder, and I was inclined to think that it wasn't. I saw the photos of Mr Grieve, and neither of these two men looked like him, in my opinion. Of course, I could be mistaken. And though the night was pretty bright, plenty of stars out, a good clear sky, I really only got a good view of one of the men. They were standing across the road from Queensberry House. I'd say directly opposite its gates. They looked like they were waiting for someone. That was what attracted my attention. I mean, that time of night, down there with all the roadworks and construction? A strange choice for a meeting. I remember speculating as I walked home. The usual things: maybe the third man had nipped off somewhere to pee; or it could be some sort of sexual encounter; or they could be about to break into the construction site . . .*

An interjection from Linford:

You really should have come forward with this at the time, Mr Cowan.

Then back to Cowan's story:

Oh, I suppose so, but you're always worried you'll get everyone excited about nothing. And these men, they didn't really look suspicious. I mean, they weren't wearing masks or carrying bags marked Swag. They were just two men who were chatting. Could have been friends who'd bumped into one another. Do you see what I mean? Both dressed quite normally, casually: denims, I think, and dark jackets, maybe training shoes. The one I got the closest look at had close-cropped hair, either dark brown or black. These big sallow eyes, like a basset-

312

hound. Cheeks to match, and a downtrodden sort of
scowl to his mouth, as if he'd just heard something that
hadn't pleased him. He was big, had to be over six feet
tall. Broad shoulders. Do you think he had something to
do with it? My God, maybe I was the last person to see
the killer . . .

'What do you think?' Linford asked.

Rebus was sifting through the other interviews.

'I know,' Linford said, 'it doesn't look like much.'

'Actually, it looks pretty good.' Linford seemed surprised
by the comment. 'Problem is, there's not enough of it. Big
guy, broad-shouldered . . . could be a hundred people who
fit.'

Linford nodded; he'd thought this through. 'But if we
can get a photofit . . . Cowan says he's willing.'

'And then what?'

'Pubs in the area, maybe he's local. Plus, a description
like that, wouldn't surprise me if he was a brickie.'

'One of the construction workers?'

Linford shrugged. 'Once we've got a photofit . . .'

Rebus made to hand the sheaf of interviews back. 'Got
to be worth a go. Congratulations.'

Linford preened visibly, reminding Rebus why he'd
started hating him in the first place. The mildest praise
and the man forgot everything else.

'And meantime,' Linford said, 'you go your own way?'

'That's right.'

'And I'm kept out of the picture?'

'Right now, Linford, that's the best place for you,
believe me.'

Linford nodded his agreement. 'So what do I do now?'

Rebus pushed open the passenger door.

'Stay away from St Leonard's till you've got that letter
written. Make sure Siobhan gets it by the end of play
today – but not before this afternoon; she needs time to

cool off. Tomorrow, maybe it'll be safe to show your face. With the stress on maybe.'

It was enough for Linford. He wanted to shake Rebus's hand. But Rebus closed the door. No way he was shaking the bastard's hand: he'd turned up a nugget, not transformed base metals into gold. And Rebus still didn't trust him, got the feeling he'd turn in his grandmother for a sniff of promotion. The question was: what would he do if he thought his job was under threat?

A bleak occasion; a bleak spot.

Siobhan was there with Rebus. A woolly suit was in attendance, too: the WPC who'd been on the scene the night 'Mackie' had jumped, the one who'd said, *You're one of Rebus's, aren't you?* A minister was present, and a couple of faces Siobhan recognised from the Grassmarket: they'd nodded a greeting towards her. She hoped they wouldn't want cigarettes today; she'd none with her. Dezzi was there, too, sobbing into a wad of pink toilet paper. She'd found some scraps of black clothing: a gypsy-style skirt, long lace shawl torn almost to streamers. Black shoes, too, a different style on either foot.

No sign of Rachel Drew; maybe she hadn't heard.

So you couldn't have called the graveside busy. Crows were calling near by, threatening to drown out the minister's few and hasty words. One of the Grassmarket pair had to keep nudging his pal, who looked like nodding off. Every time the minister said the name Freddy Hastings, Dezzi mouthed the word Chris. When it was finished, Siobhan turned on her heels and walked quickly away. She didn't want to talk to anyone, had come only from a sense of duty, something no one would thank her for.

Back at the cars, she looked at Rebus for the first time. 'What did the Farmer say to you?' she asked. 'He's taking Linford's word against ours, isn't he?' When Rebus didn't answer, she got into her car, turned the ignition and was gone. Standing by his own car, yet to unlock it, Rebus thought he had seen the beginnings of tears in her eyes.

The yellow JCB digger was going in, clawing rubble from the base. With the tenement's innards showing, the whole scene had a voyeuristic quality, yet at the same time Rebus noticed that some bystanders couldn't look. It was as if a pathologist had gone to work, exposing the body's secrets. These had been people's homes: doors they'd painted and repainted; wallpaper carefully chosen. Perhaps some young couple – newly-weds – had done the skirting boards, getting gloss on their overalls but not really caring. Light fittings, electrical sockets, switches . . . tumbling into a heap or hanging by threads of cable. And even more furtive elements of the structure: roof beams, plumbing, gaping wounds which had once been chimneys. A roaring fire at Christmas time . . . tree decorated in the corner.

The vultures had been at work: few of the better doors remained. Fireplaces had been removed, as had cisterns, wash-hand basins, baths. Water tanks and radiators . . . the scavengers would turn a profit from them. But what fascinated Rebus were the layers. Paint hidden by paint, wallpaper by wallpaper. A striped confection could be peeled to reveal hints of pale pink peony roses, and beneath that layer yet another, red-coated horsemen. A kitchen had been added to one flat, and the original kitchenette papered over. When the paper was ripped away, the original black and white tiles were revealed. Skips were being filled and loaded on to lorries, taking them to landfills outside the city where the jigsaw pieces would be covered over, a final layer for future archaeologists to scrape away.

Rebus lit a cigarette, narrowing his eyes against gusts of powder and grit. 'Looks like we're a bit on the late side.'

He was standing with Siobhan outside what had been

315

the building containing Freddy Hastings' office. She was calm now, seemed to have put Linford out of her mind as she watched the demolition. Hastings' office had been on the ground floor, with flats above. There was no sign of it now. Once levelled, contractors would commence putting up a new structure, an 'apartment complex' only a stone's throw from the new parliament.

'Someone on the council might know,' Siobhan offered. Rebus nodded: she meant, might know what had happened to the contents of Hastings' office. 'You don't look very hopeful,' she added.

'It's not in my nature,' Rebus said, inhaling the smoke, and with it a mixture of plaster dust and other people's lives.

They drove to the City Chambers on the High Street, where an official was eventually able to provide the name of a solicitor. The solicitor was based in Stockbridge. On the way there, they stopped off at what had been Hastings' home, but the present owners didn't know anything about him. They'd bought from an antique dealer who, they thought, had bought from a football player. 1979 was ancient history; New Town flats could change hands every three or four years. Young professionals bought them, one eye on the investment potential. Then they had kids, and the stairs became a chore, or they bemoaned the lack of a garden. They sold up, moved on to something bigger.

The solicitor was young, too, and knew nothing of Frederick Hastings. But he got on the phone to one of the senior partners, who was in a meeting elsewhere. A time was arranged. Rebus and Siobhan debated over whether to return to the office. She suggested a walk along the Dean Valley, but Rebus, remembering that Linford lived in Dean Village, made the excuse that his heart wasn't up to the exertion required.

Siobhan: 'I suppose you want to find a pub.'

Rebus: 'There's a good one actually, just at the corner of St Stephen's Street.'

In the end, they walked to a café on Raeburn Place. Siobhan ordered tea, Rebus decaf. A waitress apologised for the fact that they were seated in a no smoking establishment. With a sigh, Rebus put the packet away.

'You know,' he said, 'life used to be so simple.'

She nodded agreement. 'You lived in a cave, clubbed your food to death . . .'

'And little girls went to charm schools. Now, you've all got degrees from the University of Sarcasm.'

'Three words,' she said: 'pot, kettle and black.'

Their drinks came. Siobhan checked that she had no messages on her mobile.

'Okay,' Rebus said, 'it'll have to be me who asks it.'

'Asks what?'

'What are you going to do about Linford?'

'Do I know anyone called that?'

'Fair enough.' Rebus went back to drinking his coffee.

Siobhan poured some tea into her cup and lifted it with both hands. 'Did you talk to him?' she asked. Rebus nodded slowly. 'Thought so. You were spotted running out after him.'

'He told the Farmer a lie about me.'

'I know. The chief mentioned it.'

'What did you tell him?'

'The truth,' she said. They were silent, raising their cups and drinking, lowering them again as though synchronised. Rebus was nodding again, though he didn't really know why. Siobhan cracked first. 'So what did you say to Linford?'

'He's going to send you an apology.'

'That's big of him.' She paused. 'You think he means it?'

'I think he regrets what he did.'

'Only because it might have affected his glorious career.'

'You could be right. All the same . . .'

'You think I should let it drop?'

'Not exactly. But Linford's got his own leads to follow. With any luck, they'll keep him out of your way.' He looked at her. 'I think he's scared of you.'

She snorted. 'He should be.' She lifted her cup again. 'But fair enough, if he keeps out of my way, I'll keep out of his.'

'Sounds good.'

'You think the trail's gone cold, don't you?'

'Hastings?' She nodded. 'I'm not sure,' he said. 'It's amazing what you can turn up in Edinburgh.'

Blair Martine was waiting for them when they returned to the solicitors' offices. He was rotund and elderly, with a chalk-stripe suit and silver watch-chain.

'I always wondered', he said, 'whether Freddy Hastings would come back to haunt me.' In front of him on the desk sat a ten-inch-thick bundle of manila folders and envelopes, tied together with parcel string. His fingers brushed the topmost folder, came away dusty.

'How do you mean, sir?'

'Well, it was never a case for you lot, but it was a mystery all the same. He just upped and left.'

'Creditors at his heels,' Rebus added.

Martine looked sceptical. He'd obviously lunched very well, his cheeks suffused with contentment, waistcoat straining. When he leaned back in his chair, Rebus feared the buttons would pop slapstick-style.

'Freddy was not without resources,' Martine said. 'That's not to say he didn't make some bad investments; he did. But all the same . . .' He tapped the files again. Rebus was champing at the bit to be let loose on them, but knew Martine would plead client confidentiality.

'And he did leave a number of creditors,' Martine went on. 'But none of them so very significant. We had to arrange for his flat to be sold. It fetched a fair price, not quite what it might have done.'

'Enough to see off these creditors?' Siobhan asked.

'Yes, and my firm's own fees. Costly business, when someone disappears.' He paused. There was a trick hiding beneath his cuff-linked sleeve. Rebus and Siobhan stayed silent; they could see he was bursting to play it. Martine leaned forward, elbows on the desk.

'I did keep a little aside,' he said conspiratorially, 'to defray the storage costs.'

'Storage?' Siobhan echoed.

The lawyer shrugged. 'I did think Freddy might walk back into my life some day. I just never expected it to be posthumous.' He sighed. 'When is the funeral, incidentally?'

'We've just been to it,' Siobhan told him. She didn't add: with half a dozen mourners. A speedy burial, no personal eulogy from the minister. It could have been called a pauper's funeral, only Supertramp had been no pauper.

'So what exactly is it that's in storage?' Rebus asked.

'Effects from his flat: everything from pens and pencils to a rather fine Persian carpet.'

'Had your eye on that, did you?'

The lawyer glared at Rebus. 'Plus the contents of his office.'

Rebus's back stiffened visibly. 'And where', he asked, 'might we find this storage facility?'

The answer was: on a bleak stretch of road round the northern perimeter of the city. Edinburgh, being coastal, was bounded on its northern and eastern sides by the Firth of Forth. Developers and the council had big plans for Granton, at the city's northernmost extreme.

'Active imagination required,' Rebus said as they drove.

Meaning: Granton at present was an unassuming, in places ugly and brutal, region of harsh sea-wall views, grey industrial buildings and redundancy. Broken factory windows, spray paint, sooty lorries. People like Sir Terence

319

Conran had taken one look at the place and visualised a future of retail and leisure developments, Docklands-style warehouse apartments. They foresaw moneyed people moving in, jobs and homes, a whole new lifestyle.

'Any redeeming features?' Siobhan asked.

Rebus thought for a moment. 'The Starbank's not a bad boozer,' he said. She looked at him. 'You're right,' he conceded. 'That's more Newhaven than Granton.'

Seismic Storage, the premises were called. Three long rows of concrete bunkers, each one roughly three-quarters the size of a normal garage.

'Seismic,' the owner, Gerry Reagan explained, 'in that they'll survive an earthquake.'

'A real worry around here, earthquakes,' Rebus commented.

Reagan smiled. He was leading them down one of the rows. The weather was closing in, clouds gathering and a fierce wind blowing off the estuary. 'The Castle's built on a volcano,' he said. 'And do you remember those tremors a while back in Portobello?'

'Wasn't that mine workings?' Siobhan asked.

'Whatever,' Reagan said. There was constant humour in his eyes, topped off with bushy grey eyebrows. He wore metal-rimmed glasses on a chain around his neck. 'Thing is, my customers know their stuff'll be safe till kingdom come.'

'What sort of customers do you get?' Siobhan asked.

'All sorts: old folk who've moved into sheltered accommodation, no space for all their furniture. People flitting, either on their way here or heading south. Sometimes they sell up before their new place is ready. I've one or two collectors' cars, too.'

'Do they fit?' Rebus asked.

'It's snug,' Reagan conceded. 'One of them, we had to remove the bumpers. This is it.'

They'd come armed with a letter of authorisation from

Blair Martine, which Reagan now held in his hand, along with a key to unlock the up-and-over door.

'Unit thirteen,' he said, double-checking he was in the right place. Then he stooped to unlock the door, yanking it open.

As Martine had explained, Hastings' effects had first been stored in a warehouse. But then the warehouse had undergone conversion, forcing the lawyer to make other arrangements: 'I swear, him going off like that gave me more headaches than a dozen contested estates.' The effects had ended up at Seismic Storage only three years before, and Martine couldn't swear that everything was intact. He'd also told them that he hadn't known Hastings well – a few social occasions: dinners, parties. And that he'd had no dealings with Alasdair Grieve.

Siobhan's question afterwards: 'So if money wasn't why they left, what was?'

Rebus's response: 'Freddy didn't leave.'

'He left and came back,' Siobhan corrected. 'And Alasdair? Is it his body in the fireplace?'

Rebus had let that one go unanswered.

Now, as Reagan opened the door to its fullest extent, they saw that the place was a ready-made bric-a-brac shop, lacking only the cash register.

'Nice, neat job we made of it,' Reagan said, admiring his self-storage handiwork.

'Oh, dear heavens,' Siobhan gasped. Rebus was already punching numbers into his mobile phone.

'Who are you calling?' she asked.

He said nothing, straightening up when the call was answered. 'Grant? Is Wylie with you?' He grinned wickedly. 'Get a pen in your mitt, I'll give you directions. Little job here that's just perfect for the Time Team.'

Linford was back at Fettes, seated in ACC Carswell's office. He sipped his tea – china cup and saucer – while Carswell took a call. When the call was finished, Carswell lifted his own cup, held it to his lips and blew.

'Bit of a mess at St Leonard's, Derek.'

'Yes, sir.'

'I told Watson to his face, if he's got no control over his officers . . .'

'With respect, sir, a case like this one, tempers are bound to flare.'

Carswell nodded. 'I admire you for that, Derek.'

'Sir?'

'You're not the kind to drop fellow officers in the soup, even when they're at fault.'

'I'm sure I was partly to blame, sir. Nobody likes it when someone comes into an inquiry from outside.'

'So you become the scapegoat?'

'Not exactly, sir.' Linford was looking at his cup. Small blobs of oil dotted the surface. He wasn't sure if the tea, the water or the milk was to blame.

'We could transfer the investigation here,' Carswell was saying. 'Lock, stock and barrel if need be. Use Crime Squad officers to—'

'With respect, sir, it's late on in the investigation to start over from scratch. We'd lose a lot of time.' He paused. 'And it would send the budget rocketing.'

Carswell was known to like a nice, tidy budget. He frowned, took a sip from his cup. 'Don't want that,' he said. 'Not if we can help it.' He stared across the desk at Linford. 'You want to stay put, that's what you're telling me?'

'I think I can win them over, sir.'

'Well, you're braver than most, Derek.'

'Most of the team are absolutely fine,' Linford went on. 'It's just a couple . . .' He broke off, lifted his cup again.

Carswell looked at the notes he'd made for himself back in St Leonard's. 'Would that be DI Rebus and DC Clarke, by any chance?'

322

Linford said nothing; made sure his eyes didn't meet Carswell's.

'No one's irreplaceable, Derek,' the ACC said quietly. 'Believe me, no one.'

28

'It's *déjà vu* all over again,' Wylie said, as she and Hood inspected the contents. The concrete store was full almost to its roof. Desks, tables, chairs, rugs. Cardboard boxes, framed prints, a stereo system.

'This'll take days,' Hood complained. And with no Mrs Coghill to make coffee, no inviting kitchen. Just this bleak wasteland, the wind forcing tears from his eyes, rain threatening.

'Nonsense,' Rebus said. 'We're looking for paperwork. All the big items, we just put to one side. The interesting-looking stuff goes into the back of the car. We'll work shifts of two.'

Wylie looked at him. 'Meaning?'

'Meaning two clearing out the junk, and two sorting through all the papers. We'll take the stuff back to St Leonard's.'

'Fettes is closer,' Wylie reminded him.

He nodded. But Fettes was Linford's home turf. It was as though Siobhan could read his mind.

'That's even closer,' she said, nodding towards the glorified Portakabin which acted as Gerry Reagan's office.

Rebus nodded. 'I'll go square it with him.'

Grant Hood carried a portable TV out of the garage and placed it on the ground. 'Ask him if he's got a tarp, too.' He looked up. 'Rain's not far off.'

Half an hour later, the first showers blew in off the Forth, jabbing their faces and hands with needles of cold, and bringing a thick haar which seemed to cut them off from the world. Reagan had provided a large sheet of thick translucent polythene, which was going to blow away given half a chance. They'd fixed down three of its corners with bricks, leaving one open, flapping entrance. Then Reagan had a better idea: the garage two along was currently out of use. So the three of them – Hood, Wylie and Siobhan Clarke – carried the goods along to this new site while Reagan attempted to fold up his polythene sheet.

'What's the boss up to?' Hood asked Reagan.

Slitting his eyes against the rain, Reagan peered back towards his office, its lit windows like beacons of warmth and shelter against the darkening afternoon. 'Setting up the command post, that's what he told me.'

Hood and Wylie exchanged a look. 'And did that involve a kettle and a seat by the heater?' Wylie asked.

Reagan laughed.

'He said shifts,' Siobhan reminded them. 'You'll get your turn.' All the same, she wished they'd find some files or something, so she, too, would have an excuse to visit the Portakabin.

'I knock off at five,' Reagan said. 'No point staying here in the dark.'

'Any lamps we could use?' Siobhan asked. Wylie and Hood looked disappointed: a five o'clock homer sounded good to them. Reagan was looking doubtful, but for different reasons.

'We'd lock up after us,' Siobhan reassured him. 'Set the alarms or whatever.'

'I'm not sure my insurance company would be happy.'

'When are they ever?'

He laughed again, rubbed his head. 'I could stick around till six, I suppose.'

She nodded. 'Six it is then.'

Soon afterwards, they started finding the box-files. Reagan had produced a wheelbarrow, with the folded-up sheet of polythene covering its base. They loaded the files into the barrow, and Siobhan wheeled it towards the office. She pushed open the door and saw that Rebus was just finishing clearing one of the room's two desks. He'd piled all the stuff on the floor in a corner.

'Reagan said we could use this one,' he told her. He pointed to a door. 'There's a chemical toilet through there. Plus sink and kettle. Boil the water before you drink it.' She noticed there was a mug of coffee on the chair by Rebus.

'I think we could all do with a cup,' she said. She found a socket and plugged in her mobile phone, letting it charge while she filled the kettle and switched it on. Rebus went outside and started bringing the box-files in.

'It's getting pretty dark,' she said.

'How are you coping?'

'There's a light inside the garage. That's pretty much it. Mr Reagan says he can stay till six.'

Rebus checked his watch. 'So be it.'

'Just one thing,' she reminded him, 'this is the Grieve case we're working on now, right?'

He looked at her. 'We can probably swing overtime, if that's what you're thinking.'

'Might help pay for the Christmas shopping . . . if I ever get time to do any.'

'Christmas?'

'You know, festive time of year, coming up fast.'

He looked at her. 'You can just switch off like that?'

'I don't think you have to be obsessed to make a good detective.'

He went back outside, gathered more files into his arms. In the distance, he could see the three figures working in the mist – Wylie, Hood, Reagan – while their shadows danced on the pitted surface of the compound. The scene seemed timeless to him. Humans had been working like this, moving things in sub-zero gloom, for thousands of years. And to what end? So much of the past simply disappeared. But it was their job to make sure past crimes did not go unpunished, whether they be committed the day before or two decades before. Not because justice or the lawmakers demanded it, but for all the silent victims, the haunted souls. And for their own satisfaction, too. Because in trapping the guilty, they atoned for their own sins of commission and omission. How in God's name could you switch that all off for the sake of swapping some presents . . . ?

Siobhan came out to help, broke the spell. She cupped hands to her mouth and called out that she was making coffee. Cheers and clapping. The scene no longer timeless but discrete, the figures turned into personalities. Reagan thumping his gloved hands together, bouncing on his toes, glad to be part of this adventure: something to stave off the daily loneliness of his job. Hood whooping, but not breaking stride as he moved chairs from one unit to the other: the work ethic strong in him. Wylie raising her hand, announcing that she took two sugars: making sure she got what she wanted.

'Strange job, isn't it?' Siobhan commented.

'Yes,' he agreed. But she meant Reagan's.

'Every day stuck out here on your own, all these concrete boxes full of secrets and other people's stuff. Aren't you curious what else we'd find if we opened a few doors?'

Rebus smiled. 'Why do you think he's so keen to help out?'

'Because he's a generous soul?' Siobhan guessed.

'Or he doesn't want us snooping.' She looked at him. 'Reason I was indoors so long, I thought I'd take a look at his client list.'

'And?'

'Couple of names I recognised: fences who live in Pilton and Muirhouse.'

'Just along the road.' Rebus nodded. 'No way we can search without a warrant.'

'All the same, a useful piece of ammo should Mr Reagan start proving uncooperative.' He glanced at her. 'And something to bear in mind next time we pull either of them in on a charge: no point getting a search warrant for a flat in Muirhouse when the stuff's sitting in self-storage.'

They took a break, huddling in the office. Four of them: Hood said he wanted to keep going; Wylie could take his coffee out to him when she'd finished hers.

'Boy wouldn't go down well with the unions,' was Reagan's comment.

The heater was Calor gas, all three elements lit. Not much insulation in the cabin. The long narrow window to the front wore a film of condensation, with occasional beads breaking free to trickle downwards, gathering on the sill. There was one overhead bulb, and a desk lamp. The room was fuggy and yellow-bathed. Reagan accepted a cigarette from Rebus, the two men forming a huddle while the non-smoking women edged away.

'New Year resolution,' Reagan said, examining the tip of the cigarette. 'I'm giving them up.'

'Reckon you'll make it?'

The man shrugged. 'Might do, all the practice I get – two or three times a year I try calling a halt.'

'Practice makes perfect,' Rebus admitted.

'How long do you reckon this'll all take?' Reagan asked.

'We appreciate your cooperation, sir.' Said in the voice of someone who had suddenly become an official, all cigarette-sharing *bonhomie* erased. Reagan got the point: this policeman could make a nuisance of himself given the motivation. Then the door flew open and Grant Hood staggered in. He was carrying a computer screen and keyboard, pushed his way past them and dropped it on to the cleared desk.

'What do you think?' he asked, getting his breath.

'Looks ancient,' Siobhan commented.

'Not much use without the hard drive,' Ellen Wylie added.

Hood grinned. It was the answer he'd been waiting for. He reached beneath his coat, to where something was tucked into his waistband. 'Hard disks like we have weren't around back then. Slot on the side is for floppies.' He pulled out half a dozen cardboard squares, circular holes in them like old novelty records. 'Nine-inch floppies,' he said, waving them in front of him. With his free hand, he patted the keyboard. 'Probably a DOS-based WP package. Which, if that doesn't say much to any of you, means I'm going to be stuck in here.' He put down the floppies and rubbed his hands in front of the flames. 'While you lot are out there seeing if you can find any more disks.'

By the end of play, they'd emptied half the garage, and a lot of what was left looked like furniture. Rebus took three box-files away with him, thinking he'd make an evening of it at St Leonard's. The station was quiet. This time of year, pickpockets and shoplifting were the major concerns: crowds in the Princes Street stores, wallets and purses bulging. You got muggings at cash machines, too. And depression: some said it was the short bursts of daylight and longer stretches of dark. People drank themselves angry, drank until they unravelled. Bust-ups, windows smashed – bus shelters; phone boxes; shops and pubs. They took knives to their loved ones, slashed at their own wrists. SAD: Seasonal Affective Disorder.

More work for Rebus and his colleagues. More work for the A&E departments, the social workers, the courts and prisons. Paperwork mounting as the Christmas cards started to arrive. Rebus had long since given up writing cards, but people persisted in sending them to him: family, colleagues, a few of his drinking cronies.

Father Conor Leary always sent one. But Leary was still convalescing, and Rebus hadn't been to see him for a while. Hospital beds reminded him of his daughter Sammy, unconscious after the hit-and-run which had put her in a wheelchair. In Rebus's experience, Christmas was about sham get-togethers, about pretending that all was well with the world. A celebration of one man's birth, carried out with tinsel and trappings, and conducted in a haze of white lies and alcohol.

Or maybe it was just him.

There was no sense of urgency as he studied each page from the box. He kept taking coffee and cigarette breaks, stepping outside, lighting up in the car park at the rear of the station. Business correspondence: deadly dull. Newspaper clippings: commercial properties for sale and rent, some of them circled, some with double question marks in the margin. Once Rebus had identified Freddy Hastings' handwriting, he was able to tell that it was a one-man operation, no other hand at work. No secretary. And where did Alasdair Grieve fit in? Meetings: Alasdair was always mentioned at the meetings; business lunches. Maybe he was a meeter and greeter, his surname lending a certain something to the operation. Cammo's brother, Lorna's brother, Alicia's son – someone prospective clients would want to dine with.

Back inside to warm his feet and dig into the box, retrieving another batch of documents. And then another cup of coffee, a wander downstairs to talk to the night shift in the Comms Room. Break-ins, fist fights, family quarrels. Cars stolen, vandalised. Burglar alarms tripped. A missing person reported. A patient who'd absconded from his hospital ward, dressed only in pyjamas. Car smashes: black ice on the roads. One alleged rape; one serious assault.

'Quiet night,' the duty officer said.

Camaraderie on the night shift. One officer shared his sandwich snack with Rebus. 'I always seem to make one more than I need.' Salami and lettuce on wholemeal bread. A carton of orange juice if Rebus wanted one, but he shook his head.

'This is fine,' he said.

Back at his desk, he jotted notes based on his findings, flagging some of the pages by dint of fixing Post-it notes to them. Looked at the office clock and saw it was almost midnight. Reached into his pocket and checked his cigarette packet: just the one left. That decided it. He locked the files in a drawer, put his coat on, and headed out. Cut through to Nicolson Street. There were all-night shops there, three or four of them. Cigarettes and a snack on his shopping list; maybe something for tomorrow's breakfast. The street was noisy. A group of teenagers screaming for a non-existent taxi; people weaving home, cartons of carry-out food held close to them, faces bathing in steam. Underfoot: greasy wrappings, dropped gobbets of tomato and onion, squashed chips. An ambulance sped past, blue light flashing but sirenless, eerily silent amidst the street's cacophony. Conversations turned high decibel by drink. And older groups, too, well dressed, heading home from a night at the Festival Theatre or Queen's Hall.

Clusters of young people, standing in doorways and the corners of buildings. Voices low, eyes scanning. Rebus saw crime where none existed; or perhaps it was that he was attuned to the *possibility* of crime. Had the midnight revels always been this harsh and alarming? He didn't think so. The city was changing for the worse, and no amount of imaginative construction in glass and concrete could hide the fact. The old city was dying, wounded by these roars, this new paradigm of ... not lawlessness exactly, but certainly lack of respect: for surroundings, neighbours, self.

The fear was all too apparent in the tense faces of the elders, their theatre programmes tightly rolled. But there was something mixed in with the fear: sadness and impotence. They couldn't hope to change this scene; they could only hope to survive it. And back home they would collapse on the sofa, door locked and bolted, curtains or shutters closed tight. Tea would be poured into the pot, biscuits nibbled as they stared at the wallpaper and dreamed of the past.

There was a scrum outside Rebus's chosen shop. Cars

331

had drawn up kerbside, music blaring from within. Two dogs were attempting to copulate, cheered on by their youthful owners as girls squealed and looked away. Rebus went inside, the glare forcing his eyes closed for a moment. A pack of lorne sausage, four rolls. Then up to the counter for cigarettes. A white poly bag to take his purchases home. Home meant turning right, but he turned left.

He needed to pee, that was all, and the Royal Oak was near by. Just off the main drag, the place never seemed to close. Thing was, he could use their toilet without entering the bar, so it wasn't as if he was going there to drink. You walked through the doorway, and the bar was straight ahead through another door, but if you headed down the stairs, that's where the toilets were. The toilets, plus another, quieter bar. The upstairs bar at the Oak was famous. Open late, and always, it seemed, with live music. Locals would sing the old songs, but then some Spanish flamenco guitarist might do his piece, followed by a guy with an Asian face and Scots inflections playing the blues.

You never could tell.

As Rebus made for the stairs, he looked in through the window. The pub was tiny, and packed this night with gleaming faces: old folkies and hardened drinkers, the curious and the captivated. Someone was singing unaccompanied. Rebus saw fiddles and an accordion, but resting while their owners concentrated on the rich baritone voice. The singer was standing in the corner. Rebus couldn't see him, but that's where all eyes were focused. The words were by Burns:

> *What force or guile could not subdue,*
> *Through many warlike ages,*
> *Is wrought now by a coward few,*
> *For hireling traitors' wages . . .*

Rebus was halfway down when he stopped. He'd recognised one of the faces. Back up he went, his face a bit closer to the window this time. Yes, seated next to the piano: Cafferty's pal, the one from the Bar-L. What was his name? Rab, that was it. Sweating, hair slick. His face was jaundiced, eyes dull. His fist was wrapped around what Rebus took to be a vodka and orange.

And then the singer took a step forward, and now Rebus saw who it was.

Cafferty.

> *The English steel we could disdain,*
> *Secure in valour's station,*
> *But English gold has been our bane –*
> *Such a parcel of rogues in a nation . . .*

As the verse ended, Cafferty glanced towards the window. He was smiling grimly as Rebus pushed open the door, starting the final verse as Rebus made his way to the bar. Rab was watching, trying to place him perhaps. One of the barmaids took Rebus's order: a half of Eighty and a whisky. There was no conversation in the bar, respectful silence and even a tear in one patriot's eye as she sat on her stool with her brandy and Coke raised to her lips, her ragged boyfriend stroking her shoulders from behind.

When the song finished, there was applause, a few whistles and cheers. Cafferty bowed his head, lifted his whisky glass and toasted the room. As the clapping subsided, the accordionist took it as his cue to commence. Cafferty accepted a few compliments as he made his way to the piano, where he leaned down to mutter something in Rab's ear. Then, as Rebus had known he would, he came over to the bar.

'Something to ponder, come the election,' Cafferty said.

'Plenty of rogues in Scotland,' Rebus said. 'I can't see how independence would mean less of them.'

Cafferty wasn't going to rise to it. Instead, he toasted

him, emptied his glass, and ordered another. 'And one for my friend Strawman.'

'I've got one,' Rebus said.

'Be nice to me, Strawman. I'm celebrating coming home.' Cafferty eased a folded newspaper out of his pocket, placed it on the bar top. It was folded at the commercial property section.

'In the market?' Rebus asked.

'I might be,' Cafferty said with a wink.

'What for?'

'I hear there's a killing to be made, way the Old Town is now.'

Rebus nodded towards the piano, where Rab had angled his chair, the better to watch the bar. 'He's not just on the booze, is he? What is it, jellies?'

Cafferty looked over towards his minder. 'Place like the Bar-L, you take whatever you need. Mind you,' he smiled, 'I've been in cells bigger than this.'

Two glasses of malt had arrived. Cafferty added a dribble of water to his, while Rebus watched. Rab seemed to him such an unlikely companion – doubtless fine in a place like the Bar-L; you'd need muscle there. But out here, back on his home ground where he had all the men he needed, what was it tied Cafferty to Rab, Rab to Cafferty? Had something happened in jail ... or was something happening out here? Cafferty was holding the jug above Rebus's glass, awaiting a reaction. Rebus nodded eventually, and when the pouring was done raised the glass.

'Cheers,' he said.

'*Slainte*.' Cafferty took a sip, let it roll around his mouth.

'You seem surprisingly chipper,' Rebus told him, lighting a cigarette.

'What good's a long face going to do?'

'You mean apart from cheering me up?'

'Ah, you're a hard man. I sometimes wonder if you're not harder than me even.'

'Want to put it to the test?'

Cafferty laughed. 'In my current condition? And you with a face like thunder?' He shook his head. 'Another time maybe.'

They stood in silence, Cafferty applauding when the accordionist finished. 'He's French, you know. Barely a word of English.' Then, to the musician: '*Encore! Encore, mon ami!*'

The accordionist acknowledged this with a bow. He was seated at one of the tables, a guitarist beside him tuning up for the next slot. When he began to play again, something a little more sombre this time, Cafferty turned to Rebus.

'Funny, you bringing up Bryce Callan the other day.'

'Why?'

'Just that I'd been meaning to call Barry, see how old Bryce was doing.'

'And what did Barry say?'

Cafferty looked down into his drink. 'He didn't say anything. I got as far as some dogsbody, who told me he'd pass my message on.' His face was dark, but he laughed anyway. 'Wee Barry still hasn't got back.'

'Wee Barry is a big player these days, Cafferty. Maybe he can't afford to be seen with you.'

'Aye, well, good luck to him, but he'll never be a quarter the man his uncle was.' He drained his glass; Rebus felt obliged to order refills. Between times, he drained his half-pint and the blended whisky which had accompanied it, so he could now concentrate on the malt. Why the hell was Cafferty telling him all this?

'Maybe Bryce did the right thing,' Cafferty said, as their drinks came. 'Getting out like that, retiring to the sun.'

Rebus added water to both glasses. 'You thinking of following him?'

'I might at that. I've never been abroad.'

'Never?'

Cafferty shook his head. 'The ferry to Skye, that was enough for me.'

'There's a bridge these days.'

Cafferty scowled. 'Wherever they find romance, they replace it.'

Privately, Rebus didn't disagree, but he was damned if Cafferty was going to know that. 'The bridge is a lot handier,' he said instead.

Cafferty's scowl looked even more pained. But it wasn't that . . . he was in real pain. He bent forward, hand going to his stomach. Put down his drink and fumbled in his pocket for some tablets. He was wearing a dark woollen blazer with a black polo neck beneath. He shook two tablets out, washed them down with water poured into an empty glass.

'You okay?' Rebus asked, trying not to sound too concerned.

Cafferty caught his breath at last, patted Rebus's forearm as though reassuring a friend.

'Bit of indigestion, that's all.' He picked up his drink again. 'We're all on the way out, eh, Strawman? Barry could have gone the way of his uncle, but instead he's a businessman. And you . . . I'll bet most of your CID colleagues are younger, college-educated. The old ways don't work any more, that's what they'll tell you.' He opened his arms. 'If I'm a liar, let me hear it.'

Rebus stared at him, then looked down. 'You're not a liar.'

Cafferty seemed pleased to have found common ground. 'You can't be too far off retirement.'

'I've a few years in me yet.'

Cafferty raised his hands in surrender. 'The phrase more's the pity never entered my mind.'

And this time when he laughed, Rebus almost joined in. Another round of whiskies was ordered. This time, Cafferty added a vodka and fresh, which he took over to

Rab. When he came back, Rebus asked again about the bodyguard.

'Only, the way he looks tonight, I'm not sure he'd be much use to you.'

'He'd do fine in a clinch, don't you worry.'

'I'm not worried. I'm just thinking this may be the best chance I ever get to take a pop at you.'

'Take a pop at me? Christ, man, state I'm in, if you sneezed I'd be in a thousand pieces on the floor. Now come on, have another.'

Rebus shook his head. 'I've got work to do.'

'At this hour?' Cafferty's voice had risen so much, other drinkers were looking at him. Not that he was paying them any heed. 'No crows to scare off this time of night, Strawman.' He laughed again. 'Not too many of these old howffs left, eh? It's all theme pubs now. Do you remember the Castle o' Cloves?'

Rebus shook his head.

'Best pub there was. I drank there often. And now . . . well, down it came. They built a DIY store where it stood. Just up the road from your cop shop.'

Rebus nodded. 'I know the spot.'

'All changing,' Cafferty said. 'Maybe you'd be better out of the game, after all.' He lifted the glass to his lips. 'Just a thought, mind.' He finished the drink.

Rebus took a deep breath. 'Ah-choo!' Making show of sneezing across Cafferty's chest, then studying his handiwork. His eyes met Cafferty's. If looks were weapons, they'd have cleared the pub. 'You lied to me,' Rebus said quietly, walking away from the bar as the guitarist finally got his instrument in tune.

'You'll go to your grave a gobshite!' Cafferty yelled, brushing flecks of saliva from his polo neck. His voice stilled the music for a moment. 'Hear me, Strawman? I'll be dancing on your bastard coffin!'

Rebus let the door close behind him, inhaled the street's smoke-free air. Noises off: more kids heading home. He rested his head against a wall, a cold compress for his burning thoughts.

I'll be dancing on your coffin.

Strange words to come from a dying man. Rebus walked: down Nicolson Street to the Bridges, and from there down into the Cowgate. He stopped near the mortuary, smoked a cigarette. He still had his bag with him: rolls and sausage. He felt like he'd never be hungry again. His stomach was too full of bile. He sat on a wall.

I'll be dancing on your coffin.

A jig it would be, unrestrained and awkward, but a jig all the same.

Back up Infirmary Street. Back along to the Royal Oak. He kept back from the windows this time. No music: just a man's voice.

> *How slow ye move, ye heavy hours,*
> *The joyless day how dreary.*
> *It wasna sae ye glinted by,*
> *When I was wi' my dearie . . .*

Cafferty again; another of Burns' songs. His voice full of pain and pleasure, pulsing with life. And Rab, seated by the piano, eyes almost closed, breathing laboured. Two men fresh minted from the Bar-L. One dying in full voice; the other wasted on freedom.

It was wrong. It was very, very wrong.

Rebus felt it in his own doomed heart.

Part Three

Beyond
This
Mist

Yet frost under sunlight can sparkle like hope
even while muscles cramp, and the freezing damp
can whisper 'let the bottle rest for once.
There are warm mysteries beyond this mist.'

Angus Calder, 'Love Poem'

29

Jerry walked into the dole office frozen and soaked. There hadn't been any shaving foam left in the can, so he'd had to use ordinary soap, and then his last razor was in the bath, where Jayne had blunted it shaving her legs. Cue the morning's first argument. He'd nicked himself a couple of times; one of the spots wouldn't stop bleeding. And now his face was stinging from the sudden sleet, and of course as soon as he got in through the dole office door, didn't the cloud break and the sun come out?

It was a cruel city, this.

And then it turned out, after he'd waited half an hour, that his appointment wasn't at the dole office at all, but with the DSS, which was another half-hour's walk. He almost gave up and headed home, but something stopped him. Home: was that what it was? How come these days it felt like a prison, a place where his gaoler wife could nag and grind him down?

So he made for the DSS office, and they told him he was an hour late, and he started explaining but nobody was listening.

'Take a seat. I'll see what we can do.'

So he sat down with the wheezing masses, next to an old guy with a blood-curdling cough who spat on the floor when he'd finished. Jerry moved seats. The sun had dried out his jacket, but his shirt beneath was still damp, and he was shivering. Maybe he was coming down with some-thing. Three-quarters of an hour he sat there. Other people came and went. Twice he went up to the desk, where the same woman said they were trying to find him

341

'a slot'. Her mouth looked like a slot, thin and disapproving. He sat back down.

Where else was there for him to go? He thought of working in an office like Nic's, nice and warm and with coffee on tap, watching the short skirts swish past his desk, one of them leaning over the photocopier. Christ, wouldn't that be heaven? Nic was probably heading off to lunch now, out to some swank place with crisp white tablecloths. Business lunches and business drinks and deals done with a handshake. Anybody could do a job like that. But then not everybody married the boss's cousin.

Nic had phoned him last night, started given him a roasting for bottling out, running off into the night like that, but making a joke of it in the end. Jerry had caught an inkling of something: Nic was afraid of him. And then it had struck him why: Jerry could tell the cops, spill the beans. Nic *had* to keep him sweet, that was why he turned the episode into a joke, ended with the words, 'I forgive you. After all, we go back a long way, eh? The two of us against the world.'

Except that right now, it felt like Jerry was all on his own against the world, stuck here in this smelly hole, no one to help him. He was thinking back: *two of us against the world*, when had that ever been true? When had they ever been equals, partners? *What in God's name did they see in one another?* He thought maybe he had an answer for that now, too. It was a way of cheating time, because when they were together they were the same kids they'd always been. And so the things they did . . . they really *were* a game, albeit a deadly serious one.

Someone left their paper behind when they went in for their interview. Christ, and the guy had turned up twenty minutes after Jerry, yet here the bastard was, waltzing into a cubicle ahead of him! Jerry slid over, picked up the tabloid, but didn't open it. There was that bile in his gut again, that fear of what stories he might find inside: rapes, assaults, not knowing if Nic was responsible. Who knew

342

what Nic was doing behind his back, all the nights they didn't meet? And all the other stories, too: newly-weds, happy marriages, stormy relationships, sex problems, babies being born to famous mums. Everything bounced back on his own life, and all it did was make him feel worse.

Jayne: *clock's ticking*.

Nic: *time you grew up*.

The minute hand on the clock above the desk moved another notch. Clock-watching: wasn't that something you did in offices, when you weren't watching the skirts swish past? Who was to say Nic had it so good? He'd been working for Barry Hutton's company these past eight years, hadn't seen much in the way of promotion.

'Sometimes,' he'd complained to Jerry, 'that family thing can backfire on you. Barry daren't promote me or everyone'll just say it's for who I am, not what I do. Do you see?'

And then, when Cat had left him: 'That bastard Hutton's just looking to get rid of me. Now Cat's done a runner, he sees me as an embarrassment. See what she's done to me, Jerry? The cow's as good as lost me my job. Her and her bastard cousin!'

Fuming, seething, raging.

And this from a guy who lived in a £200,000 house and had a job and car! Who was it really needed to grow up? Jerry wondered about this more and more.

'He'll ditch me, Jer, soon as he gets half a chance.'

'Jayne says she's going to ditch me, too.'

But Nic hadn't wanted to hear about Jayne. His only comment: 'They're all as bad as each other, swear to God, pal.'

All as bad as each other.

He stomped back to the desk. What was he? A dummy or what? Wasn't he married, settled? Didn't he deserve a bit of respect?

Didn't he deserve that at the very least, and maybe something more besides?

The woman was there. She'd fetched herself a mug of coffee. Jerry's throat felt dry; couldn't stop shivering.

'Look,' he said, 'are you taking the piss or what?'

She had these glasses on, thick black frames. There were lipstick smears on the rim of the mug. Her hair looked dyed, and she was getting on for fat. Middle-aged, going to seed. But at the moment, she was in a position of power, and no way she was letting him interfere with that. She gave a cold smile, blinked so he saw her blue eyeshadow.

'Mr Lister, if you'll try to stay calm . . .'

Necklace hanging around her neck, all mixed in with the creases of loose skin. Big bust on her, too. Jesus, he'd never seen a chest like it.

'Mr Lister.' Trying to drag his attention back to her face. But he was transfixed, his hands gripping the edge of the desk. He saw her in the back of the van, saw himself giving her a good punch in that lipsticked mouth, ripping at the blouse, necklace sent flying.

'Mr Lister!'

She was getting to her feet. He'd been leaning further and further across the desk. And now members of staff were closing in, alerted by her yell.

'Jesus,' he said. Couldn't think of anything else to say; his whole body was shaking, head spinning. He tried to clear his head, wipe the blood from the pictures there. He was eye to eye with her for a second, and he felt she could see what he'd been thinking, every vivid frame of it.

'Oh, Jesus.'

Two big blokes coming at him; that was all he needed, get arrested. He shoved his way out of there, back into the outside world where the sun was drying the streets and everything looked eerily normal.

'What's happening?' he said. He found he was crying, couldn't stop himself. Stumbled blearily along the street, holding the wall for support. He just kept walking, breaking into a sweat eventually. It took him the best part of three hours.

He'd walked clean across town.

Grey morning. Rebus waited for the rush hour to pass before setting out.

Glasgow's Barlinnie Prison lay just off the M8 motorway. If you knew what you were looking for, you could see it in the near distance as you drove between Edinburgh and Glasgow. It sat on the edge of the Riddrie housing scheme, unsignposted until you got really close. At visiting time, you could follow the cars and pedestrians. Tattooed men in their fifties, wiry and sunken-cheeked, off to visit pals who'd got caught. Stressed mothers, kids in tow. Quiet relatives, not quite sure how things had come to this.

All of them bound for HMP Barlinnie.

The Victorian blocks sat behind high stone walls, but the reception area itself was modern. Workmen were busy on the finishing touches. A member of staff was checking visitors for drug contamination. You swiped the magic glove over them, and it came up positive if they'd recently been in contact with drugs. Positive meant no open visit: you could still go in, but only with a glass wall between you and the prisoner. Bags were being checked, and then placed inside lockers, to be retrieved on the way out. Rebus knew that the visiting area had been revamped, too, with smart new seating arrangements and even a play area for the kids.

But inside the jail, it would be the same old wings. Slopping-out was still a fact of life, and the smell permeated the interiors. There were two new wings, but restricted to sex offenders and drug users. It rankled with the 'pros', the career criminals who didn't think scum like that deserved to live, never mind the special treatment.

Another new addition was the cubicles for agent

345

interviews. This was where lawyers met their clients: glass-fronted but allowing for privacy. The Assistant Governor, Bill Nairn, seemed pleased with the renovations as he showed Rebus around. He even took Rebus into one of the cubicles, the two men sitting down opposite one another.

'Far cry from the old days, eh?' Nairn beamed.

Rebus nodded. 'I've stayed in tattier hotels.' The two men knew one another of old: Nairn had worked for the Procurator Fiscal's office in Edinburgh, and then in the city's Saughton Prison, before the promotion to the Bar-L.

'Cafferty doesn't know what he's missing,' Rebus added.

Nairn shifted in his seat. 'Look, John, I know it grates when we let one back out . . .'

'It's not that, it's *why* he's out.'

'The man's got cancer.'

'And the Guinness boss had Alzheimer's.'

Nairn stared at him. 'What are you saying?'

'I'm saying Cafferty looks pretty chirpy.'

Nairn shook his head. 'He's ill, John. You know it and I know it.'

'I know he said you wanted rid of him.' Nairn looked at him blankly. 'Because he was in danger of running the show.'

Now Nairn smiled. 'John, you've seen this place. Every door's kept locked. No easy access. Think how hard it would be for one man to run all five wings.'

'They mix though, don't they? Wood-shop, textiles, chapel . . . I've seen them wandering around outside.'

'You've seen the trusties, and always with a guard. Cafferty didn't have that level of freedom.'

'He didn't run the show?'

'No.'

'Then who does?' Nairn shook his head. 'Come on, Bill. You get drugs in here, moneylending, gang fights. You've got a scrap contract to strip anything valuable out of old wiring: don't tell me none of that stuff's been sharpened and used for a stabbing.'

'Isolated cases, John. I'm not going to deny it: drugs are the big problem here. But it's still petty stuff. And it wasn't Cafferty's bailiwick.'

'Then whose was it?'

'I'm telling you, it's not organised that way.'

Rebus leaned back in his chair, studied his surroundings: clean paint and new carpets. 'Know what, Bill? You can change the surface, but it'll take more than that to change the culture.'

'It's a start, though,' Nairn said determinedly.

Rebus scratched his nose. 'Any chance I can see Cafferty's medical records?'

'No.'

'Then can you take a look for me? Put my mind at rest.'

'X-rays don't lie, John. The hospitals here are pretty hot on cancer. It's always been a west coast growth industry.'

Rebus smiled, as was expected. A solicitor was entering the cubicle next door. The prisoner followed a few moments later. He looked young, bewildered. Remand, probably; up to court later in the day. Yet to be found guilty, but already tasting the low life.

'What was he like?' Rebus asked.

Nairn's pager had sounded. He was fumbling to switch it off. 'Cafferty?' Looking towards where the pager was clipped to his belt. 'He wasn't too bad. You know how it is with career villains: serve their time, just part and parcel of the job, like a temporary relocation.'

'You think he's changed?'

Nairn shrugged. 'Man's older.' He paused. 'I'm assuming power's shifted in Edinburgh while he's been away.'

'Not so you'd notice.'

'He's back to his old ways, then?'

'He's not ready for the Costa del Sol just yet.'

Nairn smiled. 'Bryce Callan, now there's a name from the vaults. Never did manage to lock him up, did we?'

'Not for want of trying.'

'John . . .' Nairn looked down at his hands, which rested on the table top. 'You used to come and visit Cafferty.'

'So?'

'So it's more than just the usual cop/villain thing with you two, isn't it?'

'How do you mean, Bill?'

'I'm just saying . . .' He sighed. 'I'm not sure what I'm saying.'

'You're saying I'm too close to Cafferty? Maybe obsessed, not objective?' Rebus was remembering Siobhan's words: you didn't need to be obsessed to be a good cop. Nairn looked about to argue. 'I agree a hundred per cent,' Rebus went on. 'Sometimes I feel closer to that bastard than I do . . .' He bit off the ending: *to my own family.* Frankly, most of the time it felt like no contest. 'That's why I'd rather he was in here.'

'Out of sight, out of mind?'

Rebus leaned forward, looked around. 'Strictly between us?' Nairn nodded. 'I'm scared what'll happen, Bill.'

Nairn held his gaze. 'He's planning to have a go at you?'

'If what you say is true, what's he got to lose?'

Nairn was thoughtful. 'What about you?'

'Me?'

'Say he's going to die, natural causes. Doesn't that cheat you? No chance of *you* trying to get at *him?* One final victory.'

One final victory.

'Bill,' Rebus chastised, 'do I look the sort to you who'd have any truck with that?'

The two men smiled. Next door, the prisoner's voice was rising.

'But ah havnae done nuthin'!'

Nairn tutted. 'Double negatives,' he said.

'Thought these booths were soundproofed?' Rebus said. Nairn's shrug told him they'd done their best. Then Rebus

348

had a thought. 'What about someone called Rab, released about the same time as Cafferty?'

Nairn nodded. 'Rab Hill.'

'Rab was Cafferty's bodyguard?'

'I wouldn't go that far. They were only on the same wing for four, five months.'

Rebus frowned. 'Way Cafferty tells it, they were best pals.'

Nairn shrugged. 'Prison makes for strange alliances.'

'Rab's not coping too well with the outside world.'

'No? You'll excuse me if my heart doesn't bleed.'

The voice from next door again: 'How many times dae ah huv tae tell ye?'

Rebus got to his feet. *Strange alliances* he was thinking. Cafferty and Rab Hill. 'How did it come about, Cafferty's cancer?'

'How do you mean?'

'How was it diagnosed?'

'Usual way. He hadn't been feeling too hot. Took him in for tests, and bingo.'

'Just do me one favour, Bill. Look at our friend Rab. Medical records, whatever you've got. Will you do that for me?'

'Know something, John? You're harder work than half my prisoners.'

'Then pray a jury never finds me guilty.'

Bill Nairn was about to laugh that off, until he saw the look in Rebus's eyes.

By the time he got to Seismic Storage, Ellen Wylie and Siobhan Clarke had finished emptying the container. On the spare desk in Reagan's office sat eight columns of paperwork. The women were warming themselves by the heater, mugs of tea in their hands.

'What now, sir?' Wylie asked.

'St Leonard's,' Rebus said. 'That interview room you were using as an office, we'll take them there.'

'So no one else can see them?' Siobhan guessed.

Rebus looked at her. Her face was pink with cold, nose shiny. She was wearing ankle boots with socks over black woollen tights; a pale grey scarf accentuating the colour in her cheeks.

'Have you got two cars?' Rebus asked. The women agreed that they had. 'Load them up, and I'll see you back at base, okay?'

He left them to it, drove to the South Side and was smoking a cigarette in the car park when the Chief Super arrived in his Peugeot 406.

'Mind if I have a word, sir?' Rebus asked, in place of any greeting.

'Out here or in the warm?' Farmer Watson hoisted his briefcase, checked his watch. 'I've a noon appointment.'

'This'll only take a minute.'

'Fair enough. My office, soon as you've finished out here.'

The Farmer went in, closed the door. Rebus nipped his cigarette, tossed it, and followed.

Watson was firing up the coffee-maker when Rebus knocked at his open door. He glanced up, nodded for Rebus to enter. 'You look rough, Inspector.'

'I was working late.'

'What on?'

'The Grieve case.'

The Farmer looked at him again. 'Is that true?'

'Yes, sir.'

'Only, from what I hear, you're involving yourself in everything but.'

'I think the cases tie up.'

With the machine on, the Farmer retreated behind his desk. He sat down and motioned for Rebus to do the same, but Rebus stayed standing.

'Progress?'

'Getting there, sir.'

'And DI Linford?'

'He's working his own leads.'

'But the two of you are in contact?'

'Absolutely, sir.'

'And Siobhan's keeping out of his way?'

'He's keeping out of *hers*.'

The Chief Super seemed dissatisfied. 'I'm getting no end of flak.'

'From Fettes?'

'And beyond. Someone from the Scottish Secretary's office was on to me first thing this morning, wanting results.'

'Hard to run an election campaign', Rebus guessed, 'with a murder inquiry ongoing.'

The Farmer stared at him coldly. 'Almost his exact words.' His eyes narrowed a fraction. 'So what's on your mind?'

Now Rebus sat down, leaning forward, elbows on knees. 'It's Cafferty, sir.'

'Cafferty?' Whatever he'd been expecting, Watson hadn't been expecting this. 'What about him?'

'He's out of the Bar-L and back here.'

'So I've heard.'

'I want a watch kept on him.' There was silence in the room as Rebus waited in vain for the Chief Super to comment. 'I think we need to know what he's up to.'

'You know we can't do that without good reason.'

'His rep's not enough?'

'Lawyers and the media would have a field day. Besides, you know how stretched we are.'

'We'll be more stretched once Cafferty gets started.'

'Started on what?'

'I bumped into him last night.' He saw the look on his chief's face. 'Completely by accident. Thing was, he'd been browsing the *Scotsman*'s commercial property section.'

'So?'

'So what's he after?'

351

'Turning a profit, maybe.'

'That's more or less what he said.'

'Well then?'

Only it wasn't the way he'd put it: *a killing to be made* . . .

'Look,' the Farmer rubbed his temples, 'let's just get on with the work at hand. Clear up the Grieve case and I'll think about Cafferty. Deal?'

Rebus nodded distractedly. The door was still ajar. A knock came, and a uniform appeared round it. 'Visitor for DI Rebus.'

'Who is it?'

'She didn't say, sir. Just told me to tell you she'd not brought any peanuts. Said you'd understand.'

Rebus understood.

30

Lorna Grieve was in the waiting area. He unlocked the interview room, then remembered that Freddy Hastings' stuff was piled up in there. So he told her there was a change of plan, led her across the road to the Maltings.

'You have to be drunk before you can talk to me?' she teased. She was dressed to the tens: tight red leather trousers tucked into knee-high black boots; a black silk blouse with plunging neckline, black suede jacket open over it. More than enough make-up, and her hair freshly styled. She was carrying shopping bags from a couple of boutiques.

Rebus ordered fresh orange and lemonade for himself. She seemed to think her words had forced him into it, rose to the occasion by asking for a Bloody Mary.

'Mary, Queen of Scots, isn't it?' she said. 'Head chopped off, that's the bloody part.'

'I wouldn't know.'

'Never drunk one? Perfect pick-me-up.' She waited for a joke, but he didn't offer one. Nodded when the barmaid asked if she wanted Lea and Perrin's. They sat at a table inlaid with squares. She admired the pattern.

'It's so people can play chess,' Rebus explained.

'Loathsome game. Takes for ever, and at the end it all falls apart. No sense of climax.' Another pause. Again, Rebus wasn't biting.

'Cheers,' he said.

'First one today.' She took a gulp of her drink. Rebus doubted her veracity: he considered himself something of an expert, and would say she'd had at least a couple of belts already.

'So what can I do for you?' The commerce of the everyday: people wanting things from people. Sometimes it was an exchange, sometimes not.

'I want to know what's happening.'

'Happening?'

'The murder inquiry: we're being kept in the dark.'

'I don't think that's true.'

She lit a cigarette; didn't offer him one. 'Well, *is* anything happening?'

'We'll let you know as soon as we can.'

She straightened her back. 'That's not good enough.'

'I'm sorry.'

She narrowed her eyes. 'No, you're not. The family should be told—'

'In point of fact, it's the widow we'd talk to first.'

'Seona? You'll have to get in the queue. She's a media darling now, you know. Papers, TV ... falling over themselves for a photo of the "brave widow", carrying on where her husband left off.' She modulated her voice, imitating Seona Grieve: ' "It's what Roddy would have wanted." Like hell it is.'

'How do you mean?'

'Roddy may have seemed the quiet type, but there was steel in him, too. His wife running for MSP? He wouldn't have wanted that. It turns *her* into the martyr rather than him. He's already being forgotten about, except when she dusts off the corpse in the great cause of publicity!'

There were only the two of them in the bar; all the same, the barmaid gave a warning look.

'Easy,' Rebus said.

Her eyes were liquid with tears. Rebus got the feeling they weren't for anyone but Lorna herself: the lost one, the forgotten one. 'I've got the right to know what's going on.' Her eyes were clearing as she looked at him. 'Special rights,' she said in a low voice.

'Look,' he said, 'what happened that night—'

'I don't want to hear it.' She shook her head, steadied herself with another gulp of Bloody Mary, reducing it to ice.

'Whatever you're going through, if I can help I will, but don't resort to blackm—'

She was on her feet. 'I don't know why I came.'

He stood up, grabbed her hands. 'What have you taken, Lorna?'

'Just some . . . My doctor prescribed them. Not supposed to mix with alcohol.' Her eyes were everywhere but on him. 'That's all it is.'

'I'll get a patrol car to run you—'

'No, no, I'll find a cab. Don't worry.' She modelled a smile for him. 'Don't worry,' she repeated.

He picked her bags up for her; she seemed to have forgotten they were there. 'Lorna,' he said, 'have you ever met a man called Gerald Sithing?'

'I don't know. Who is he?'

'I think Hugh knows him. He runs a group called the Knights of Rosslyn.'

'Hugh keeps that side of his life separate. He knows I'd laugh at him.' She was on the verge of laughing now; she was on the verge of more than laughter. Rebus led her from the bar.

'Why do you ask?' she said.

'Doesn't matter.' He saw Grant Hood waving from across the road. In the distance, Siobhan Clarke and Ellen Wylie were unloading their cars. Hood dodged the traffic.

'What's up?' Rebus asked.

'The reconstruction,' Hood told him breathlessly. 'We've got a printout.'

Rebus nodded thoughtfully, then looked towards Lorna Grieve. 'Maybe you should see this,' he said.

So they went into St Leonard's and took her to an empty office. Hood fetched the computer graphic while

Rebus provided tea. She wanted two sugars; he added a third, watched her drink.

'What's the mystery?' she asked.

'It's a face,' he explained slowly, studying her. 'The university in Glasgow put it together for us from a skull.'

'Queensberry House?' she guessed, amused by his look of surprise. 'Not all the brain cells have emigrated to a better place. Why do you want me to see it?' Then that, too, came to her. 'You think it might be Alasdair?' She started shaking; Rebus realised his mistake.

'Maybe it'd be better if—'

Rising to her feet, she knocked the tea on to the floor, but seemed not to notice. 'Why? What would Alasdair be doing . . . ? He sends postcards.'

Rebus was cursing himself for being an insensitive bastard, short-sighted, unsubtle, twisted.

And then Grant Hood was in the doorway, brandishing the picture. She snatched it from him, stared at it intently, then burst out laughing.

'It's nothing like him,' she said. 'You bloody imbecile.'

Imbecile: he hadn't got to that one yet. He took the sheet from her. It was a good likeness of someone, but he had to agree: judging by the paintings in Alicia Grieve's studio, this was not her son. The face was a completely different shape, hair a different colour . . . cheekbones, chin, forehead . . . No, whoever it was in the fireplace, it wasn't Alasdair Grieve.

That would have been too simple. Rebus's life had never been simple; no reason to suppose it would start now.

Wylie was in the doorway, too, alerted by the laughter: not a regular sound in a police station.

'He thought it was Alasdair,' Lorna Grieve was saying, pointing at Rebus. 'He told me my brother was dead! As if one wasn't enough.' There was poison in her eyes. 'Well, you've had your little laugh, and I hope you're happy.' She stormed out of the office and down the corridor.

'Go after her,' Rebus told Wylie. 'Make sure she finds

the way out. And here . . .' He stooped down, retrieved the shopping bags. 'Give her these.'

She stared at him for a moment.

'Go!' he yelled.

'I hear and obey,' Ellen Wylie muttered. After she'd gone, Rebus slumped back down on his chair, rubbed both hands through his hair. Grant Hood was watching him.

'Not looking for tips, I hope,' Rebus told him.

'No, sir.'

'Because if you are, here's the best I can offer: study what I do, and then strive to do the exact fucking opposite. That way, you might make something of yourself.' He dragged his hands down his face, stared at the picture.

'Who the hell are you?' he asked. For some reason, he knew Skelly was the key, not just to Hastings' suicide and the four hundred grand, but to Roddy Grieve's murder, too . . . and maybe a lot more besides.

They sat in the cramped interview room, door closed to passers-by. People in the station were beginning to talk about them, calling them 'the Manson family', 'the Lodge', 'the swingers' club'. Hood was seated in the corner. He had the computer set up. Its screen was weird: black background, orange writing. He'd warned that the disks might be corrupted. Rebus, Wylie and Clarke sat round the centre table, box-files at their feet, the computer-generated image of the Queensberry House victim in front of them.

'You know what we have to do?' Rebus told them. Wylie and Clarke shared a look, sceptical of that 'we'.

'MisPers,' Wylie guessed. 'Back into the files and try to match this with one of the photos.'

Rebus nodded; Wylie shook her head. He turned to Hood: 'Any problems?'

'Seems to be running fine,' Hood said, hammering keys two-fingered. 'Printer connection's a problem. None of the ones we've got will fit. Might have to scour the second-hand shops.'

'So what's on the disks?' Siobhan Clarke asked.

He looked at her. 'Give me a chance.' And got back to work. Ellen Wylie lifted the first box-file on to the table and opened it. Rebus hoisted up three more, patted them.

'I've already done these,' he said. The others looked at him. 'Late night,' he said, winking.

Just so they knew he wasn't slacking.

Lunch consisted of sandwiches. By the time they broke at three for coffee, Hood was beginning to get somewhere with the disks.

'The good news', he said, unwrapping a chocolate bar, 'is that the computer was a late addition to Hastings' office.'

'How do you work that out?'

'The stuff on the disks, it's all dated '78, early '79.'

'My box-file goes back to '75,' Siobhan Clarke complained.

'*Wish You Were Here,*' Rebus said. 'Pink Floyd. September, I think it was. Much underrated.'

'Thank you, Professor,' Wylie said.

'You lot were still at nursery, I presume?'

'I'd really like to print this stuff out,' Grant Hood mused. 'Maybe if I phoned around the computer shops ...'

'What sort of stuff are we talking about?' Rebus asked.

'Bids on land. You know, gap sites, all that.'

'Where?'

'Calton Road, Abbey Mount, Hillside ...'

'What was he planning to do with them?'

'Doesn't say.'

'He wanted *all* of them?'

'Looks that way.'

'That's a lot of property,' Wylie commented.

'Well, a lot of building sites anyway.'

Rebus left the room, came back with an *A–Z*. He circled

Calton Road, Abbey Mount and Hillside Crescent. 'Tell me he had plans for Greenside,' he said. Hood sat back down at the computer. They waited.

'Yep,' he said. 'How did you know?'

'Take a look. He was drawing a circle around Calton Hill.'

'Why would he do that?' Wylie asked.

'1979,' Rebus stated. 'The devolution referendum.'

'With the parliament sited there?' Siobhan guessed.

Rebus nodded. 'The old Royal High School.'

Wylie was seeing it now. 'With the parliament there, all that land would have been worth a fortune.'

'He took a gamble on Scotland voting Yes,' Siobhan said. 'And he lost.'

'I wonder,' Rebus said. 'Did he have the money in the first place? Even back in the seventies – which is prehistory for you lot – those areas weren't exactly cheap.'

'What if he didn't have the money?' Hood asked.

It was Ellen Wylie who answered: 'Then someone else did.'

They knew what they were after now: financial records; clues that someone other than Hastings and Alasdair Grieve had been a partner in the business. They stayed late, Rebus reminding them that they could head home if they liked. But they were working as a team – uncomplaining, focused – and no one was about to break the spell. He got the feeling it had nothing to do with overtime. Out in the corridor, taking a breather, he found himself alone with Ellen Wylie.

'Still feel hard-done-by?' he asked.

She stopped, looked at him. 'How do you mean?'

'You thought I was using the pair of you; just wondering if that's still how you feel.'

'Keep wondering,' she said, moving off.

At seven o'clock, he treated them to dinner at Howie's

Restaurant. They discussed the case, progress and theories. Siobhan asked when the devolution vote had taken place.

'March first,' Rebus told her.

'And Skelly was killed early in '79. Could it have happened straight after the election?'

Rebus shrugged.

'They finished in the basement at Queensberry House on March eighth,' Wylie said. 'A week or so later, Freddy Hastings and Alasdair Grieve do a runner.'

'As far as we know,' Rebus added.

Hood, cutting into his gammon, just nodded. Rebus, big spender, had splashed out on a bottle of the house white, but they weren't making inroads. Siobhan was sticking to water; Wylie had taken a glass of wine but had yet to touch it. Hood had finished his glass but refused a refill.

'Why is it I'm seeing Bryce Callan?' Rebus said.

There was silence around the table for a moment, then Siobhan: 'Because you want to?'

'What would have happened to the land?' Rebus asked.

Hood: 'It would have been developed.'

'And what does Callan's nephew do?'

Clarke: 'He's a developer. But back then he was a labourer.'

'Learning the ropes.' Rebus swallowed some wine. 'Land around Holyrood, any idea what it's worth now they're building the parliament there rather than Calton Hill or Leith?'

'More than it was,' Wylie guessed.

Rebus was nodding. 'And now Barry Hutton's eyeing up Granton, the Gyle, God knows where else.'

'Because that's his job.'

Rebus was still nodding. 'Bit easier if you've got something your competitors haven't.'

Hood: 'You mean strongarm tactics?'

Rebus shook his head. 'I mean friends in the right places.'

*

'AD Holdings,' Hood said, tapping the screen. Rebus stood over him, eyes squinting at the orange letters. Hood pinched the bridge of his nose, squeezed his own eyes shut, then opened them and shook his head briskly, as if to shake off cobwebs.

'Long night,' Rebus agreed. It was nearly ten; they were on the verge of calling a halt. A lot of good work done, but still – as Rebus had been the first to pun – nothing concrete.

And now this.

'AD Holdings,' Hood repeated. 'Seems that's who they were in bed with.'

Wylie had the phone book open. 'Not in here.'

'Probably gone bust,' Siobhan guessed. 'If they ever existed.'

Rebus was smiling. 'Bryce Callan's initials?'

'BC,' Hood supplied. Then he got it: 'BC, AD.'

'A little private joke. AD was going to be BC's future.' Rebus had already been busy on the phone, asking a couple of retired colleagues about Bryce Callan. He'd sold up late in '79. Some of what he'd sold had gone to the upstart Morris Gerald Cafferty. Cafferty had started on the west coast, 1960s muscle for loan sharks. Drifted down to London for a time, post-Krays and Richardson. Made his name and learned his trade.

'There's always an apprenticeship, John,' Rebus had been told. 'These guys don't come fully formed from the womb. And if they don't learn, we put them away . . . and we keep on putting them away.'

But Cafferty had learned fast and well. By the time he'd reached Edinburgh, associated with Bryce Callan's operation, and then branching out on his own, he'd shown a propensity for not making mistakes.

Until he'd met John Rebus.

And now he was back, and Callan, his old employer, was tied to the case. Rebus tried to make a connection, but couldn't.

Bottom line: late in '79, Callan threw in the towel. Or, put another way, headed overseas to where Britain's extradition laws didn't apply. Because he'd had enough? Or had his fingers burned? Or because he was worried about something . . . some crime that could come straight back to him?

'It's Bryce Callan,' Rebus said now, 'it's got to be.'

'Which just leaves the one little problem,' Siobhan reminded him.

Yes: proving it.

31

It took them the best part of the next day, Thursday, to set
everything up. Trawls through company records; phone
calls. Rebus spent over an hour talking to Pauline Carnett,
his contact at the National Criminal Intelligence Service,
then another hour talking to a retired chief superintendent who had spent eight fruitless years in the 1970s
pursuing Bryce Callan. When Pauline Carnett called him
back, after she'd spoken to Scotland Yard and Interpol,
she had a Spanish telephone number. 950 code: Almeria.

'I once went there on holiday,' Grant Hood said. 'Too
many tourists; we ended up trekking into the Sierra
Nevadas.'

'We?' Ellen Wylie said, raising an eyebrow.

'Me and a mate,' Hood mumbled, his neck reddening.
Wylie and Siobhan shared a wink and a smile.

They would have to make the call from the Chief
Super's office: his was the only one with a speaker phone.
Besides, international calls were blocked in the rest of the
station. Chief Superintendent Watson would be present,
but that didn't leave much room. It was decided that the
three junior officers would be kept out, but a recording
made.

If the interviewee agreed.

Rebus sent Siobhan Clarke and Ellen Wylie in to
negotiate with the Farmer. His first two questions to them:
'Where's DI Linford? What's his take on this?'

Rebus had briefed them; they'd talked their way around
Linford, pressed their case again until the Farmer, worn
down, nodded his agreement.

With everything set up, Rebus sat in the Chief Super's chair and hit the buttons. The Chief Super himself was seated across the desk, in the chair Rebus usually occupied.

'Try not to get used to it,' had been the Farmer's comment.

The phone was picked up at the other end; Rebus hit the record button. A woman's voice: Spanish.

'Could I speak to Mr Bryce Callan, please?'

More Spanish. Rebus repeated the name. Eventually the woman went away. 'Housekeeper?' Rebus guessed. The Farmer just shrugged. Now someone else was picking up the receiver.

'Yes? Who's this?' Annoyed. Maybe a siesta interrupted.

'Is that Bryce Callan?'

'I asked first.' The voice deep, guttural: no trace that he was losing his Scottish inflections.

'I'm Detective Inspector John Rebus, Lothian and Borders Police. I'd like to speak to Mr Bryce Callan.'

'Fucking good manners you lot have got these days.'

'That'll be the customer relations training.'

Callan let out a wheezy laugh, rolling it into a cough. Catarrh: smoker. Rebus made to light a cigarette of his own. The Farmer was frowning, but Rebus ignored him. Two smokers having a chat: instant rapport.

'So what can you do me for?' Callan asked.

Rebus kept his tone light. 'Is it okay if I record this, Mr Callan? Just so I've got a record.'

'You might have one, son, but my sheet's clean. No criminal convictions.'

'I'm aware of that, Mr Callan.'

'So what's this about?'

'It's about a company called AD Holdings.' Rebus glanced at the sheets of paper spread out on the desk. They'd done their work: could prove the company was part of Callan's little empire.

There was a pause on the line.

'Mr Callan? You still there?' The Farmer was off his chair, drawing the waste bin over so Rebus could flick his ash into it. Then he went to open a window.

'I'm here,' Callan said. 'Call me back in an hour.'

'I'd really appreciate it if we could . . .' Rebus realised he was talking to the dialling tone. He cut the call.

'Bugger,' he said. 'Now he's got time to fix a story.'

'He doesn't have to talk to us at all,' Farmer Watson reminded him.

Rebus nodded.

'And now he's gone, you can put that bloody thing out,' the Farmer added. Rebus stubbed his cigarette against the side of the bin.

They were waiting for him in the corridor, expectant faces collapsing as he shook his head.

'He said to call back in an hour.' He checked his watch.

'He'll have a story by then,' Siobhan Clarke said.

'What do you want me to do?' Rebus snapped.

'Sorry, sir.'

'Ach, it's not your fault.'

'He's given himself an hour,' Wylie said, 'but that means we've got an hour, too. Make a few more calls, keep going through Hastings' paperwork . . .' She shrugged. 'Who knows?'

Rebus nodded his approval. She was right: anything was better than waiting. So they went back to work, fuelled by tins of soft drinks and background music courtesy of a cassette machine provided by Grant Hood. Instrumental stuff – jazz, classical. Rebus had been dubious at first, but it did help stave off the boredom. Farmer's orders: keep the volume down.

Siobhan Clarke agreed: 'If it got out that I listened to jazz, I'd never be able to show my face.'

An hour later, it was back upstairs to the Farmer's office. Rebus left the door open this time; felt it was the least they deserved. Watson didn't seem to notice. Called again, and this time it rang and rang. Callan wasn't going to answer; of course he wasn't.

But he did. No housekeeper this time, and straight to the point.

'You got a conference facility?'

The Chief Super nodded. 'Yes,' Rebus said.

Callan gave him a number to ring: Glasgow code. The name was C. Arthur Milligan – Rebus knew him as 'the Big C', a nickname he shared, seemingly happily, with cancer. And Milligan was like cancer to police officers and the Procurator Fiscal's office. He was one of the really big defence solicitors, worked a lot with the advocate Richie Cordover, Hugh's brother. If you had Big C by your side, and Cordover defending you in court, you had the sharpest edge there was.

At a price.

The Farmer was showing Rebus how to work the conference call. Milligan's voice: 'Yes, Inspector Rebus, can you hear me?'

'Loud and clear, sir.'

'Hiya, Big C,' Callan said. 'I'm hearing you, too.'

'Good afternoon, Bryce. How's the weather out there?'

'God knows. I'm stuck indoors because of this arsehole.' Meaning Rebus. 'Look, Mr Callan, I really do appreciate—'

Milligan interrupted. 'I believe you wish to record your conversation with my client. Who else is present?'

Rebus identified the Chief Super, didn't bother mentioning the others. Milligan and Callan had a discussion about the taping. At last, it was agreed the recording could begin. Rebus hit the button.

'That's us,' he said. 'Now if I could just—'

Milligan again: 'If I could just say at the outset, Inspector, that my client is under no obligation of any kind to answer what questions you may have.'

'I appreciate that, sir.' Trying to keep his voice level.

'And he's only talking to you out of a sense of public

duty, even though the United Kingdom is no longer his chosen country of residence.'

'Yes, sir, and I'm very grateful.'

'Are you charging him with anything?'

'Absolutely not. This is for information only.'

'And this tape wouldn't be produced in a court of law?'

'I shouldn't think so, sir.' Choosing his words carefully.

'But you can't be definite?'

'I can only speak for myself, sir.'

There was a pause. 'Bryce?' Milligan asked.

'Fire away,' Bryce Callan said.

Milligan: 'Fire away, Inspector.'

Rebus took a moment to compose himself, looking at the documents on the desk as he fished his cigarette out of the bin and relit it.

'What are you smoking?' Callan asked.

'Embassy.'

'Tuppence a bloody packet out here. I stick to cigars these days. Now get on with it.'

'AD Holdings, Mr Callan.'

'What about them?'

'Your company, I believe.'

'Nope. I had a few shares, but that's as far as it went.'

Eyes were on Rebus from the doorway: *we know that's a lie*. But Rebus didn't want to catch Callan out, not this early on. 'AD were buying up parcels of land around Calton Hill, using another business as a front. Two men: Freddy Hastings and Alasdair Grieve. Ever meet either of them?'

'You're going back how far?'

'Late 1970s.'

'Bloody hell, lot of water been passed since then.'

Rebus repeated the two names.

'If you'd care to tell my client what this is about, Inspector,' Milligan said, sounding curious himself.

'Yes, sir. It's a question of a sum of money.'

'Money?' Now Callan was hooked, too.

'Yes, sir, quite a lot of money. We're trying to find a home for it.'

Stares from the doorway: he hadn't told them how he'd play it.

Callan was laughing. 'Well, look no further, chum.'

'How much money?' the lawyer asked.

'Even more than Mr Callan will be paying you for your services this afternoon,' Rebus told him. More laughter from Callan, and a warning look from the Farmer: it didn't do to wind up people like the Big C unnecessarily. Rebus concentrated on his cigarette. 'Four hundred thousand pounds,' he said at last.

'A not inconsiderable sum,' Milligan admitted.

'We think Mr Callan might be able to claim it,' Rebus told him.

'How?' Callan sounding cagey; wary of traps.

'It belonged to a man called Freddy Hastings,' Rebus explained. 'Belonged in the sense that he carried it around with him in a briefcase. At one time, Mr Hastings was a property developer, working with AD Holdings to buy land near Calton Hill. This was in late '78 and early '79, prior to the referendum.'

Milligan: 'And if there had been a Yes result, the land would have been worth a fortune?'

Rebus: 'Possibly.'

'What does this have to do with my client?'

'In later years, Mr Hastings lived as a down and out.'

'With all that money?'

'We can only speculate why he didn't spend it. Maybe he was holding it for someone. Maybe he was afraid.'

'Or off his rocker,' Callan added. But the remark was bravado; Rebus could tell he was thinking about things.

'The point is, AD Holdings, of which we believe Mr Callan was prime mover, was using Hastings to make bids on all this land.'

'And you think Hastings just pocketed the money?'

'It's one theory.'

'So the money would belong to AD Holdings?'

'It's possible. Mr Hastings left no family, no will. The Treasury will claim it if no one else does.'

'That would be a shame,' Milligan said. 'What do you say, Bryce?'

'I've already told him, I only had a few shares in AD.'

'You wish to add to that? Perhaps elucidate?'

'Well, it might have been more than a few shares, now you mention it.'

Rebus: 'You had dealings with Mr Hastings?'

'Yes.'

'Using his company as a front for buying land and property?'

'Maybe.'

'Why?'

'Why what?'

'You already had a company – AD Holdings. In fact, you had dozens of companies.'

'I'll take your word for it.'

'So why did you need to hide behind Hastings?'

'Work it out for yourself.'

'I'd rather you told me.'

Milligan interrupted: 'And why is that, Inspector?'

'Mr Milligan, we need to be clear about whether Mr Callan here and Freddy Hastings did business together. We need some sort of proof that the money could conceivably have belonged to Mr Callan.'

Milligan was thoughtful. 'Bryce?' he said.

'As it happens, he *did* take money off me, and then scarpered.'

Rebus paused. 'You notified the police, of course?'

Callan laughed. 'Of course.'

'Why not?'

'Same reason I used Hastings as a go-between. Filth were trying to drag my good name down, all sorts of lies and accusations. I wasn't just buying land.'

'You were going to build on it?'

'Houses, clubs, bars . . .'

'And you'd have needed planning permission, which Mr Hastings, with his credentials, might have found easier to come by.'

'See? You've worked it out all by yourself.'

'How much did Hastings take?'

'Best part of half a mil.'

'You must have been . . . displeased.'

'I was raging. But he'd disappeared.'

Rebus looked towards the doorway. It explained why Hastings had changed identity so radically. It explained the money, but not why he hadn't spent it.

'What about Hastings' partner?'

'Did a runner at the same time, didn't he?'

'He doesn't seem to have got any of the money.'

'You'd have to talk to him about that.'

Milligan interrupted again. 'Bryce, any chance you've got paperwork proving any of this? It would help validate any claim.'

'I might have,' Callan conceded.

'Forgeries won't count,' Rebus warned. Callan tutted. Now Rebus sat forward in his chair. 'But thanks for clearing that up. It brings me to a connected series of questions, if you don't mind?'

'Go ahead,' Callan said breezily.

Milligan: 'I think perhaps we should—'

But Rebus was off and running. 'I don't think I said how Mr Hastings died: he committed suicide.'

'Not before time,' Callan snapped.

'He did so shortly after the prospective MSP Roddy Grieve was murdered. That's Alasdair's brother, Mr Callan.'

'So?'

'And also shortly after the discovery of a corpse in one of the old fireplaces at Queensberry House. You'll remember that, Mr Callan?'

'What do you mean?'

'I just mean, maybe your nephew Barry told you about Queensberry House.' Rebus picked up a sheet of paper, checked the facts. 'He was working there early in 1979, around the time of the devolution vote. That's when you found out that all the land you'd been buying up wasn't going to be a gold mine after all. It's also probably when you learned that Hastings had been skimming. Either that or he'd just kept all the loot on one of the deals and pretended to you it had gone through. You'd only find out later that it hadn't, and by then he'd have done a runner.'

'What's that got to do with Barry?'

'He was working for Dean Coghill.' Rebus picked up another sheet. Milligan was trying to interrupt, but no way Rebus was letting him. Ellen Wylie was bouncing on her toes, willing him on. 'I think you were putting pressure on Coghill. You got him to take on Barry. Barry was working for you at the time. I think you put Barry in there to screw things up for Coghill. It was like an apprenticeship.'

Callan – Rebus could imagine his face suffused with blood: 'Here, Milligan, you going to let him talk to me like this?'

Milligan; not Big C; not pal or chum. Oh yes, Callan was fizzing.

Rebus talked right across the pair of them. 'See, the body went into the fireplace same time your boy Barry was there, same time you were finding out that Hastings and Grieve had ripped you off. So my question to you, Mr Callan, is: whose body is it? And why did you have him killed?'

Silence, and then the explosion: Callan screaming; Milligan threatening.

'You lousy conniving—'

'Must strongly object to the—'

'Come on the phone with a load of shit about four hundred grand—'

'Unwarranted attack on someone with no criminal

record in this or any other country, a man whose reputation—'

'I swear to God, if I was there you'd need to slap me in chains to stop me smacking you one!'

'I'm waiting,' Rebus said, 'any time you want to hop on a plane.'

'Just you watch me.'

Milligan: 'Now, Bryce, don't let this appalling situation goad you into . . . Isn't there a senior officer present?' Milligan checked his notes. 'Chief Superintendent Watson, isn't it? Chief Superintendent, I must protest in the strongest terms about these underhand tactics, entrapping my client with tales of an unclaimed fortune . . .'

'The story's true,' Watson said into the speaker phone. 'The money's here. But it seems to be part of a wider mystery, and one which Mr Callan could help clear up by flying back here for a proper interview.'

'Any recording made today is, of course, inadmissible in a court of law,' Milligan said.

'Really? Well,' the Farmer said, 'I leave questions like that to the Fiscal's office. Meantime, am I right in thinking that your client has yet to deny anything?'

Callan: 'Deny? What do I need to deny? You can't touch me, you bastards!'

Rebus imagined him on his feet, face turned a colour no hours of tanning would ever match, gripping the receiver in his fist, strangling the tormentor it had become.

'You admit it then?' Watson asked, his voice all naïve sincerity. He winked towards the doorway as he spoke. If Rebus didn't know better, he'd say the man was beginning to enjoy himself.

'Piss off!' Callan growled.

'I think you can take that as a denial,' Milligan said tonelessly.

'I think you're probably right,' Watson agreed.

'Away to hell, the lot of you!' Callan yelled. There was a click on the line.

'I think Mr Callan has left us,' Rebus said. 'Are you still there, Mr Milligan?'

'I'm here, and I really do feel the need to protest in the strongest—'

Rebus cut the connection. 'I think we just lost him,' he told the room. There were whoops from the doorway. Rebus got up. Watson reclaimed his chair.

'Let's not get too carried away,' he said as Rebus switched off the tape-recorder. 'Pieces are beginning to fit, but we still don't know who did the killing, or even who was killed. Without those two pieces, all the fun we've just had with Bryce Callan counts for nothing.'

'All the same, sir . . .' Grant Hood was grinning.

Watson nodded. 'All the same, DI Rebus showed us the way to that man's black heart.' He looked at Rebus, who was shaking his head.

'I didn't get enough.' He hit the rewind button. 'I'm not sure I got anything.'

'We know what we're dealing with, and that's half the battle,' Wylie said.

'We should bring in Hutton,' Siobhan Clarke added. 'It seems to revolve around him, and at least *he's* here.'

'All he has to do is deny it,' Watson reminded her. 'He's not a man without influence. Drag him in here, it would reflect badly on us.'

'Can't have that,' Clarke grumbled.

Rebus looked to his boss. 'Sir, it's my shout. Any chance you can join us?'

The Farmer glanced at his watch. 'Just the one then,' he said. 'And a packet of mints for the car home – my wife can smell alcohol on my breath at twenty paces.'

Rebus brought the drinks to the table, Hood helping. Wylie just wanted cola from the gun. Hood himself was on a pint of Eighty. For Rebus: a half and a 'hauf'. A single malt for the Farmer, and red wine for Siobhan Clarke. They toasted each other.

'To teamwork,' Wylie said.

The Farmer cleared his throat. 'Speaking of which, shouldn't Derek be here?'

Rebus filled the silence. 'DI Linford is following up a line of inquiry of his own: a description of Grieve's possible murderer.'

The Chief Super met his eyes. 'Teamwork should mean just that.'

'You don't have to tell me, sir,' Rebus said. 'I'm usually the one out in the cold.'

'Because that's where you've wanted to be,' the Chief Super reminded him. 'Not because we wouldn't let you in.'

'Point taken, sir,' Rebus said quietly.

Clarke put down her glass. 'It's my fault really, sir, blowing up the way I did. I think John just thought there'd be less tension if DI Linford was kept at a distance.'

'I know that, Siobhan,' Watson said. 'But I also want Derek appraised of what's been going on.'

'I'll talk to him, sir,' Rebus said.

'Good.' They sat in silence for a minute. 'Sorry if I put a damper on things,' the Farmer said at last. Then he drained his glass and said he'd better be off. 'Just get my round in first.' They assured him he didn't need to, that it wasn't expected, but he got the round in anyway. When he'd gone, they could feel themselves relax. Maybe it was the alcohol.

Maybe.

Hood brought draughts over from the bar, and commenced a game against Clarke. Rebus said he never played.

'I'm a bad loser, that's my problem.'

'What I hate is a bad winner,' Clarke said, 'the kind that rubs your nose in it.'

'Don't worry,' Hood said, 'I'll be gentle with you.'

The lad was definitely coming out of himself, Rebus thought. Then he watched as Siobhan Clarke took her opponent apart, getting a crown while her own top row was still covered.

'This is brutal,' Wylie said, comforting Hood by ruffling his hair. When a second game was set up, Wylie and Hood swapped places. Hood sat across from Rebus now, and drained his first pint, replacing it with the one the Chief Super had bought.

'Cheers,' he said, taking a sip. Rebus raised his glass to him. 'I can't drink whisky,' Hood confided. 'Gives me blazing hangovers.'

'Me, too, sometimes.'

'Then why do you drink it?'

'The pleasure before the pain: it's a Calvinist thing.' Hood looked at him blankly. 'Never mind,' Rebus told him.

'He had it all wrong, you know,' Siobhan Clarke said, as Wylie concentrated on her next move.

'Who did?'

'Callan. Using a front company so the plans stood a better chance of going through. There was an easier route.'

Wylie glanced over towards the men. 'Wonder if she's going to tell us?'

'I think she wants us to guess first,' Rebus said.

Wylie jumped one of Clarke's draughts; Clarke retaliated. 'Simple really,' she said. 'Why not just pay off the planners?'

'Bribe the council?' Hood smiled at the thought.

'Bloody hell,' Rebus said, staring into his drink. 'Maybe that's it . . .'

A comment he refused to explain, even when they threatened to make him play draughts.

'I'll never crack,' he said, making light of it. But inside, his mind was buzzing with new possibilities and permutations, some of them including Cafferty's face. He sat there wondering what the hell he could do about them . . .

32

Rebus and Derek Linford, the canteen at Fettes police HQ, Friday morning. Rebus nodded towards familiar faces: Claverhouse and Ormiston, Scottish Crime Squad, tucking into bacon rolls. Linford glanced in their direction.

'You know them?'

'I'm not in the habit of nodding at strangers.'

Linford looked at the slice of toast cooling on his plate. 'How's Siobhan?'

'All the better for not seeing you.'

'She got my note?'

Rebus drained his cup. 'She hasn't said anything.'

'Is that a good sign?'

Rebus shrugged. 'Look, you're not suddenly going to be pals again. She could have reported you as a stalker, for Christ's sake. How would that have gone down in Room 279?' Rebus pointed upstairs with his thumb.

Linford's shoulders slumped. Rebus got up, fetched a fresh cup of coffee. 'Anyway,' he said, 'there's some news.' He went on to explain about the links between Freddy Hastings and Bryce Callan. The tension came back into Linford's shoulders. He was forgetting about Siobhan Clarke.

'So how does Roddy Grieve enter the equation?' he asked.

'That's what we don't know,' Rebus admitted. 'Revenge for the way his brother ripped off Callan?'

'And Callan waits twenty years?'

'I know, I can't see it either.'

Linford stared at him. 'But there's something, isn't there? Something you're not telling me?'

Rebus shook his head. 'But do yourself a favour: look into Barry Hutton. If it *was* Callan, he had to have someone here.'

'And Barry fits the bill?'

'He's his nephew.'

'Any evidence he's not just the Rotarian businessman?'

Rebus gestured towards Claverhouse and Ormiston. 'Ask Crime Squad, maybe they'll know.'

'From what little I know of Hutton, he doesn't fit the witness description of the man on Holyrood Road.'

'He has employees, doesn't he?'

'Chief Superintendent Watson's already warned that Hutton has "friends": how do I go snooping without raising hackles?'

Rebus looked at him. 'You don't.'

'I don't go snooping?' Linford seemed confused.

Rebus shook his head. 'You don't *not* raise hackles. Look, Linford, we're cops. Sometimes you have to step out from behind the desk and get in people's faces.' Linford didn't look convinced. 'You think I'm setting you up for something?'

'Are you?'

'Would I admit it if I was?'

'I suppose not. I'm just wondering if this is some sort of . . . test.'

Rebus stood up, coffee untouched. 'You're getting a suspicious mind. That's good, goes with the territory.'

'And what territory is that?'

But Rebus just winked, walked away with hands in pockets. Linford sat there, drumming his fingers on the table, then pushed his toast away and got up, too, walked over to where the two Crime Squad detectives were sitting.

'Mind if I join you?'

Claverhouse gestured to the spare chair. 'Any friend of John Rebus's . . .'

'. . . is probably after some bloody big favour,' Ormiston said, completing his colleague's thought.

Linford sat in his BMW in the only spare bay at the front of Hutton Tower. Lunchtime: workers were streaming out of the building, returning later with sandwich bags, cans of soft drink. Some stood on the steps, smoking the cigarettes they couldn't smoke indoors. It hadn't been easy to find the place: he'd driven through a building site, the road surface not yet finished. A wooden board – CAR PARK FOR REGISTERED PERSONNEL ONLY. But one free space, which he accepted gladly.

He'd got out of the BMW, checking the wheels were intact after the rutted and pitted roadway. Sprays of grey mud radiating from his wheel arches. Car wash at day's end. Back in the driving seat, watching the parade of sandwiches, baps and fresh fruit, he regretted not eating that breakfast toast. Claverhouse and Ormiston had whisked him upstairs, but their search on Hutton had drawn a blank other than some parking fines and the fact that his mother's brother was one Bryce Edwin Callan.

Rebus had said, in effect, that there was no subtle way to go about this, that he would have to announce himself and his intentions. He had no good reason to walk into the building and demand a line-up of every member of staff. Even if Hutton had nothing to hide, Linford couldn't see him agreeing. He'd want to know why, and when told would refuse the request outright and be on the phone to his lawyer, the newspapers, civil rights . . . And now that Linford thought about it, wasn't this looking more and more like a wild-goose chase dreamed up by Rebus – or maybe even Siobhan – to punish him? If he walked into trouble, *they'd* be the ones to profit from it.

All the same . . .

All the same, didn't he deserve it? And if he went along,

might he be forgiven? Not that he was about to walk into the building, but surveillance . . . studying each employee as they left the building. It was worth an afternoon. And if Hutton himself should leave, he would follow, because if Grieve's murderer didn't work here, there was always the chance that he'd meet up with Hutton anyway.

A contract killing . . . revenge. No, he still didn't see it. Roddy Grieve hadn't been killed for anything in his personal or professional life – not that Linford could find. Admittedly, his family was barmy, but that in itself didn't constitute a motive. So why had he died? Had he been in the wrong place at the wrong time, seen something he shouldn't have? Or was it to do with the person he was about to become rather than the person he was? Someone hadn't wanted him as an MSP. The wife came to mind again; again he dismissed her. You didn't kill your spouse just so you could stand for parliament.

Linford rubbed his temples. The smokers on the steps were throwing him looks, wondering who he was. Eventually, they might tell Security, and that would be that. But now a car was approaching, stopping. Its driver sounded his horn, gesturing towards Linford. And now he was getting out, stomping towards the BMW. Linford slid his window down.

'That's my space you're in, so if you wouldn't mind . . . ?'

Linford looked around. 'I don't see any signs.'

'This is staff parking.' A glance at a wristwatch. 'And I'm late for a meeting.'

Linford looked towards where another driver was getting into his car. 'Space there for you.'

'You deaf or what?' Angry face, jaw jutting and tensed. A man looking for a fight.

Linford was just about ready. 'So you'd rather argue with me than get to your meeting?' He looked to where the other car was leaving. 'Nice spot over there.'

'That's Harley. He takes his lunch hour at the gym. I'll

be in the meeting when he gets back, and that's *his* space. Which is why *you* move your junk heap.'

'This from a man who drives a Sierra Cosworth.'

'Wrong answer.' The man yanked Linford's door open. 'The assault charge is going to look bloody good on your CV.'

'You'll have fun trying to make a complaint through broken teeth.'

'And you'll be in the cells for assaulting a police officer.'

The man stopped, his jaw retreating a fraction. His Adam's apple was prominent when he swallowed. Linford took the opportunity to reach into his jacket, showing his warrant card.

'So now you know who I am,' Linford said. 'But I didn't catch your name . . . ?'

'Look, I'm sorry.' The man had turned from fire to sun, his grin trying for embarrassed apology. 'I didn't mean to . . .'

Linford was taking out his notebook, enjoying the sudden reversal. 'I've heard of road rage, but parking rage is a new one on me. They might have to rewrite the rule book for you, pal.' He peered out at the Sierra, took down its registration. 'Don't worry about your name.' He tapped the notebook. 'I can get it from this.'

'My name's Nic Hughes.'

'Well, Mr Hughes, do you think you're calm enough now to talk about this?'

'No problem, it's just that I was in a hurry.' He nodded towards the building. 'You've got some business with . . . ?'

'That's not something I can discuss, sir.'

'Course not, no, it's just that I was . . .' The sentence trailed off.

'You'd best get to your meeting.' The revolving door was moving, Barry Hutton coming out, buttoning his suit. Linford knew him from newspaper photos. 'I was just off anyway, as it happens.' Linford beamed at Hughes, then reached for the ignition. 'Spot's all yours.' Hughes stepped back. Hutton, unlocking his own car – a red Ferrari – saw him.

'Fuck's sake, Nic, you're supposed to be upstairs.'

'Right away, Barry.'

'Right away's not good enough, arsehole!'

And now Hutton was looking at Linford, frowning. He tutted. 'Letting someone use your space, Nic? You're not the man I thought you were.' Grinning, Hutton got into the Ferrari, but then got out again, came over to the BMW.

Linford thinking: *I've blown it; he knows my face now, knows my car. Following him is going to be a nightmare . . .* '*You don't* not *raise hackles . . . Get in people's faces.*' Well, he'd got in the Cosworth driver's face, and here was his reward, Barry Hutton standing in front of the BMW, pointing towards him.

'You're a cop, aren't you? Don't ask me how it is you lot stick out, even in a motor like that. Look, I told the other two, and that's all I'm saying, right?'

Linford nodded slowly. The 'other two': Wylie and Hood. Linford had read their report.

'Good,' Hutton said, turning on his heels. Linford and Hughes watched as the Ferrari's engine fired, that low rumble like money in the bank. Hutton kicked up dust as he raced out of the car park.

Hughes was staring at Linford. Linford stared back. 'Do something for you?' he said.

'What's going on?' The man had trouble getting the words out.

Linford shook his head, smallest of victories, and put the Beamer into gear. Crawled out of the car park, wondering if it was worth trying to catch up with Hutton. Saw Hughes in his rearview. Something not right about the man. The warrant card hadn't just pacified him, it had freaked him out.

Something to hide? It was funny how even church

381

ministers could break into a sweat when there was a copper in front of them. But this guy . . . No, he looked nothing like the description. All the same . . . all the same . . .

At the lights on Lothian Road, Barry Hutton was three cars in front. Linford decided he'd nothing to lose.

33

Big Ger Cafferty was on his own, parked outside Rebus's flat in a metallic-grey Jaguar XK8. Rebus, locking his own car, pretended he hadn't seen him. He walked towards the tenement door, hearing the electric hum of the Jag's window sliding down.

'Thought we might take another drive,' Cafferty called.

Rebus ignored him, unlocked the door, and went into the stairwell. As the door closed behind him, he stood there, debating with himself. Then he opened the door again. Cafferty was out of the car, leaning against it.

'Like the new motor?'

'You bought it?'

'You think I stole it?' Cafferty laughed.

Rebus shook his head. 'I just thought you might have been better off hiring, seeing how you're on the way out.'

'All the more reason for indulging myself while I'm here.'

Rebus looked around. 'Where's Rab?'

'Didn't think I'd need him.'

'I don't know whether to be flattered or insulted.'

Cafferty frowned. 'By what?'

'You coming here without a minder.'

'You said it yourself the other night: that was the time to take a pop at me. Now how about that drive?'

'How good a driver are you?'

Cafferty laughed again. 'It's true I'm a bit rusty. I just thought it might be more private.'

'For what?'

'Our little chat about Bryce Callan.'

*

They headed east, through the one-time slums of Craig-millar and Niddrie, now falling to the bulldozers.

'I've always thought', Cafferty said, 'that this should be the ideal spot. Views to Arthur's Seat, and Craigmillar Castle behind you. Yuppies would think they'd died and gone to heaven.'

'I don't think we say yuppies any more.'

Cafferty looked at him. 'I've been away a while.'

'True.'

'I see the old cop shop's gone.'

'Just moved around the corner.'

'And great God, all these new shopping centres.'

Rebus explained that it was called The Fort. Nothing to do with Craigmillar's old police station, whose nickname had been Fort Apache. They were past Niddrie now, following signs to Musselburgh.

'The place is changing so fast,' Cafferty mused.

'And I'm ageing fast just sitting here. Any chance of you getting to the point?'

Cafferty glanced in his direction. 'I've been making the point all along, it's just you've not been listening.'

'What is it you want to tell me about Callan?'

'Just that he called me.'

'He knows you're out, then?'

'Mr Callan, like many a wealthy expat, likes to keep abreast of Scottish current affairs.' Cafferty glanced at him again. 'Nervous, are you?'

'Why do you ask?'

'Your hand's on the door handle, like you're ready to bale out.'

Rebus moved his hand. 'You're setting me up for something.'

'Am I?'

'And I'd bet three months' salary there's nothing wrong with you.'

Cafferty kept his eyes on the road. 'So prove it.'

'Don't worry.'

'Me? What have I got to worry about? It's you that's the nervous one, remember.' They were silent for a moment. Cafferty slid his hands around the steering wheel. 'Nice car, though, isn't it?'

'And doubtless purchased with the honest sweat of your brow.'

'Others do my sweating for me. That's what makes a successful businessman.'

'Which brings us to Bryce Callan. You couldn't even get to speak to his nephew, and suddenly he calls you out of the blue?'

'He knows I know you.'

'And?'

'And he wanted to know what I knew. You haven't made yourself a friend there, Strawman.'

'Inside, I'm crying.'

'You think he's mixed up in these murders?'

'Are you here to tell me he isn't?'

Cafferty shook his head. 'I'm here to tell you that his nephew's the one you should be looking at.'

Rebus digested this.

'Why?' he asked at last.

Cafferty just shrugged.

'Does this come from Callan?'

'Indirectly.'

Rebus snorted. 'I don't get it. Why would Callan dump Barry Hutton in it?' Cafferty shrugged again. 'It's a funny thing . . .' Rebus went on.

'What?'

Rebus stared out of his window. 'Here we are coming into Musselburgh. Know what its nickname is?'

'I forget.'

'The Honest Toun.'

'What's funny about that?'

'Just that you've brought me here to feed me a load of shite. It's *you* that wants to see Hutton get burned.' He stared at Cafferty. 'I wonder why that should be?'

The sudden anger in Cafferty's face seemed to give off a heat all of its own. 'You're mad, do you know that? You'd ignore any crime sitting in your path, sidestep it just so you could give *me* a bloody nose. That's the truth, isn't it, Strawman? You don't want anyone else; you just want Morris Gerald Cafferty.'

'Don't flatter yourself.'

'I'm trying to do you a favour here. Get you a bit of glory *and* maybe keep Bryce Callan from killing you.'

'So when did you become the UN peacekeeper?'

'Look . . .' Cafferty sighed; some of the blood had left his cheeks. 'Okay, maybe there *is* something in it for me.'

'What?'

'All you need to know is there's more in it for John Rebus.' Cafferty was indicating, bringing the car to a halt kerbside on the High Street. Rebus looked around; saw just the one landmark.

'Luca's?' In summer, the café had queues out the door. But this was winter. Mid-afternoon and the lights were on inside.

'Used to be the best ice cream around,' Cafferty was saying, undoing his seat belt. 'I want to see if it still is.'

He bought two vanilla cones, brought them outside. Rebus was pinching his nose, shaking his head incredulously.

'One minute Callan's putting a contract on me, the next we're eating ice cream.'

'It's the small things you savour in this life, ever noticed that?' Cafferty had already started on his cone. 'Now if there was racing on, we could have had a flutter.' Musselburgh Racecourse: the Honest Toun's other attraction.

Rebus tasted the ice cream. 'Give me something on Hutton,' he said, 'something I can use.'

Cafferty thought for a moment. 'Council junkets,' he said. 'Everyone in Hutton's line of work needs friends.' He paused. 'The city might be changing, but it still works the same old way.'

Barry Hutton went shopping: parked his car in the St James Centre and hit a computer shop, John Lewis department store, and then out on to Princes Street and the short walk to Jenners. He bought clothes, while Derek Linford pretended to study a range of neckties. The shops were all busy enough; Linford knew he hadn't been spotted. He'd never done surveillance before, but knew the theory. He bought one of the ties – pale orange and green stripes – and swapped it for his own plain maroon.

The man Hutton had seen in the company car park had worn the maroon tie: different tie, different man.

Across the road to the Balmoral Hotel, afternoon tea with a man and a woman: business, briefcases open. Then back to the car park and the crawl to Waverley Bridge, traffic building as the rush hour neared. Hutton parked on Market Street, made for the rear entrance to the Carlton Highland Hotel. He was carrying a sports holdall. Linford made the deduction: health club. He knew the hotel had one – he'd almost joined it, but the fees had put him off. His thinking at the time: way to meet people, the city's movers and shakers. But at a price.

He bided his time. There was a bottle of water in the glove compartment, but he knew he daren't drink anything – just his luck to be off having a pee when Hutton came out. Ditto eating. His stomach was growling; café just along the road . . . He searched the glove compartment again, came up with a stick of chewing gum.

'*Bon appetit*,' he said to himself, unwrapping it.

Hutton spent an hour in the club. Linford was keeping a record of his movements, and duly noted the time to the minute. He was alone when he came out, his hair damp from the shower, holdall swinging. He had that sheen, that scrubbed confidence which came with a workout.

Back into his car, and heading towards Abbeyhill. Linford checked his mobile phone. The battery was dead. He plugged it into the cigar lighter, got it charging. He wondered about calling Rebus, but to say what exactly? To ask his consent? *You're doing the right thing; keep at it.* The action of a weak man.

He wasn't weak. And here was the proof.

They were on Easter Road now, Hutton busy on his own mobile. The whole trip he'd been carrying on conversations, hardly ever glancing in rearview or side mirrors. Not that it would have mattered – Linford was three cars back.

But then suddenly they were in Leith, taking side roads. Linford hung back, hoping someone would overtake, but there was nobody there, nobody but the suspect and him. Left and right, the roads getting narrower, tenements either side of them, front doors opening directly on to the pavement. Children's playgrounds, broken glass sparkling in the headlights. Dusk. Hutton pulling over suddenly. Down by the docks, Linford guessed. He didn't know this part of town at all; tried to avoid it: schemes and hard-man dives. Weapons of choice: the bottle and the kitchen knife. The assaults tended to be on friends and 'loved ones'.

Hutton had parked outside one of the hard-man dives: a tiny pub, with narrow curtained windows seven feet off the ground. Solid-looking door: you'd think the place was locked. But Hutton knew better, pushed open the door and walked straight in. He left his holdall on the Ferrari's front seat, shopping bags in the back, the whole lot in full view.

Stupid or confident. Linford would bet the latter. He thought of the Leith pub in *Trainspotting*, the American tourist asking for the toilet, the schemies following him in, divvying the spoils after. That was this kind of pub. The place didn't even have a name, just a sign outside advertising Tennent's Lager. Linford checked his watch, entered the details in his log. A textbook surveillance. He checked his phone for messages. There weren't any. He knew the singles club was having a night out, starting at nine. He wasn't sure whether to go or not. Maybe Siobhan would be there again – it wasn't her case now but you never knew. He hadn't heard any stories about him being at the club that night, so probably Siobhan had kept her word, not said anything to anyone. That was good of her, considering . . . He'd given her the ammo, and after what he'd done, she still hadn't used it.

Then again, what *had* he done? Loitered outside her flat like a lovelorn teenager. Not such a heinous crime, was it? It had only been the three times. Even if Rebus hadn't found him . . . well, he'd have given up soon enough, and that would have been an end of it. It was down to Rebus really, wasn't it? Landing him in it with Siobhan, leaving him marginalised at work. Christ, yes, exactly what Rebus had wanted all along. One in the eye for the Fettes fast-stream. He could rise to chief constable and it would be there, hanging over him. Rebus would be retired, of course, maybe even have drunk himself to death, but Siobhan would be around, unless she went off to get married, have kids.

Always with the power to hurt him.

He didn't know what to do about that. The ACC had told him, no one's irreplaceable.

He passed the time reading whatever was in the car: owner's manual, service log, some leaflets from the passenger-side pocket: tourist attractions; old grocery lists . . . He was poring over his map book, looking at how much of Scotland he didn't know, when his phone sounded, shocking him with its sudden shrill cry. He picked it up, fumbled to switch it on.

'It's Rebus,' the voice said.

'Something happened?'

'No, it's just . . . nobody'd seen you this afternoon.'

'And you were worried?'

389

'Let's say I was curious.'

'I'm following Hutton. He's in a pub down in Leith. Been in there . . .' He checked his watch. 'An hour and a quarter.'

'Which pub?'

'No name above the door.'

'Which street?'

Linford realised that he didn't know. He looked around, saw nothing to help him.

'How well do you know Leith?' Rebus asked. Linford felt his confidence ebb.

'Well enough,' he said.

'So are you North Leith or South? Port? Seafield? What?'

'Near the port,' Linford spluttered.

'Can you see any water?'

'Look, I've been on his tail all afternoon. He did some shopping, had a business meeting, went to his health club . . .'

Rebus wasn't listening. 'He's got a pedigree, whether he's straight or not.'

'How do you mean?'

'I mean he used to work for his uncle. He probably knows more about this sort of thing than you do.'

'Look, I don't need you to tell me about—'

'Hello? Anyone home? What do you do when you need a pee?'

'I don't.'

'Or something to eat?'

'Ditto.'

'I said you should look at people who work for him. I didn't mean like this.'

'Don't tell me how to do my job!'

'Just don't go into that pub, okay? I've half an idea where you are, I'll come down there.'

'There's no need.'

'Try and stop me.'

'Look, this is *my*—' But Linford's caller had gone.

He cursed silently, tried calling Rebus back. 'I'm sorry,' said the recording, 'but the phone you have called may be switched off . . .'

Linford cursed again.

Did he want Rebus here, sharing his inquiry, sticking his nose in? *Meddling?* Soon as he arrived, he'd be told where he could go.

The pub door rattled open. All the time Hutton had been inside – one hour and twenty minutes – no one else had gone in or come out. But now here he was, emerging, bathed in light from the open door. And there was another man with him. They stood chatting in the doorway, Linford, parked across the road and down a ways, peering at this new figure. He ticked off the Holyrood description in his mind, came up with a close match.

Denims, dark bomber jacket, white trainers. Black cropped hair. Big round eyes and a permanent-looking scowl.

Hutton punched the man's shoulder. The man didn't seem too happy about what was being said. He put out a hand for Hutton to shake, but Hutton wasn't having any of it. Went and unlocked his Ferrari, started the engine and headed off. The man looked like he was going to turn back into the pub. Linford had a new scenario now: in he walks with Rebus as back-up, takes the man in for questioning. Not a bad day's work.

But the man was just shouting his goodbyes to someone. Then he headed off on foot. Linford didn't think twice, slid from his car, made to lock it, then remembered the little squeak of acknowledgement which the alarm made. Left it unlocked.

Forgot to take his mobile.

The man seemed drunk, weaving slightly, arms hanging loose. He went into another pub, came out again scant minutes later, stood by the doorway lighting a

391

cigarette. Then back on his travels, stopping to talk to someone he seemed to know, then slowing as he fished a mobile phone out of his jacket and took a call. Linford patted his own pockets, realised the mobile was back in his car. He'd no idea where they were, tried memorising the few street names on show. Another pub: three minutes and out again. A short cut down a lane. Linford waited till the suspect had turned left out of the lane before entering it himself, sprinting to the other end. A housing scheme now, high fences and curtained windows, sounds of TVs and kids playing. Dark passageways smelling faintly of urine. Graffiti: Easy, Provos, Hibs. More walkways, the man pausing now, knocking at a door. Linford sticking to the shadows. The door opened and the man stepped quickly inside.

Linford didn't think it was a last stop. No keys, so probably not his home. He checked the time again, but had left his notebook back in the car, lying on the seat with the mobile. The BMW unlocked. He gnawed at his bottom lip, looked around at the concrete maze. Could he find his way back to the pub? Would his pride and joy be there if he did?

But Rebus was on his way, wasn't he? He'd work out what had happened, keep guard till Linford came back. He took a couple of steps further back into the darkness, plunged his hands into his pockets. Bloody freezing.

When the blow came, it came silently and from behind. He was unconscious before he hit the ground.

34

Jayne had gone and done it this time. She wasn't at her mum's. The old crone told him: 'Just said to tell you she was going to a friend's, and don't bother asking which one because she said it was better I didn't know.' She had her arms folded, filling the doorway of her semi-detached.

'Well, thanks for helping me save my marriage,' Jerry replied, heading back down the garden path. Her dog was sitting by the gate. Nice little thing, name of Eric. Jerry gave it a kick up its arse and opened the gate. He was laughing as Jayne's mum swore at him above Eric's yelps and howls.

Back at the flat, he went on another recce, see if she'd left any clues for him to find. No note, and at least half her clothes had gone. She hadn't been in a temper. Evidence of this: one of his boxes of 45s was sitting on the floor, a pair of scissors next to it, but she hadn't touched the records. Maybe a peace offering of sorts? Couple of things knocked off shelves, but put that down to her being in a hurry. He looked in the fridge: cheese, marge, milk. No beer. Nothing to drink in any of the cupboards either. He emptied his pockets on to the couch. Three quid and some change. Christ almighty, and when was the next giro due? Best part of a week away, was it? Friday night, and all he had was three quid. He searched drawers and down the back of the couch and under the bed. A grand total haul of a further eighty pence.

And the bills, staring at him from the noticeboard in the kitchen: gas, electric, council tax. Plus, somewhere, the rent and telephone. Phone bill had only come in that morning, Jerry asking Jayne why she had to spend three hours a week on the blower to her mum who only lived round the corner?

He went back through to the living room, dug out 'Stranded' by The Saints. B-side was even faster – 'No Time'. Jerry had all the time in the world; thing was, he felt utterly stranded.

The Stranglers next, 'Grip', and he wondered if he would strangle Jayne for putting him through this.

'Get a grip,' he told himself.

Made a cup of tea and tried working out his options, but his mind wasn't up to thinking. So he slumped back on to the sofa. At least he could play his music now, any time he liked. She'd taken her tapes with her – Eurythmics, Celine Dion, Phil Collins. Good riddance, the lot of them. He went along three doors to Tofu's pad and asked if he had any blow. Tofu offered to sell him a quarter.

'I just need enough for a joint. I'll give it back.'

'What? After you've smoked it?'

'I mean I'll owe you it.'

'Yeah, you will. Like you still owe me for last Wednesday.'

'Come on, Tofu, just one measly hit.'

'Sorry, pal, no more tick from Tofu.'

Jerry jabbed a finger at him. 'I'll remember this. Don't think I won't.'

'Aye, sure thing, Jer.' Tofu closed the door. Jerry heard the chain rattle back across it.

Inside the flat again. Feeling itchy now, wanting some *action*. Where were your friends when you needed them? Nic . . . he could phone Nic. Tap him for a loan if nothing else. Christ, with the stuff Jerry knew, he had Nic over a barrel. Make the loan more of a weekly retainer. He checked the clock on the video. Gone five. Would Nic be at work, or maybe at home? He tried both numbers: no luck. Maybe he was out on the pull, a few drinks in the wine bar with some of the short skirts from the office. No place in that picture for his old comrade-in-arms. The only thing Jerry was useful for was as a punchbag, somebody to make Nic look good because *he* looked bad.

A stooge, plain and simple. They were all laughing at him: Jayne, her mum, Nic. Even the woman at the DSS. And Tofu . . . he could almost *hear* that bastard's laughter, sitting snug in his padlocked flat with his bags of grass and nuggets of hash, bit of music on the hi-fi and money in his pocket. Jerry picked up the coins one by one from around him on the couch and tossed them at the blank TV screen.

Until the doorbell rang. Jayne, had to be! Okay, he had to pull himself together, act casual. Maybe be a bit huffy with her, but grown-up about it. Things happened sometimes, and it was down to those involved to . . . More ringing. Hang on, she'd have her keys, wouldn't she? And now the banging of a fist on the door. Who did they owe money to? Were they taking away the TV? The video? There was precious little else.

He stood in the hallway, holding his breath.

'I can see you, you tosser!'

A pair of eyes at the letter box. Nic's voice. Jerry started moving forward.

'Nic, man, I was just trying to get you.'

He unsnibbed the door and it flew inwards, driving him backwards and on to his arse. He was pulling himself upright when Nic gave him another push that sent him sprawling. Then the door slammed shut.

'Bad move, Jerry, really, *really* bad move.'

'What're you talking about? What've I done this time?'

Nic was sweating profusely. His eyes were darker and colder than ever before, and his voice was like a chisel.

'I never should've told you,' he hissed.

Jerry was back up on his feet. He slid along the wall and into the living room. 'Told me what?'

'That Barry wanted me out.'

'What?' This wasn't making sense to Jerry; he was

panicking that it was his fault, that it would make sense if only he'd concentrate.

'It wasn't enough to grass me to the pigs—'

'Whoah, hold on—'

'No, *you* hold on, Jerry. Because when I'm finished with you . . .'

'I didn't do anything!'

'Grassed me up *and* told them where I work.'

'I never!'

'They've been talking to Barry about me! There was one sitting in the car park this afternoon! He'd been there for hours, sitting in *my* space! Now why else would he be there, eh?'

Jerry was shaking. 'Loads of reasons.'

Nic shook his head. 'No, Jer, just the one. And you're so fucking stupid you think I won't take you with me.'

'Christ's sake, man.'

Nic had brought something from his pocket. A knife. A bloody great carving knife! And Jerry noticed that he was wearing gloves, too.

'I swear to God, man.'

'Shut up.'

'Why would I *do* that, Nic? Think for a minute!'

'Your bottle's gone. I can see you shaking from here.' Nic laughed. 'I knew you were weak, but not this bad.'

'Look, man, Jayne's gone and I—'

'Jayne's the last thing you have to worry about.' There were thumps on the ceiling. Nic glanced up. '*Shut it!*'

Jerry saw a half-chance, dived through the doorway and into the kitchen. The sink was full of dishes. He plunged a hand in, pulled out forks, teaspoons. Nic was on him. Jerry chucked the lot at him. He was screaming now.

'Call the police! You upstairs, get on to the cops!'

Nic swung with the knife, caught Jerry on his right hand. Now a current of blood flowed down his wrist, mixing with the dishwater. Jerry cried out in pain, lashed out with a foot, caught Nic smack on the kneecap. Nic lunged again, and Jerry pushed past him, back into the living room. Tripped and fell. Fell over the box of 45s, scattering them. Nic was coming, his feet grinding one of the records into the floor.

'Bastard,' he was saying. 'You won't be saying a word against me.'

'Nic, man, you've lost it!'

'It wasn't enough, Cat leaving me, you had to rub my nose in it. Well, pal, it's *you* that's the rapist here. I just drove the van. That's what I'll tell them.' There was a sick grin on his face. 'We got into a fight, it was self-defence. That's what I'll say. See, I'm the one with the brains here, Jerry-fucking-nobody. The job, the mortgage, the car. And *I'm* the one they'll believe.' He raised the knife, and Jerry lunged. Nic sort of wheezed, and froze for a second, mouth agape, then angling his chin to stare down at where the scissors protruded from his chest.

'What were you saying about brains, man?' Jerry said, rising to his feet as Nic slumped face forwards on to the floor.

He sat back down on the couch, Nic's body twitching once or twice and then falling still. Jerry ran his hands through his hair. He examined his cut. It was a deep wound, and about three inches long. Hospital job, stitches. He knelt down, searched Nic's pockets and came up with the keys to the Cosworth. Nic had never let him drive it, never once offered.

Now, at last, he had a choice. Sit here and wait it out? Get his story straight for the cops? Self-defence was the truth of it. Maybe the neighbours would tell what they'd heard. But the cops . . . the cops knew Nic was the rapist. And they also knew there were two men involved.

Stood to reason it was him: Nic's pal from way back, the underachiever, Nic's killer. They'd get witnesses who'd identify him from the nightclubs. Maybe there were clues in the van.

Not such a difficult choice then, in the end. He tossed

the keys, caught them, and headed out of the flat. Left the door wide open. Pigs would only kick it in otherwise.

He wondered if Nic would have thought of that.

35

Rebus was renewing his old acquaintance with the rougher end of the Leith pub scene. Not for him the charming, rejuvenated taverns of The Shore or the gleaming Victorian hostelries to be found on Great Junction Street and Bernard Street. For the nameless howffs, the spit 'n' sawdusts, you had to look slightly further afield, charting streets which few Scottish Office brogues from the HQ down the road ever trod. He had drawn up a shortlist of four – drew a blank with the first two. But at the third, saw Linford's BMW parked eighty yards away, under a busted street light: smart enough to park where he wouldn't easily be spotted. Then again, every second street light was busted.

Rebus tucked his Saab behind the BMW. He flashed his lights: no response. Got out of his car and lit a cigarette. That's all he was: a local lighting a cigarette. But his eyes were busy. The street was quiet. There was light in the high windows of Bellman's Bar – its name from years back. What it was called now was anybody's guess. Probably nobody who drank there knew, or cared.

He walked past the BMW, glancing inside. Something on the passenger seat: mobile phone. Linford couldn't be far. Taking that piss maybe, the one he'd said he wouldn't need. Rebus smiled and shook his head, then saw that the BMW's doors weren't locked. He tried the driver's side. By the interior light he could see Linford's notebook. He reached for it, started reading, but the light went off. So he slipped into the driver's seat, closed the door, and flipped the light back on again. Meticulous in every detail, but that didn't count for anything if you were spotted. Rebus went back outside, inspected the few parked cars. They were ageing and ordinary, the kind that passed each MOT with a backhander to a friendly mechanic. He wouldn't place Barry Hutton as the owner of any of them. Yet Hutton had driven here. Did that mean he'd left?

Did that mean Linford had missed him?

Suddenly, this began to seem like the best-case scenario. Rebus started to think of others, not half as appealing. He walked back to the Saab and called in, got St Leonard's to check any activity in Leith. They got back to him pronto: quiet night so far. He sat there, smoking three or four cigarettes, killing the packet. Then he walked over to Bellman's and pushed open the door.

Smoky inside. No music or TV. Just half a dozen men, all standing at the bar, all staring at him. No Barry Hutton; no Linford. Rebus was taking coins from his pocket as he approached.

'Cigarette machine?' he asked.

'Havenae got one.' The man behind the bar was practising a scowl. Rebus blinked sleepily.

'Any packs behind the bar?'

'Naw.'

He turned to look at the drinkers. 'Any of you guys sell me some?'

'A pound each,' came the lightning response. Rebus snorted.

'That's criminal,' he said.

'Then fuck off and buy them somewhere else.'

Rebus took his time studying the faces, then the bar's blunt décor: three tables, a linoleum floor the colour of ox blood, wood panelling on the walls. Pictures of yester-year's page three girls. A dartboard gathering cobwebs. He couldn't see any toilets. There were only four optics behind the bar, and two taps: lager or export.

'Must do a roaring trade,' he commented.

'I didn't know you'd booked a floor show tonight, Shug,' one drinker said to the barman.

'The floor's where he'll end up,' the barman said.

'Easy, boys, easy.' Rebus held up his hands in appeasement, started backing away. 'I'll be sure to tell Barry that this is what you call hospitality.'

They weren't falling for it, stayed silent until Shug the barman spoke. 'Barry who?' he said.

Rebus shrugged, turned and walked out.

It was another five minutes before he got the call. Derek Linford: already on his way to the Infirmary.

Rebus paced the corridor: didn't like hospitals; liked this one less than most. This was where they'd brought Sammy after the hit and run.

At just after eleven, Ormiston appeared. Police officer attacked, Fettes and Crime Squad always took an interest.

'How is he?' Rebus asked. He wasn't alone: Siobhan was seated with a can of Fanta, looking shell-shocked. More officers had looked in – including the Farmer and Linford's boss from Fettes, the latter pointedly ignoring Rebus and Siobhan.

'Not good,' Ormiston said, searching in his pockets for change for the coffee machine. Siobhan asked him what he needed, handed over some coins.

'Did he say what happened?'

'Doctors didn't want him talking.'

'But did he tell you?'

Ormiston straightened up, plastic cup in hand. 'He got whacked from the back, and a few kicks for good measure. Best part of a broken jaw, I'd say.'

'So he probably wasn't in a chatty mood,' Siobhan said, looking at Rebus.

'They've pumped him full of drugs anyway,' Ormiston said, blowing on the liquid in his cup and eyeing it speculatively. 'Is this coffee or soup, would you say?'

Siobhan shrugged.

'He did write something down,' Ormiston said at last. 'Bugger seemed keen enough about that.'

'What did it say?' Siobhan asked.

Ormiston glanced towards Rebus. 'I might be para-phrasing, but it was along the lines of: Rebus knew I was there.'

'What?' Rebus's face was like stone. Ormiston repeated the words for him.

Siobhan looked from one man to the other. 'Meaning what?'

'Meaning,' Rebus said, slumping into a chair, 'he thinks I did it. Nobody else knew where he was.'

'But it had to be whoever he was following,' Siobhan argued. 'Stands to reason.'

'Not Derek Linford's reason.' Rebus looked up at her. 'I phoned him, said I was on my way down. Could be I set him up, grassed him to whoever was in the bar. Or could be I was the one who whacked him.' He looked to Ormiston for confirmation. 'That how you see it, Ormie?'

Ormiston said nothing.

'But why would you . . . ?' Siobhan's question trailed off as she saw the answer. Rebus nodded, letting her know she was right. Revenge . . . jealousy . . . because of what Linford had done to Siobhan.

That was Linford's thinking. The way he saw the world, it made perfect sense.

To Linford's mind, it was perfect.

Siobhan was sitting outside the hospital in her car, debating whether to visit the patient or not, when she heard the call on her radio.

Be on the lookout for a black Ford Sierra Cosworth, driver may be Jerry Lister, wanted for questioning concerning a major incident, code six.

Code six? The codes were always changing – all except code twenty-one, officer requiring assistance. Right now a code six was suspicious death – usually meaning homicide. She called in, was told that the victim's name was Nicholas Hughes. He'd been stabbed to death with a pair of scissors, his body found by Lister's wife on her return home. The woman was now being treated for shock. Siobhan was thinking back to that night, the night she'd taken the short cut through Waverley. She'd taken it because of the two men in the black Sierra, one of them saying to the other, *Lesbian, Jerry*, and now a man called Jerry was on the run in a black Sierra.

She'd tried to get away, and in doing so had ended up involved with a tramp's suicide.

The more she thought about it, the more she couldn't help wondering . . .

36

The Farmer was apoplectic.

'Whose idea was it for him to be tailing Barry Hutton in the first place?'

'DI Linford was using his own initiative, sir.'

'Then how come I see your grubby little prints all over this?'

Saturday morning, they were seated in the Farmer's office. Rebus was edgy to start with: he had a pitch to sell, and couldn't see his boss going for it.

'You've seen his note,' the Farmer continued. ' "Rebus knew". How the hell do you think that looks?'

There was so much tension in Rebus's jaw, his cheeks were aching. 'What does the ACC say?'

'He wants an inquiry. You'll be suspended, of course.'

'Should keep me out of your way till retirement.'

The Chief Super slammed both hands against his desk, too angry to speak. Rebus took his chance.

'We've got a description of the guy seen hanging around Holyrood the night Grieve was murdered. Add to this the fact that he drinks in Bellman's, and there's a good chance we can nab him. Bellman's won't give us anything; it's the sort of pub where they look after their own. But I've got snitches in Leith. We're looking for a hard man, someone who uses that pub almost as an office. With a few officers, I think I can—'

'He says *you* did it.'

'I know he does, sir. But with respect—'

'How would it look if I put you in charge of the

investigation?' The Farmer suddenly looked tired, beaten half to death by the job.

'I'm not asking to be put in charge,' Rebus said. 'I'm asking you to let me go to Leith, ask some questions, that's all. A chance to clear my own name if nothing else.'

Watson leaned back in his chair. 'Fettes are going ape-shit as it is. Linford was one of theirs. And Barry Hutton under unauthorised surveillance – know what that would do to any case against him? The Procurator Fiscal will have a seizure.'

'We need evidence. That's why we need someone in Leith with a few contacts.'

'What about Bobby Hogan? He's Leith based.'

Rebus nodded. 'And I'd want him there.'

'But you want to be there, too?' Rebus stayed silent. 'And we both know you'll go there anyway, no matter what I say.'

'Better to have it official, sir.'

The Farmer ran a hand over the dome of his head.

'Sooner the better, sir,' Rebus prompted.

The Chief Super started shaking his head, his eyes on Rebus. 'No,' he said, 'I don't want you down there, Inspector. It's just not something I can sanction, bearing in mind the flak from headquarters.'

Rebus stood up. 'Understood, sir. I don't have permission to go down to Leith and ask my informants about the attack on DI Linford?'

'That's right, Inspector, you don't. You're awaiting suspension; I want you close by when word comes through.'

'Thank you, sir.' He headed for the door.

'I mean it. You don't leave St Leonard's, Inspector.'

Rebus nodded his understanding. The Murder Room was quiet when he reached it. Roy Frazer was reading a paper. 'Finished with this?' Rebus asked, picking up another. Frazer nodded. 'Chicken *phal*,' Rebus explained, rubbing his stomach. 'Hold all my calls and let everyone know the shunkie's off-limits.'

Frazer nodded and smiled. Saturday morning on the bog with the paper: everyone had done it at one time.

So Rebus headed out of the station and into the car park, jumped into his Saab and got on the mobile to Bobby Hogan.

'I'm ahead of you, pal,' Hogan said.

'How far?'

'Sitting outside Bellman's waiting for it to open.'

'Waste of time. See if you can track down some of your contacts.' Rebus flipped open his notebook, read the description of the Holyrood man to Hogan as he drove.

'A hard man who likes rough pubs,' Hogan mused when he'd finished. 'Now where the hell would we find anyone like that in Leith these days?'

Rebus knew a few places. It was 11 a.m., opening time. Grey overcast morning. The cloud hung so low over Arthur's Seat, you could pick out the rock only in shifting patches. Just like this case, Rebus was thinking. Bits of it visible at any one time, but the whole edifice ultimately hidden.

Leith was quiet, the day keeping people indoors. He drove past carpet shops, tattoo parlours, pawnbrokers. Laundrettes and social security offices: the latter were locked for the weekend. Most days, they'd be doing more business than the local stores. Parked his car in an alley and made sure it was locked before leaving it. At twelve minutes past opening, he was in his first pub. They were serving coffee, so he had a mug, same as the barman was drinking. Two ancient regulars watched morning television and smoked diligently: this was their day job, and they approached it with the seriousness of ritual. Rebus didn't get much out of the barman, not so much as a free refill. It was time to move on.

His mobile went off while he was walking. It was Bill Nairn.

'Working weekends, Bill?' Rebus said. 'How's the overtime?'

'The Bar-L never closes, John. I did what you asked, checked out our friend Rab Hill.'

'And?' Rebus had stopped walking. A few shoppers moved around him. They were mostly elderly, feet hardly clearing the pavement. No cars to take them to the retail parks; no energy to take the bus uptown.

'Not much really. Released on his due date. Said he was moving through to Edinburgh. He's seen his parole officer there . . .'

'Illnesses, Bill?'

'Well, yes, he did complain of a dicky stomach. Didn't seem to clear up, so he had some tests. They were all clear.'

'Same hospital as Cafferty?'

'Yes, but I really don't see . . .'

'What's his Edinburgh address?'

Nairn repeated the details: it was a hotel on Princes Street. 'Nice,' Rebus said. Then he took down the parole officer's details, too. 'Cheers, Bill. I'll talk to you later.'

The second bar was smoky, its carpet tacky with the previous night's spillage. Three men stood drinking nips, sleeves rolled up to show off their tattoos. They examined him as he entered, seemed not to find his presence objectionable enough to arouse comment. Later in the day, with sobriety a dull memory, things would be different. Rebus knew the barman, sat down at a corner table with a half-pint of Eighty and smoked a cigarette. When the barman came to empty the ashtray of its single dowp, it gave time for a couple of muted questions. The barman replied with little twitches of the head: negative. He either didn't know or wasn't saying. Fair enough. Rebus knew when he could push a bit harder, and this was not one of those times.

He knew as he left that the drinkers would be talking about him. They'd smelt cop on him, and would want to know what he'd been after. The barman would tell them: no harm in that. By now it would be common knowledge – and when one of their own was attacked, the police always went in quickly and with prejudice. Leith would be expecting little else.

Outside, he got on the phone again, called the hotel and asked to be put through to Robert Hill's room.

'I'm sorry, sir. Mr Hill's not answering.'

Rebus cut the call.

Pub three: a relief barman, and no faces Rebus recognised. He didn't even stay for a drink. Two cafés after that, Formica tables pockmarked with cigarette burns, the vinegary haze of brown sauce and chip fat. And then a third café, a place the men from the docks came to for huge doses of reviving cholesterol, as if it were more doctor's surgery than eating place.

And seated at one of the tables, scooping up runny egg with a fork, someone Rebus knew.

His name was Big Po. Sometime doorman for pubs and clubs of the parish, Po's past included a long stint in the merchant navy. His fists were nicked and scarred, face weathered where it wasn't hidden by a thick brown beard. He was massive, and watching him squashed in at the table was like watching a normal-sized adult seated in a primary-school classroom. Rebus had the impression that the whole world had been built on a scale out of kilter with Big Po's needs.

'Jesus,' the man roared as Rebus approached, 'it's been a lifetime and a half!' Flecks of saliva and egg peppered the air. Heads were turning, but didn't stay turned long. No one wanted Big Po accusing them of nosing into his business. Rebus took the proffered hand and prepared for the worst. Sure enough, it was like a car going through a crusher. He flexed his fingers afterwards, checking for fractures, and pulled out the chair opposite the man mountain.

'What'll you have?' Po asked.

'Just coffee.'

'That counts as blasphemy in here. This is the blessed church of St Eck the Chef.' Po nodded towards where a fat, elderly man was wiping his hands on a cook's apron and nodding towards him. 'Best fry-up in Edinburgh,' Po roared, 'is that right, Eck?'

Eck nodded again, then got back to his skillet. He looked the nervous sort, and with Big Po on the premises, who could blame him?

When a middle-aged waitress came out from behind the counter, Rebus ordered his coffee. Big Po was still busy with his fork and egg yolk.

'Be easier with a spoon,' Rebus suggested.

'I like a challenge.'

'Well, could be I've another for you.' Rebus paused while the coffee arrived. It was in a see-through Pyrex cup with matching saucer. In some cafés, they were becoming trendy again, but Rebus had the feeling this was an original. He hadn't asked for milk, but it was already added, with bubbles of white froth breaking on the surface. He took a sip. It was hot and didn't taste of coffee.

'So tell me what's on your mind,' Big Po said.

Rebus gave him the background. Po listened as he ate, finishing with a mopping-up operation involving the addition to the bare greasy plate of a liberal squirt of brown sauce, and two further slices of toast. Afterwards, Big Po tried sitting back, but there wasn't really the room. He slurped at his mug of dark brown tea and tried to turn his bear growl into something mere mortals might recognise as an undertone.

'Gordie's the man to talk to about Bellman's; used to drink there till they barred him.'

'Barred from Bellman's? What did he do, machine-gun the place or ask for a gin and tonic?'

Big Po snorted. 'I think he was shagging Houton's missus.'

'Houton being the owner?'

Po nodded. 'Big bad bastard.' Which meant a lot, coming from him.

'Is Gordie a first or last name?'

'Gordie Burns, drinks in the Weir O'.'

Meaning the Weir O' Hermiston, on the shore road out towards Portobello. 'How will I know him?' Rebus asked.

Po reached into his blue nylon windcheater, brought out a mobile phone. 'I'll give him a call, make sure he's there.'

As he did so, knowing the number by heart, Rebus stared out of the steamed-up window. At call's end, he thanked Po and stood up.

'Not finishing your coffee?'

Rebus shook his head. 'But this is on me.' He walked up to the counter, handed over a fiver. Three fifty for the fry-up, cheapest coronary in town. On his way back past Big Po's table, he patted the man's shoulder, slid a twenty into the windcheater's breast zip-up pocket.

'God bless you, young sir,' Big Po boomed. Rebus couldn't have sworn to it, but as he closed the door behind him he got the feeling the big man was ordering another breakfast.

The Weir O' was a civilised sort of pub: car park out front, and a chalkboard advertising a range of 'home cooked fayre'. As Rebus stepped up to the bar and ordered a whisky, a drinker, two along, started finishing up. By the time Rebus's drink arrived, the man was leaving, telling his companion that he'd be back in a wee while. Rebus took a minute or two to savour his own drink, then made for the door. The man was waiting for him around the corner, where the view was of disused warehouses and slag heaps.

'Gordie?' Rebus asked.

The man nodded. He was tall and gangly, late thirties with a long, sad face and thinning, ill-cut hair. Rebus made to hand him a twenty. Gordie paused just long enough to let Rebus know he had some pride, then pocketed the note.

'Make it quick,' he said, eyes darting from side to side. Traffic was thundering past, lorries mostly, travelling too quickly to take note of the two men.

Rebus kept it brief: description; pub; attack.

'Sounds like Mick Lorimer,' Gordie said, turning to walk away.

'Whoah,' Rebus said. 'What about an address or something?'

'Mick Lorimer,' Gordie repeated, heading back into the pub.

John Michael Lorimer: known as Mick. Previouses for assault, entering lockfast premises, housebreaking. Bobby Hogan knew him, which was why they took Lorimer to Leith cop shop, let him sweat there for a little while before starting the questioning.

'We're not going to get much out of this one,' Hogan warned. 'Vocabulary of about a dozen words, half of which would make your granny shriek.'

And he'd been waiting for them, seated quietly in his two-storey house just off Easter Road. A 'friend' had let them in, and Lorimer had been in a chair in the living room, newspaper open on his lap. He'd said almost nothing, not even bothering to ask them why they were there, why they were asking him to go down to the station with them. Rebus had taken an address from the girlfriend. It was on the housing scheme where Linford had been attacked. Which was fair enough: even if they proved it was Lorimer Linford had been following, he now had an alibi – went to his girlfriend's, didn't leave the flat all night.

Convenient and cost-effective; no way she'd suddenly

change her story, not if she knew what was good for her. From her washed-out eyes and slow movements, Rebus would guess she'd had a pretty good education at the hands of Mick Lorimer.

'Are we wasting our time, then?' Rebus asked. Bobby Hogan just shrugged. He'd been on the force as long as Rebus; both men knew the score. Getting them into custody was just the opening bell of the bout, and most times the fight seemed fixed.

'We've got the line-ups anyway,' Hogan said, pushing open the door to the interview room.

Leith police station wasn't modern, not like St Leonard's. It was a solid late-Victorian design, reminding Rebus of his old school. Cold stone walls covered with maybe their twentieth layer of paint, and lots of exposed pipework. The interview rooms were like prison cells, sparse and dulling the senses. Seated at the table, Lorimer looked as much at home as he had in his own living room.

'Solicitor,' he said as the two detectives entered.

'Think you need one?' Hogan asked.

'Solicitor,' Lorimer repeated.

Hogan looked to Rebus. 'Like a broken record, isn't he?'

'Stuck in the wrong groove.'

Hogan turned back to Lorimer. 'We get you for six hours to ourselves without as much as a whiff of legal advice. That's what the law says.' He slipped his hands into his trouser pockets. All he was doing, the gesture said, was having a bit of a chat with a friend. 'Mick here', he told Rebus, 'used to be one of Tommy Telford's doormen, did you know that?'

'I didn't,' Rebus lied.

'Had to make himself scarce when Tommy's little empire blew up.'

Rebus was nodding now. 'Big Ger Cafferty,' he said.

'We all know Big Ger wasn't happy about Tommy and his gang.' A meaningful look towards Lorimer. 'Or with anyone connected to them.'

Rebus was standing in front of the table now. He leaned down so that his hands rested on the back of the empty chair. 'Big Ger's out. Did you know that, Mick?'

Lorimer didn't so much as blink.

'Large as life and back in Edinburgh,' Rebus went on. 'Maybe I could put you in touch with him . . . ?'

'Six hours,' Lorimer said. 'Nae bother.'

Rebus glanced towards Hogan: so much for that.

They took a break, stood outside smoking cigarettes.

Rebus was thinking aloud. 'Say Lorimer killed Roddy Grieve. Putting aside the question of why, we think Barry Hutton was behind it.' Hogan was nodding. 'Two questions really: first, was Grieve meant to die?'

'Wouldn't put it past Lorimer to get a bit overzealous. He's one of those guys, gets the red mist once he gets started.'

'Second,' Rebus went on, 'was Grieve meant to be found? Wouldn't they try hiding the body?'

Hogan shrugged. 'That's Lorimer again; hard as nails but not half as sharp.'

Rebus looked at him. 'So say he cocked up: how come he's not been punished?'

Now Hogan smiled. 'Punish Mick Lorimer? You'd need a big army. Either that or you'd want to lull him, get him when his guard was down.'

Which reminded Rebus . . . He called the hotel again. There was still no sign of Rab Hill. Maybe face to face would be better. He needed Hill on his side. Hill was the proof, which was why Cafferty was keeping him close.

If Rebus could get to Rab Hill, he could put Cafferty away again. There was almost nothing he wanted more in the world.

'It'd be like Christmas,' he said aloud. Hogan asked him to explain, but Rebus just shook his head.

Mr Cowan, who'd given them the description of the man on Holyrood Road, took his time over the line-up, but picked out Lorimer eventually. While the prisoner went back to his cell, the others were led away to be given tea and biscuits until their second appearance. They were students mostly.

'I get them from the rugby team,' Hogan explained. 'When I need a few bruisers. Half of them are training to be doctors and lawyers.'

But Rebus wasn't listening. The two men were standing outside the station's front door, enjoying a cigarette. And now an ambulance had drawn up, and its back doors were being opened, a ramp lowered. Derek Linford, face heavily bruised, head bandaged and with a surgical collar around his neck. He was in a wheelchair, and as the orderly pushed him closer, Rebus could see wiring around his jaw. His pupils had a drugged blankness to them, but when he spotted Rebus his vision cleared a little, his eyes narrowing. Rebus shook his head slowly, a mixture of sympathy and denial. Linford looked away, trying for a measure of dignity as his wheelchair was turned, the better to get it up the steps.

Hogan flicked his cigarette on to the road, just in front of the ambulance. 'You staying out of it?' he asked. Rebus nodded.

'Think I'd better, don't you?'

He'd smoked two more cigarettes before Hogan reappeared.

'Well,' he said, 'he gave us the nod: Mick Lorimer.'

'Can he talk?'

Hogan shook his head. 'Mouth's full of metal. All he did was nod when I gave him the number.'

'What does Lorimer's lawyer say?'

'Not too happy. He was asking what medicines DI Linford had taken.'

'Are you charging Lorimer?'

'Oh, I think so. We'll try assault to start with.'

'Will it get far?'

Hogan blew out his cheeks. 'Between you and me?

Probably not. Lorimer's not denying being the man Linford followed. Problem with that is, it opens a whole other can of worms.'

'Unauthorised surveillance?'

Hogan nodded. 'Defence would have a field day in court. I'll talk to the girlfriend again. Maybe there's a grudge there . . .'

'She won't talk,' Rebus said with some confidence. 'They never do.'

Siobhan went to the hospital. Derek Linford was propped up with four pillows at his back. A plastic jug of water and tabloid newspaper for company.

'Brought a couple of magazines,' she said. 'Didn't know what you liked.' She laid the carrier bag on the bed, found a chair near by and brought it over. 'They said you can't talk, but I thought I'd come anyway.' She smiled. 'I won't ask how you're feeling: no point really. I just wanted you to know, it wasn't John's fault. He'd never do something like that . . . or let something like that happen to someone. He's not that subtle.' She wasn't looking at him. Her fingers played with the handles on the carrier bag. 'What happened between us . . . between you and me . . . it was my fault, I see that now. I mean, mine as much as yours. It's not going to help anyone if you . . .' She happened to glance up, saw the fire and mistrust in his eyes.

'If you . . .' But the words died in her mouth. She'd rehearsed a little speech, but could see now how little difference it would make.

'The only person you can blame is the person who did this to you.' She glanced up again, then looked away. 'I'm wondering if that loathing is for me or for John.'

She watched him slowly reach for his tabloid, bringing it down on to the bedcover. There was a biro attached to it. He unclipped it and drew something on the paper's front page. She stood up to get a better look, angling her neck. It was a rough circle, as big as he could make it, and it stood, she quickly realised, for the world, for everything, the whole damned lot.

The subject of his loathing.

'I missed a Hibs match to come here,' she told him. 'That's how important this is to me.' He just glared. 'Okay, bad joke,' she said. 'I'd have come anyway.' But he was closing his eyes now, as if tired of listening.

She gave it a couple more minutes, then walked out. Back in her car, she remembered a call she had to make: the slip of paper with the number was in her pocket. It had only taken her twenty minutes to find it amongst the paperwork on her desk.

'Sandra?'

'Yes.'

'I thought you might be out shopping or something. It's Siobhan Clarke.'

'Oh.' Sandra Carnegie didn't sound exactly pleased to hear her.

'We think the man who attacked you has ended up getting himself killed.'

'What happened?'

'He was stabbed.'

'Good. Give whoever did it a medal.'

'Looks like it was his accomplice. He got a sudden attack of conscience. We caught him heading for Newcastle down the A1. He's told us everything.'

'Will you do him for murder?'

'We'll do him for everything we can.'

'Does that mean I'll have to testify?'

'Maybe. But it's great news, isn't it?'

'Yeah, great. Thanks for letting me know.'

The phone went dead in Siobhan's hand. She made an exasperated sound. Her one planned victory of the day snatched away.

'Go away,' Rebus said.

'Thanks, I will.' Siobhan pulled out the chair and sat

416

down opposite him, shrugged her arms out of her coat. She'd already bought her drink: fresh orange topped up with lemonade. They were in the back room of the Ox. The front room was busy: Saturday early evening, the football crowd. But the back room was quiet. The TV wasn't on. A lone drinker over by the fire was reading the *Irish Times*. Rebus was drinking whisky: no empties on the table, but all that meant was he was taking his glass back for a refill each time.

'I thought you were cutting down,' Siobhan said. He just glared at her. 'Sorry,' she said, 'I forgot whisky's the answer to the world's problems.'

'It's no dafter than yogic flying.' He raised the glass to his mouth, paused. 'What do you want anyway?' Tipped the glass and let the warmth trickle into his mouth.

'I went to see Derek.'

'How is he?'

'Not talking.'

'Poor bastard can't, can he?'

'It's more than that.'

He nodded slowly. 'I know. And who's to say he's not right?'

Her frown brought a little vertical crease to the middle of her forehead. 'How do you mean?'

'It was me told him to go chasing Hutton's men. In effect, I was telling him to tag a murderer.'

'But you weren't expecting him to—'

'How do you know? Maybe I *did* want the bugger hurt.'

'Why?'

Rebus shrugged. 'To teach him something.'

Siobhan wanted to ask what: humility? Or as punishment for his voyeurism? She drank her drink instead.

'But you don't know for sure?' she said at last.

Rebus made to light a cigarette, then thought better of it.

'Don't mind me,' she said.

But he shook his head, slid the cigarette back into its

417

packet. 'Too many today as it is. Besides, I'm outnumbered.' Nodding towards the *Irish Times*. 'Hayden there doesn't smoke either.'

Hearing his name, the man smiled across, called out, 'For which relief, much thanks,' and went back to his reading.

'So what now?' Siobhan asked. 'Have they suspended you yet?'

'They have to catch me first.' Rebus began playing with the ashtray. 'I've been thinking about cannibals,' he said. 'Queensberry's son.'

'What about him?'

'I was wondering whether there are still cannibals out there, maybe more than we think.'

'Not literally?'

He shook his head. 'We talk about getting a roasting, chewing someone up, eating them for breakfast. We say it's a dog-eat-dog world, but really we're talking about ourselves.'

'Communion,' Siobhan added. 'The body of Christ.'

He smiled. 'I've always wondered about that. I couldn't do it, that wafer turning to flesh.'

'And drinking the blood . . . that makes us vampires as well.'

Rebus's smile broadened, but his eyes said that his thoughts were elsewhere.

'I'll tell you a strange coincidence,' she said. She went on to tell him about the night at Waverley, the black Sierra and the singles club rapist.

He nodded at the story. 'And I'll tell you a stranger one: that Sierra's licence number was found in Derek Linford's notebook.'

'How come?'

'Because Nicholas Hughes worked for Barry Hutton's company.' Siobhan made to form a question, but Rebus anticipated it. 'Looks like complete coincidence at this stage.'

Siobhan sat back and was thoughtful for a moment. 'Know what we need?' she said at last. 'I mean in the Grieve case. We need corroboration, witnesses. We need someone who'll talk to us.'

'Better get the Ouija board out then.'

'You still think Alasdair's dead?' Waited till he'd shrugged. 'I don't. If he was six feet under, we'd know about it.' She broke off, watching Rebus's face clear suddenly. 'What did I say?'

He was looking at her. 'We want to talk to Alasdair, right?'

'Right,' she agreed.

'Then all we have to do is issue the invitation.'

She was puzzled now. 'What sort of invitation?'

He drained his glass, got to his feet. 'You better do the driving. Knowing my luck recently, I'd wrap us round a lamp-post.'

'What invitation?' she repeated, struggling to get her arms into the sleeves of her coat.

But Rebus was already on his way. As she passed the man with the newspaper, he raised his glass and wished her good luck.

His tone implied that she'd need it.

'You know him then,' she complained, heading for the outside world.

37

The funeral of Roderick David Rankeillor Grieve took place on an afternoon of steady sleet. Rebus was at the church. He stood towards the back, hymnary open but not singing. Despite the short notice, the place was packed: family members from all over Scotland, plus establishment figures – politicians, media, people from the banking world. There were representatives from the Labour hierarchy in London, playing with their cuff links and checking their silent pagers, eyes darting around for faces they ought to know.

At the church gates, members of the public had gathered, ghouls on the lookout for anyone worth an autograph. Photographers, too, with deadlines to meet, wiping beads of water from zoom lenses. Two TV crews – BBC and independent – had set up their vans. There was a protocol to be observed: invitees only in the churchyard. Police were patrolling the perimeter. With so many public figures around, security was always going to be an issue. Siobhan Clarke was out there somewhere, mingling with the public, scrutinising them without seeming to.

The service seemed long to Rebus. There wasn't just the local minister: the dignitaries had to make their speeches, too. Protocol again. And, filling the front pews, the immediate family. Peter Grief had been asked if he'd sit with his aunts and uncles, but preferred to be with his mother, two rows back. Rebus spotted Jo Banks and Hamish Hall, five rows ahead of his own. Colin Carswell, the Assistant Chief Constable, was wearing his best uniform, looking slightly piqued that there wasn't room for him in the row in front, where so many distinguished invitees had crammed themselves that they had to rise and sit in single, fluid movements.

Speech after speech, the centre aisle decked with wreaths. Roddy Grieve's old headmaster had spoken haltingly and softly, so that each clearing of the throat from the pews drowned out half a sentence. The coffin, dark polished oak, gleaming brass handles, was resting on a trestle. The hearse had been a venerable Rolls-Royce. Limos clogged the narrow streets around the church, some of the cars sporting national flags – representatives from the various Edinburgh consulates. Out on the path, Cammo Grieve had given Rebus a half-twist of his mouth, a sombre smile of greeting. He'd done most of the organising, drawing up lists of names, liaising with officials. After the interment, there was to be a finger buffet at a hotel in the West End. Fewer invitees to this function: family and close friends. There'd be a police presence – security again – but provided by the Scottish Crime Squad.

As another hymn got under way, Rebus slipped from the back of the congregation and out into the churchyard. The burial site was eighty yards away, a family plot containing the deceased's father and one set of grand-parents. The hole had already been dug, its edges covered with lengths of green baize. There was melt water in the bottom of the grave. The mound of earth and clay sat ready to one side. Rebus smoked a cigarette, paced the area. Then when he'd finished, he didn't know what to do with the dowp: nicked it and popped it back into the packet.

He heard the church doors opening, the organ music swelling. Walked away from the graveside and took up position at a nearby grouping of poplars. Half an hour later it was all over. Howls and handkerchiefs, black ties and lost looks. As the mourners filtered away, their emotions went with them. What was left was industry, as the diggers got busy filling in the hole. Car doors, engines revving. The scene was cleared in minutes. The churchyard was just that again: no voices or cries, just a crow's defiant call and the crisp working of shovels.

Rebus moved further away, towards the rear of the church building, but keeping the graveside in view. Trees and headstones camouflaging him. The headstones were worn almost smooth. He got the feeling very few these days were privileged to have their resting place here. There was a much larger purpose-built cemetery across the road. He picked out a few names – Warriston, Lockhart, Milroy – and read evidence of infant mortality. Hellish to lose a son or daughter. Now Alicia Grieve had lost two.

An hour he waited, feet growing icy as the damp penetrated his shoe soles. The sleet wasn't letting up, the sky a hard grey shell, muffling the life beneath. He didn't smoke; smoke might draw attention. Even kept his breathing slow and regular, each exhalation a billowing indication of life. Just a man coming to terms with mortality, graveyard memories of past family, past friends. Rebus had ghosts in his life: they came hesitantly these days, not sure how welcome they'd be. Came to him as he sat in darkness, incidental music playing. Came to him on the long nights when he had no company, a gathering of souls and gestures, movement without voice. Roddy Grieve might join them some day, but Rebus doubted it. He hadn't known the man in life, and had little to share with his shade.

He'd spent all day Sunday in pursuit of Rab Hill. At the hotel, they admitted that Mr Hill had checked out the previous evening. A bit of pressing, and Rebus was informed that Mr Hill hadn't been seen for a day or two beforehand. Then Mr Cafferty had explained that his friend had been called away. He'd settled the account, keeping his own room open, date of departure uncertain. Cafferty was the last person Rebus wanted to talk to about

Hill. He'd been shown the bedroom – nothing had been left behind. As staff said, Mr Hill had brought only the one canvas duffel bag with him. Nobody'd seen him leave.

Rebus's next stop had been Hill's parole officer. It had taken him a couple of hours to track down her home phone number, and she'd been none too pleased to have her Sunday disturbed.

'Surely it can wait till tomorrow.'

Rebus was beginning to doubt it. Eventually she'd given him what she could. Robert Hill had attended two interviews with her. He wasn't due to see her again until the following Thursday.

'I think you'll find he misses that appointment,' Rebus told her, putting down the receiver.

He'd spent his Sunday evening parked outside the hotel; no sign of either Cafferty or Hill. Monday and Tuesday he'd been back at St Leonard's, while his future was debated by people so far up the ladder they were little more than names to him. In the end, he was kept on the case. Linford hadn't been able to offer any real evidence to support his claim, but Rebus got the feeling it was more to do with PR. Gill Templer, the rumour went, had argued that the last thing the force needed was more bad publicity, and pulling a well-known officer from a high-profile inquiry would have the media vultures hovering.

Her approach had gone straight to the deepest fears of the High Hiedyins. Only Carswell, the story went, voted for Rebus's suspension.

Rebus still had to thank her.

He looked up now and saw a cream trench coat moving across the grass towards the grave, hands deep in pockets, head bowed. Moving briskly, and with definite purpose. Rebus started moving, too, eyes never leaving the figure. A man, tall, thick hair slightly tousled, giving an impression of boyishness. He was standing graveside as Rebus approached. The diggers were still working, nearly done now. The headstone would come later. Rebus felt slightly dizzy, the way gamblers sometimes did when long odds romped home. Three feet behind the figure now . . . Rebus stopped, cleared his throat. The man's head half-turned. His back straightened. He began to walk away, Rebus following.

'I'd like you to come with me,' he said quietly, his performance watched by the gravediggers. The man said nothing, kept moving.

Rebus repeated the request, this time adding: 'There's another grave you should see.'

The man slowed, but didn't stop.

'I'm a police officer, if that's what you're worried about. You can check my warrant card.'

The man had stopped on the path, only a yard or two inside the gate. Rebus moved around in front of him, seeing the full face for the first time. Sagging flesh, but suntanned. Eyes which spoke of experience and humour and – above all – fear. A cleft chin, showing flecks of grey stubble. Weary from travel, mistrustful of this stranger, this strange land.

'I'm Detective Inspector Rebus,' Rebus said, holding up the warrant card.

'Whose grave?' It was said almost in a whisper, no sign of native accent.

'Freddy's,' Rebus said.

Freddy Hastings had been buried in a barren spot in a sprawling cemetery on the other side of the city. No marker had been erected, so that they stood by an anonymous soft hillock, the bare earth covered patchily with sections of turf.

'There weren't many turned out for this one,' Rebus said. 'Couple of fellow officers, old flame, couple of winos.'

'I don't understand. How did he die?'

'He killed himself. Saw something in the paper, and decided, God knows why, that he'd had enough of hiding.'

'The money . . .'

424

'Oh, he spent some of it at first, but after that ... Something made him leave it untouched, for the most part. Maybe he was waiting for you to show up. Maybe it was just the guilt.'

The man didn't say anything. His eyes were glassy with tears. He reached into his pocket for a handkerchief and wiped at his face, shivering as he replaced it.

'Bit parky this far north, eh?' Rebus said. 'Where have you been living?'

'The Caribbean. I run a bar there.'

'Bit of a ways from Edinburgh.'

He turned towards Rebus. 'How did you find me?'

'I didn't have to: *you* found *me*. All the same, the paintings helped.'

'Paintings?'

'Your mother, Mr Grieve. She's been putting you on canvas ever since you left.'

Alasdair Grieve wasn't sure if he wanted to see his family.

'At this time,' he argued, 'it might be too much.'

Rebus nodded. They were seated in an interview room at St Leonard's. Siobhan Clarke was there, too.

'Don't suppose', Rebus said, 'you want your visit here trumpeted from the Castle ramparts?'

'No,' Grieve agreed.

'Incidentally, what name do you go by these days?'

'My passport says Anthony Keillor.'

Rebus wrote the name down. 'I won't ask where you got the passport.'

'I wouldn't tell you if you did.'

'Couldn't shrug off every link with the past, though, could you? Keillor, short for Rankeillor.'

Grieve stared. 'You know my family.'

Rebus shrugged. 'When did you find out about Roddy?'

'A few days after it happened. I thought of coming back then, but didn't know what good it would do. Then I saw the funeral announcement.'

'I wouldn't have thought it would make the Caribbean papers.'

'The Internet, Inspector. The *Scotsman* online.'

Rebus nodded. 'And you thought you'd take the chance?'

'I always liked Roddy ... thought it was the least I could do.'

'Despite the risks?'

'It was twenty years ago, Inspector. Hard to know after that length of time ...'

'Just as well it was me at that graveside and not Barry Hutton.'

The name brought back all sorts of memories. Rebus watched them pass across Alasdair Grieve's face. 'That bastard,' Grieve said at last. 'Is he still around?'

'Land developer of the parish.'

Grieve scowled, muttered the word 'Christ'.

'So,' Rebus said, leaning forward, resting his elbows on the table, 'I think maybe it's time you told us who the body in the fireplace belongs to.'

Grieve stared at him again. 'The what?'

When Rebus had explained, Grieve started to nod.

'Hutton must have put the body there. He was working at Queensberry House, keeping an eye on Dean Coghill for his uncle.'

'Bryce Callan?'

'The same. Callan was grooming Barry. Looks like he did a good job of it, too.'

'And you were in cahoots with Callan?'

'I wouldn't call it that.' Grieve half rose from the table, then stopped. 'Do you mind? I get a bit claustrophobic.'

Grieve began pacing what floor space there was. Siobhan was standing by the door. She smiled reassuringly at him. Rebus handed him a photo – the computer-generated face from the fireplace.

'How much do you know?' Grieve asked Rebus.

426

'Quite a bit. Callan was buying up lots of land around Calton Hill, presumably with both eyes on a new parliament. But he didn't want the planners knowing it was him, so he used Freddy and you as a front.'

Grieve was nodding. 'Bryce had a contact in the council, someone in the planning department.' Rebus and Siobhan exchanged a look. 'He'd given Bryce a promise on the parliament site.'

'Bloody risky, though: it was all down to how the vote went in the first place.'

'Yes, but that looked solid at first. It was only later the fix went in, the government making damned sure it wouldn't happen.'

'So, Callan had all this land and now nothing was going to happen to make it worth anything?'

'The land was still worth something. But he blamed us for everything.' Grieve laughed. 'As if *we'd* rigged the election!'

'And?'

'Well . . . Freddy had been playing silly buggers with the figures, telling Callan we'd had to pay more for the land than was the case. Callan found out, wanted the difference back plus the money he'd paid as a fee for fronting the whole thing.'

'He sent someone round?' Rebus guessed.

'A man called Mackie.' Grieve tapped the photo. 'One of his thugs, a real piece of work.' He rubbed at his temples. 'Christ, you don't know how strange it feels, saying all this at last . . .'

'Mackie?' Rebus prompted. 'First name Chris?'

'No, not Chris: Alan or Alex . . . something like that. Why?'

'It's the name Freddy took for himself.' Guilt again? Rebus wondered. 'So how did Mackie end up dead?'

'He was there to scare us into paying, and he could be *very* scary. Freddy just got lucky. There was a knife he kept in his drawer, a sort of letter opener. Took it with him

427

that night for protection. We were supposed to be meeting Callan, sort it all out. Car park off the Cowgate, late night . . . the pair of us were scared shitless.'

'But you went anyway?'

'We'd discussed doing a runner . . . but, yes, we went anyway. Hard to turn down Bryce Callan. Only Bryce wasn't there. It was this guy Mackie. He gave me a couple of whacks on the head – one of my ears still doesn't work properly. Then he turned on Freddy. He had this gun, hit me with the butt. I think Freddy was going to get worse . . . I'm sure of it. He was the one in charge, Callan knew that. It was self-defence, I'd swear to it. All the same, I don't think he meant to kill Mackie, just . . .' He shrugged. 'Just stop him, I suppose.'

'Stabbed him through the heart,' Rebus commented.

'Yes,' Grieve agreed. 'We could see straight off he was dead.'

'What did you do?'

'Dumped him back in his car and ran for it. We knew we had to split up, knew Callan would have to kill us now, no two ways about it.'

'And the money?'

'I told Freddy I didn't want anything to do with it. He said we should meet, a year to the day, a bar on Frederick Street.'

'You didn't make the meet?'

Grieve shook his head. 'I was someone else by then, somewhere I was getting to know and like.'

Freddy had travelled, too, Siobhan was thinking: all the places he'd told Dezzi about.

But a year to the day, when Alasdair didn't show, Freddy Hastings had walked into the building society on George Street, just round the corner from Frederick Street, and opened an account in the name of C. Mackie . . .

'There was a briefcase,' Siobhan asked.

Grieve looked at her. 'God, yes. It belonged to Dean Coghill.'

'The letters on it were ADC.'

'I think Dean's his second name, but he liked it better than the first. Barry Hutton brought us one lot of cash in that briefcase, boasted how he'd taken it from Coghill; "Because I can, and there's nothing he can do about it." ' He shook his head.

'Mr Coghill's dead,' Siobhan said.

'Chalk up another victim to Bryce Callan.'

And though Coghill had died of natural causes, Rebus knew exactly what Grieve meant.

Rebus and Siobhan, a powwow in the CID suite.

'What've we got?' she asked.

'Lots of bits,' he acknowledged. 'We've got Barry Hutton heading out to check on Mackie, finding the body. Not far from Queensberry House, so he takes the body there, walls it in. Chances were, it wouldn't be found for centuries.'

'Why?'

'Couldn't have the police asking questions, I suppose.'

'How come no one called Mackie ended up posted a MisPer?'

'Mackie belongs to Bryce Callan, no one to mourn him or post him missing.'

'And Freddy Hastings kills himself when he reads the story in the paper?'

Rebus nodded. 'The whole thing's coming back again, and he can't deal with it.'

'I'm not sure I understand him.'

'Who?'

'Freddy. What made him do what he did, living like that . . .'

'There's a slightly more pressing concern,' Rebus told her. 'Callan and Hutton are getting away with this.'

Siobhan was leaning against her desk. She folded her arms. 'Well, in the end, what did they *do*? They didn't kill

Mackie, they didn't push Freddy Hastings off North Bridge.'

'But they made it all happen.'

'And now Callan's a tax exile, and Barry Hutton's a reformed character.' She waited for him to say something, but he didn't. 'You don't think so?' Then she remembered what Alasdair Grieve had said in the interview room.

'A contact in the council,' she quoted.

'Someone in the planning department,' Rebus quoted back.

38

It took them a week to get everything together, the team working flat out. Derek Linford was convalescing at home, drinking his meals through a straw. As someone commented, 'Every time an officer takes a kicking, the brass has to reward them.' The feeling was Linford would be going on a promotion shortlist. Meantime, Alasdair Grieve was acting the tourist. He'd got himself a room at a bed and breakfast on Minto Street. They weren't letting him leave the country, not quite yet. He'd surrendered his passport, and had to report each day to St Leonard's. The Farmer didn't think they'd be charging him with anything, but as the witness to a fatal assault, a case-file would have to be prepared. Rebus's unofficial contract with Grieve: stay put, and your family needn't know you're back.

The team compiled their case. Not just the Roddy Grieve team, but Siobhan and Wylie and Hood, Wylie making sure she had a desk by a window: her reward, she said, for all the hours in the interview room.

They had help from further afield, too – NCIS, Crime Squad, the Big House. And when they were ready, there was still work to be done. A doctor had to be arranged, the suspect contacted and informed that a solicitor might be a good idea. He would know they'd been asking questions; even in his state, he'd have to know – friends tipping him the wink. Again, Carswell argued against Rebus's involvement; again, he was voted down, but only just.

When Rebus and Siobhan turned up at the detached,

walled house on Queensferry Road, there were three cars in the driveway: both doctor and solicitor had already arrived. It was a big house, 1930s vintage, but next to the main artery between the city and Fife. That would knock £50k from the value, easy; even so, it had to be worth a third of a million. Not bad for a 'toon cooncillor'.

Archie Ure was in bed, but not in his bedroom. To avoid the stairs, a single bed had been erected in the dining room. The dining table now sat out in the hall, six formal chairs upended and resting on its polished surface. The room was redolent of illness: that stuffy, fusty smell of sweat and unbrushed teeth. The patient sat up, breathing noisily. The doctor had just finished his examination. Ure was hooked up to a heart monitor, his pyjama top unbuttoned, thin black wires disappearing beneath circles of flesh-toned tape. His chest was near hairless, falling with each laboured exhalation like a punctured bellows.

Ure's solicitor was a man called Cameron Whyte, a short, meticulous-looking individual who, according to Ure's wife, had been a family friend for the past three decades. He was seated on a chair at the bedside, briefcase on his knees and a fresh pad of A4 lined paper resting atop it. Introductions had to be made. Rebus did not shake Archie Ure's hand, but did ask how he was feeling.

'Bloody fine till all this nonsense,' was the gruff response.

'We'll try to be as quick as we can,' Rebus said.

Ure grunted. Cameron Whyte went on to ask some preliminary questions, while Rebus opened one of the two cases he was carrying and brought out the cassette machine. It was a cumbersome piece of kit, but would record two copies of the interview and time-stamp each one. Rebus went over the procedure with Whyte, who watched carefully as Rebus set the date and time, then broke open two fresh tapes. There were problems with the flex, which just barely stretched from the wall socket, and then with the double-headed microphone, whose lead just made it to the bed. Rebus shifted his own chair, so that he was seated in a claustrophobic triangle with lawyer and patient, the mike resting on top of the duvet. The whole process had taken the best part of twenty minutes. Not that Rebus was hurrying: he was hoping the wait might bore Mrs Ure into retreating. She did disappear at one point, returning with a tray containing teacups and pot. Pointedly, she poured for the doctor and lawyer, but told the police officers to 'serve yourselves'. Siobhan did so smilingly, before moving back to stand by the door, there being no chair for her – and little enough room for one. The doctor was seated at the far side of the bed, beside the heart monitor. He was young, sandy-haired, and seemed bemused by the whole scene being acted out before him.

Mrs Ure, unable to get next to her husband, stood by the solicitor's shoulder, making him twitch with discomfort. The room grew hotter, stuffier. There was condensation on the window. They were at the rear of the house, with a view on to a sweeping expanse of lawn, ringed by trees and bushes. A bird table had been fixed into the ground near the window, tits and sparrows visiting from time to time, peering into the room, dismayed by the quality of service.

'I could die of boredom,' Archie Ure commented, sipping apple juice.

'Sorry about that,' Rebus said. 'I'll see what I can do to help.' He was opening his second case, pulling out a fat manila folder. Ure seemed momentarily transfixed by its sheer weight, but Rebus pulled out a single sheet and laid it on top, creating a makeshift desk much like the lawyer's.

'I think we can start,' Rebus said. Siobhan crouched on the floor and activated the recorder. Nodded to let him know both tapes were rolling. Rebus identified himself for the record, then asked the others present to do likewise.

'Mr Ure,' he said, 'do you know a man called Barry Hutton?'

It was one question Ure had been expecting. 'He's a property developer,' he said.

'How well do you know him?'

Ure took another sip of juice. 'I run the council's planning department. Mr Hutton always has schemes coming before us.'

'How long have you been head of planning?'

'Eight years.'

'And before that?'

'How do you mean?'

'I mean, what positions did you fill.'

'I've been a councillor for the best part of twenty-five years; not many posts I haven't filled at one time or another.'

'But mostly planning?'

'Why bother asking? You already know.'

'Do I?'

Ure's face twisted. 'Quarter of a century, you make a few friends.'

'And your friends tell you we've been asking questions?'

Ure nodded, went back to his drink.

'Mr Ure nods,' Rebus said, for the benefit of the tape. Ure looked up at him. There was a measure of loathing there, but something in the man was prepared to enjoy this game, because that's what it was to him: a game. Nothing they could pin on him; no need to say anything incriminating.

'You were on the planning board in the late seventies,' Rebus went on.

''Seventy-eight to '83,' Ure agreed.

'You must have come across Bryce Callan?'

'Not really.'

'What does that mean?'

'It means I know his name.' Both Ure and Rebus watched the lawyer scratch a note on his pad. Rebus noticed he was using a fountain pen, his letters tall and

434

slanting. 'I don't recall his name ever cropping up on a planning application.'

'How about Freddy Hastings?'

Ure nodded slowly: he'd known this name would come up, too. 'Freddy was around for a few years. Bit of a wide boy, liked to gamble. All the best developers do.'

'And was Freddy a good gambler?'

'He didn't last long, if that's what you're getting at.'

Rebus opened the file, pretending to check something. 'Did you know Barry Hutton back then, Mr Ure?'

'No.'

'I believe he was dipping a toe in the water at that time.'

'Maybe so, but I wasn't on the beach.' Ure wheezed out a laugh at his joke. His wife stretched an arm across the solicitor, touched her husband's hand. He patted hers. Cameron Whyte looked trapped. He'd had to stop scratching on his pad, seemed relieved when Mrs Ure withdrew the arm.

'Not even selling the ice creams?' Rebus asked. Both Ures, husband and wife, glared at him.

'No need to be glib, Inspector,' the lawyer drawled.

'I apologise,' Rebus said. 'Only it wasn't cones you were selling, was it, Mr Ure? It was information. As a result of which, to coin a phrase, you ended up with the lolly.' Behind him, he could hear Siobhan choke back a laugh.

'That's a strong accusation, Inspector,' Cameron Whyte said.

Ure turned his head towards his lawyer. 'Do I need to deny that, Cam, or do I just wait for him to fail to prove it?'

'I'm not sure I *can* prove it,' Rebus admitted guilelessly. 'I mean, we know someone in the council tipped off Bryce Callan about the parliament site, and probably about land in the area that could be available for purchase. We know someone smoothed the way for a lot of plans put forward by Freddy Hastings.' Rebus fixed eyes with Ure. 'Mr

Hastings' business partner of the time, Alasdair Grieve, has given us a full statement.' Rebus searched in the folder again, read from a transcript: 'We were told there wouldn't be any problems with consents. Callan had that under control. Someone in planning was making sure.'

Cameron Whyte looked up. 'I'm sorry, Inspector, maybe my ears aren't what they were, but I failed to hear my client's name mentioned there.'

'Your ears are fine, sir. Alasdair Grieve never knew the mole's name. Six people on the planning committee at that time: could have been any one of them.'

'And presumably,' the lawyer went on, 'other members of council staff had access to such information?'

'Perhaps.'

'Everyone from the Lord Provost down to the typing pool?'

'I wouldn't know, sir.'

'But you *should* know, Inspector, otherwise such flimsy allegations could get you into serious trouble.'

'I don't think Mr Ure will want to sue,' Rebus said. He kept stealing glances at the heart monitor. It wasn't as good as a lie detector, but Ure's rate had leapt in the past couple of minutes. Rebus again made a show of glancing at his notes.

'A general question,' he said, again fixing eyes with Ure. 'Planning decisions can make people millions of pounds, can't they? I don't mean the councillors themselves, or whoever else is responsible for taking the decisions . . . but the builders and developers, anyone who owns land or property near the development site?'

'Sometimes, yes,' Ure conceded.

'So these people, they need to be on good terms with the decision-makers?'

'We're under constant scrutiny,' Ure said. 'I know *you* think we're probably all bent, but even if someone wanted to take a backhander, chances are they'd be found out.'

'Which means there's a chance they wouldn't?'

'They'd be a fool to try.'

'Plenty of fools around, if the price is right.' Rebus glanced back down at his notes. 'You moved into this house in 1980, is that right, Mr Ure?'

It was Whyte who answered. 'Look, Inspector, I don't know what you're insinuating—'

'August 1980,' Ure interrupted. 'Money from my wife's late mother.'

Rebus was ready. 'You sold her house to pay for this one?'

Ure was immediately suspicious. 'That's right.'

'But she had a two-bedroom cottage in Dumfriesshire, Mr Ure. Hardly comparable to Queensferry Road.'

Ure was silent for a moment. Rebus knew what he was thinking. He was thinking: if they've dug that far back, what else do they know?

'You're an evil man!' Mrs Ure snapped. 'Archie's just had a heart attack, and you're trying to kill him off!'

'Don't fret, love,' Archie Ure said, trying to reach out for her.

'Again, Inspector,' Cameron Whyte was saying, 'I must protest at this line of questioning.'

Rebus turned to Siobhan. 'Any more tea in that pot?' Ignoring the flurry of voices; the doctor getting out of his chair, concerned at his patient's state of agitation. Siobhan poured. Rebus nodded his thanks. He turned back to them again.

'Sorry,' he said, 'I missed all that. Point I was going to make is that if there's money to be made on projects in Edinburgh, how much more power would someone have if they were in charge of planning for the whole of Scotland?' He sat back, sipped the tea, waited.

'I don't follow,' the lawyer said.

'Well, the question was really for Mr Ure.' Rebus looked at Ure, who cleared his throat before speaking.

'I've already said, at council level there are all sorts of

437

checks and scrutinies. At national level, they'd be multiplied tenfold.'

'Doesn't quite answer the question,' Rebus commented affably. He shifted in his chair. 'You were runner-up to Roddy Grieve in the ballot, weren't you?'

'So?'

'With Mr Grieve dead, you should have taken his place.'

'If *she* hadn't stuck her oar in,' Mrs Ure spat.

Rebus looked at her. 'I'm assuming that by "she" you mean Seona Grieve?'

'That's enough, Isla,' her husband said. Then, to Rebus: 'Say your piece.'

Rebus shrugged. 'It's just that by rights, with the candidate out of the way, the nomination should have been yours. No wonder you got a shock when Seona Grieve stepped forward.'

'Shock? It nearly killed him. And now you come in here, stirring it—'

'I said be quiet, woman!' Ure had turned on to one side, leaning on an elbow, the better to confront his wife. The beeping of the heart monitor seemed louder to Rebus. The patient was being coaxed on to his back by his doctor. One of the wires had come loose.

'Leave me alone, man,' Ure complained. His wife had folded her arms, her mouth and eyes reduced to narrow, angry fissures. Ure took another sip of juice, lay his head back against the pillows. His eyes were focused on the ceiling.

'Just say your piece,' he repeated.

Rebus all of a sudden felt a pang of pity for the man, a bond that recognised their common mortality, their pasts paved with guilt. The only enemy Archie Ure had now was death itself, and such self-knowledge could change a man.

'It's a supposition really,' Rebus said quietly. He was shutting them all out; it was just him and the man in the bed now. 'But say a developer had someone in the council

438

he could trust to make the right decision. And say this councillor was thinking of running for parliament. Well, if they got in ... with all that experience behind them – over twenty years mostly spent in city planning – they'd be odds-on for a similar post. Planning supremo for the new Scotland. That's a lot of power to wield. The power to say aye or nay to projects worth billions. All that knowledge, too: which areas are going to get redevelopment grants; where this factory or that housing development is going to be sited ... Got to be worth something to a developer. Almost worth killing for ...'

'Inspector,' Cameron Whyte warned. But Rebus had pulled his chair as close to the bed as he could get it. Just him and Ure now.

'See, twenty years ago, I think you were Bryce Callan's mole. And when Bryce moved away, he handed you on to his nephew. We've checked: Barry Hutton hit a golden streak early on in the game. You said it yourself, a good developer is a gambler. But everyone knows the only way to beat the house is if you cheat. Barry Hutton was cheating, and you were his edge, Mr Ure. Barry had high hopes for you, and then Roddy Grieve ended up selected in your place. Barry couldn't have that. He decided to have Roddy Grieve followed. Maybe only so he could be "persuaded", but Mick Lorimer went too far.' Rebus paused. 'That's the name of the man who killed Roddy Grieve: Lorimer. Hutton hired him; we know that.' He could feel Siobhan shifting uneasily behind him – the tape running, catching him saying something they couldn't yet prove.

'Roddy Grieve was drunk. He'd just been selected and wanted a look at his future. I think Lorimer watched Roddy Grieve climb the fence into the parliament site and then followed him. And suddenly, with Grieve out of the way, it was your show again.' Now Rebus narrowed his eyes thoughtfully. 'What I can't figure out is the heart attack: was it because you realised a man had been

439

murdered, or was it when Seona Grieve stepped into her husband's shoes, depriving you all over again?'

'What do you want?' Ure's voice was hoarse.

'There's no evidence, Archie,' the lawyer was saying.

Rebus blinked, his eyes never leaving Ure's. 'What Mr Whyte says is not quite true. I think we've got enough to present in court, but not everyone would agree. We need just that little bit more. And I think you want it, too. Call it a legacy.' His voice was almost a whisper now; he hoped the recorder was catching it. 'After all the shit, a clean break of sorts.'

Silence in the room, except for the monitor, its bleeping slower now. Archie Ure raised himself up so he was sitting unsupported. He crooked a finger, beckoning Rebus closer. Rebus half rose from his chair. A whisper in his ear: it wouldn't make the tape. All the same, he needed to hear . . .

Ure's breathing sounded even more laboured this close, hot rasps against Rebus's neck. Grey bristles on the man's cheeks and throat. Hair oily. When washed, it would be soft and fluffy like a baby's. Talcum powder, that sweet masking smell: his wife probably used it on him, stopping bed sores.

Lips close to his ear, grazing it at one point. Then the words, louder than a whisper, words everyone was meant to hear.

'Nice fucking try.'

And then wheezing laughter, rising in volume, filling the room with sudden, violent energy, drowning out the doctor's advice, the machine's staccato arrhythmia, the wife's pleas. The lawyer's glasses were knocked flying as she lunged at her husband, sensing something. As Whyte leaned down to retrieve them, Isla Ure half clambered across his back. The doctor was studying the machine, pushing Archie Ure back down on to the bed. Rebus stood back. The laughter was for him. The defiance was for him. The red-veined eyes, bulging from their sockets, were for him. All that was demanded of Rebus was that he play the part of spectator.

For now the laughter had a choked, rending sound to it, disappearing in a white noise of gargled froth as the face turned puce, the chest falling and refusing to rise. Isla Ure shrieking now.

'*Not again, Christ! Not again!*'

Cameron Whyte was rising to his feet, glasses back in place. His teacup had been knocked over, a brown stain spreading across the pale pink carpet. The doctor was speaking, Siobhan springing forward to help: she'd had the training. So had Rebus, come to that, but something held him back: the audience didn't clamber on to the stage. The performance had to belong to the actor.

While the doctor issued instructions, he was sliding his body atop his patient, readying himself for CPR. Siobhan was ready to administer mouth-to-mouth. Pyjama shirt wide open, fists flattened one on the other, right at the centre of the chest . . .

The doctor started, Siobhan counting for him.

'One, two, three, four . . . one, two, three.' She pinched the nose, blew into the mouth. Then the doctor started pushing again, almost lifting himself off the bed with the effort.

'*You'll break his ribs!*'

Isla Ure was sobbing, knuckles to her mouth. Siobhan's mouth locked on to the dying man's. Breath of life.

'Come on, Archie, come on!' the doctor roared, as if decibels could counter death. Rebus knew, or feared he knew: if you wished for death, it came for you all too easily. Every step you took, it shadowed your thoughts, waiting for that invitation. It sensed despair, and tiredness and resignation. He could almost sense it in the room. Archie Ure had willed death upon himself, consumed it readily and with that final relished bellow, because it was the only possible victory.

Rebus couldn't despise him for it.

'Come on, come on!'

'. . . three, four . . . one, two . . .'

The lawyer stood pale-faced, one arm missing from his glasses, snapped underfoot. And Isla Ure, head down by her husband's ear, voice cracked to the point of unintelligibility.

'*Allu . . . archmon . . . allu-yoosweess . . .*'

For all the noise, the sweeping chaos of the room, it was an echo of laughter which filled Rebus's ears. The final, stripped-down laughter of Archie Ure. His eyes gazed past the bed, caught movement behind the window. The bird table, a robin clinging to its underside, head turned towards the human pantomime within. First robin he'd seen this winter. Someone had told him once they weren't seasonal, but if that were the case, then why did you only ever see them in the cold months?

One more question to add to the list.

Two, three minutes had passed. The doctor was tiring. He checked for a pulse in the throat, then put his ear to the chest cavity. The wires were hanging dislodged. The monitor making no sound at all; just three red LED letters where numbers had previously been:

ERR

Now flashing to a new message:

RESET

The doctor slid his feet off the bed and on to the floor. Cameron Whyte had picked up the teacup. His spectacles sat at the wrong angle on his face. The doctor was pushing his hair back from his forehead, sweat gleaming in his eyelashes and dripping from his nose. Siobhan Clarke's lips looked dry and pale, as if some of the life had been sucked from them. Isla Ure was lying across her husband's face, shoulders juddering. The robin had flown off, its spirit unfettered by doubt.

John Rebus bent down, retrieved the microphone from the floor. 'Interview ends at . . .' He checked his watch.

'Eleven thirty-eight a.m.'

Eyes turned to him. When he stopped the tapes, it was as if he'd switched off Archie Ure's life-support.

39

Fettes HQ, the office of the Assistant Chief Constable. Colin Carswell, the ACC (Crime), listened to the jumble of noises which made up the last five minutes of the recording.

You had to be there, Rebus felt like telling him. He identified: the moment when Ure sat up, beckoning him closer . . . the moment flecks of foam had appeared at the corners of his twisted mouth . . . the sound of the doctor climbing on to the bed . . . and that dull static was the mike hitting the floor. From then on, everything was muffled. Rebus turned the bass down, upped the treble and volume. Even so, most of the sounds were indistinct.

Carswell had the two reports – Rebus's and Siobhan Clarke's – on the desk in front of him. He'd moistened his thumb before perusing them, lifting each page by a corner. Between them, they'd put together a second-by-second account of Archie Ure's demise, their timings matched to the tape.

There was one other copy of the tape, of course. It had been handed over to Cameron Whyte. Whyte said that Ure's widow was considering a claim against the police. That's why they were here in the ACC's office. Not just Rebus, but Siobhan and the Farmer, too.

More static: that was the mike being picked up. *Interview ends at . . . eleven thirty-eight a.m.*

Rebus stopped the tape. Carswell had listened to it twice now. After the first listen, he'd asked a couple of questions. Now he sat back, hands pressed together in front of his nose and lips. The Farmer made to mimic him, saw what he was doing and lowered his hands, pressing them between his legs instead. Then, seeing this as an unflattering pose to strike, he removed them quickly, laid them on his knees.

'Prominent local politician dies under police questioning,' Carswell commented. He might have been repeating a newspaper headline, but in fact so far they'd managed to keep the truth away from the newshounds. The lawyer had seen the sense of it, and had prevailed with the widow: a headline like that, and people would begin asking questions. Why had police wanted to talk to the recent heart-attack victim? She had enough to cope with without all that.

And she had concurred, while at the same time urging Whyte to 'sue the bastards for every penny'.

Words which acted like a frozen sword to the spines of the High Hiedyins at the Big House. So, just as Cameron Whyte and his team were doubtless poring over the tape, looking to build their case, the lawyers for Lothian and Borders Police were already seated in a room along the corridor, ready to take delivery of the evidence.

'A fatal error of judgement, Chief Superintendent,' Carswell was telling the Farmer. 'Sending someone like Rebus into a situation like that. I had my doubts all along, of course, and now I find myself vindicated.' He looked at Rebus. 'I wish I could take some pleasure in that.' He paused. 'A fatal error,' he repeated.

Fatal error, Rebus was thinking. ERR RESET.

'With respect, sir,' the Farmer said, 'we could hardly be expected to know . . .'

'Sending someone like Rebus to interview a sick man is tantamount to unlawful killing.'

Rebus clenched his jaw, but it was Siobhan who spoke. 'Sir, Inspector Rebus has been invaluable to this investigation throughout.'

'Then how come one of our best officers ends up with his face wired together? How come a long-time Labour councillor is in one of the fridges at the Cowgate? How

445

come we don't have a single solitary conviction? And bloody unlikely to get one now.' Carswell pointed to the tape machine. 'Ure was as good a shout at it as we were going to get.'

'There was nothing wrong with the line of questioning,' the Farmer said quietly. He looked like he wanted to go sit hunched in a corner till gold-watch day.

'Without Ure, there's no case,' Carswell persisted, his attention focused on Rebus. 'Not unless you think Barry Hutton will crack under your rapier-like assault.'

'Give me a rapier and let's see.'

Carswell threw him a furious look. The Farmer started apologising.

'Look, sir,' Rebus interrupted, eyes fixed on the ACC, 'I feel as badly about this as anyone. But we didn't kill Archie Ure.'

'Then what did?'

'Maybe a guilty conscience?' Siobhan offered.

Carswell leapt to his feet. 'This whole investigation has been a farce from the start.' He was pointing at Rebus. 'I hold *you* responsible, and so help me I'll make sure you pay for it.' He turned to the Farmer. 'And as for you, Chief Superintendent . . . well, it's not a very pretty end to your career, is it?'

'No, sir. But with respect, sir . . .'

Rebus could see a change in Watson's demeanour.

'What?' Carswell asked.

'Nobody asked your blue-eyed boy to keep tabs on Hutton. No one told him to head off into a Leith housing scheme in pursuit of a possible murder suspect. Those were *his* decisions and they got him where he is now.' The Farmer paused. 'I think you're putting up a smokescreen so everyone will conveniently forget those facts. The officers here . . .' the Farmer looked at them, '*my* officers . . . also have your protégé pegged as a peeper. Something else you've conveniently ignored.'

'Careful now . . .' Carswell's eyes were boring into the Farmer.

'I think that time's past, don't you?' The Farmer pointed to the tape machine. 'Same as you, I've listened to that tape, and I can't see a damned thing wrong with DI Rebus's methods or his line of questioning.' He stood up, face to face with Carswell. 'You want to make something of it, fine. I'll be waiting.' He started heading for the door. 'After all, what have I got to lose?'

Carswell told them to get the hell out, but it was too late: they were already gone.

Down in the canteen, they left the food on their plates, pushed it around, feeling numb, and didn't talk very much. Rebus turned to the Farmer.

'What happened there?'

The Chief Super shrugged, tried to smile. The fight had gone out of him again; he looked exhausted. 'I just got fed up, simple as that. Thirty years I've been on the force . . .' He shook his head. 'Maybe I've just had a bellyful of the Carswells. Thirty years, and he thinks he can talk to me like that.' He looked at the pair of them, tried out a smile.

'I liked your parting shot,' Rebus said: ' "What have I got to lose?" '

'Thought you might,' the Farmer said. 'You've used it on me often enough.' Then he went to fetch three more coffees – not that they'd finished the first ones; he just needed to be moving – and Siobhan leaned back in her chair.

'What do you think?' she asked.

'Golgotha via Calvary,' he said. 'And don't bother looking for the return portion.'

'Not that you like to exaggerate.'

'Know what really sticks in my craw? We might be crucified for this, and that bastard Linford's going to get a peg up.'

'At least we can eat solids.' She tossed the fork on to her plate.

40

'Why here?' Rebus said.

He was walking across a frozen lawn in Warriston Crematorium's garden of remembrance. Big Ger Cafferty was wearing a black leather flying-jacket with fur collar, zipped to the chin.

'Remember, you came on a run with me once, years back?'

'Duddingston Loch.' Rebus was nodding. 'I remember.'

'But do you remember what I told you?'

Rebus thought for a moment. 'You said we're a cruel race, and at the same time we like pain.'

'We thrive on defeat, Strawman. And this parliament will put us in charge of our own destinies for the first time in three centuries.'

'So?'

'So it's maybe a time for looking forward, not back.' Cafferty stopped. His breath came out as a grey vapour. 'But you . . . you just can't leave the past alone, can you?'

'You brought me to a garden of remembrance to tell me I'm living in the past?'

Cafferty shrugged. 'We all have to live with the past; doesn't mean we have to live *in* it.'

'Is this a message from Bryce Callan?'

Cafferty looked at him. 'I know you're going after Barry Hutton. Think you'll get a result?'

'It's been known to happen.'

Cafferty chuckled. 'Something I know to my cost.' He started walking again. The only things visible in the flower beds were roses, their branches clipped back, looking brittle and stunted but with the promise of renewal hibernating within. *That's us*, Rebus thought, *thorns and all*. 'Morag died a year back,' Cafferty was saying. Morag: his wife.

'Yes, I heard.'

'They said I could go to the funeral.' Cafferty kicked at a stone, sent it flying into a flower bed. 'I didn't go. The guys in the Bar-L, they thought that made me hard.' A wry smile. 'What do you think?'

'You were scared.'

'Maybe I was at that.' He looked at Rebus again. 'Bryce Callan isn't as forgiving as I am, Strawman. You managed to put me away, and you're still walking around. But now Bryce knows you're after Barry, he's got to have you put out of the game.'

'Then he goes away, too.'

'He's not that stupid. Remember: where there's no body, there's no crime.'

'I'll just disappear?'

Cafferty was nodding. 'Whether you get your precious result or not.' He stopped walking. 'Is that what you want?'

Rebus stopped, looked around as if enjoying the view for the last time. 'What's it to you?'

'Maybe I like having you around.'

'Why?'

'Who else cares about me?' Cafferty chuckled again. In the distance, Rebus could see Cafferty's car – the grey Jag – the Weasel standing beside it, not quite daring to rest against its paintwork. Shuffling his feet in an effort to defrost them.

'Speaking of no body, no crime . . . where's Rab Hill?'

Cafferty looked at him. 'Yes, I heard you'd been asking.'

'It's Rab that has cancer, not you. He went for tests, came back with the news and told his good friend.' Rebus paused. 'You switched X-rays somehow.'

449

'NHS,' Cafferty said. 'Don't pay those doctors half what they're worth.'

'I'm going to prove it, you know that.'

'You're a cop with a vendetta. Not much a poor citizen like me can do about that.'

'Maybe I could ease up a little,' Rebus said.

'In return for . . . ?'

'Testify against Bryce Callan. You were there in '79, you know what was going on.'

Cafferty shook his head. 'That's not the way to play it.'

Rebus stared at him. 'Then what is?'

Cafferty ignored the question. 'It's a cold place this, isn't it?' he said instead. 'When they bury me, I want it to be somewhere warm.'

'You'll be going somewhere warm,' Rebus told him. 'Might even be a bit *too* warm.'

'And you're on the side of the angels, eh?' They were heading for the car now. Rebus stopped; his Saab was parked the other side of the chapel. Cafferty didn't check; he half waved and kept on walking. 'Next funeral I go to will probably be yours, Strawman. Anything you want put on your headstone?'

'How about "Died peacefully in his sleep, aged ninety"?'

Cafferty laughed with the confidence of the immortal.

Rebus turned, retraced his steps. He was out in the open, and his shoulders jerked when he heard a sharp report, but it was only the Weasel slamming shut the door of the Jag. Rebus walked round to the front of the chapel, opened the door and stepped inside. There was an anteroom, a big book of remembrance open on a marble-topped table. A red silk marker kept it open at the day's date on the previous year: eight names, meaning eight cremations that day, eight grieving families who might or might not turn up to pay their respects. No . . . that wasn't right. Not the date of cremation . . . these were dates of death. He kept the place but started at the back of the book, letting the as-yet-empty sheets slide through his fingers. There'd be names in there eventually. If Cafferty was right, his wouldn't be among them: he'd just disappear. He didn't know how he felt about that. Didn't feel anything really. Today's date: no names entered as yet. But cars had been pulling away as he'd been arriving, a teenager peering out at him from the back seat of a limousine, black tie knotted awkwardly at the throat.

Yesterday: no names; too soon. Day before that: none. Then it was back to the weekend. Friday: nine names – the cremations had probably taken place yesterday. Rebus looked down the list, neat entries made in black ink by someone with a gift for calligraphy. Fountain pen: thick downstrokes, tapering flicks. Dates of birth, maiden names . . .

Bingo.

Robert Wallace Hill. Known as Rab.

He'd died the previous Friday. The funeral had probably taken place yesterday, the ashes scattered over the garden of remembrance: the reason Cafferty had come here, paying his respects to the man who'd been his ticket out of jail. Rab, his body riddled with cancer. Rebus saw it all now. Rab, with his release date coming, the cancer a cruel blow. Taking the news back to the Bar-L, confiding in Cafferty, who'd feigned illness, gone for tests himself, arranging the switch of records, some bribe or threat to a doctor. Rab pumped full of painkillers, his release date almost coinciding with Cafferty's. Doubtless paid well: money for a decent send-off, an envelope thick with banknotes finding its way to any family left behind.

Rebus somehow doubted Cafferty would return to the chapel a year down the line. He'd have more important things on his mind. He'd be back in business. And Rab? Well, hadn't Cafferty said it himself: *a time for looking forward, not back.* Christmas was on its way. 1999 would bring the Scottish Parliament back to Edinburgh. In the spring, they'd flatten the old brewery, start constructing the glass boxes which would eventually house the MSPs.

Glass walls: the theme was openness, accountability. Okay, till then they'd be meeting in a church hall on The Mound, but even so . . .

Even so. So what?

'And then you die,' he muttered to himself, turning to leave the chapel.

He got on his mobile to the mortuary, asked Dougie who'd done the autopsy on Rab Hill. The answer: Curt and Stevenson. He thanked Dougie, punched in Curt's number. He was thinking of Rab's body: ashes now. *Where there's no body, there's no crime.* But there'd be the autopsy report, and when it showed up the cancer, Rebus would have evidence enough to have Cafferty re-examined.

'It was an overdose,' Curt explained. 'He'd been a user in prison, got a bit too greedy when he came out.'

'But when you opened him up, what else did you find?' Rebus was holding the phone so tightly, his wrist was hurting.

'Family were against it, John.'

Rebus blinked. 'A young man . . . suspicious death.'

'Some religious thing . . . church I'd never heard of. Their lawyer put it in writing.'

I'll bet he did, Rebus thought. 'There was no autopsy?'

'We did as much as we could. Chemical tests were clear enough . . .'

Rebus cut the call, screwed shut his eyes. A few flakes of snow fell on his lashes. He was slow to blink them away.

No body, no evidence. He shivered suddenly, remembering Cafferty's words: *Yes, I heard you'd been asking.* Asking about Rab Hill. Cafferty had known . . . known that Rebus knew. So easy to administer an overdose to a sick man. So easy for someone like Cafferty, someone with so much to lose.

41

The few days running up to Hogmanay were a nightmare. Lorna had sold her story to a tabloid – Model's Night-Time Romp With Murder Case Cop. Rebus's name hadn't been mentioned . . . not yet.

It was a move which might ostracise her from husband and family alike, but Rebus could see why she'd done it. There was a middle-page spread, showing her to her best in diaphanous clothing, face and hair done to the nines. Maybe it was the relaunch she thought she needed. Maybe it was a case of using what she had.

A moment's notoriety.

Rebus could see his career crumbling before him. To keep herself in the news, she'd have to name names, and Carswell would pounce. So Rebus went to see Alasdair, and made him a proposition. Alasdair phoned his sister at High Manor, talked her round. They were on the phone forty minutes, at the end of which Rebus handed Alasdair's passport back and wished him good luck. He'd even driven him out to the airport. Grieve's parting words to him: 'Home in time for New Year.' A handshake and a brief wave of farewell. Rebus had felt obliged to warn that they might need him back to give testimony. Grieve had nodded, knowing he could always refuse. Either that or keep moving . . .

Rebus wasn't working on Hogmanay. A trade-off because he'd been on call over Christmas. The town had been quiet, which hadn't stopped the cells filling up. Sammy had sent him a present: the CD edition of the Beatles' *White Album*. She was staying down south, visiting her mum. Siobhan had left her present to him in his desk drawer: a history of Hibernian FC. He flicked through it during the dead hours, hours when he'd no need to be at the station. When he wasn't reading about the Hibs, he was poring over case-notes, trying to restructure them into something more acceptable to the Procurator Fiscal. He'd had a series of meetings with various advocates depute. So far, they were of the opinion that the only person they could try with any hope of securing a conviction was Alasdair Grieve: accessory to . . . fleeing the scene of . . .

Another good reason for putting Grieve on the plane.

And now it was Hogmanay, and everyone was talking about how bad the television had been. Princes Street would fill tonight, maybe two hundred thousand revellers. The Pretenders were playing, almost reason enough to go along, but he knew he'd stay home. He wasn't risking the Ox: too close to the mayhem, and getting there would be difficult. Barriers had been erected, ringing the city centre. So he'd headed to Swany's instead.

When he was a kid, all the mothers would be out bleaching their front steps, busy house cleaning: you had to see the New Year in with a clean house. There'd be sandwiches and stovies for the drinkers. Chimes at midnight: someone tall and dark waiting outside, carrying bottle and lump of coal, plus something to eat. Welcoming the New Year with a knock at the door. Songs and 'doing a turn'. One of his uncles had played harmonica, an aunt might sing with a tear in her eye, a catch in her throat. Tables groaning with black bun and shortie, Madeira cake, crisps and peanuts. Juice in the kitchen for the kids, maybe homemade ginger beer. Steak pie sitting in the oven, waiting to be cooked for lunch. Strangers would see a light on, knock and be welcomed in. Anyone was welcome into your home, on that night if no other.

And if no one came . . . then you sat and waited. You didn't go out until you'd been 'first-footed': it was bad

454

luck. One aunt had sat alone for a couple of days; everyone thought she was at her daughter's. Elsewhere: songs in the street, handshakes, drunken reminiscence and prayers for a better year to come.

The old days. And now Rebus was old himself, heading home from Swany's at eleven. He'd see the New Year in alone, and would go out tomorrow even though he'd had no first foot. Maybe he'd walk under a ladder, too, and step on every crack in the pavement.

Just to show that he could.

His car was parked one street over from Arden Street – no spaces available near his flat. He unlocked the boot and extracted his carry-out: a bottle of Macallan, six bottles of Belhaven Best, paprika crisps, dry roasted peanuts. There was a pizza in the freezer, and some sliced tongue in the fridge. Enough to see him through. He'd been saving the *White Album*; could think of worse ways to see in the New Year.

One of them was standing by his tenement door: Cafferty.

'Would you look at us?' Cafferty said, opening his arms. 'Both on our ownios, this of all nights!'

'Speak for yourself.'

'Oh, right,' Cafferty said, nodding, 'you're hosting the social event of the year – I'd forgotten. A bevvy of beauties are on their way as I speak, scented and mini-skirted.' He paused. 'Merry Christmas, by the way.' He tried handing something to Rebus, who wasn't of a mind to take it. Something small and shiny . . .

'Twenty fags?'

Cafferty shrugged. 'An impulse buy.'

Rebus had three packets waiting for him upstairs. 'Keep them,' he said. 'Maybe I'll get lucky and you'll get cancer.'

Cafferty tutted. His face seemed huge, moon-like in the sodium light. 'I thought we'd take a drive.'

Rebus stared at him. 'A drive?'

'Where d'you fancy: Queensferry, Portobello . . . ?'

'What's so urgent?' Rebus put his carrier bags down; they clinked musically as they came to rest.

'Bryce Callan.'

'What about him?'

'You don't have a case, do you?' Rebus didn't respond. 'Won't get one either. And I haven't noticed any worry lines on Barry Hutton's brow.'

'So?'

'So maybe I can help.'

Rebus shuffled his feet. 'And why would you do that?'

'I might have my reasons.'

'Reasons you didn't have ten days ago when I asked?'

'Maybe you didn't ask nicely enough.'

'Then I've got some bad news: my manners haven't improved with age.'

Cafferty smiled. 'Just a drive, Strawman. You can do your drinking, and fill me in on the case.'

Rebus narrowed his eyes. 'Land developer,' he mused. 'It would be branching out, wouldn't it?'

'Easier to do if you can take over an existing business,' Cafferty admitted.

'Barry Hutton's business? I put him away, you step in. I can't see Bryce being too happy.'

'My problem.' Cafferty winked. 'Let's go for that drive. Stick a note on the door, let the glamour models know the party's shifted back an hour.'

'They won't be happy. You know what models are like.'

'Overpaid and underfed, you mean? Would that be the opposite of yourself, DI Rebus?'

'Ha ha.'

'Careful now,' Cafferty warned. 'This time of the season, a split side can take ages to heal.'

Somehow, they'd been moving while they talked, and Rebus was surprised to find that he'd picked up his carrier bags, too. Now they stood by the Jag. Cafferty yanked open the driver's door, slid in behind the steering wheel in a single, practised movement. Rebus stood there a moment longer. Hogmanay, last day of the year: a day for paying debts, balancing the books . . . a day for finishing things.

He made to get in.

'Sling the booze in the back,' Cafferty suggested. 'I've a hip flask in the glove compartment, twenty-five-year-old Armagnac. Wait till you taste this stuff. I'm telling you, it would turn a heathen into John the fucking Baptist.'

But Rebus had extracted the Macallan from one of his bags. 'I'll stick to my own,' he said.

'Not a bad drop either.' Cafferty was making a great effort not to be offended. 'Make sure you waft some of it my way, so I can at least inhale.' He turned the ignition. The Jaguar purred like the cat it resembled. And suddenly they were moving, looking to the outside world like nothing more suspicious than two friends out for a jaunt. South to the Grange, and further south to Blackford Hill, then east towards the coast. And Rebus talked, as much for his own benefit as Cafferty's. About the pact two business friends had made with a devil called Bryce Callan, a pact which would lead to a killing. About how the killer waited in vain for his friend to return, living rough – a disguise against detection, or a route to penitence? Past lessons learned by Barry Hutton, now a successful businessman, seeing an opportunity for fresh riches and increased fame: replaying that game from twenty years before, determined that his man on the council would become his player in parliament . . .

At the end of the story Cafferty seemed thoughtful, then said, 'So it's tainted before it begins?'

'Maybe,' Rebus replied, putting the bottle back to his mouth. Portobello: that's where they looked to be headed, maybe park by the harbour and sit with windows open. But Cafferty headed on to Seafield Road and started driving towards Leith.

'There's some land up this way I'm thinking of buying,'

he explained. 'Got some plans drawn up, builder called Peter Kirkwall did the costings.'

'For what?'

'Leisure complex – restaurant, maybe a cinema or health club. Some luxury flats parked on top.'

'Kirkwall works with Barry Hutton.'

'I know.'

'Hutton's sure to find out.'

Cafferty shrugged. 'Something I just have to live with.' He gave a smile Rebus couldn't read. 'I heard about this plot of land next to where they're building the parliament. It sold for three-quarters of a million four years ago. Know what its price is now? Four million. How's that for a yield?'

Rebus pushed the cork back into the bottle. This stretch of road was all car dealers, wasteland behind, and then the sea. They headed up a narrow, unlit lane, its surface uneven. A large metal fence at the far end. Cafferty stopped the Jag, got out and took a key to the padlock, pulled the heavy metal chain free and pushed the gates open with his foot.

'What's there to see?' Rebus asked, uneasy now, as Cafferty got back into the driving seat. He could run, but it was a long way to civilisation, and he was dead beat. Besides, he was done running.

'It's all warehouses just now. If you coughed too loud, they'd collapse. Easy enough to bulldoze, and there's a quarter-mile of seafront to play with.'

They drove through the gates.

'A quiet place for a chat,' Cafferty said.

But they weren't here to chat; Rebus knew that now. He turned his head, saw that another car was following them into the compound. It was a red Ferrari. Rebus turned back to Cafferty.

'What's going on?'

'Business,' Cafferty said coldly, 'that's all.' He stopped the Jag, pulled on the handbrake. 'Out,' he ordered. Rebus didn't move. Cafferty got out of the car, left his door open. The other car had pulled up alongside. Both sets of headlamps stayed on dipped, illuminating the cracked concrete surface of the compound. Rebus focused on one of the weeds, its jagged shadow crawling up the wall of one of the warehouses. Rebus's door was pulled open. Hands grabbed at him. He heard a soft click as his seat belt was unlocked, and then he was being dragged out, thrown on to the cold ground. He took his time looking up. Three figures, silhouetted against the headlamps, breath billowing from their dark faces. Cafferty and two others. Rebus started getting to his feet. The single malt had fallen from the car, smashed on the concrete. He wished he'd taken one more hit of it while he had the chance.

A boot to the chest had enough force to send him on to his backside. He put his hands out behind him, steadying himself, so that he was unprotected when the next blow came. To the face this time, connecting with his chin, cracking his head back. He felt the snap as bones in his neck uttered a complaint.

'Can't take a warning,' a voice said: not Cafferty's. A thin man, younger. Rebus narrowed his eyes, shielded them with a hand as though peering into the sun.

'It's Barry Hutton, isn't it?' Rebus asked.

'Pick him up,' was the barked response. The third man – Hutton's man – pulled Rebus to his feet as though he were made of cardboard, held him from behind.

'Gonny teach you,' Hutton hissed. Rebus could make out the features now: face tight with anger, mouth downturned, nose pinched. He was wearing black leather driving gloves. A question – absurd under the circumstances – flashed through Rebus's mind: *wonder if they were a Christmas present?*

Hutton hit him with a fist, connecting with Rebus's left cheek. Rebus rode the blow, but still felt it. As he turned his face, he caught a glimpse of the man pinning him from behind. It wasn't Mick Lorimer.

'Lorimer isn't with you tonight, then?' Rebus asked. Blood was pooling in his mouth. He swallowed it. 'Were you there the night he killed Roddy Grieve?'

'Mick just doesn't know when to stop,' Hutton said. 'I wanted the bastard warned off, not on a slab.'

'You just can't get the staff these days.' He felt the grip around his chest tighten, forcing the breath from his lungs.

'No, but there always seems to be a smart-arsed cop around when you least need it.' Another blow, this time bursting Rebus's nose open. Tears pounded from his eyes. He tried blinking them away. Oh, Jesus Christ, that hurt.

'Thanks, Uncle Ger,' Hutton was saying. 'That's one I owe you.'

'What else are partners for?' Cafferty said. He took a step forward, and now Rebus could see his face clearly. It was dead of any emotion. 'You wouldn't have been this careless, Strawman, not five years back.' He stepped back again.

'You're right,' Rebus said. 'Maybe after tonight I'll retire.'

'You'll do that all right,' Hutton said. 'A nice long rest.'

'Where'll you put him?' Cafferty asked.

'Plenty of sites we're working on. A nice big hole and half a ton of concrete.'

Rebus wrestled, but the grip was fierce. He raised a foot, stomped hard, but his captor was wearing steel toecaps. The grip tightened, like a thick metal band, crushing him. He let out a groan.

'But first, a bit more fun,' Hutton was saying. He came close, so his face was inches from Rebus's. Then Rebus felt pain explode behind his eyeballs as Hutton's knee thudded into his groin. Bile rose in his throat, the whisky seeking the quickest exit route. The grip loosened, fell away, and he dropped to his knees. Mist in front of his eyes, thick as haar, the sea singing in his ears. He wiped his hand across his face, clearing his vision. Fire was spreading out from his groin. Whisky fumes at the back of his throat. When he tried breathing through his nose, huge bubbles of blood expanded and popped. The next blow caught him on the temple. A kick this time, sending him rolling across concrete to end hunched foetus-like on the ground. He knew he should get up, take the fight to them. Nothing to lose. Go down kicking and scratching, punching and spitting. Hutton was crouching in front of him, pulling his head up by the hair.

There were explosions in the distance: the fireworks at the Castle, meaning it was midnight. The sky was lit with coloured blooms, blood-red, aching yellow.

'You'll stay hidden a sight longer than twenty years, believe me,' Hutton was saying. Cafferty was standing just behind him, holding something. Light from the fireworks glinted from it. A knife, blade had to be eight or nine inches. Cafferty was going to do it himself. A determined grip on the handle. This was the moment they'd been coming to, ever since the Weasel's office. Rebus almost welcomed it: Cafferty rather than the young thug. Hutton had camouflaged his criminality well, the veneer thick and brightly polished. Rebus would take Cafferty every time . . .

But now the sea was washing over all of it, washing Rebus, cleaning him with its flow of noise, building in his ears to a deafening roar, the shadows and light blurring, becoming one . . .

Fade to grey.

42

He woke up.

Frozen, aching, as if he'd spent the night in a sepulchre. His eyes were crusted. He prised them open. Cars all around him. Couldn't stop shivering, body temperature dangerously low. He rose shakily to his feet, held on to one of the cars for support. Garage forecourt; had to be Seafield Road. He broke the crust of blood in his nostrils, started breathing fast. Get that blood pumping round his body. His shirt and jacket were spattered with blood, but no wounds, no sign that he'd been stabbed or slashed.

What the hell is this?

It wasn't light yet. He angled his watch to the nearest street lamp: three thirty. Started patting his pockets, found his mobile and entered the access code. Got the night shift at St Leonard's.

Is this heaven or hell?

'I need a car,' he said. 'Seafield Road, the Volvo concession.'

He ran on the spot while he waited, patting himself with aching arms. Still couldn't stop shivering. The patrol car took ten minutes, two uniforms emerging from it.

'Christ, look at you,' one of them said.

Rebus stumbled into the back seat. 'That heating on full blast?' he asked.

The uniforms got into the front, closed their doors. 'What happened to you?' the passenger asked.

Rebus thought the question over. 'I'm not sure,' he said at last.

'Happy New Year anyway, sir,' the driver said.

'Happy New Year,' the passenger added.

Rebus tried to form the words; couldn't. Slouched down in the seat instead and concentrated on staying alive.

He took a team back to the compound. The concrete surface was like a skating rink.

'What's happened here?' Siobhan Clarke asked.

'Wasn't like this,' Rebus answered, fighting to keep his balance. The hospital had been reluctant to let him go. But his nose wasn't broken, and though he might be seeing some blood in his urine, there wasn't any sign of internal injury or infection. It was one of the nurses who'd made the comment: 'Lot of blood for a busted nose.' She was studying his clothes at the time. It had made him think: lacerations and grazes to the face, a cut on the inside of the cheek and a bloody nose. He had spatters of blood all over him. Saw the knife again, Cafferty standing behind Barry Hutton . . .

And now, standing pretty much where he'd been only ten hours before . . . nothing except the sheet of ice.

'It's been hosed down,' he said.

'What?'

'They hosed away the blood.'

He began to walk back towards the car.

Barry Hutton wasn't home. His girlfriend hadn't seen him since the previous evening. His car was parked outside his office block, locked and with the alarm set, no sign of the keys. No sign of Barry Hutton either.

They found Cafferty at the hotel. He was enjoying morning coffee in the lounge. Hutton's man – now Cafferty's, if he hadn't been all along – was reading a paper at a neighbouring table.

'I've just found out what they're charging come the millennium,' Cafferty said of the hotel. 'Shysters, the lot of them. Wrong line of work, you and me.'

Rebus sat down opposite his nemesis. Siobhan Clarke introduced herself, stayed standing.

'Two of you,' Cafferty mused. 'That means corroboration.'

Rebus turned to Siobhan. 'Go wait outside.' She didn't move. 'Please.' She hesitated, then turned and stomped off.

'A fiery one that.' Cafferty laughed, sitting forward, face suddenly showing concern. 'How are you, Strawman? Thought I was going to lose you there.'

'Where's Hutton?'

'Christ, man, how should I know?'

Rebus turned to the bodyguard. 'Go to Warriston Crem, check the name Robert Hill. Cafferty's minders tend to live short lives.' The man stared at him blankly.

'Has Barry not turned up, then?' Cafferty was feigning amazement.

'You killed him. Now you step into his shoes.' Rebus paused. 'Which was the plan all along?'

Cafferty just smiled.

'What's Bryce Callan going to say?' Rebus watched the smile broaden still further. He began nodding. 'Bryce okayed it? This was where it was always headed?'

Cafferty spoke in an undertone. 'You can't go around bumping off people like Roddy Grieve. It's bad for everyone.'

'But you *can* murder Barry Hutton?'

'I saved your neck, Strawman. You owe me.'

Rebus pointed a finger. 'You took me there. You set the whole trap, and Hutton walked into it.'

'You both walked into it.' Cafferty was almost preening. Rebus wanted to stick a fist in his face, and Cafferty knew it. He looked around at the elegant surroundings. Chintz and antimacassars, chandeliers and sound-deadening carpets. 'Wouldn't do, really now, would it?'

'I've been thrown out of better places than this.' Rebus glowered. 'Where is he?'

Cafferty sat back. 'You know the story about the Old Town? Reason it's so narrow and steep, there's some big serpent buried under it.' He waited for Rebus to get it; decided to supply the punchline himself. 'Room for more than one snake under the Old Town, Strawman.'

The Old Town: the building works around Holyrood – Queensberry House, Dynamic Earth, *Scotsman* offices ... hotels and apartments. So many building sites. Lots of good, deep holes, filling with concrete ...

'We'll look for him,' Rebus said. Cafferty's words in the garden of remembrance: *where there's no body, there's no crime.*

Cafferty shrugged. 'You do that. And be sure to hand your clothes in as evidence. Maybe his blood's mixed in there with yours. Maybe it'll be *you* who has to do some explaining. Me, I was here all evening.' He waved an arm casually. 'Ask around. It was a hell of a party, a hell of a night. By next Hogmanay ... well, who knows what we'll all be doing? We'll have our parliament by then, and this ... this will all be history.'

'I don't care how long it takes,' Rebus warned. But Cafferty just laughed. He was back, and in charge of *his* Edinburgh, and that was all that mattered ...

Acknowledgements

I'd like to thank the following: Historic Scotland, for providing a tour of Queensberry House; The Scottish Office Constitution Group; Professor Anthony Busuttil, University of Edinburgh; the staff at Edinburgh Mortuary; staff at St Leonard's police station and Lothian and Borders Police HQ; the Old Manor Hotel, Lundin Links (especially Alistair Clark and George Clark).

The following books and guides were helpful: 'Who's Who in the Scottish Parliament' (a supplement provided with *Scotland on Sunday*, the issue of 16 May 1999); *Crime and Criminal Justice in Scotland* by Peter Young (Stationery Office, 1997); *A Guide to the Scottish Parliament* edited by Gerry Hassan (Stationery Office, 1999); *The Battle for Scotland* by Andrew Marr (Penguin, 1992).

The lyrics to 'Wages Day' are by Ricky Ross. The track can be found on the Deacon Blue albums *Raintown* and *Our Town: the Greatest Hits*.

I'd also like to thank Angus Calder for permission to quote from his poem 'Love Poem', and Alison Hendon, who brought another poem to my attention and gifted me the title of this book.

For further information on the remarkable Rosslyn Chapel, visit its website at www.ROSSLYNCHAPEL.org.uk

PROLOGUE

1

The girl screamed once, only the once.

Even that, however, was a minor slip on his part. That might have been the end of everything, almost before it had begun. Neighbours inquisitive, the police called in to investigate. No, that would not do at all. Next time he would tie the gag a little tighter, just a little tighter, just that little bit more secure.

Afterwards, he went to the drawer and took from it a ball of string. He used a pair of sharp nail-scissors, the kind girls always seem to use, to snip off a length of about six inches, then he put the ball of string and the scissors back into the drawer. A car revved up outside, and he went to the window, upsetting a pile of books on the floor as he did so. The car, however, had vanished, and he smiled to himself. He tied a knot in the string, not any special kind of knot, just a knot. There was an envelope lying ready on the sideboard.

2

It was 28th April. Wet, naturally, the grass percolating water as John Rebus walked to the grave of his father, dead five years to the day. He placed a wreath so that it lay, yellow and red, the colours of remembrance, against the still shining marble. He paused for a moment, trying to think of things to say, but there seemed nothing to say, nothing to think. He had been a good enough father and that was that. The old man wouldn't have wanted him to waste his words in any case. So he stood there, hands respectfully behind his back, crows laughing on the walls around him, until the water seeping into his shoes told him that there was a warm car waiting for him at the cemetery gates.

He drove quietly, hating to be back here in Fife, back where the old days had never been 'good old days,' where ghosts rustled in the shells of empty houses and the shutters went up every evening on a handful of desultory shops, those metal shutters that gave the vandals somewhere to write their names. How Rebus hated it all, this singular lack of an environment. It stank the way it had always done: of misuse, of disuse, of the sheer wastage of life.

He drove the eight miles towards the open sea, to where his brother Michael still lived. The rain eased off as he approached the skull-grey coast, the car throwing up splashings of water from a thousand crevasses in the road. Why was it, he wondered, that they never seemed to fix the roads here,

3

while in Edinburgh they worked on the surfaces so often that things were made even worse? And why, above all, had he made the maniacal decision to come all the way through to Fife, just because it was the anniversary of the old man's death? He tried to focus his mind on something else, and found himself fantasising about his next cigarette.

Through the rain, falling as drizzle now, Rebus saw a girl about his daughter's age walking along the grass verge. He slowed the car, examined her in his mirror as he passed her, and stopped. He motioned for her to come to his window.

Her short breaths were visible in the cool, still air, and her dark hair fell in rats-tails down her forehead. She looked at him apprehensively.

'Where are you going, love?'

'Kirkcaldy.'

'Do you want a lift?'

She shook her head, drops of water flying from her coiled hair.

'My mum said I should never accept lifts from strangers.'

'Well,' said Rebus, smiling, 'your mum is quite right. I've got a daughter about your age and I tell her the same thing. But it is raining, and I *am* a policeman, so you can trust me. You've still got a fair way to go, you know.'

She looked up and down the silent road, then shook her head again.

'Okay,' said Rebus, 'but take care. Your mum was quite right.'

He wound his window up again and drove off, watching her in his mirror as she watched him. Clever kid. It was good to know that parents still had a little sense of responsibility left. If only the same could be said of his ex-wife. The way she had brought up their daughter was a disgrace. Michael, too, had given his daughter too long a leash. Who was to blame?

Rebus's brother owned a respectable house. He had

4

followed in the old man's footsteps and become a stage hypnotist. He seemed to be quite good at it, too, from all accounts. Rebus had never asked Michael how it was done, just as he had never shown any interest or curiosity in the old man's act. He had observed that this still puzzled Michael, who would drop hints and red herrings as to the authenticity of his own stage act for him to chase up if he so wished.

But then John Rebus had too many things to chase up, and that had been the position during all of his fifteen years on the force. Fifteen years, and all he had to show were an amount of self-pity and a busted marriage with an innocent daughter hanging between them. It was more disgusting than sad. And meantime Michael was happily married with two kids and a larger house than Rebus could ever afford. He headlined at hotels, clubs, and even theatres as far away as Newcastle and Wick. Occasionally he would make six-hundred quid from a single show. Outrageous. He drove an expensive car, wore good clothes, and would never have been caught dead standing in the pissing rain in a graveyard in Fife on the dullest April day for many a year. No, Michael was too clever for that. And too stupid.

'John! Christ, what's up? I mean, it's great to see you. Why didn't you phone to warn me you were coming? Come on inside.'

It was the welcome Rebus had expected: embarrassed surprise, as though it were painful to be reminded that one still had some family left alive. And Rebus had noted the use of the word 'warn' where 'tell' would have sufficed. He was a policeman. He noticed such things.

Michael Rebus bounded through to the living-room and turned down the wailing stereo.

'Come on in, John,' he called. 'Do you want a drink? Coffee perhaps? Or something stronger? What brings you here?'

Rebus sat down as though he were in a stranger's house, his back straight and professional. He examined the panelled walls of the room – a new feature – and the framed photographs of his niece and nephew.

'I was just in the neighbourhood,' he said.

Michael, turning from the drinks cabinet with the glasses ready, suddenly remembered, or did a good impersonation of just having remembered.

'Oh, John, I forgot all about it. Why didn't you tell me? Shit, I hate forgetting about Dad.'

'Just as well you're a hypnotist then and not Mickey the Memory Man, isn't it? Give me that drink, or are you two getting engaged?'

Michael, smiling, absolved, handed over the glass of whisky.

'Is that your car outside?' asked Rebus, taking the glass. 'I mean the big BMW?'

Michael, still smiling, nodded.

'Christ,' said Rebus. 'You treat yourself well.'

'As well as I treat Chrissie and the kids. We're building an extension onto the back of the house. Somewhere to put a jacuzzi or a sauna. They're the in thing just now, and Chrissie's desperate to keep ahead of the field.'

Rebus took a swallow of whisky. It turned out to be a malt. Nothing in the room was cheap, but none of it was exactly desirable either. Glass ornaments, a crystal decanter on a silver salver, the TV and video, the inscrutably miniature hi-fi system, the onyx lamp. Rebus felt a little guilty about that lamp. Rhona and he had given it to Michael and Chrissie as a wedding present. Chrissie no longer spoke to him. Who could blame her?

'Where is Chrissie, by the way?'

'Oh, she's out doing some shopping. She has her own car

now. The kids will still be at school. She'll pick them up on the way home. Are you staying for something to eat?'

Rebus shrugged his shoulders.

'You'd be welcome to stay,' said Michael, meaning that Rebus wouldn't. 'So how's the cop-shop? Still muddling along?'

'We lose a few, but they don't get the publicity. We catch a few, and they do. It's the same as always, I suppose.'

The room, Rebus was noticing, smelled of toffee-apples, of penny arcades.

Michael was speaking:

'This is a terrible business about those girls being kidnapped.'

Rebus nodded.

'Yes,' he said, 'yes, it is. But we can't strictly call it kidnapping, not yet. There hasn't been a demand note or anything. It's more likely to be a straightforward case of sexual assault.'

Michael started up from his chair.

'Straightforward? What's straightforward about that?'

'It's just the terminology we use, Mickey, that's all.' Rebus shrugged again and finished his drink.

'Well, John,' said Michael, sitting, 'I mean, we've both got daughters, too. You're so casual about the whole thing. I mean, it's frightening to think of it.' He shook his head slowly in the world-wide expression of shared grief, and relief, too, that the horror was someone else's for the moment. 'It's frightening,' he repeated. 'And in Edinburgh of all places. I mean, you never think of that sort of thing happening in Edinburgh, do you?'

'There's more happening in Edinburgh than anyone knows.'

'Yes.' Michael paused. 'I was across there just last week playing at one of the hotels.'

'You didn't tell me.'

It was Michael's turn to shrug his shoulders.

'Would you have been interested?' he said.

'Maybe not,' said Rebus, smiling, 'but I would have come along anyway.'

Michael laughed. It was the laughter of birthdays, of money found in an old pocket.

'Another whisky, sir?' he said.

'I thought you were never going to ask.'

Rebus returned to his study of the room while Michael went to the cabinet.

'How's the act going?' he asked. 'And I really *am* interested.'

'It's going fine,' said Michael. 'In fact, it's going very well indeed. There's talk of a television spot, but I'll believe that when I see it.'

'Great.'

Another drink reached Rebus's willing hand.

'Yes, and I'm working on a new slot. It's a bit scary though.' An inch of gold flashed on Michael's wrist as he tipped the glass to his lips. The watch was expensive: it had no numbers on its face. It seemed to Rebus that the more expensive something was, the less of it there always seemed to be: tiny little hi-fi systems, watches without numbers, the translucent Dior ankle-socks on Michael's feet.

'Tell me about it,' he said, taking his brother's bait.

'Well,' said Michael, sitting forward in his chair, 'I take members of the audience back into their past lives.'

'Past lives?'

Rebus was staring at the floor as if admiring the design of the dark and light green carpet.

'Yes,' Michael continued, 'Reincarnation, born again, that sort of thing. Well, I shouldn't have to spell it out to you, John. After all, *you're* the Christian.'

'Christians don't believe in past lives, Mickey. Only future ones.'

Michael stared at Rebus, demanding silence.

'Sorry,' said Rebus.

'As I was saying, I tried the act out in public for the first time last week, though I've been practising it for a while with my private consultees.'

'Private consultees?'

'Yes. They pay me money for private hypnotherapy. I stop them smoking, or make them more confident, or stop them from wetting the bed. Some are convinced that they have past lives, and they ask me to put them under so that they can prove it. Don't worry though. Financially, it's all above board. The tax-man gets his cut.'

'And do you prove it? Do they have past lives?'

Michael rubbed a finger around the rim of his glass, now empty.

'You'd be surprised,' he said.

'Give me an example.'

Rebus was following the lines of the carpet with his eyes. Past lives, he thought to himself. Now there was a thing. There was plenty of life in *his* past.

'Well,' said Michael, 'remember I told you about my show in Edinburgh last week? Well,' he leaned further forward in his chair, 'I got this woman up from the audience. She was a small woman, middle-aged. She'd come in with an office-party. She went under pretty easily, probably because she hadn't been drinking as heavily as her friends. Once she was under, I told her that we were going to take a trip into her past, way, way back before she was born. I told her to think back to the earliest memory she had . . .'

Michael's voice had taken on a professional but easy mellifluence. He spread his hands before him as if playing to an audience. Rebus, nursing his glass, felt himself relax a

9

little. He thought back to a childhood episode, a game of football, one brother pitted against the other. The warm mud of a July shower, and their mother, her sleeves rolled up, stripping them both and putting them, giggling knots of arms and legs, into the bath . . .

'. . . well,' Michael was saying, 'she started to speak, and in a voice not quite her own. It was weird, John. I wish you *had* been there to see it. The audience were silent, and I was feeling all cold and then hot and then cold again, and it had nothing to do with the hotel's heating-system by the way. I'd done it, you see. I'd taken that woman into a past life. She was a nun. Do you believe that? A *nun*. And she said that she was alone in her cell. She described the convent and everything, and then she started to recite something in Latin, and some people in the audience actually *crossed* themselves. I was bloody well petrified. My hair was probably standing on end. I brought her out of it as quickly as I could, and there was a long pause before the crowd started to applaud. Then, maybe out of sheer relief, her friends started to cheer and laugh, and that broke the ice. At the end of the show, I found out that this woman was a staunch Protestant, a Rangers supporter no less, and she swore blind that she knew no Latin at all. Well, *somebody* inside her did. I'll tell you that.'

Rebus was smiling.

'It's a nice story, Mickey,' he said.

'It's the truth.' Michael opened his arms wide in supplication. 'Don't you believe me?'

'Maybe.'

Michael shook his head.

'You must make a pretty bad copper, John. I had around a hundred and fifty witnesses. Iron-clad.'

Rebus could not pull his attention away from the design in the carpet.

'Plenty of people believe in past lives, John.'

10

Past lives . . . Yes, he believed in some things . . . . In God, certainly . . . But past lives . . . Without warning, a face screamed up at him from the carpet, trapped in its cell.

He dropped his glass.

'John? Is anything wrong? Christ, you look as if you've seen . . .'

'No, no, nothing's the matter.' Rebus retrieved the glass and stood up. 'I just . . . I'm fine. It's just that,' he checked his watch, a watch with numbers, 'well, I'd better be going. I'm on duty this evening.'

Michael was smiling weakly, glad that his brother was not going to stay, but embarrassed at his relief.

'We'll have to meet again soon,' he said, 'on neutral territory.'

'Yes,' said Rebus, tasting once again the tang of toffee-apples. He felt a little pale, a little shaky, as though he were too far out of his territory. 'Let's do that.'

Once or twice or three times a year, at weddings, funerals, or over the telephone at Christmas, they promised themselves this get-together. The mere promise now was a ritual in itself, and so could be safely proffered and just as safely ignored.

'Let's do that.'

Rebus shook hands with Michael at the door. Escaping past the BMW to his own car, he wondered how alike they were, his brother and him. Uncles and aunts in their funeral-cold rooms occasionally commented, 'Ah, you're both the spitting image of your mother.' That was as far as it went. John Rebus knew that his own hair was a shade of brown lighter than Michael's, and that his eyes were a shade of green darker. He knew also, however, that the differences between them were such that any similarities were made to look unutterably superficial. They were brothers without any sense of brother-hood. Brotherhood belonged to the past.

11

He waved once from the car and was gone. He would be back in Edinburgh within the hour, and on duty another half-hour after that. He knew that the reason he could never feel comfortable in Michael's house was Chrissie's hatred of him, her unshakeable belief that he alone had been responsible for the break-up of his marriage. Maybe she was right at that. He tried ticking off in his mind the definite chores of the next seven or eight hours. He had to tidy up a case of burglary and serious assault. A nasty one that. The CID was undermanned as it was, and now these abductions would stretch them even more. Those two young girls, girls his own daughter's age. It was best not to think about it. By now they would be dead, or would wish that they were dead. God have mercy on them. In Edinburgh of all places, in his own dear city.

A maniac was on the loose.

People were staying in their homes.

And a screaming in his memory.

Rebus shrugged, feeling a slight sensation of attrition in one of his shoulders. It was not his business after all. Not yet.

Back in his living-room, Michael Rebus poured himself another whisky. He went to the stereo and turned it all the way up, then reached underneath his chair and, after a little fumbling, pulled out an ashtray that was hidden there.